AND IN TH

by G.M

This book was originally published by Simon and Schuster in Australia, under my name Graeme Hague in 2002, and subsequently over time was re-released in various formats and by different publishers including being licensed to Readers Digest in Australia and The Netherlands.

Finally, the publishing rights have reverted to myself, and I've taken the opportunity to release the novel independently. In the process, it's undergone some fine-tune editing, and I've had to fix a few errors caused by file conversions from those early releases—hopefully I got them all!

So essentially, this version is still the novel that was published back in 2002, and some readers may realise they've read it before. Still, the subject is timeless, and one newspaper review described it as: "Giving the soldiers (and women) of Gallipoli and the Great War a haunting voice. It is a story that should never be forgotten."

And In The Morning is my contribution to ensuring that doesn't happen.

Graeme Hague.

And In The Morning

by GRAEME HAGUE

First published in 2002

This edition published in February 2023

Copyright for all editions owned by G.M.Hague.

This ebook is licensed for your personal enjoyment only. This ebook may not be re-sold or given away to other people. If you would like to share this book with another person, please purchase an additional copy for each recipient. If you're reading this book and did not purchase it, or it was not purchased for your use only, then please purchase your own copy. Thank you for respecting the hard work of this author.

In the interests of allowing readers to freely exchange this Ebook between their own personal devices I've not applied any Digital Rights Management restrictions myself, although there may be some DRM in place beyond my control according to the format you've purchased (for example, Amazon's Kindle). Therefore I'd appreciate it, if you didn't support digital piracy by freely distributing this book. If you'd like any information or simply want to get in touch my website is at www.graemehague.com.au and my email address is mail@graemehague.com.au. My Facebook page is under the name Graeme Hague.

Acknowledgements

I haven't written a novel yet without a salute to the skills of Selwa Anthony, but this book in particular is a testimony to her guidance and expertise.

Matt Fletcher read the early drafts of the first chapters. So did David and Elizabeth Partridge, who fortunately pointed out the cows were the wrong colour. And thanks to the many unseen people over the internet who cheerfully provided advice and information on a wide range of things from aspirins to x-ray machines *circa* 1915.

This novel was written on White Rocks Farm, Brunswick Junction, Western Australia.

I've composed and recorded a soundtrack album to accompany this book. It includes two ambient tracks that reflect the narrative of the book, while other songs are more of a progressive rock style and perhaps not to everyone's taste. And don't worry, there are no spoilers in the lyrics. I'll be making it available on selected streaming services. Please write or check my website, if you'd like to know more about the music for *And In The Morning*.

The wonderful cover design is by Jennifer Givner, Acapella Book Cover Design.

Extract of a letter from Lieutenant Ledward, 23rd Brigade, 8th Division (British Army) after a successful counterattack, without any artillery support (as requested) by Australian troops against a vastly superior German force in March 1918.

'It is my considered opinion that the Australians, in 1918, were better in a battle than any troops on either side. They were not popular. They had a contempt for Britishers to begin with–that is, some Australians voiced such a contempt. I myself heard the expression, "Not bad for a Britisher" used by one about some successful feat of British arms. They were untidy, undisciplined, cocky, not nice enough even for the taste of Thomas Atkins, but it seems to me indisputable that a greater number of them were personally indomitable, in the true sense of the word, than any other race. I am glad they were on our side.'

***

From *For the Fallen (September 1914)* by Laurence Binyon (1869-1943) The fourth stanza of his poem, often reproduced on war memorials around the world:

They shall grow not old, as we that are left grow old
Age shall not weary them, nor the years condemn
At the going down of the sun ***and in the morning***
We will remember them

Contents

And In The Morning

G.M.Hague

Rose Preston

Rose Preston was no angel when it came to her behaviour, especially if you asked her father. His only daughter was headstrong, stubborn and ungrateful for all the worldly advantages he'd given her in a lifetime of hard work. Success hadn't come easily, and was not to be taken lightly, especially by young ladies. Rupert Preston had put Rose through a private college for the best education. He let her buy the finest clothes, shoes and trinkets regardless of the expense, and as she'd grown older, encouraged her to see the better things Melbourne society had to offer. By then, she was slim and pretty, so it had never been difficult to arrange a suitable escort to the opera or the latest concerts. Strangely though, the young men rarely asked twice. It took a while for Rupert to understand why.

His daughter scared the hell out of them. Rose had even—God forbid—gone to Flemington for the Cup and joined the ranks of flirting women with their outrageous hats and high fashions. An altogether immoral display of behaviour, in Rupert's opinion, parading themselves like prize poultry on offer. There was no place for females at the racetrack. Gambling and horses were gentlemen's pursuits and not to be sullied by the presence of wives or young girls. Rose had been able to convince her father, however, that things were changing and told him that if he expected her to be a knowledgeable member of Melbourne's upper classes, she needed to taste forbidden fruit for herself at least once. Everyone was doing it. And how could she hold her own in conversation at the next party, if her father never let her venture beyond the four walls of their St Kilda home?

She'd smiled her beautiful, impish smile that reminded Rupert so much of her late mother, and as usual, it melted his resolve.

Ten years after his wife, Jean, had died of pneumonia and Rose had turned twenty, Rupert gave in to his daughter's latest badgering and agreed that she could go to Europe for an extended holiday. She was old enough now to be trusted to behave properly on the long sea journey, especially with her older brother, Donald, to watch over her. There were relatives in England for both of them to meet. Rupert's uncle had offered places to stay and a chance to live among the real upper classes, and that was important for Rose's future. There was even a possibility that she would find a potential husband who didn't run away after their first meeting.

One stipulation Rupert made was that Rose didn't go beyond the shores of the United Kingdom, no matter how strong the temptation to experience the Continent. The rumbling of war approaching in Europe was clear, even on the opposite side of the world. Most people believed it would soon erupt into a beautiful chaos of mounted charging men on fine horses, gloriously settling their country's differences on the battlefield and clearing the political air once and for all. Just as wars had done for hundreds of years.

Not Rupert, who had paid close attention to the bitter, spiteful Boer conflict in South Africa, and he'd heard stories that would never be printed in any newspaper. The men returning from that war never spoke of gallantry or their comrades dying gloriously. Modern warfare could be dreadful and he didn't want his daughter anywhere near it. The Germans were more civilised than the Boers, but you never knew for certain. No, it was best to be cautious and forbid her crossing the Channel.

Any war in Europe would never touch the shores of England herself. So Rupert felt comfortable with the idea of Rose's travelling there. She was the right age to be trusted, Donald was with her, and although she was impressionable, she would learn a great deal about being a proper lady from those who knew. Rupert's aunt, for example, was a model of social etiquette, and acquainted with all the right people.

Rose would be safe in London for the duration of any hostilities, if they occurred, and any fighting wouldn't last for long. Warfare over the wide, open spaces of the South African plains had taken years because of the sheer size of the country. Any dispute that might flare up in Europe would be quickly resolved. It was the way things were done there.

Rupert had decided not to accompany Rose himself. His business was textiles and cloth, and a war in Europe, no matter how brief, would create a huge demand for material for uniforms, blankets and canvas for tents as the forces mobilised. Australia might even put together a token force herself, although it was doubtful that any trained men would make it across the oceans in time to take part. Regardless, if war came, the situation would need adept and aggressive business dealings, and it wouldn't be the time for dallying in the social circles of London, trying to find your daughter a suitable husband. Rupert would be needed here in Australia, at the head of his organisation, making the most of opportunities.

***

Three months later, nobody could ever have predicted the swiftness of events that swept the world into the worst war in living history. As the German armies invaded Belgium and killed thousands every day, Rupert tried desperately to contact Rose in London and convince her to return. He'd changed his mind quickly. The massive conflict might well spill over the Channel onto English soil after all, and he wanted her home.

Rose was still in the capital, he knew, but she was oddly out of reach. Donald's telegrammed replies were infuriatingly vague too. Finally, to Rupert's amazement, Donald admitted he was returning to Australia alone.

Rose was staying behind to train as a nurse.

***

Her best intentions were soon thwarted by the sheer size of the task. No one had time to train women properly to become fully qualified nurses, although the need was desperate. Makeshift hospitals all over England were filled beyond capacity with wounded soldiers. Tens of thousands of them. At great cost, the British Expeditionary Force had halted the German advance and the stalemate of trench warfare known as "the Western Front" had begun.

There was little room for walking wounded in these hospitals, so men were discharged whenever possible. The injuries of those who stayed were often ghastly. The twentieth century hadn't just brought more efficient ways of killing men, it was also newly adept at cobbling the shattered pieces back together, keeping human beings barely recognisable alive with morphine after they'd been hastily sewn up at surgeons' tables on the battlefield to be eventually delivered in appalling condition to the long rows of hospital beds in England. Many soldiers would have been better off left to die. Some finally did, after they'd endured the agony of the journey home.

Under these circumstances, Rose became a VAD, a member of the Voluntary Aid Detachment, working in a converted hospital near the docklands. The VAD did the dirtiest jobs. They cleaned the grime and blood from the new arrivals, or sorted through the clothing of those who had died. The survivors stank of filth, excrement and their own infection. Removing field dressings was the worst job because they were always glued to the wounds, and the shock of pain could kill the patient. It was the VADs who prepared these men for the doctors, nurses and surgeons, who in turn could be contemptuous of anything not done properly. The volunteers took the brunt of their short tempers, brought on by exhaustion and frustration. Some of the VADs succumbed to the pressure themselves and faded away, unable to face the horrors anymore. Others, like Rose, earned a grudging respect from the doctors and were asked to do worse.

Rose Preston, the little girl of her father's dreams who grew up enough to parade with the social elite at the Melbourne Cup, could always be relied upon to hold a man's gangrenous limb while the surgeon sawed through the bone.

She had two uniforms, and each shift the one she wore was literally soaked with blood. Her last task every evening was to wash that day's uniform in the huge, steaming boilers of the hospital, then press the other one in readiness for the morning. Given the fickle English weather, everyone hung their alternate clothing in this basement to dry in the boiler's heat. With so many volunteers, she was never alone and it was the only place there was any real social interaction. The girls stood in their underwear or dressing gowns and chatted wearily through the steam and noise as they washed or ironed.

By December 1914, the opposing armies in France and Belgium were completely locked together and began a period of consolidation, rather than attack. Winter snows bogged everything down anyway. The daily number of casualties, though still horrifying by any standard, was reduced. At the same time, the medical authorities in England started to catch up on the initial flood of wounded and more hospitals were operating, so the workloads eased.

When she read in the *Times* that Australia had formed its own army, Rose felt no strong guilt about leaving. She *did* feel a real urge to serve among her own countrymen—to nurse soldiers who came from familiar places and to be a part of the Australian effort to defeat the Germans, whom she'd grown to hate. Without doubt, there would be hospital units created too. Although it was assumed that the new army would naturally come to Europe and fight in France, and she might be able to arrange to meet them in England, Rose preferred to travel home first. It was a chance to see her father, whose letters still hinted at a strong disapproval, and the sea trip was an opportunity to escape the bitter cold of London's winter and have a decent rest, which she desperately needed.

She left without ceremony, saying only brief goodbyes to the few friends she'd made, then sailed two weeks before Christmas to arrive home in early January.

Home again

'You look well, Rose.'

As soon as he'd spoken, her father turned away to empty his pipe into the cold fireplace. It was mid-summer in the southern hemisphere and the maid had put a flower arrangement in the hearth to hide the blackened bricks. Rupert didn't care. He rapped the wooden bowl against the stone and let the burned tobacco fall on the petals, leaving dark specks. But it gave him a moment he needed. Frankly, the appearance of his daughter had shocked him. Rose looked thin, rather than petite as he remembered, and the lack of weight showed in her face. Her hands, held steady on her lap, were roughened from work, the fingernails trimmed close. Her beautiful long hair was gone, cut into a short pageboy style. Rupert wasn't to know that this prevented it falling into men's wounds as she bent over them.

'Thank you, Father,' Rose murmured, her head lowered. Despite all that had happened since she'd left for England in the first place, Rose still expected her father to express his disapproval about what she'd done. Time wouldn't have healed the anger, but she wasn't afraid or ashamed. Just resigned and wanting to get the moment over with.

Rupert did have every intention of making his feelings known, but he was suddenly at a loss for words. Whenever he was upset, he liked to straighten his lean frame, hook his thumbs into the small pockets of his waistcoat, and puff reflectively on his pipe. It gave his antagonist time to think about what he or she had done. Consider the possibility of their guilt. The blue smoke was supposed to surround him with a calm, controlled aura, but this time he'd forgotten to even fill the damned pipe. He did so now, his fingers fumbling. He'd waited nearly twelve months to reprimand his little girl, but he was faced by a confident young woman instead. A woman with added years in her sad eyes.

He tried, 'I would hope your little adventure is over?'

'I would hardly call it an adventure, Father. Don't you read the newspapers?'

'Of course.' The snap in his voice crept through and he checked himself. It was important to keep composed. He lit the tobacco and dragged deeply. The early morning sunlight coming from a window cut shafts through the drifting tendrils of smoke.

'It's been a bad business over there,' he said. 'Why do you think I wanted you home?' When she didn't answer he asked more kindly, 'Anyway, the journey back must have given you a nice rest?'

'The Germans are using submarines more and more. I think it would have been safer on a hospital ship because they don't sail blacked-out. Our captain preferred to stay dark like the freighters, believing the risk was less, even though we were clearly a passenger liner.' Rose inclined her head to say it was now a pointless argument, since they'd arrived safely. 'I couldn't sleep much during the nights for worrying. I mainly dozed on deck in the daytime.'

'Good God, no one's going to sink an unarmed passenger liner,' Rupert said gruffly. 'Not even the Germans.'

'No, you're probably right.'

Unexpectedly, she smiled at him, displaying new creases in the corners of her eyes. Rupert couldn't tell if she was being condescending or not, but he lost the will to chastise her further. He wasn't even sure he could.

'Well, you're back home safe and sound. That's all that matters, I suppose. I've been very angry with you for a long time, but now...' He went over and kissed the top of her head. She smelled of carbolic soap, not the perfume he expected. In turn, she caught the familiar tobacco smells that lingered in his clothing, mixed with the same mild cologne he always bought. She reached up, found his hand and gave it a squeeze.

'It's good to be home, Father. Honestly.'

He seemed satisfied with that and patted the back of her fingers with his free hand.

'Emily Strathbury has already arranged a welcoming party for you,' he said. 'Just afternoon tea tomorrow at three. I said you wouldn't mind, even though you've only just got home—I wasn't to know your ship would be late, after all. She asked me last week. I expect they'll be keen to hear what you've been up to.'

Rose visibly blanched and pulled her hand away. It was highly unlikely the circle of women she'd mixed with before would be wanting to hear stories of amputating ruined limbs and stroking the fevered foreheads of dying boys, telling them they'd be *just fine*. No, the girls would be hungry for romantic tales of Florence Nightingale, falling in love with handsome cavalry officers with crooked smiles and one arm in a clean, white sling.

What could she say? Should she make up the stories they wanted to hear?

Rose didn't want to relive her experiences herself. Not yet.

'I–I don't know about that, Father. I'm still very tired.'

'It's just afternoon tea, Rose.' He frowned. 'And rather difficult to call off at this late stage. If you'd arrived home on time, it wouldn't be such a problem.'

'There was a U-boat warning and the ship changed course,' Rose explained. 'It added two extra days.' She thought of the scene awaiting her. Emily Strathbury's house had a back veranda surrounded by tall, creeping vines.

During this hot season, everyone would be seated there on the painted, wrought-iron furniture, the table in the centre. All the girls' clothing would be white or pastel coloured because of the heat. The gardener would discreetly spray water on the vine leaves and the breeze passing through would be pleasantly cool. A nice way to spend the afternoon, but not an occasion for Rose's stories.

She looked up to see her father with pressed lips, annoyed and uncertain how to deal with this reluctance. His daughter was almost a stranger to him, and with a softening heart Rose realised this. A small part of her was disappointed that he either didn't know what she'd been doing for the last six months, or refused to consider it. Did he appreciate how difficult it would be for her to just step back into her old life?

She gave in. 'All right, I'll go. I'll have an early night tonight, then I'll be fine. You don't have to change anything.'

'Good girl,' he smiled. He pulled a watch from his pocket and clicked his tongue in dismay. 'I'm already late for the office. We're very busy right now—' he stopped guiltily. Profiteering from the war wasn't something you talked about. 'Well, you can imagine why. What will you do for the rest of the day?'

'Have a long bath. I might even stay in it all day.'

That was more like the mischievous, spoilt Rose he knew. 'You do whatever you want. You've earned it.' He gave her another kiss, again on her hair. 'I'll remind Harriet that you'll be home. She'll probably make you a special lunch, so don't disappoint her by declining.'

'I won't.'

'Donald gets back tomorrow morning. He has a surprise for you.' He winked. 'I promised not to tell.'

'Is he still mad at me too?' she asked, fondly.

'You'll have to ask him yourself.' His tone implied that Donald, always mild-mannered, could hardly still be angry with his only sister.

'We'll all be together again,' she said. 'Won't that be lovely?'

He made one last attempt at scolding her. 'Yes, and about time too. Now, I must get going.' He nodded farewell and walked briskly from the room, his mind already on business matters.

After he'd left, for a long time Rose sat absolutely still and watched dust motes twist in the sunlight. Everything was so serene and peaceful. She couldn't get used to it.

***

The following morning, Rose was on edge. It felt strange having little, or even nothing, to do. At least some of the sadness had leaked from her soul, the confrontation with her father done with and the memories of the hospital slowly fading in these vastly different surroundings, and after six weeks on board the ship. The night before, Rupert had explained in proud detail how the family business was growing. It had been good for Rose to simply sit and listen, take in the news and nod appreciatively when she knew it was expected. Later, they'd played chess and she had found herself smiling widely, then chuckling, when she beat her father in just a few minutes. She didn't notice that the sound of her laughter seemed to take him by surprise.

Today, some of her discomfort returned and it was difficult to know why. She fidgeted in the garden, trying to enjoy the sunshine before it got too warm. She dutifully admired the carefully tended roses and clucked over the vegetable patch that Godfrey, the gardener, had established. Then, as she bent over a patch of peas and quickly stole one to taste, half-angry words came from behind.

'I should give you a damned thrashing while you're like that, for all the trouble you put me through.'

Rose laughed as she straightened up at her brother Donald's voice. She turned with a smart reply on her lips but froze as she saw him.

Donald was in uniform, the khaki of a soldier with two corporal's stripes on the shoulders. The flat cap sat rakishly on the back of his head. For a long moment, neither of them moved.

'Hey, aren't you glad to see me?' He held his arms out wide, but in his sparkling eyes was the hint of alarm at her dismay.

'God, of course I am.' She recovered and ran forward to embrace him. 'You took me by surprise, that's all.'

Donald crushed her in a hug, lifting her right off the ground. He was tall and powerfully built. Their father often joked that he obviously hadn't come from the Preston side of the family. Rose felt the familiar rough texture of a military uniform under her fingers and against her face, bringing back flashes of bad memories. At least it smelled clean and new. Donald let her go, putting his hands on her shoulders to hold her at arm's length and inspect her.

He said seriously, but with a smile, 'You need a bloody good feed and a few days in bed, from the look of you.'

She didn't want to argue. 'True, I need a bit of a holiday at least. That's why I'm here.'

He heard something unsaid and looked at her suspiciously. 'What? You're going back? Have you told Father?'

'No, I haven't made any decisions,' she said, deliberately vague. 'So don't put any ideas in Father's head, please. He's only just forgiven me for staying in England in the first place.'

'You're telling me? I'm the one who pretended I couldn't understand his telegrams, remember?' Donald stabbed himself in the chest with a finger.

'And I love you for it.' Rose stood on her toes and kissed him on the cheek.

'Now, I suppose this is your surprise?' She gestured at his uniform.

'Do you like it? Not just the threads, but these too.' He tapped the stripes. 'I'm leadership material, they reckon.'

'Which means the Germans will shoot you first. The snipers prefer killing officers and NCOs, you know.' The words were out of her mouth before she could stop them. Donald's smile vanished and he looked hurt. Instantly, she felt dreadful and put her hand on his arm.

'I'm sorry. That was a terrible thing to say. I don't know what came over me.'

'Yes, steady on,' he said softly, then he shrugged it off. 'Look, to be honest, you probably do know more about the business than I, after all that time nursing the wounded and hearing all sorts of stories, I suppose. So don't worry, I'll take heed of what you say and lead my men gallantly from the bottom of a very deep trench.' His smile came back and he gave her a mock bow. 'No charging out in front of the troops, waving the jolly old flag, I promise.'

'Good, Donald. Make sure you don't.' She hoped he meant it, though it was unlikely. She told herself to try harder at keeping the dark thoughts of the war at bay. It was a beautiful morning, filled with the colours and smells of the garden. Bees were humming inside the flowers and butterflies scattered aside from their path. Now her lovely brother was here too. She should enjoy herself, while she could.

She purposely changed the subject as they linked arms and started walking slowly back towards the house. 'What are your plans until Father comes home?'

'I don't have any, actually.'

'I've got to go to afternoon tea with Emily Strathbury and the rest. Want to come?' As she explained, she realised that her persistent unease came from dreading the party.

'Tea with a bunch of prattling females? Absolutely not. I just took a vow of cowardice, remember? You insisted on it. You're on your own there, little sister.'

She groaned. 'I didn't think you'd go. You're not a very good brother after all, are you?'

'The worst,' he agreed, laughing.

***

Emily was two years older than Rose and in the past had adopted a protective manner towards her, as if she were a big sister. Rose would have called Emily her best friend, without considering her exactly a *confidante*. The two women had exchanged only a few letters while Rose was in England, the tyranny of distance taking its toll, and if they were both truthful, it had been a poor attempt at keeping in touch. The gap between the subject matter of their letters was as vast as the ocean that separated them. Emily wrote about the petty gossip, engagements and marriages of their mutual friends, all within the affluent circles she moved in. Rose tried to tell Emily about the cramped flat she shared with two other VADs, because her Rupert's relatives lived too far away from the hospital. And the rationing that affected almost everything. She'd written some heavily censored stories about the hospital and her nursing duties, but not many. Good news mostly, about men who recovered.

With a taxi chugging noisily away up the street behind her, Rose walked the long garden path to the Strathburys' house. When she was halfway there, Emily opened the front door and called out happily.

'The intrepid traveller returns! And alone, no less. Where's that handsome brother of yours? He was supposed to come too. I told your father.'

Rose waited until she had reached the porch before exchanging a quick hug. 'Hello, Emily. Donald had some important business to deal with. He wants to get all that rubbish out of the way, so he can relax.' The devil got hold of her and she added with a sly smile, 'Why don't you invite him over for dinner one evening? I'm sure he'd like to see you.'

The prospect of having Donald to herself appealed to Emily and put gleam in her eye. 'Good idea,' she said, arching an eyebrow. 'Anyway, *do* come in.

We're all out the back on the porch. It's too nice a day to be indoors.'

She bustled off down the hallway, expecting Rose to follow. It was a bit anticlimactic, as if Rose had been away for merely a long weekend, not a whole year. Rose noted that her friend had put on some weight, or perhaps she was used to the more gaunt appearance of her colleagues back in England—hard work and rationing took their toll. Emily struck her as *fleshy* in a prosperous sort of way. The flowing pale blue dress with its white lace hid her figure mostly, but the fullness showed in her face and hands.

Then Rose silently chastised herself for being unfairly judgemental. *What did she expect*? The war had hardly touched Australia yet and Emily looked healthy, for God's sake. There was nothing wrong with that.

'Look who's here,' Emily was saying delightedly as they emerged from the house. Rose held her breath and put on her best smile, bracing herself for a crowd of excited, welcoming faces, some of which she wouldn't even know. She was relieved to see only four other girls seated at the wrought-iron table. They were all friends from her past, people who had shared other parties or concerts—the usual events. Two of them, Belinda Johnson and Julie-Anne Merriweather, had gone to the same school as Rose, as classmates. The others, Tiffany Schultz and Susanne Corbett, had met her some years before and always attended the social gatherings of their clique. Emily's parents were nowhere to be seen.

Rose moved around the table and accepted brief embraces and pecks on the cheek from all of them. She noticed Susanne was well into a pregnancy and offered her congratulations. The husband was somebody Rose didn't know. Finally she sat at the last vacant chair and waited while a maid, who had appeared from nowhere, poured a cup of tea.

Emily said, 'I thought I'd keep this little party nice and intimate. I didn't want to overwhelm you with too many people.'

'Thank you. That's very thoughtful.' Rose *was* grateful, and now felt even more guilty about her unkind thoughts on Emily's figure.

'God, you look so–so grown up,' Emily laughed at herself. The others joined in.

Rose smiled. 'Being away from home for a while does that,' she shrugged.

'Especially in Europe,' Emily winked.

'Well, in London.'

'That's European enough for me!'

On cue, everyone laughed again.

The conversation began with comparisons between the way of life overseas and in Australia. Belinda was the only one who had travelled and eagerly swapped anecdotes with Rose, while the rest listened jealously. Rose was glad to keep things going this way, dreading the moment when the chatter would address her work and everything else she'd been doing—as it would, eventually.

An hour passed. The tea flowed and Rose wondered if these girls had some secret way of controlling their bladders, because hers was starting to feel the pressure. But every time a cup was poured, or the bowl of sugar was offered, it stretched the afternoon out a fraction more, and brought her closer to an acceptable time when she could make her apologies and leave. Anything, including gallons of tea, was better than telling tales of her VAD experiences. Because it was summer, the day was long and the sun stayed unco-operatively high in the sky, so it looked as if the afternoon would never end. The chatter flowed around Rose. She nibbled on the sandwiches and cream cakes brought by the maid, who seemed to have nothing better to do. The Strathburys had the maid and a cook, plus a full-time gardener. In comparison, Rose's father employed just Harriet as a live-in housemaid who also prepared meals. Godfrey, the gardener, was shared with half a dozen other families.

Talk of Rose's nursing came from out of the blue and took her by surprise, just as she was about to ask for a taxi to make her escape. They were discussing Susanne's new husband and the impending baby.

'What about you, Rose?' Emily asked her. 'You must have left a thousand broken hearts behind here, when you sailed. Did you wreak similar havoc in London? You haven't got a husband back there that you haven't told us about?'

'No, of course not.' She tried to laugh it off.

'Surrounded by doctors and soldiers all day?' Emily gave her a disbelieving look. 'Medical students may be poor as church mice, but once they get qualified with a nice little practice somewhere, they can be quite attractive.' She glanced suggestively at the others. 'Or perhaps a major general is more to your taste.'

'Nothing less than a brigadier will do, I'm told,' Belinda chipped in, giggling.

'I didn't meet anyone like that,' Rose admitted. 'My ward was for enlisted men only. The officers were treated elsewhere.'

'Well, naturally,' Emily nodded easily and sipped her tea.

The anger came suddenly, as it always did for Rose. She frowned. 'No, in fact there's nothing natural about it at all.'

Something about her upper-class surroundings this afternoon, the hovering servants and the girls' educated accents, had already brought back the spark of a resentment born in London. Now Emily's comments fanned it into a flame.

Rose began believing that class distinction, which she'd gladly taken for granted before the war, was often unfair and pointless. In her opinion, all the wounded were brought down to the same level by a bullet or shrapnel. The men all made the same sacrifice. But the officers enjoyed a subtle favouritism, such as a larger ward and more space between the beds. Perhaps it was a false impression because the flowers and gifts for the officers tended to come from more prosperous families, which made everything look better. Still, she couldn't help being offended by it, and the enlisted casualties with nothing to occupy their minds except pain and sometimes bitterness, often hinted at the same.

Making things worse now, with these feelings souring Rose's mood, Emily had unwittingly opened the door to the very conversation Rose wanted to avoid. She bit her lip in dismay.

'Yes, what exactly did you do?' Emily asked, with sudden sympathy and ignoring the argument. 'You never quite explained in your letters.'

After a small hesitation, Rose decided to forge on as quickly as possible. Refusing to discuss it would have been churlish. 'I wanted to be a nurse, but it was easier to volunteer as a nurse's aide and start work straight away.'

A mixture of revulsion and fascination crossed Belinda's face, 'So you worked in the wards. With the wounded men?'

'That's right.' Rose decided that she wouldn't mention assisting the surgeons.

'That must have been awful. How did you ever cope?'

'The wounded are suffering more. You simply remember that.'

'Yes, I think you were very brave,' Emily announced loudly, as if it had been her idea for Rose to volunteer.

'Not really,' Rose smiled wanly.

'It's all the fault of those dreadful Germans,' Julie-Anne said in a whisper. 'I hear they were raping women and killing children in Belgium.' She looked pointedly at Susanne, who paled and put a hand on her swelling belly.

'The Germans,' Belinda agreed knowledgably. 'Terrible people. They're descended from the barbarians of old. That's why we call them *Huns* now.'

Emily said quickly in an odd tone, 'Now Belinda, not all Germans are quite so unpleasant.' Her eyes were darting at Tiffany Schultz, who looked very uncomfortable.

Belinda's fingers flew to her mouth. 'Oh! I didn't mean—well, not *everyone*.' She reached over and touched Tiffany's arm. 'Goodness, you're not really a German anyway. I mean, you were born here.' She faltered, the damage already done. No one knew what to say and a silence dragged out.

'You're not the only ones to think we're German,' Tiffany said in a small voice. 'People have been wrecking our front fence. Pulling the palings off as they pass at night. And shouting out horrible things. We had to take our name off the front of the house, but it was too late. Everyone knows where we live.'

This brought gasps all around except from Rose. Similar things had happened in London to families of German descent, before they were taken away and interned as aliens.

'What is the world coming to?' Emily said heavily. 'Honestly, I wish they could keep their damned war to themselves.' This was strong language for her, and some of her guests shifted uneasily in their seats.

Rose felt her anger flare again. 'It's our war too,' she said, a little harshly.

'Well, of course, Australia is sending troops. And we absolutely should, I agree. The king has called for every able-bodied man...' Emily was flustered by Rose's attitude. 'But I mean, it's got nothing to do with *us*, has it?'

'With whom, exactly?'

In the spark of a disagreement between the two friends, the brief sympathy for Tiffany Schultz had evaporated. Her woes were forgotten as the girls blinked nervously at Emily, their leader, and Rose who dared to question her.

In the tense atmosphere, Emily gestured at everyone uncertainly. 'People like us, I mean. Wars are fought by... well... others. A few gentlemen officers might regard the army as a career, but otherwise rank and file soldiers come from the working class.'

A cold pit of disgust formed in Rose's stomach. She knew it was unreasonable. Emily couldn't be expected to understand the first thing about this war, and she hardly represented the majority of Australians who were urging their country to get into the fight and defeat the Germans. But again the references to class distinction disturbed Rose too much to let them pass without comment.

In a steely voice, she asked, 'Do you know how many French soldiers were killed in the first week of the German invasion?'

Emily made a frustrated noise. 'That's hardly something I would take an interest—'

'Forty-seven thousand,' Rose cut her off. 'That's *killed*, Emily. It doesn't include how many were wounded. It was 47,000 men dead in a week. Half of those were in a single day.'

It wasn't the sort of thing young ladies discussed. They were staring almost fearfully at Rose now, but she didn't care. Julie-Anne was blushing with her discomfort. A longer silence threatened to become embarrassing.

Finally Emily laughed briefly. 'Goodness, that can't be right. I don't think the entire French *army* is that big. You must have been listening to too much of that... what do they call it? Propaganda.'

'Actually, the real figure is probably more,' Rose told her with an icy calm. 'But the French government fears it's demoralising enough. My point is that the Germans don't care who they slaughter. It didn't matter where the French soldiers were educated, or how prosperous their families were. Where they lived.'

Belinda broke in desperately, trying to defuse the situation. 'But there's nothing we can do about it, is there? That's what Emily was trying to say.'

Rose turned on her. 'There's plenty we can do. Women don't have to be useless their entire lives. Especially people like us, who are lucky enough to be able to make some choices for themselves.'

Emily had regained some of her poise and she let her disapproval show. 'That's fine for you to say. You've had your Florence Nightingale adventure, so now you think you can come home and criticise us. Why didn't you stay in London, if it's so important to you?'

'I've come back to join the Australian army,' Rose snapped back. 'And if they won't have me, I will go back to London.'

It was half a challenge to the girls and they looked uneasily at each other.

Susanne spoke first. 'I think that's admirable of you, Rose,' she said quietly. 'But not everyone is in a position to be so helpful. You should remember that.' She ran a hand over her swollen belly. 'In fact, it's time I got home and had a rest. I like to be cheerful when Roger gets home. It's easier, if I've closed my eyes for a few minutes before he arrives.'

She struggled to her feet, perhaps exaggerating the extra weight she carried. Everyone except Rose stood with her and offered helping hands.

'I'll get someone to go and hail you a taxi,' Emily said kindly, moving towards the back door. 'It won't take long.'

Rose stopped her. 'Please, get one for me too.'

Emily's answer was cold as she paused at the entrance. 'Of course.'

Rose stayed seated, feeling that everyone's eyes were staring crazily at her. It was as if she were covered in blood, the way she used to be after a shift in the ward. Then Tiffany touched her shoulder and asked softly, 'Would you like to share a taxi with me, Rose? We're both going in the same direction.'

'Yes, thank you. That's a good idea,' Rose said, looking up and managing a smile.

Everyone waited awkwardly on the front porch for the taxis to arrive. One of the servants needed to walk to the main road and flag them down. In the meantime, Emily wasn't going to let Rose off the hook and maintained her icy manner. When the taxi finally came, it was a relief.

Sitting side-by-side in the back of the car, Tiffany and Rose found conversation difficult. The motor was too loud and they were jolted around painfully by the harsh suspension.

As they pulled up outside Tiffany's home, Rose was saddened by the damage to the fence and garden. The war with its hatred was touching Australia after all. More wooden palings were missing and shrubs had been uprooted, leaving black craters of soil in the green lawn.

'Don't worry, it's my treat,' Rose said gently, as she watched Tiffany stand outside the car, head bent to hide sudden tears as she fumbled in a tiny purse for some coins. The driver looked at the damage suspiciously, came to his own conclusions and frowned.

Tiffany nodded gratefully and put one gloved hand on the car's open window. Her eyes glittered in the late afternoon sunshine.

She said timidly, 'You've changed, Rose. A lot.'

An automatic apology came to the tip of Rose's tongue, but she stopped it. 'I know,' she said instead. 'And I'm glad.'

'Yes, perhaps you're right,' Tiffany agreed, reluctantly.

'Please take care of yourself.'

'Oh, I expect Father's got it all sorted out.'

'Fathers always do.'

Rose leaned forward to remind the driver of the next address and they pulled away with a roar and a cloud of smoke. Despite being smothered by the fumes, Tiffany stayed and waved until the car turned a corner.

***

Rose broke the news to her father the next morning at breakfast. The three of them were sitting around the dining room table. Rupert and Donald were at either end and she was between them. Sunlight streamed through the lace curtains and glinted off the silverware. Feeling nervous about the impending argument, she hardly touched her food, and Rupert noticed.

'Are you ill, Rose?' he asked, a fork halfway to his mouth. 'I hope it's not something you picked up on the boat?'

She sighed. 'No, I'm fine. It's just that I have something to tell you.'

Rupert glanced at Donald, who suddenly had to concentrate fiercely on his ham and eggs. 'It's obviously going to be something unpleasant,' Rupert said carefully.

'It depends on your point of view.'

That made him even more wary. Rose took a breath, squared her shoulders and looked him in the eye. 'I've decided I'm going to join the Australian Army Nursing Service. I want to travel back to Europe with them, with our own army. Do something useful.'

Rupert went still, then put his cutlery down with a decisive *click*. Donald felt obliged to stop eating too and sat awkwardly, his hands on the table. At that moment, Harriet came in with a fresh pot of tea and placed it where they could all reach. She felt the tension and fled quickly.

'That's disappointing to hear,' Rupert said tightly. 'I'm not sure I approve. You've only just turned twenty-one, after all. You're hardly of an age to be making these sorts of decisions for yourself.'

Rose could tell he was searching for a means to stop her, as she'd expected. However, he hadn't burst into anger, although she was prepared for it. Not yet, anyway. He was shrewd enough to realise that he couldn't really prevent her from doing anything. Not in a legal sense. But she couldn't afford to live anywhere without her allowance.

'I don't need your approval,' she told him quietly, and winced. 'I can only hope for your support.'

'Support? Support for what? My daughter ignoring everything I've ever done for her, just so she can continue an irresponsible life of high adventure?' His voice was rising.

She matched his tone. 'Tending wounded men is hardly high adventure.'

'The army has *men* trained for such things. And it's not the life I envisaged for my daughter.'

'I'll have you know it's something I do well.' Rose surprised herself. 'A damned sight better than you probably realise.'

His eyebrows flew up at her language and he struggled to reply.

Donald started to rise. 'I think perhaps I should—'

'Sit down, Donald,' Rupert snapped at him instead. 'This is a family matter and the three of us are all the family we have.'

Something in his words struck a chord in Rose and she wondered if this, after all, hinted at her father's greatest fear. Was he afraid of being left alone? Without doubt, Donald would be going overseas. Possibly for years, if the latest estimates of the war's duration were accurate. Rose could be gone for the same amount of time and her father would be left in the house by himself, with only the maid for company.

Rupert let out a long breath through his nose. 'I was hoping to have you around the home for a little while. In fact, no—' he corrected himself. 'I was *actually* hoping you'd get a little more serious about settling down. This is not the time to be wandering around the world.'

'And find a husband, you mean?' she asked, gently now. 'That's hardly likely.

All the good men are going overseas to fight.'

'Don't joke, Rose.'

'I'm not joking, Father.'

'Did you know about this?' Rupert asked Donald, who looked startled.

'Not at all. I'm just as surprised as you are, Father.'

After a suspicious glare at his son, Rupert turned back to Rose and accused her, 'You planned this before you even got off the boat, didn't you? Why didn't you say something earlier?'

'I've only been home for three days.'

He snorted but didn't answer. Rose watched him pick up his cutlery again and he began sawing angrily at the ham. Donald took it as encouragement to finish his own breakfast, but he did so slowly in case it somehow got him into more trouble.

'It's not as if I'm talking about leaving today,' she told them both. 'I'm not even sure the nursing service will have me.'

'Exactly,' Rupert was encouraged. 'Aren't you being presumptuous? Changing bedpans in a London hospital is hardly qualifications for being accepted into the army.'

'Changing bedpans?' Rose choked back a renewed sudden anger. 'Is that what you think I did? What *any* of us did?'

'How the devil should I know? How many letters did you write us in the past year? Three? Four at the most? Oh, for God's sake!' Rupert threw his napkin aside. He stood up from the table and stalked out of the room. A moment later, they heard the front door open.

They stayed seated in the silence. Donald kept eating for a few seconds, then put down his knife and fork and said lightly, 'There, that wasn't so bad, was it? I thought Father might go completely berserk. Old age has mellowed him, it seems.'

'Father never goes completely berserk,' she reminded him. 'Don't be silly.'

He pulled a face. 'Just trying to cheer things up a bit.'

She pushed her chair back. 'I'll go and talk to him.'

He looked doubtful, but changed his mind with a shrug, leaned over and used his fork to steal the ham from her plate. 'This will go cold then,' he explained innocently.

Rupert stood on the front path and breathed deeply in the fresh morning air. It was something he did every time he got upset and needed to think. Rose walked silently up behind him and put her arms around his waist, resting her cheek against his back. She felt him go rigid for a second, then relax with a sigh.

'I know what I'm doing, Father,' she said softly.

'No doubt you think you do,' he replied heavily. 'But you're only a child.'

'You're right about one thing. I've got the rest of my life to worry about husbands and children of my own. But I'm not a child anymore. I've seen too much.'

'You should never have seen it in the first place.' His hands came down to cover hers. 'And I should never have let you go to London.'

'There was nothing wrong with that. Everything *else* in the world went bad.'

'Yes, I suppose you're right.'

They stayed like this in a comfortable silence for some time, then the moment was shattered by a high scream of pain carrying clearly from the end of the street. Rupert broke her embrace, went to the fence and leaned over to see. A main thoroughfare was only six houses away. A tram had stopped across the t-junction and a small crowd had gathered around it. Everything looked bright and colourful in the sunshine, but obviously something was wrong.

'Some fool has been hurt by a tram again,' he told Rose over his shoulder. 'It happens all the time. They try to cross the tracks just as the trams move off.

The damned drivers should take more care, too...' He paused, then added sombrely, 'It looks rather serious.'

He was surprised by Rose pushing past him through the gate to hurry down the road towards the tram. 'Rose? What are you doing?'

'Going to see if I can help,' she shouted back.

'There are already more than enough people,' he began, then shook his head in exasperation. 'Besides, it's time for me to leave for work,' he called, with no hope of stopping her.

A few cars had parked now, their owners getting out to look. Hard against the side of the tram about a dozen jostling, talking people were standing around a crumpled figure at their feet. Several others hung out the windows of the tram to see. One man was bent down beside the victim, but didn't seem to be doing much. Rose forced her way through the crowd and crouched beside the injured man too. She heard some muttering from the people behind her as she did, but ignored it.

It was a youth, perhaps sixteen years old. He'd somehow slipped in the path of the moving tram and the wheels had severed one of his legs just above the knee, even slicing through the cloth of his trousers. He lay in an uncomprehending daze now, groaning horribly, shaking, his eyes glazing over as he tried to focus on the newcomer. A wide pool of blood spread from the reddened stump, making the onlookers slowly edge backwards. The man by the youth's side was the tram driver.

'This is no place for you, miss,' he said automatically, but Rose ignored him too. He was in nearly as much shock as the boy.

'Either help, or get out the way,' she rasped at him. The driver jerked back in surprise, but he stayed.

The tarmac was already hot from the morning sun and it stank of spilt oil and horse droppings. Rose could feel the sticky warmth through the knees of her dress as she knelt. The smell of the boy's blood wafted up around her. The tram at her shoulder was like a huge iron beast, waiting impatiently.

She snapped off the boy's braces from one side, then shoved a hand under his body to get the other end. 'Find his leg,' she told the driver, puffing with the effort of moving the boy's weight.

'What?' he asked, staring at her numbly.

'*Find the rest of his leg,*' Rose nearly shouted in his face.

'Oh–oh, yes,' he muttered, but he cast around ineffectually without rising, not really looking. Some of the crowd did the same, half-heartedly shuffling about and gazing at the ground as if they were looking for a lost penny. Rose felt a rage grow in her and she was about to yell at them all.

Then a voice came calmly from one of the windows above them. 'It will be *under* the tram, you fools.'

Rose looked up to see the face of a man watching. He was upset but controlled. 'Yes, of course. Thank you,' she called back coolly, then turned to the driver. 'You heard him. Look under the tram—and someone find a blanket.'

The driver did a double-take, realising that she expected him to crawl under the wheels. He went reluctantly.

As they tried to drag the severed limb out, Rose used the first brace to tie a tourniquet above the bleeding stump. By now, the youth was unconscious. She didn't think he would live because of the amount of blood he'd already lost, but she had to try. Someone dropped a checked blanket next to her and after releasing the other trouser brace, she quickly tucked it around the boy, leaving the injured leg exposed. Then somebody gingerly pushed the rest of the severed limb next to her.

Some of the onlookers gasped when Rose picked it up without a second thought and started to rip at the laces of the boot and drag it off. Next, she shook the dead limb out of the trousers. She wasn't interested in the leg, she wanted the cloth of the pants. She used it like a sock, pulling it partially over the bloody stump, then wrapping the remainder like a turban around the upper leg. She used the second brace to tie it in place. Now the injury was protected from further dirt, if nothing else.

She stood up painfully, her knees protesting from the hard tarmac. It had all taken less than two minutes, but with the rush of adrenalin it felt like hours. 'We need to get him off the road,' she announced.

With the dreadful injury covered, there were plenty of willing helpers to pick the youth up and place him on the grassy verge under the shade of a tree.

Then the crowd began to melt away. Passengers on the tram were also getting down from the carriage and trying to hail taxis. The show, it seemed, was over—apart from the large bloodstain and the white, pathetic limb lying beside it. In the distance, the jangling bell of an ambulance came closer.

By the time the ambulance men loaded the boy onto a stretcher and put him into the van, he was barely alive. Rose watched in silence. Nobody asked who had done the rudimentary first aid, although the two knee-high bloodstains on her dress where she'd knelt on the road gave her away. One of the van's crew went over and retrieved the rest of the leg. A policeman was talking to the driver now, and they were joined by the conductor. They kept on looking at Rose.

Her mood changed and she didn't want to have anything more to do with things. Almost all the onlookers had gone, and for the first time she noticed her father. Seeing her look at him, he came over and put an arm around her shoulder.

'I'll walk you to the house, then I'll come back and talk to the police myself,' he said gently.

Rose let him lead her. She wasn't shocked or upset, just suddenly too tired to speak. As they moved through their front gate, Rupert put his lips to his daughter's hair and spoke softly. 'And I'll talk to some contacts I have in the army. I've got a few now, what with supplying thousands of blankets and such.' Then he cleared his throat roughly before adding in a tone of resignation, mixed with pride, 'You're right. I'd say they might find you quite useful.'

Anzac Cove, 1915

In May 1915, the invading Australian and New Zealand forces held a small beachhead just north of Gaba Tepe on the Gallipoli Peninsula. Beyond the narrow beach itself the terrain was utterly unsuitable for fighting a war. It was mostly desert-like, with sheer, high cliffs and deep gullies of loose sand and rocks. Trees were sparse. Prickly, stunted bushes with dry, green leaves and sharp branches provided no shade and no comfort. Our imaginations will always fall short of the truth about how harsh this region can be with its unrelenting heat in summer and freezing snows during winter. It was a difficult, perhaps impossible place to attempt an invasion. The conditions killed men of both sides as readily as enemy bullets.

The Anzac position resembled a child's spread hand. The stubby fingertips were the extremes of their advance and ended in short sections of trenches. The land between the fingers was impassable with high, unclimbable crests and valleys too low and exposed to any fire from above. Some parts were mountainous. So although there was a definitive "front line" and the Turkish forces faced the Anzacs with corresponding defences, most of the fighting occurred in distinct areas. There was no continuous line of trenches like those that had developed in Belgium and France. On Gallipoli, a pitched battle in one area might as well have been on the other side of the world because of the natural barriers between.

The Anzac soldiers became known as "diggers", after their leader General Sir Ian Hamilton's famous directive to "dig, dig, dig, until you are safe" rather than abandon the landings after the first disastrous day. And dig they did, not just at the beginning, but as part of their attacking strategy. The soldiers would tunnel or "sap" forward from their existing trenches towards the Turks, establish outposts of armed resistance, then expand their digging sideways to eventually link up these advanced pockets and form a new front trench line.

This is what the Anzacs did all day, and all night. They attacked forward when they could, defended their gains grimly at all costs (and sometimes lost) and dug ceaselessly at the treacherous soil, trying to improve their hopeless situation. The arid, hilly land seemed to hate them as much as the Turks did. Their food rations were inadequate and fresh drinking water was in severe short supply, carried up from the beach by hand. Rifle and machine gun fire was constant from both sides—an incredible amount of ammunition was expended each day.

Artillery shells plucked at the landscape and its hiding soldiers remorselessly, causing random casualties.

The noise of all this cannot be imagined. Looking back today, our mind's eyes are clouded by faded photographs and artists' hurried, impressionist brushstrokes. Nothing can be seen clearly.

But the written words of countless diaries and letters home haven't changed over the long years. We still have the soldiers' stories, clear and undiminished by time.

Jonathon

Jonathon White sat on the fire step with his back against the forward trench wall, his legs splayed out carelessly. Men walking past stepped over, some of them muttering apologies or warnings, but most ignoring him. He was smoking a cigarette, wearily tipping his head back to send the smoke shooting upwards. The trenches were deep here, the floor seven feet below the crumbling edge of the parapet: deep enough to allow men to walk upright in safety. The walls of dry yellow soil cascaded in small landslides as the men squeezed around each other, their shoulders rubbing against the edges. Every day soldiers cleared the latest falls and used sandbags to shore up the unstable parts. The constant digging caked the men's skin with dust and got into their clothing. It filled their hair and made them look old.

A machine gun opened up somewhere close, drowning the noise of the constant rifle fire. Jonathon could feel the loud firing beat through the air, the hammering noise painfully loud. He could even hear the tinkling of the brass cartridges as they fell about the gunner's feet. He listened hard, but held off unwinding his tall, lean frame from its comfortable position just yet. The gunner was one of their own. No one was panicking about an attack. There were no warning whistles, and there was no discordant bugling from the Turks.

The gun stopped abruptly and somebody laughed in the silence.

'I'm glad you think it's bloody funny,' Jonathon muttered, waiting.

Within seconds, a Turkish gun raked their section of the trench in reply. Men on either side of him crouched down quickly. Instinctively he ducked as bullets crackled overhead. Some chipped into the ground in front of the parapet, sending a spray of dirt over the lip onto his head and shoulders. He snarled a curse, feeling the sand sneak down the back of his shirt.

'Did you *have* to do that?' he called when the gunfire stopped. It got another laugh. Disgusted, Jonathon flicked his cigarette butt up and out of the trench.

All along the trench, men were risking shots at the enemy, poking their heads up and firing quickly. Among them other soldiers, like Jonathon, rested. On a quiet day like today there was little sense in wasting valuable ammunition. The men took turns in maintaining a respectable rate of fire, that was all.

The Turks did the same back. Their Mausers made a flat, cracking sound different from the explosive bang of the Lee Enfields, and bullets buzzed past like angry insects. Shouted orders from both sides carried across the land on this gentle spring morning. There was a bright sun and a slight breeze, which none of them could enjoy without exposing themselves. At least the breeze came from the west, across the ocean behind the Anzac beachhead, so for now, the stench from the corpses in no-man's-land was carried forward into the Turkish positions.

Someone sat heavily down beside Jonathon and caused another avalanche of soil from the wall. He stopped a growl of complaint when he saw that it was his friend, Robert Thornton.

'G'day, Robert,' he said casually.

'Jonno,' Robert nodded slowly, as he always did. He was immediately absorbed in rolling a cigarette, his rifle dropped to lean against the fire step. Robert's hands worked between his raised, wiry knees. He had been thin and awkward-looking from the start. Now, after a few weeks of their strict rations, he looked starved.

'Want one?' He offered the open tin.

'Got one,' Jonathon touched another smoke he had behind his ear, hidden by his fair hair. 'So, you heard anything?' It was a common greeting among the men, who thrived on rumours and stories.

'Yeah, Willow wants to do one of his trench raids tonight.' As he licked the gum of the cigarette paper, Robert stole a look at his friend.

'What? Jesus...' Suddenly angry, Jonathon stared at the dirt next to his boots. 'This is our last night. Can't it wait? We've done all right this time. Why go and ruin it?'

Their stint in the front trenches was nearly over and they'd suffered only a few casualties. The next morning would see them having a brief rest in the rear, although instead of fighting they would be carrying water, ammunition and supplies back to the very trenches they'd just left. That meant walking steadily up and down the hills, the men fully laden and struggling to keep their footing. With the enemy snipers and artillery, it was hardly a rest. But that was how the men saw it.

'Exactly,' Robert said, nodding again as he lit up. 'Willow probably doesn't want us leaving the line without feeling we've done something useful.'

'Just bloody surviving is useful enough.'

'Yeah, well... maybe he won't ask you.' Robert shook the match out.

'Pig's arse.'

Jonathon was well known for his excellent night vision, so he was a natural choice for any operations after dark. Willow always *asked* men to be a part of the raids, but no one ever refused. It just wasn't done.

'Shit, you *always* go,' Robert said. 'Willow knows that, so maybe he won't ask.'

'What's the moon tonight?'

'Ah—no, no moon. It's gone already.' Avoiding his friend's eyes, Robert took off his cap and ran a hand through his thick black hair. It stood up in wet spikes.

'So he'll ask, for sure.'

Robert's silence agreed. Putting the cap back on, he said, 'Hell, I don't know why we even bother with the damned things.'

'To give the Turks the shits. Nothing else—well, maybe to grab a German.'

Jonathon shrugged. 'They're running the show over there. The Turks are just hired help in their own country.'

'What the hell does it matter?'

'That's not for us to know, is it?' With a sigh, Jonathon got to his feet. A soldier beside them called Hanson looked down when he felt Jonathon's touch. 'Dougie, take a break. I'll keep an eye out.'

Gratefully, Hanson sat down. Jonathon took his place on the fire step, but before he chanced a look over the top, he heard Robert mutter in surprise.

'Hey, take a look at this.'

Sergeant Tom Carter was making his way along the trench, a strange-looking rifle in his hands. The weapon had an assortment of timber pieces, mirrors and strings fastened to the stock. 'Here's the thing, lads,' he said cheerfully. 'Have you seen the periscopes some of the men are using? This is the next bright idea. Damned clever.' He lifted the rifle to show them.

Jonathon stepped back down to have a closer look.

Robert eyed the contraption doubtfully. 'Does it work?'

'There's only one way to find out, isn't there?' The sergeant's smile said he already knew.

Soldiers nearby paused in their shooting to watch, but beyond the small audience, the desultory exchange of rifle fire went on. Another machine gun rattled in the distance. As if to mark the occasion, the Turkish force's largest artillery gun *whoofed* a shell overhead to explode among the beach supply lines. The noise echoed around the hills.

No one mentioned it. Nicknamed "Big Bertha", the gun was well beyond the reach of any answering shot, so there was nothing to say.

Climbing onto the fire step, Carter balanced the modified rifle over the parapet's edge above. He had to bend and squint at a mirror that jutted down from the shoulder stock. He swivelled his body awkwardly to take aim. Then carefully, like man trying to hook a fish nibbling on a bait, Carter wound a string slowly around his finger.

He yanked and the rifle fired, bucking backwards from the trench lip. Carter deftly let the rifle fall and caught it.

He turned and grinned. 'See?'

'Did you hit anything?' Jonathon asked for everyone.

'Don't know.'

'Wonderful,' Robert said. 'Are we all supposed to make these things?'

'Especially you,' Carter nodded. 'Since you're always sitting on your arse having a smoke. This way, you don't have to get up at all.' Robert decided not to answer.

Carter's mood changed as he looked at Jonathon. 'Willow's doing a trench raid tonight, so he'll be chasing you up, no doubt.'

'Yeah, I heard.'

'I reckon you don't have to go. You're always doing them. Tell him you're crook, if you like, and you've had the shits all day. I'll back you up.'

'Christ, now *there's* a good excuse,' Robert muttered. Most of the troops suffered diarrhoea from the poor rations and water, but only the extreme cases stopped fighting.

'You know what I mean—' Carter began impatiently and glared at him.

'Don't worry. I'll go, if he asks me,' Jonathon cut him off.

Carter and Robert exchanged a glance, then the sergeant said, 'Good man. Those sharp eyes of yours can make all the difference, you know. *I'll* be happier to have you along, anyway.'

'Are you going?'

'Well, I thought I might save someone else the trouble.' Carter shrugged it away, but Jonathon felt uncomfortable. Carter had offered him a chance to escape because he knew Jonathon had done his fair share of the dangerous raids, but he'd still volunteered himself.

'So all right, what's the point?' Jonathon asked wearily. 'What are they hoping to find this time?'

'More Hun officer sightings.' Carter suddenly laughed wryly. 'A full colonel this time, no less. At this rate, within a week someone'll spot the fucking Kaiser himself manning a machine gun.'

Robert was frowning. 'You know, I wouldn't know a German colonel if he bit me on the arse.'

'Who would? Still, the brass swallowed the story and Willow stuck his hand up to go and have a look. Maybe we'll find a uniform, or some papers—I dunno.'

'And maybe we'll find half the Turkish garrison waiting in the trench.'

'We, Robert?' Jonathon grinned, but the smile didn't reach his eyes. 'Are *you* coming, too?'

'Why the hell not?' Robert spat to one side, avoiding their looks. After a silence he added, 'Like the sergeant says, it'll save someone else the trouble of going.'

Another burst of Turkish machine gun fire swept across the parapet above, showering down dirt. Everyone ducked again, the men on the fire step cursing loudly as they hurriedly turned away. The Australian gun sent a burst back.

'I'll tell Willow you're both in,' Carter yelled above the racket of firing. 'Meet us at his dugout at 2300. We'll be going soon after.'

Jonathon waved, not bothering to shout back over the noise, but when Carter was gone he rounded on Robert. 'You bloody idiot. What did you go and do that for?'

'To watch your back,' Robert shouted. 'While you're trying to see everything else, I suppose. Shit, what difference does it make?'

The machine gun stopped and in the silence Jonathon lowered his voice. 'There'll always be someone else to do that. What if we both get knocked? Who's going to milk the bloody cows back home then?'

'Your little brother, of course. Joseph can do 'em all. That suits me.' Robert started to laugh until he saw that his friend wasn't joking.

They came from neighbouring farms near the tiny town of Brunswick Junction in Western Australia. Although they had known each other all their lives, as two young boys in a small community would, they hadn't purposely joined the army together. It just happened that way and their casual friendship became close.

Jonathon squinted at him. 'What, don't you *want* to go home?'

'Sure,' Robert shrugged too quickly. 'Well, I think so. I mean, hell, I sure don't want to stay here.' He gazed thoughtfully at the soldiers on the fire step. They were beginning to shoot towards the Turkish lines again. 'It's not going to feel the same though, is it? Back home.'

Jonathon didn't answer for a while. 'No, I suppose it isn't,' he said finally.

***

Rifles cracked from all directions and machine guns chased noisily after fleeting targets. At Lone Pine, where the lines came within forty yards of each other, hand-bombs were exchanged. The Turks used small round missiles, which the Australians retrieved like cricket balls to hurl back. Their own grenades were mainly homemade things—jam tins packed with explosive, then any loose metal pieces. The nails from storage crates were a favourite.

All day, like some reliable deadly town clock, Big Bertha lobbed shells onto the Anzac beaches.

A permanent cloud of brown dust and cordite rolled away from the peninsula. Depending on the wind, it either went back into the hills and escarpments behind the Turkish lines, or out across the Anzac positions to the open ocean. Either way, always taking with it the smell of the dead and the stink of tens of thousands of men living underground.

After nightfall, the fighting continued. The soldiers couldn't see to aim, but they kept shooting and lobbing bombs into the darkness.

Willow's bunker was elaborate compared with most, especially since they'd only been landed two weeks. There were two real chairs among the usual upturned packing crates. Incredibly, he had a wide rug in the centre, but it was almost indistinguishable from the surrounding dirt now. The place was dug deep enough that there was no need to stoop, although the hanging oil lamps still had to be avoided. Maps and plans adorned the walls. These were army things, but they gave an impression of decoration until you looked closely. A stretcher with a neatly folded blanket was against one side. A makeshift table and one of the chairs were on another. Items of clothing hung from hooks thrust into the walls. The bunker had a feeling of permanency in a place where a major attack could overrun them at any moment.

Six men crowded inside. A similar number lingered beyond the curtained doorway, listening in. The air was thick with tobacco smoke. It shivered regularly as Turkish artillery shells slammed into the ground nearby. The noise after the initial detonation was a low rumble that shook the walls. Major Willow found himself pressed into one corner. He kept glancing at a map beside him, conscious that everyone knew it was probably not worth a damn because everything changed so much, and those that had been supplied for the landings had often proved hopelessly inaccurate from the start.

Willow was a thin, narrow-shouldered man with a moustache and thick black hair that he constantly brushed away from his forehead. He was Australian, but affected a cultured English accent more suitable, he believed, for an officer in this new army. It took an effort to keep up and often slipped when he was drunk or upset. Now his voice was piping as well, struggling to overcome the sporadic bombardment and an Anzac machine gun that periodically blasted at the Turkish lines and interrupted him with what seemed an uncanny sense of timing.

'Okay, everyone listen closely,' he began, peering in the poor light at the map. 'We'll jump from Bill's sector.' Around him the murmured conversation stopped, but he found the right place and tapped the map with his finger. 'It's a fair hike to the Turkish trenches, but that's good in some ways. They wouldn't expect a raid to come from such a distance. Also, they launched an attack at us across the same spot two days ago. It failed, of course, and now the place is littered with their dead. Plenty to hide behind when they throw flares.' He waited for someone to comment, but no one did. Six pairs of eyes, blinking with the smoke, watched him impassively.

'This straight part of their trench system hasn't changed since the day we got here. That makes it likely there's several large bunkers built into the walls, preventing any alterations. Probably for officers. This, and the fact that they're not too close to our lines, could mean that our German friends will be living there in comparative safety. Somewhere they can eat their sausage in peace, hey?'

The joke fell flat and wiped the smile off his face.

Carter spoke up quickly. 'Is this where they spotted the German officer, sir? The colonel?'

'Ah—no, it was opposite Lone Pine.' Willow looked annoyed. 'But still, this is a more likely place to try.'

'If the bunkers are even there, sir.'

'Yes, if the bunkers are *there*. As I'm sure they will be, Carter.'

'What if they're not?'

Willow sighed impatiently. 'We'll get the hell out again and come back. There's only so much we can do and the Turks will be stirred up to buggery. We don't want to be taking a midnight stroll along their lines. We get in, and *out*, of this section only. And bloody quick. Nothing else, for God's sake—or do you want to stay for supper?'

They smiled wryly, some with relief, at the hint that Willow didn't like this raid either. They'd already suffered foolish orders too often and it sounded like he wouldn't be taking even the smallest unnecessary risk.

Outside, a Turkish machine gun took its turn to send rounds cracking directly over the top of the bunker. Automatically they lowered their heads or hunched their shoulders, despite the corrugated iron ceiling above with its layer of protective sandbags.

'And what about *that* bastard?' someone snarled, when the firing stopped.

'Forget it.' Willow shrugged. He was studying his pocket watch. 'We'll be shadowed by a small rise. He can't touch you.' He flipped the lid on the watch closed with a decisive snick. 'All right, we'll go over in ten minutes. Last chance for a smoke, drink, or whatever you need to do. Just don't go too far.'

Everyone shuffled out into the trench, pushing past the men who'd been gathered at the bunker's opening. Jonathon and Robert worked their way along the narrow walkway until they found a vacant part of the fire step. Here, they sat and rolled a cigarette from their own tins. Both of them frowned at the tobacco between their fingers in the shadows. Then a flare was thrown nearby, flooding the area with a shimmering white light. Robert turned his face up to watch the glare reflect off the closest hills, and his skin looked a deathly pale.

'Burn 'em all up now, Abdul,' he said grimly. 'Keep it nice and dark for when we're out there.'

'You can hear them coming,' Jonathon said, lighting his smoke. 'The flares, I mean. Plenty of time to lie like you're dead after the fuse pops, but before they chuck 'em. Just don't move afterwards, that's all. Until it's gone.'

'That can be bloody ages,' Robert said, thrusting the cigarette in his lips between his friend's cupped hands for the last of the match. He took an appreciative drag. 'What if you're smack in the middle of crawling over a body? You're getting shit all over you. It's a bit hard to wait for the fucking flare to go away then.'

'You've always got time, if you listen.' Jonathon glanced at him. 'You've done this before.'

'Sure, but both times we were over the top and into the other side before you even had a chance to get scared. There was none of this creeping over a bloody mile of no-man's-land first.'

'It's about the only place there is miles to crawl over,' Jonathon said ruefully. 'I wish there were more of it. I get sick of these bastards breathing down our necks all day.'

The flare extinguished itself and the night closed in again, even darker after the glare. To their left, a burst of rifle fire and excited yelling told them someone had seen movement in front of the lines—or thought he had. Now the soldiers would blaze away at a spot in the blackness until they tired of the effort. These moments rarely brought a result, but helped them survive the night.

Robert said quietly, 'Christ, do you think we'll ever get out of here?'

'No doubt about it,' Jonathon nodded unseen. 'We wouldn't still be here if we couldn't. Someone'll come up with something, you watch.'

'You really believe that?'

'Yep.' He pushed himself upright. 'Come on. Willow will be foaming at the mouth by now.'

They were the last two to arrive at the jump-off point. It was only a small group, but Carter made a point of counting each man out loud before turning to Willow.

'All thirteen present, sir. Including yourself, of course.'

'Thank you, Sergeant. I hope no one's superstitious,' Willow said lightly.

A man called Harris said, 'Maybe six of us will get shot straight away.

Seven's supposed to be a lucky number.'

'Nobody's going to get shot,' Carter snapped. 'Not if we keep our wits about us and our bloody heads low.'

'Yes, the sergeant's right. We'll all be fine,' Willow added calmly, putting a hand on Carter's shoulder. 'Besides, once we nab our Hun, that'll make fourteen of us. That's twice as lucky as seven. Right, Harris?'

Robert leaned close to Jonathon and whispered, 'If we keep yapping about bloody bingo all night, we won't be going at all. Suits me.'

Jonathon didn't get a chance to reply. Willow was telling them once more the pre-arranged passwords to get them safely back into their own trenches if they got split up. He'd already gone over these in the bunker meeting, but always reminded his men of details like this at every opportunity, as if he didn't trust them to remember anything. He finished by saying, 'We stay close and watch each other's tails. That way, we'll all come back together safe and sound. Now, is everyone ready? Time to go.'

Without waiting further, Willow led the way, his revolver held poised in front of him. The soldiers followed with Carter bringing up the rear. He had a rifle and a holstered pistol.

They crawled inch by inch with exaggerated care, their limbs in slow motion. The sporadic firing around them could always hide any sounds they made, but any movement seen in no-man's-land would bring an instant reaction. The patrol watched for shifting in the night too. In case the Australians crept head-on into a Turkish raid coming their way.

The first bodies loomed only yards from the Anzac lines. The bulky silhouettes against the flashes of gunfire looked like large rocks half-buried in the earth. These were the Turks who had made it the furthest during the attack, more by sheer luck than bravery, before being cut down. Some had fallen at the very lip of the Australian trenches, but the diggers dragged those in later and used the corpses for shoring up sandbag emplacements. It was simpler than filling the hessian sacks with soil, and the smell, in all the stench of the battlefield, soon went unnoticed.

During the Turkish offensive a few days before, the Anzacs let the waves of attackers get close. The enemy were easier to shoot at point-blank range and the sheer numbers running at them, screaming defiantly or calling to Allah, prevented the Turks' own machine guns from providing covering fire. The diggers had gunned them down with near impunity.

Tonight, the dead men provided cover. Plenty of it. Even in the harsh light of a flare, the raiding party needed only to stay absolutely still to be lost among the countless other bodies on the open ground. Some Turks had dropped on top of one another and created piles of dead flesh that could hide them completely.

The raiding party kept in two curved lines, the centre of each pressing forward and concentrating on the ground ahead while the others worried about their flanks. The second line was supposed to offer covering fire if things went wrong. Jonathon was beside Carter, in the middle of the front line, with Robert just to his right and slightly behind. Their progress should have been steady, but the training book manoeuvre didn't allow for encountering the dead Turks every few feet, nor did it ever envisage the trench system they had just left or were supposed to attack. At best, keeping in touch with their comrades and always moving forward was all they could do.

Jonathon sensed, rather than knew, when Robert lost touch with the rest of the line. He was close enough to Carter to reach out, tap his ankle and tell him to stop. Carter crabbed around and put his face near Jonathon's.

'What's up?'

'Robert's fallen back.'

'Do you think he's hurt?' It was unlikely. No gunfire had come their way.

'Dunno. I didn't hear anything.'

'The next lads should find him. Help him catch up.'

Almost unseen, Jonathon stared irritably at Carter. 'I want to know if he's okay. Something bad could be happening.'

They were talking about someone most likely within twenty yards of them. But with the darkness and littered corpses hiding everything, and the danger in calling out, Robert was as good as a mile away.

'Christ.' Carter looked over his shoulder. The other two men in his wave, including Willow, were crawling ahead unaware that they were alone. 'Stay here. I'll try and stop Willow and come back.'

'All right—damn it,' Jonathon touched Carter on the shoulder. He felt guilty now. Robert was probably fine and would loom out of the night as soon as Carter was gone.

***

Robert was trapped by a dying Turk. The enemy was a large man lying on his side, so Robert decided to use the corpse's bulk to raise his own head high and look for trouble ahead. He figured men in the opposing trenches would be used to the bigger shape and his own added presence wouldn't be noticed. But what he didn't allow for was being seen by the dead man himself.

The Turk's eyes opened wide in shock, the whites gleaming in the night. In the moment it took Robert to register what was happening, he realised at least that the man wasn't going to make a noise. Not yet, anyway. The Turk must have been hanging on to his life with an intense effort. Salvation had arrived in the darkness, stirring him from his coma, but what if he cried out something that gave the game away? *Got them all killed?* Robert wasn't even sure the man had seen him. The glazed eyes were open, but maybe unseeing. Perhaps the sound of Robert's approach had alerted him, but the Turk was blind from his injuries. A long minute passed while Robert froze, trying to decide. It was worse knowing that the others were going on ahead.

'I can't help you, mate,' he finally whispered, when the Turk hadn't moved again. Then Robert winced, knowing it was a mistake to have spoken aloud. If there had been any doubt about his identity, the foreign words had ended it.

The Turk started to breathe raggedly, gathering strength to make a noise. His eyes were rolling with fear or maybe a last hope.

'Shit, don't start...' Robert grated between his teeth. He knew no words of Arabic apart from the insults the Anzacs yelled from the trenches. This man could cry out anything that might reveal to a listening enemy that someone was out there in no-man's-land with him. Someone other than the dead and wounded.

There was firing about a hundred yards to Robert's left, but it was just harassment from the Australian lines to keep the Turks awake and on edge. For the moment, it masked the noises coming out of the dying man, but his bubbling breath began to whine in his throat and Robert could see that his body was trembling with the effort.

'Stay fucking *quiet*,' he tried angrily, but it was no good. Even as he spoke, Robert was reaching for his bayonet in its scabbard.

He didn't bother attaching it to his rifle because with so little strength left, if the Turk did try to grapple with him, it wouldn't be for long.

Keeping the blade hidden in one hand and cradling his rifle awkwardly with the other, Robert edged up hard against the Turk by pushing himself with his legs. He shut his ears to the man's sounds, which were near sobs now, either of fear or relief. Robert caught the man's terrible stench. The stink of loosened bowels, blood and decaying flesh. Clearly he'd been out here for days, one of the first to fall during the attacks. It was incredible that he was alive at all, and that didn't make killing him like this any easier.

Robert placed the point of his bayonet against the Turk's chest. For an instant he felt the knife rise and fall with the man's desperate gasps, and he choked back a sudden surge of bile in his throat as he pushed hard on the bayonet. It sank in less than an inch before Robert began sliding backwards through the dirt.

'Oh Jesus,' he spat, appalled at the cruel mess he was making of this. He dropped his rifle and crawled close again, this time hooking his free arm over the Turk's shoulder. The intimate contact with the stinking man made Robert's nausea threaten more, but the extra leverage allowed him to shove the knife in to its hilt. The Turk jerked slightly beneath him, then the life he'd held onto so grimly ended with a silent shudder. After so long and desperate a fight for survival, it was finished in a second. That fact wasn't lost on Robert as he rolled quickly away, pulling the bayonet out as he did.

All the man's effort and prayers had been wasted. Robert felt disgusted with himself and sprawled on his stomach, staring with loathing at corpse. As if to taunt him a flare popped, then exploded into its brilliant glare around them. He stayed absolutely still under the blank stare of the Turk he had just killed. Every detail of the body was starkly revealed including the fresh wound in his chest.

After an eternity the flare sputtered out.

'Robert? What the hell are you doing?'

The hissed words made him jump with fright. He could just make out the dark form of someone creeping towards him. With relief, he knew it was Carter's voice.

'I got caught up,' Robert whispered back fiercely with a shake in his voice. 'This bastard wasn't dead.'

'We were thinking *you* were,' Carter growled. 'Bloody Jonathon wouldn't keep going until he'd checked. I'm telling you, I don't know why they gave me these bloody stripes. You bastards never do as you're fucking told. Now, come on.' In the dark, Carter jabbed a thumb over his shoulder. 'You're about thirty yards astray from the rest of us.'

He moved away, expecting Robert to follow.

Letting out a long sigh, Robert felt around and found his rifle, then began to crawl after him.

The delay to the raiders meant their carefully planned formation was spoiled. Now all thirteen men were bunched around an impatient Willow, who decided it was useless to try and re-establish any proper structure.

'Just spread out,' he said, after a glare at Robert and Carter. 'Or a wretched mortar will collect the bloody lot of us.' He set off towards the Turkish lines again.

Feeling oddly guilty, everyone else fanned out slightly and followed.

The success of the Anzacs' defensive tactics during the attacks now began to work against the raiding party. The closer they got to the Turkish lines, the fewer bodies littered the landscape, so there was less cover and the chances of being seen were greatly increased. The plan was for Willow to judge the distance at which the Australians could rush the trenches. Half the men would split up into two groups and seal each end of the section of trench attacked. The others would secure the space between, subduing any resistance and capturing prisoners. If all went well, the Anzacs would briefly occupy a small part of the Turkish lines.

It was a calculated risk. None of this allowed for potentially dropping into a section unexpectedly packed with Turkish troops and finding themselves hopelessly out-numbered. It *did* take into account that any enemy counter-attack would be from either end within the trench itself. For the Turks to move across the open ground above, or forward from their reserve lines, involved too much risk. Machine guns waiting for them in the Anzac trenches ensured that.

For the Anzacs, everything depended on surprise, working fast when the moment called for it, and getting back out before the Turks could organise a strong response.

Willow stopped and made a low chopping motion with his hand, telling the others to halt. It had to be passed back from one man to the next. In the darkness, everyone bunched up again before they got the message. This was as close as Willow was prepared to crawl. Ahead about twenty yards was the Turkish trench line, which looked oddly devoid of movement. Not even the glow of a cigarette or a slight change in the shadows as men on the fire step shifted their weight, or turned their heads to talk to someone near.

Willow's voice suddenly came clearly. 'All right, everyone. In we go.'

He rose and ran almost neatly forward, the practised gait of an officer in control. The rest of the raiding party followed. They needed to hit the trench together. Anyone going in alone for just a second would be killed. There were no savage war cries, but some of the men shouted in alarm when they discovered, as they fell, the reason for the lack of any movement. The trench was very deep and the fire step narrow. Miss it, and you were dropping nearly nine feet.

The next fifteen seconds were an eternity of confusion filled with the flash of muzzle blasts and deafening rifle shots in that confined space. The Anzacs spread quickly to either side, killing everyone they met—although there were surprisingly few. Later, in hindsight, the decimation of the Turkish troops during the daytime attacks made sense of this. Few of the enemy had been left to man this section for fear of depleting other parts of the line. Jonathon and Robert were with the raiders, dropping into the centre of the attack and searching for prisoners, documents or anything that might be of value. In those first mad moments neither fired a shot. The only Turks nearby were dealt with by others. Then Jonathon noticed in the trench's rear wall a canvas doorway. There were more at intervals along the section. A few yards away, Willow was already leading a probe into one.

'In here,' Jonathon told Robert. 'You pull the rag. I'll go first.' He flattened himself against the soil next to the entrance and tensed himself, ready.

Robert did the same on the other side, his wide eyes white in the gloom. A flare landing somewhere close by flooded everything with glare. Jonathon didn't know which side had thrown it, but it helped their cause. Perhaps it was part of Willow's planning—he couldn't remember. Robert cautiously grasped a corner of the canvas door and wrenched it aside.

It was dangerous. No one had brought any bombs, and besides, the crude wick arrangements might have worked against them. With the fuse length uncertain, the Turks had a chance to throw them back out at the last moment, killing their attackers. So Jonathon crouched down and ducked his head around the corner for a moment, his rifle thrust with it. Even dropping below where the enemy might aim in anticipation, he still expected to be shot in the face or bludgeoned.

This dugout was empty. A single paraffin lamp flickered on a wooden crate and showed everything. He checked again, searching for anything official-looking. There was nothing.

'Next one,' Jonathon called. Robert was crowding in behind and had to back out again quickly. They moved away from Willow's team towards their end of the captured line. The fighting had stopped, the few Turks encountered dead or made prisoner. By now, the Anzacs at both ends of their position would be anxiously awaiting a counter-attack along the trench. Surrounded by the noise from the rest of the battleground, their area was eerily quiet.

They repeated the manoeuvre at the next dugout, this time with Robert going in first.

'Bugger all,' he announced, reversing out from under a blanket doorway. He'd taken a fraction too long to make up his mind and Jonathon, fearing the worst, had been on the verge of hauling him back by his trousers. Men were known to freeze when they were confronted by the enemy close up.

'Jesus, don't do that,' Jonathon rasped at him. Robert just winked.

The two of them trotted the short distance to the next entrance. The flare was in its last dying seconds and Jonathon wanted to use the light while he could. The dugout was within reach of the Australians guarding that end of the trench and he took time to gesture a silent question, *had they checked the bunker*? One of the men shook his head before turning his attention back to the possible threat from the other direction.

'Okay,' Jonathon took his position beside the doorway.

'Third time lucky,' Robert grinned humourlessly. He yanked the blanket away.

Jonathon repeated his trick and stayed low. The scene inside the bunker took him completely by surprise. His finger tightened on the trigger, and he came within a hair's breadth of shooting before he stopped.

A young German officer, bare-headed but dressed neatly and clean in his full uniform, sat calmly at a table. Two candles lit the space. The officer looked at Jonathon as if he fully expected him, like a guest invited for dinner, and indeed a thick half of sausage and a wedge of yellow cheese were on the table in front of him.

Wary of a trap, Jonathon moved slowly further inside. Without taking his eyes off the German, he called over his shoulder, 'We got one here, Robert.'

Robert scuffled in behind, tense and ready for a fight. He let out an oath.

'Bloody hell! Sausage an' all. I thought Willow was only joking.'

Jonathon laughed nervously. 'Cover him for a second, will you?'

Robert pointed his weapon straight at the German's head. Jonathon kept away from the line of fire and moved close enough to snatch the food from the table. He stuffed it into his pockets. The officer didn't show a flicker of emotion, staring down Robert's rifle. Jonathon lifted his own gun again.

'All right, move out of here,' he snapped, jerking the barrel towards the doorway. He didn't expect the German to understand anything more than rudimentary signs.

But the officer replied in calm, perfect English, 'To be shot outside by your compatriots? I don't think so.'

Robert swore again, then grinned.

'No one's going to shoot you,' Jonathon said, recovering quickly. 'You're a prisoner. We're taking you back.'

'I'd prefer to stay here, thank you.'

'Don't be bloody stupid.' Jonathon raised his rifle slightly and now the officer flinched. His face wasn't only pale with fear, the flesh was white. He must have arrived from the homeland only days before, not long enough to tan or even burn red. And he was young, too. About Jonathon's age.

Jonathon rasped, 'You don't have a fucking choice. Get moving.'

The rattle of small arms fire, along with alarmed shouts, burst loudly beyond the doorway. The Turks were beginning to probe back into their captured trench. The Anzacs holding that end of the line called anxiously for the others to hurry and get the job done. It was time to leave.

Robert said matter-of-factly, 'I can't be bothered arguing, Jonno.' He aimed purposely at the German's face. 'He'll have papers. Let's shoot him and get going.'

Jonathon glanced at the doorway, considering it, then shrugged.

'Wait,' the German said quickly. 'I'm coming.' As he stood, the candles flickered. Robert moved aside. A shove in the back sent their prisoner stumbling into the trench outside and wrenched the blanket off its pegs as he went.

They took him to Willow.

'Well done,' Willow cried, peering at the German in the darkness. He almost clapped him on the shoulder as if he were an old friend they'd found. 'Makes all this worth the effort. Carter and I will take him from here. You lads go back and help the others keep the bastards at arm's length. Listen for my three shots into the air. That's the sign to go over the top again and head for home.'

Jonathon and Robert barely had time to travel the short distance back to the men holding their end of the line before Willow's distinct, timed shots rang out.

'Give 'em something to think about,' someone called. Everyone let off a fusillade of rifle fire down the trench to keep the Turks out of sight. Then they all scrambled onto the fire step, over the lip of the trench and back into no-man's-land.

Out in the open, the running soldiers converged. There was no attempt at stealth now, just an effort to get across the dangerous, exposed ground. Little could be seen except for each man's weaving silhouette against gunfire flashing in the distance. Nobody needed warning that the Turks would soon throw a flare.

It came when they'd made half the distance and their pace was slowed by having to dodge the Turkish corpses. Some of them weren't bothering and trod on the bodies like stepping-stones. In their haste, no one heard the popping of the flare, or perhaps it was masked by gunfire. The magnesium glare took them by surprise, starkly revealing both the landscape and them racing across it. An instant later, a Turkish machine gun chattered after them, sweeping hopefully and too fast among them before concentrating on the raiding party's position. By then, they were all down on the ground.

Jonathon screamed at Robert, '*Shit, are you all right?*' But the noise of the machine gun nearly drowned him out. There was the deadly whirring of rounds over their heads. More firing came from the Australian lines, wary attempts to cover the raiders' return without shooting their own men. And there were shouts of encouragement.

'I'm okay,' Robert called back, his face deathly in the flare. 'But Pete's got one in the foot. See him?'

Jonathon could hear the man groaning in pain. He picked out a writhing shape beyond Robert. 'Can you get him back?'

'Are you going to help me?'

'I think I saw Carter go down. I want to make sure he's okay.'

'Christ—' Robert spat out some dirt and hesitated. 'Okay, but be bloody careful.'

'What the hell do you expect?'

The machine gun was keeping up a ceaseless rate of fire over their heads. Sometimes it dropped down, probing unsuccessfully among the corpses, smacking wetly into the dead flesh. The Turks knew where their enemy was and were feeding fresh belts into the gun without pause. They didn't want to give the Australians a chance to get up and run again.

Jonathon crawled between the bodies, using each for cover and stopping only when the bullets were directly overhead. He'd glimpsed Carter moments before the firing started, then seen him fall heavily and knew that he hadn't just dived for safety.

The flare was low, in a dip of the ground, silhouetting everything. Jonathon couldn't tell which sprawled human shape was a dead Turk or a fallen Australian until he got close. The machine gun kept coming back, as if it had a personal vendetta against him. Maybe the gunners had glimpsed his movement among the corpses and were hoping to scare him into revealing himself more.

He rolled into a deep shell hole, relieved to escape from the stream of bullets above. The crater was rare, perhaps a shortfall from Big Bertha, because neither side was using field artillery so large. Right now, though, Jonathon didn't care about such details. He was just grateful for the protection.

Then he was instantly raising his rifle again, realising he wasn't alone in the hole. One of the shadowy figures spoke quickly.

'It's me, Jonno. Take it easy.' The words were laboured, filled with pain.

'Christ, Tom? Are you all right? I've been looking for you.' Staying below the lip of the crater, Jonathon dragged himself across to Carter.

'Don't block my view. Look out for this bastard.'

Jonathon twisted around and saw another man in the shell hole with them. It was the young German officer, his white face clear as he watched them both. He held himself hard against the opposite side of the crater, seemingly pinned there by the revolver Carter had pointed at him.

'Are you hit?' Jonathon asked.

Carter grunted a pain-racked laugh. 'What do you reckon, I'm having a kip? One in the guts, another in my fucking leg.'

The flare blacked out. Jonathon cursed and awkwardly searched for Carter's wounds by running his hands through his clothing. The sergeant didn't complain but swore at the effort of keeping his revolver on the German.

'I can still *see* you,' he hissed across the shell hole. 'If I even think you're trying to move, I'll shoot.'

The German didn't answer.

'Is he hurt too?' Jonathon asked quietly, still probing the wet, sticky uniform. The blood was warm and easy to find. The injury was bad, but it might have missed the stomach. He was worried about the lung though. And the leg had been shot right through the calf muscle.

'No,' Carter said. 'Bloody figures, doesn't it? But he took his time to get over being shit-scared. Otherwise, he would have got away.'

'Well that's good, because I need him to help carry you.'

'No,' Carter snapped with surprising strength. 'Get him back to the lines first and come back for me with a stretcher. He could be important. I don't want to have copped this for nothing.'

'Shit, Tom. He knows nothing,' Jonathon replied angrily. 'He hasn't been out here long enough. You can tell.'

'I don't care.'

'I won't carry him,' the German interrupted. 'And you can't force me. Take him yourself and leave me here.'

Jonathon couldn't tell if the man was trying to bargain for his freedom, or was simply terrified of going out into the open. It was possible the Turks knew about the shell hole and guessed it was where Jonathon was hiding.

'See?' Carter whispered, weaker already. 'Take the bastard back first, then come and get me.'

'No, wait,' Jonathon said. 'Give me your revolver.'

Careful not to give their captive even a moment of safety, Carter let him take the pistol from his hand.

'Right,' Jonathon kept it on the German. 'You're going to help me get this man back to our lines, or I'll shoot you now.'

The German steeled himself. 'I'm your prisoner. You cannot shoot me in cold blood.'

'I don't give a shit about rules. I'm going to get my friend back to medical help. Make up your mind, because I'm not going to leave you here.'

There was a silence as the German weighed up his chances. 'I give you my word I'll stay here until you've had time to escape,' he said. 'And I'm unarmed.

I can't hurt you.'

The machine gun fire stopped abruptly. Jonathon glanced up at the empty air. Others were firing close, but nothing near them.

'We're going now,' he said harshly. 'Get over here and lift him under the arms. I'll get his legs. We're going to run—*that* way.' He jerked his head towards the Anzac lines.

'And we'll all be killed,' the German said. 'What's the use? It's better to stay here—'

Without another word, Jonathon shot him three times, aiming for the chest. Even in the dark, he didn't want to see that face shatter. The German was killed instantly without a cry, but Carter groaned a feeble protest.

'What's the bloody difference?' Jonathon snarled, but he was shaken.

'He could have had important information,' Carter said, every word getting softer.

'Bullshit. He didn't know a bloody thing.'

Suddenly another voice called from beyond the shell hole. '*Coming in.*'

Two bodies flung themselves into the crater. It was a soldier named Tanner and a corporal called Streeth. Both of them had been in the raiding party.

'We heard you arguing,' Tanner said in disbelief. 'Who's here?'

'Carter's hurt bad,' Jonathon said. 'We've got to get him back. The other bloke's dead.'

'One of ours?'

'No.'

'We'd better get a move on,' Streeth decided. 'Before that bloody machine gun wakes up. You ready?'

'As ever.'

With the three of them, it was easier. Tanner and Streeth grabbed an arm each while Jonathon took Carter's feet. Bending low, slung rifles banging against their hunched backs, they scurried across the open ground. They nearly dropped Carter as each of them tried to sidestep a Turkish corpse in different directions. It was almost comical, but Carter didn't complain because he was unconscious—or dead. At first it seemed a miracle that the Turkish machine gun wasn't chasing them, until Jonathon saw two Australian guns raking the enemy position from its flanks, keeping the gunners down. Being sniped at from somewhere else was still a real possibility, but luck stayed with them until they tumbled into the Anzac lines.

Flat on the floor of the trench and gasping for breath, Jonathon called for a stretcher, but one had already appeared. Carter was rolled onto it and hurried away.

'Hey, is he still alive?' Jonathon called after them. No one answered.

Then Robert was standing beside him, looking down. Oddly calm, he held out a cigarette, already lit.

'Christ... is he okay, Robert? Did you see?' His hand shook as he snatched the smoke.

'He's still alive,' Robert nodded slowly. 'Didn't look good though. What about you?'

'Fine. I'm fine.' Jonathon didn't sound like it. He dragged long on the cigarette and filled his lungs. The burning tip glowed brightly in the dark.

'We lost two other blokes for sure, and Pete's missing half his foot. Must have been one of those explosive bullets we've been hearing about.'

'Bastards.'

'Yeah, and Willow's asking everyone where the bloody German got to. Any idea?'

'That's easy. I shot him.'

Robert hesitated. 'Fair enough. But you might have to explain that to Willow.'

'He wouldn't help carry Carter. I wasn't going to leave him behind to just walk home, was I? So I knocked him.'

'Too right. Anyone else would do the same. I guess Willow won't mind.' His friend's casual tone was a mockery. It cut through Jonathon's shock and made him laugh harshly.

'Mind? He'll be mad as a cut snake.'

'Probably. Still, what're you supposed to do?'

'That's right, exactly.' Jonathon ground the cigarette butt angrily into the wall. 'What the hell are you supposed to do?'

***

A week later, there was mail. Jonathon and Robert were given theirs on the beach where they'd been unloading ammunition from a navy pontoon. Corporal Streeth, who had been promoted to sergeant, replacing Carter, handed over the letters and let them take a short break to read them. They sat in the shade of piled-up stores, oblivious of the snap of snipers' bullets that regularly flicked at the sand or tore chunks from the wooden crates.

'From Joseph,' Jonathon showed Robert one of the two envelopes he'd been given. The other was from his parents. The letter from Joseph soon soured his mood.

'Oh shit,' he said, just stopping short of crumpling the paper.

'What's wrong?' Robert was labouring through a long letter from his mother.

'Bloody Joseph. He's heard about our fooling around in Egypt and he's going to join up before he misses out on all the *fun*.'

'What? But he's too young.'

'He won't be next month.'

Robert checked the date on his own letter. 'This mail's six weeks old. But he must have heard about the landings by now. All the casualties. Maybe they'll change his mind?'

'Not Joseph. It'll make him more determined.'

'What about the farms? Who's going to look after them?' Robert looked thoughtful. 'Perhaps they won't let him go.'

'You've got to be joking.' Jonathon nodded towards a line of laden stretchers being carried towards the emptying pontoon. Only a few had blankets to cover the wounded men. As for the rest, their bloodied bandages and hanging, useless limbs were there for all to see. 'I think we'll be taking every man we can get.'

Robert gave up arguing as a seaplane rattled overhead. The novelty of it made them both watch until the plane's clattering motor faded in the distance.

'Hey, someone told me Carter got onto a hospital ship, no problems,' Robert said suddenly.

'If he lasted that long, he's got a good chance of pulling through.' Jonathon's mind was still on Joseph's letter.

'They've got real nurses on board—women, I mean,' Robert said. 'It can't be all bad, getting looked after by some pretty girl. My mum says I should marry a nurse.'

'Don't get too excited. Any nurse who agreed to marry you would be old and fat, and ugly like all the nursing sisters. If those girls could get married, they wouldn't bother being bloody nurses, believe me. That's how it works.'

'Thanks a lot.' Robert shook his head sadly. 'Couldn't you let me dream for just a bit?'

Jonathon shrugged and gave him a lop-sided grin. 'Yeah, sorry. Perhaps you're right. Maybe Tom's having his bandages changed right now by a beautiful nurse who falls in love at the drop of a hat. With blokes like you.'

'And she looks like an angel,' Robert added.

Jonathon nodded. 'All right, *and* she looks like an angel.'

Joseph

The view from up here always made Joseph dream. The higher he walked, the better it got. It was like flying with the birds, or taking to the air in one of those hot-air balloons he'd read about.

The wide expanse of their farm was changing from the golden hay of summer to a hint of new grass. There had been some good early autumn rains. In another month or so it would be deep green pasture as far as the eye could see. From where Joseph sat eating his lunch on a log, halfway into the hills, he could look down onto the roof of their farmhouses and pick out the smoking chimney in the main homestead. He recognised a tiny speck as his mother, crossing to the dairy. The cows in the far paddock were only brown dots. It would take some time for them to return for the afternoon milking, he figured idly. The ribbons of tracks between the paddocks had darkened with overnight rain.

He was up on the slopes, grubbing trees—he cleared them by digging around the bases, cutting the roots with an axe as deep as he could, then in a few weeks' time any trees that hadn't died and fallen over of their own accord could be pulled down easily by a team of horses. It was back-breaking work, but Joseph had been doing it since he was old enough to swing a shovel. His father had acquired this extra land behind their property cheaply because it was higher and more difficult to cultivate. The easiest way to get around that, Benjamin White had apparently decided, was to send his son up to do the work while he stayed on the lower ground with their neighbour, Will Thornton, and made fence posts.

They were working hard to expand both properties. Demand for everything had gone up dramatically with the need to supply an army overseas. The Whites aimed to increase butter production by enlarging their dairy stock, hence the need for extra fenced land and more grazing space. It would have been better had Jonathon stayed, but he had gone into the AIF.

A new sound attracted Joseph's attention. He gazed towards the south and found the tell-tale plume of a steam train coming their way. The tracks ran along the boundary of the farm, and he was able to watch it for some time. When the train drew level with the buildings, the driver hooted a long greeting on the whistle. Immediately the windows filled with madly gesticulating arms, some holding hats. It was too far for Joseph to see any faces, but he imagined they'd all be looking out eagerly, wondering who the train engineer had saluted, but waving anyway. There'd been another recruitment drive in the district and the carriages were again full of excited, soon-to-be soldiers on their way to Perth. The casualty figures from the war in Europe hadn't dampened their enthusiasm to join the fight and now that it was well known the AIF were training in Egypt—although it didn't make much sense—the exotic lure of such a far-off place alone was enough to entice the adventurous. The prospect of getting into a fight with the Germans afterwards was a bonus.

The train disappeared behind the trees to become just a thick worm of smoke moving north, but the powerful chugging of the engine echoed around the hills behind Joseph for a long time.

Without moving, he no longer saw the sweeping farmland of Western Australia. Instead, he imagined the yellow sands of Egypt stretching to the horizon. Majestic pyramids towered into the sky and lines of camels twisted like ants around them. Somewhere close by would be the crowded bazaars of Cairo, the sidewalk markets filled with long-robed Arabs offering charms and secret talismans. The noise was exhilarating.

These were mental pictures Joseph had from Jonathon's letters. At first, it was supposed to be a secret where the AIF were camped and training, but obvious references from his brother such as, "I don't miss Mother, because there's plenty of other *mummies* around here," and "All we get to eat are SANDwiches," slipped past the censors. All the soldiers writing home did the same until their location became common knowledge and the authorities gave up trying to deny it. Finally the newspapers had been allowed to admit what they'd known all along and printed stirring stories of the soldiers' preparations, along with anecdotes of Australians enjoying themselves in the bars and cafes of Cairo. The only real mystery remaining was why the Australian army was training there in the first place. It seemed an odd, unsuitable land for learning how to defeat Germany.

Joseph felt prompted to pull the last of Jonathon's letters out of his pocket and read it all again. The paper was well-thumbed and starting to tear at the creases because he carried it with him everywhere and it had been some time since they'd received anything new. He almost didn't need to read the single page, he knew the letter so well. Still, he took in each word eagerly, reliving every moment of his brother's adventure as it were his own. He'd already written back to Jonathon saying that he'd be joining up as soon as possible. It just wasn't fair that he should get all the fun, although their parents might have something different to say on that subject.

Finishing it once more, Joseph sighed, ended his lunch with a swig of milk from his canteen, and slid off the log to start work again.

He kept going until the sun was low. There was little point in heading home earlier, since his father would find him something else to do while there was still daylight to do it. Joseph left the tools beside the last tree. For certain, he'd be back in the morning to carry on with the job. Swinging his satchel over one shoulder, he tramped down the hill to the house.

His mother, Maxine, met him on the porch before he had a chance to kick his boots off.

'Joseph, have you got time to try for some rabbits?' she asked him cheerfully. 'I need two for tomorrow.'

He looked around, trying to decide. The sunset had shrunk to a haze in the west and the light was almost gone, but a few minutes remained.

'Sure, I'll give it a go,' he told her.

Maxine reached behind the door to bring out a gun. 'Be careful,' she said as always, and handed it over. 'And your father's still out there somewhere. Don't shoot him by mistake.'

'He'd have to look like a pretty big rabbit,' Joseph smiled, tilting the rifle towards the light coming from the house to check that it was loaded. There were a few more rounds in his satchel and he rummaged around for them, but found only four. He showed her. 'Wish me luck. It looks like I'll be back soon.'

'I'll tie up the dogs.' She went around the corner of the house, whistling loudly.

There was a sunken creek bed about five hundred yards from the house. The water flowed all year, but slowed to a trickle in the middle of summer. Joseph's father had rigged a gravity-feed tank further up the hill where the current was always good, running a long pipe back to the house, then on to the dairy. But at the lower levels the creek slowed and twisted through its ancient course crowded by drooping gums along the banks that created a miniature valley.

The rabbits burrowed under the fallen logs and ventured out in the evening. Joseph had used traps before, when his mother gave him some notice. Otherwise he needed to go shooting, as he did now.

He approached the area carefully, although the likelihood of arriving undetected was small. There was no breeze, but the new season was making its presence felt and he shivered. Grey shapes darted away from his path. Inquisitive ears poked up from behind a hillock, but Joseph ignored them and settled himself on a raised rock with the rifle pointing upright, the butt propped on his knee. He composed himself, then waited, keeping absolutely still. The creek gurgled pleasantly nearby. In the distance, his father called a farewell to Will Thornton and the sound drifted among the hills. Then almost complete silence.

He wondered if there were rabbits in Egypt, and then he couldn't imagine a country *without* them. Rabbits were like flies, everywhere.

The shadows deepened.

And In The Morning

Were rabbits the same colour in Egypt? The same shape?

A loping, dark shadow emerged from under a bank. It didn't look Joseph's way, but moved to a clump of green grass and began nibbling. Either it didn't know he was there, or it had decided he wasn't a threat. A second appeared beside a log and started foraging. Joseph held his breath, waiting just a little longer to see if a better shot came, but the night was racing to beat him. He raised the rifle and aimed at the rabbit near the log. Oblivious of its impending death, it chewed calmly at the grass.

The rifle cracked and the rabbit convulsed in the air, dead before it hit the ground. Already, Joseph wasn't watching. His hand flew to the bolt, the next bullet held between the second and third fingers like a cigarette, and with an impressive, deft movement he ejected the spent round and reloaded. He turned to the first rabbit, upright and startled, ready to take flight. It ran as Joseph took aim, becoming a bouncing streak in the gloom. Joseph fired at a point just in front of its head. The bark of the rifle slapped back in an echo from the countryside.

The rabbit fell in a heap.

Joseph lowered the rifle and allowed himself a satisfied, 'Hmmm.' That second shot had been tricky, but he didn't often miss.

He picked up the carcasses in one hand, his rifle in the other, and walked back to the house. He hung the rabbits high on the back porch out of reach of the dogs and went inside.

The house had been built by his father, before the boys were born. Over the years it had been added to, improved, damaged by storms, repaired and even plundered to fix another building. Now it was a home, filled with furniture his mother had collected, the walls covered in knick-knacks and pictures, the windows heavily curtained to keep out the winter chill. In all the rooms, the rough timber and beams of the building were almost completely hidden by Maxine's decorations.

Joseph hadn't realised just how cold it had become until he felt the warmth of the kitchen fire. Maxine was at the stove, boiling vegetables, and he could smell the beef roasting in the oven. The Whites and the Thorntons had shared a steer and were eating a lot of fresh meat until Maxine would have to salt the remainder to preserve it. Joseph's father, Benjamin, was sitting at the table and writing in a journal by an oil-lamp. His rimless glasses reflected the orange flame. The property had electricity from a wind generator, but on a still night like this it wasn't worth turning on.

'Are they a good size?' Maxine asked Joseph. She didn't doubt he'd been successful.

'As good as usual,' he told her, flopping into a chair beside his father. 'It's like there's a never-ending supply down there.'

'They breed all right,' Benjamin grunted, without lifting his eyes from the scratching pen. 'I won't put the herd down there for fear they'll break their damned legs in the burrows.'

'They're good for a stew and soup every week,' Maxine reminded him.

'And that's all they're good for,' he grumbled back.

'Did Will have any news from Robert?' Joseph asked, eagerly.

Benjamin looked at him over the top of his glasses. 'He gets his papers and the mail tomorrow, as you well know.'

'I just thought he might have gone in early for once.'

'The words on the paper won't change for reading them a day sooner.'

'But we haven't heard anything new for *ages*. A new letter could have been waiting in town all week.'

Benjamin sighed at his son's impatience and put down his pen. 'I'm well aware of that, but Will and I are not going to waste half the day, every day, going in to check. We've got important work to finish and the newspapers never get it right at first anyway. Jonathon's probably on the move towards the fighting at last. His letters won't get through for a while, so the papers won't be able print anything for the sake of secrecy—' He stopped, seeing his wife's back stiffen in dismay.

He added quickly, 'Of course, I'm sure Jonathon's all right.'

Unaware of the change of mood, Joseph said blithely, 'The war will be over before I get a chance to see any of it.'

'I'm sure your mother won't be too disappointed about that.'

Joseph glanced at her. 'I'm not interested in getting into any fight,' he said unconvincingly. 'It's just an opportunity to see some of the world.'

'I don't want both of you gone,' she said unhappily. 'Perhaps if Jonathon came home first.'

'I don't think it can work like that,' Joseph said. 'Besides, I'm old enough to join up next month. There's no chance he'll be back before then.'

'And who's going to help your father around the farm?'

With a wounded look, Joseph appealed to his father for help, but Benjamin shrugged. 'Your mother's right. I can't do it on my own.'

His tone already admitted the truth. Despite all the authority he could muster as a father, or by insisting on any obligation to their livelihood, Benjamin knew he couldn't stop Joseph from leaving too. The war sucked in all the men, young and old, like a huge ocean wave that broke over the country and left behind the women, children and the aged as it washed away. God knew, there were days Benjamin wished he could go himself, but he was too old. It was a dangerous business, yet the lure of adventure was still strong.

'You and Will could work for each other, like you do now,' Joseph was explaining. 'I'm sure you'd manage.'

Benjamin raised his eyebrows. 'So now you're an expert on running this farm?'

'No,' Joseph backed off. 'Not at all. I'm saying you two are the real experts. You don't need me.'

It was a clever answer that got him out of trouble, and Benjamin only just suppressed a smile. Maxine dropped some plates on the table noisily between them.

'Let's at least wait until your birthday to discuss it,' she said almost harshly. 'Perhaps we'll have heard more from John by then.'

'That's a good idea,' Benjamin said gently, and fixed Joseph with a look. 'Another month never hurt anyone.'

***

The next day, Will Thornton arrived late as usual after his customary trip into Brunswick to collect the newspapers and mail. Benjamin was already sawing at some wooden posts with Joseph's help. They stood ankle-deep in the sawdust. The hundreds of fence posts around the farm had all been made here. In the morning sunshine, without any wind, the strong smell of the cut timber lingered around them.

Will rode up in a hurry and reined his horse in urgently, but as he dismounted he seemed oddly reluctant to deliver his news.

'No letters from the boys,' he said tersely, tugging at the straps of his saddlebags. He rarely bothered with greetings. 'Just the papers.' He dragged out a bundle and held the top one towards Benjamin. Will's face was blank, carefully controlled.

'They've landed,' he told them both flatly.

Benjamin snatched the paper. 'What? Where? And they're already fighting?'

'They're calling it an *amphibious* landing.' Will struggled with the word. 'It's like an invasion from the sea. In Turkey somewhere.'

Benjamin hastily flapped the newspaper open and scanned the front page. He had to hold it at arm's length because he didn't have his glasses. With so much information at one glance, it was difficult to know what to read first. Joseph crowded in to see over his father's shoulder.

Finally Benjamin said, 'Gallipoli, it's called. I remember it. The Royal Navy has been bombarding some forts there, but they came off second-best.' His voice trailed away in dismay as it appeared in the stories that, despite the patriotic tone and positive outlook of the reporting, the landings hadn't gone well.

'Looks like we've had a lot of casualties too,' Will said sombrely. 'They don't say how many exactly, or who.'

'Shit,' Benjamin read quickly, his attention shifting between the different articles. Then, taking a deep breath and letting the paper drop he said, 'I'd better go and find Maxine.'

As he walked away, Joseph called out, 'Dad? Can I read some?'

Benjamin absently looked down at the newspaper still in his hand. There was nothing in it that Maxine needed to see. The news was bad enough without the painful details. 'Yes, sure,' he held it out.

Will Thornton squatted on one of the sawn logs, his head in his hands, as he listened to Joseph read out sections of the stories enthusiastically. The veiled reports of high casualties and few territorial gains didn't concern Joseph. He certainly didn't think of them as meaning the possible death of his brother or Robert.

'This all happened over a week ago.' Joseph looked at the dates.

'It could all be finished by now,' Will said quietly. 'Christ, I hope those lads are all right.'

This, coming from a man never prone to unnecessary emotion, made Joseph frown at the paper and wonder about the truth between the lines.

'They'll be fine,' he said after a while. 'I'm sure of it.'

Will nodded. 'Yeah, there's no point in worrying. Robert knows how to look after himself.'

When his father returned, Joseph tramped up into the hills to continue his tree grubbing. But he spent most of the time staring off into the distance, trying to see things on the other side of the world among the unimaginable fury of battle in a far-off land. He simply couldn't picture what it must be like. He could see his brother's face streaked with dirt and gunpowder, his expression intent as the war screamed around him. But beyond this, imagination failed him. Only one thing was certain. Jonathon and the men around him needed all the help they could get.

Things weren't going too well.

By the end of the day, Joseph had resolved to tell his parents that he was joining up immediately. One month was so little time that the recruiting officers would be sure to turn a blind eye. Joseph had heard of much younger boys getting through the system. The army was after keen new soldiers and he looked old enough.

If he were truthful, Joseph had imagined arriving at the battlefield just in time to save his brother and everyone else. He was destined to be a hero, and waiting another four weeks didn't fit that dream.

***

That evening, his mother's silent worrying changed Joseph's mind and he was no longer sure what to do about announcing his plans. There was a train to Perth early the next morning and he intended to be on it.

After dinner, he went to his room and packed a few belongings into a suitcase. It didn't take long. As he folded the few clothes, he had to acknowledge that he was meaning to sneak away in the morning. It made him feel terrible, but confronting his mother would be worse.

Before he could finish, his father knocked briefly on the door and came in.

He stared at the suitcase and there was a long silence.

'Were you just going to creep away in the night?' he asked finally.

Joseph felt his face flush. 'No, Father. I wanted to talk about it at dinner, only Mother was too upset. I didn't know how to start.'

'And this wouldn't upset her more, for God's sake?'

‘I was only getting ready. I still wanted to tell you both.’ The half-lie hung uncomfortably in the air. Benjamin didn’t challenge it.

He went on, still deeply upset, ‘You can’t go like this. I’ll tell your mother myself, later tonight. In the morning, we’ll all go together to the station.’

It took a moment to understand the words. When their meaning became clear, a weight lifted from Joseph’s shoulders, though he was still stabbed by guilt. ‘Are you sure...’ Tears came to his eyes and he tried to blink them away. His father nodded slowly and squeezed his son’s shoulder.

‘No, not at all. You know, I’m not sure about any of this. But I won’t let you run away to the war without saying goodbye.’ Benjamin dropped his head and left.

Joseph felt that so much more needed to be said, but his father was already gone.

That night, he couldn’t sleep from excitement and nerves about the next day. Later, through the thin walls he heard strange sounds and he realised it was his mother crying. The sound tore at his heart, it was so desolate and hopeless. And there was the low murmur of his father trying to comfort her.

Joseph felt like crying too and buried his face in the pillow. It was too late to change his mind now. He could never live with himself.

***

Maxine went about the early morning with a forced cheerfulness as if Joseph was leaving for boarding school, or an extended holiday, but her eyes were red-rimmed. Nobody mentioned the war or his signing up. Jonathon had been farewelled like a conquering hero, off on a great quest. Even with the news from Europe, they hadn't known the reality back then.

A satchel was added to his luggage with food for the train trip and a flask of tea. Joseph spent most of his time wandering awkwardly about the house, filling in the minutes. The sun wasn't up. The train would pass through just after dawn, if by chance it was running on schedule, and it would take a while to travel into Brunswick in the sulky first. The Whites hadn't succumbed to buying anything motorised, like a truck or a car, yet. Vehicles were becoming more common in the area every day and with the extra demands placed on the farm by war production, Benjamin had reluctantly given the matter thought, but done nothing about it.

This morning, teaming up the horses gave him the excuse to avoid the kitchen.

Finally there was nothing left to do except make the journey to the station. Everyone rugged up against the dawn chill and Joseph secretly wondered what he was going to do with all this clothing when he got to Egypt. His two bags were thrown on the back. The horses stamped, snorting clouds from their nostrils, and the sulky jerked as everyone climbed on. Benjamin took the reins and without fanfare they were off, *clip-clopping* down the dirt driveway to the main road. In the east, the dawn was slow because of the high ground behind the farm, building to an orange glow above the hills.

When they crossed the railway and turned towards town, Joseph suddenly realised that he was leaving for a long time. He looked back now, across the cleared fields, thinking that he might not see home again for years. He said nothing as Maxine's hand slipped into his and held it tight.

It was too long a trip for complete silence, so they chatted about Benjamin's plans for the farm and what he hoped to have in place for both his sons when they returned. Joseph made suggestions as if he would be a part of it. Maxine tried to join in, but she wasn't convincing, and Brunswick crept close as the sky grew steadily brighter.

The station was busy and the train already there, shrouded in leaking steam as it waited for several farmers to load their wares. Joseph held the horses while Benjamin went to arrange his son's travel. This wasn't a passenger train and Joseph would be riding hard in one of the freight cars. In peacetime, it would need favours exchanged and maybe a sly shilling or two in the right hand. Now the magic words, "He's going to join up," were enough to open all doors.

With everything set, the three of them stood around the sulky and stared towards the train, willing it to move and force them to end this painful parting.

'You should both go home,' Joseph said after a while. 'This train's not going anywhere just yet and you've got work to do. The cows will be wondering what's gone wrong.'

'No, we'll stay until you leave. See you on your way,' Benjamin said resolutely. Maxine nodded and suddenly clung to Joseph's arm.

'Please. It doesn't make sense,' he pleaded. This drawn-out farewell was getting too much. 'We should say goodbye now, without being rushed by the train leaving. It's better that way.'

'We might not see you for a long time,' Maxine protested quietly.

'I'll be *back*, Mother. Sooner than you think, probably. It makes no difference if we say our goodbyes now or in half an hour's time, except that you've got better things to do than stand around here forever. This train could be here all morning.'

'It doesn't feel right to just leave you,' she whispered.

'And there's something else,' he said with a sudden idea. 'When the train passes the farm, I want to wave madly like everyone else does and know that somebody's waving back. It would feel special, coming from my own home.'

Maxine's grip loosened slightly and at that moment Benjamin caught his son's eye and nodded. He needed to end it too.

'Come on, Maxine,' he said gently. 'Let's say goodbye now, and with luck we'll be able to wave from beside the track at home.'

She started to cry in earnest and wrapped Joseph in a suffocating hug. He held her tightly as long as he could, then carefully pushed her away to shake his father's hand. The clasp seemed to last forever.

With the physical contact finally broken, his parents reluctantly climbed into the sulky and stared down at him.

'Yes, I'll be careful,' he said with a smile, before they had a chance.

'Tell Jonathon we love him very much too,' Maxine said.

'First thing, as soon as I see him.'

'Make us proud, Joseph,' Benjamin called too loudly, his voice rough.

'I will, Father.'

Benjamin flicked the reins and the horses pulled away into a tight circle. Joseph stepped back to let them pass. Once they had turned, there was only his father's straight back and his mother, twisted in the seat to see him, to wave at. When the sulky had almost gone and Joseph thought he could drop his aching arm, his father turned around too and lifted his hand high in salute.

***

The train left an hour later. Plenty of time for his parents to get home. As the farm approached, Joseph threw open the wide door of the freight car and stood in the entrance. The wind of the train's passage made his eyes water as he waved furiously in the general direction of the house. No one was waiting beside the track. Then he looked towards the hills, in case anyone had climbed up there for a better vantage point. At last, he realised that both his mother and father would be in the dairy milking, so he looked over there, still waving crazily. A second later, trees obscured his view.

He'd seen no one, and with the tears in his eyes, he'd scarcely seen even the farm. He could only trust that his parents had heard the approaching train, or seen the smoke, done as he'd asked and waved back. It felt like the most important thing in the world, as if it demonstrated their belief that he would be coming back.

Deep inside, and with a sense of shock, for the first time Joseph wished he could be so sure about that.

The Cease Fire

'That bloody sniper's got to go.'

Sergeant Streeth spat the words out as he held the dying man's head in his lap, hopelessly offering comfort. The bullet had gone through above his right eye and exited in a shattered mess at the top of his neck. He wouldn't last long. Two men stamped urgently into the trench, holding a stretcher.

'Keep your damned heads down,' Streeth snapped at them. They flung themselves to the dirt floor. The sergeant rolled his eyes and made a disgusted noise.

'It's that fucking loop-hole,' he nodded at Robert Thornton, jerking a gory thumb at the firing position. 'The bastard's got it down pat. He can put a bullet through it with his eyes closed. Sandbag the damned thing, so no one else tries to use it.'

'He's a bloody good shot, you know,' Robert said admiringly, eyeing the loop-hole. 'We should try and knock him, or he's just going to win prizes somewhere else.'

'Now that's a good idea,' Jonathon spoke up dryly beside him. 'Are *you* going to go out there and shoot him? I reckon he might have something to say about that.'

Everyone in the trench was crouching, two dozen of them dusty and tired and pinned below the parapet, at first by a

Turkish machine gun that had appeared overnight, and now by this sniper. Any attempt to see through the narrow gaps in the sandbagging would be fatal. Two men had been shot already, one killed instantly and the second probably dead before the stretcher could get him to the beach. This sap was new and narrow, so the men had to shuffle awkwardly to allow room for the stretcher-bearers to do their work. Only the firing positions had raised steps. The soldiers avoided exposing themselves to the loophole like men ducking a swinging lantern. In the low morning sun, the trench was mostly shaded, but they could sense it was going to be a hot day. Already, the water bottles were being passed for careful sips.

'Maybe we'd better try something,' Streeth agreed reluctantly. 'If they keep our heads down like this, the Turks will try an attack soon enough.' No one answered him, but all watched silently as the stretcher-bearers carried the wounded soldier away. Then Streeth added tersely, 'Jonesy, go with them and bring back a periscope. Willow will have one.'

Jones scampered after them like an eager pup. He was young and always keen. But the Turkish machine gunners had obviously glimpsed the movement because they sprayed the lip of the trench with a long burst that kicked dirt and rocks down onto the Australians.

'Yeah, we *know,*' someone snarled.

'Snipers, I *hate* bloody snipers,' Robert growled after the firing stopped, and shook the soil from his slouch hat.

'That was the machine gun, Robert,' someone said blandly. 'Haven't you learned the bloody difference yet?'

'Aren't you the funny bastard?'

Some of the men laughed, but nervously.

Around them, the battle for the peninsula raged on with a renewed vigour, as it usually did during the first few hours of the day. The crack of rifle and machine gun fire echoed around the hills. In their section, with nobody attempting to fire back, it felt oddly calm.

'I don't like this,' Jonathon muttered. 'Half the Turkish army could be crawling towards us right now, and we can't see 'em. Somebody has to have a look soon.'

'Wait for the periscope,' Streeth said uncertainly.

'We can't wait all day, Nick.'

Streeth sighed, then swore. 'All right. Give me a leg-up here, where he won't expect it. I'll have a quick look.'

Jonathon and Robert arranged themselves on either side of him, then grasped each other's hands, crossing their grip. Robert asked Streeth innocently, 'Aren't you going to take your boots off?'

'Don't give me the shits, Robbo,' Streeth muttered, clearly anxious. Robert silently took his hat off and put it on top of their joined hands.

'There, tread on that, if you have to,' he grumbled, and winked at Jonathon.

As an afterthought, Streeth removed his own hat and braced himself for the jump. He took a deep breath, launched himself upwards and stared out over the lip of the trench. Robert and Jonathon grunted with the effort of holding his weight. Streeth stayed like this for only a moment, then dropped and a shot rang out as he fell.

'Christ,' he yelled and collapsed in panic to the bottom of the trench, taking the other two with him. 'That went through my *hair*.'

'He's fast *and* a good shot,' Robert said. 'We need him on our side.'

'For God's sake—is everything clear, Nick?' Jonathon asked for everyone, ignoring Robert's joking.

'No, there's no one out there.' Streeth shook his head, then ran a hand across his scalp and checked his fingers. 'Jesus, that was close.'

'Did you see him? Do you know where the shot came from?'

'Not a chance.'

'We'll be buggered if we don't find out where he is.' Jonathon frowned. 'We have to try and keep *his* head down for a change.' He suddenly plucked Robert's hat from his head, which his friend had just finished straightening.

'Hey, use your own.'

Jonathon hurried out of his reach. He took the hat to the loophole where the two men had been killed. Nobody had placed a sandbag in the gap yet. Carefully, he balanced the hat on the barrel of his rifle and edged it near.

'Shit, Jonno. He's not going to fall for *that* old—' Robert was cut off by another shot. The hat spun off the rifle and a spurt of soil kicked out from the back of the trench. 'Great,' he said. 'Now you've stuffed my bloody hat.'

Jonathon examined the hat. 'He's over there, somewhere.' He pointed. 'You can tell by the angle. I reckon he's camped in with the machine gun. Makes sense.'

'One protects the other.' Streeth nodded unhappily. 'Could we reach it with a bomb?'

'Someone good might. With the right bomb. Not too big, but not too small either.'

A voice came from further down the trench. 'Get Phil Withers. He's got a good arm. I saw him take six for twenty-three last year. Dry pitch, too.'

'But he's a *spin* bowler,' someone else sneered.

'But he fields from the *outer,* you—'

'All right,' Streeth said shortly.

Jones slid untidily into the trench in a shower of soil, cradling a makeshift periscope against his chest.

'Well done, Jonesy.' Streeth snatched the periscope and immediately used it to look over the parapet. He didn't watch for long. This sniper was obviously capable of shooting the mirror, given enough time. 'It's still clear,' he announced, before turning back to Jones. 'Now go and find Phil Withers. Bring him and half a dozen decent bombs back here. If anyone complains, tell them we need him real bad.'

'He's sapping at Lone Pine,' someone called. 'I saw him yesterday.'

Gasping for air, Jones looked as if he were about to protest, but nodded and rushed away.

While they waited for him to return, the mood in the trench eased. With Streeth darting along the line and sneaking the periscope up for periodic checks, the chances of being surprised lessened. His antics became almost a game, amusing the men as he tried to second-guess the sniper each time by never raising the mirror twice in the same place.

'He's going to get you, Nick,' Robert said in a sing-song voice, after another bullet slapped into the soil only moments after Streeth lowered the periscope. It was the third time the sniper had tried a shot.

'Shut up,' Streeth snarled back, shaken, even though it was the periscope rather than him at risk. 'Where the hell is this cricket hero?'

'Maybe it's morning tea break.' Robert squatted and began to roll a cigarette.

Streeth was not in the mood for jokes. He chanced another quick glance through the periscope.

'I think I just saw the gunners,' he said loudly to no one in particular. 'Over to the right, near the very end of their line. Dunno about the sniper.'

The Turkish machine gun opened fire, pounded the lip of their trench and sent everyone ducking and cursing. The high bullets ripped through the air with a snapping sound. A few rounds sneaked through the loop-hole and into the rear trench wall. When the firing stopped, Streeth called out to ask if there were any casualties. No one was hurt, but some of the men were still cursing.

Jones suddenly reappeared, followed by a second soldier who moved just as fast out of the communication trench, but with less fuss. He was a lanky, awkward-looking man with a private's uniform hung emptily on his narrow shoulders.

'Phil Withers,' he introduced himself calmly to Streeth, holding out his hand. Streeth shook it automatically.

'Nick Streeth,' he replied, adding as he tapped the corporal's stripes on his arm, 'But it's Sergeant. They bumped me up a few days ago.' Withers nodded and seemed unimpressed.

Streeth asked, 'Did Jonesy tell you what's going on?'

'You've got a sniper.'

'And a dead-eye dick too. This bastard's good. We can't do a thing until we get rid of him.'

Between their feet, from a sack, Jones was tipping a handful of bombs onto the trench floor. Withers bent down and picked one, hefting it in his hand.

'How far away is he?'

'Forty, maybe fifty yards away. And he's in a machine gun nest. You'll do well, if you get them too. Can you throw that far?'

Withers looked doubtful. 'On a good day, perhaps, with a bloody cricket ball.' He eyed the bomb. It was a jam tin packed with explosive and some small rounded pebbles. Four inches of black fuse dangled from the top. 'But I'll give it a go, of course.'

Jonathon was nearby. 'You can't have a look,' he said. 'You'll be throwing blind. This bloke will knock you, soon as you stick your head up.'

'But you can have a squizz through here first,' Streeth countered, showing Withers the periscope. 'It'll give you a rough idea where you're going. Get close, and that might put their heads down long enough for us to have a real good look.'

Withers studied the top of the trench as if it might give him a clue to the machine gun's whereabouts. The morning sun was high enough to be in his eyes now, and he squinted.

'Where do you reckon it is?' he asked again.

'About forty yards, at an angle to us like this,' Streeth chopped the air with his hand. He sounded eager, trying to persuade Withers. 'I reckon you can do it easy.'

Withers wasn't convinced. 'I'll throw one first,' he said. 'And you have a look, while they're still under cover.'

'Fair enough. Got a match?'

There followed a minute of debating whether or not the fuse on the first bomb should be trimmed. No one could decide how long it would last. Having it thrown back at them by the Turks would be disastrous. Finally, they left it alone and Robert cupped a match to the wick. Everyone stood back. In the narrow space, Withers barely had room to swing his arm.

The makeshift bomb sailed gracefully out, black against the clear blue sky above and trailing a trace of smoke. Crouched in the trench, the Anzacs stared at each other in anticipation of the explosion. When it hadn't happened seconds later, they were nervous and expected to hear the jam tin thud to earth somewhere nearer, hurled back by the Turks.

Streeth mouthed a frightened, '*Jesus Christ,*' at Jonathon and the bomb cracked loudly from close to the enemy line. The stones struck some corrugated iron in a vicious hail. Foreign curses and cries to Allah floated across the space.

Eager to see, Streeth threw himself against the front wall so hard he winded himself, but he stayed upright with the periscope to his face.

'Smoke's clearing,' he called out painfully. 'It's got to be close.' A long ten seconds passed. 'There! Just to the left, but a good length—*damn.*' He dropped down.

The machine gun had started firing again, though not at Streeth. The Turks were firing desperately out across no-man's-land without aiming, obviously afraid that the bomb indicated an attack. After a long burst the fusillade paused, then with a more deliberate aim it raked the Australian trench. Instinctively the soldiers ducked lower, except for Withers, who ignored the bullets tearing through the air above him. He was calmly picking among the selection of bombs again for something similar to the last one. When Robert crawled close, offering to trim the fuse, Withers waved him off.

'I'll wait longer instead,' he yelled against the racket of firing.

The deadly hammering stopped. Withers gestured at Robert for another match, just as if he were asking for his cigarette. Robert obliged, and with the fuse lit, those close by stared fearfully at the sputtering flame as Withers counted off seconds. There was plenty of time, but a lit bomb in the trench still made for anxious moments. Then Withers threw it with a grunt.

He'd timed it exactly. There were no screams from the Turks, probably because they had taken cover.

Unless Withers had scored a direct hit.

'Closer, but to the right now,' Streeth disappointed them. The sun reflected by the mirrors made a bright square of light on his face. 'We'd better hurry up. The stupid bastards will soon figure out that if we can reach *them* with a tin of fucking bully beef, they'll be able to bomb us, no problem.'

The Turkish hand bombs were rounded, purpose-made devices shaped like a ball and perfect for throwing.

'Hope you brought your bat,' Robert grinned at Withers. The air above them came alive with the Turkish machine gun firing once more in retaliation, an almost obligatory sweep of the Australian position from one end to the other and back again.

Jonathon manoeuvred himself close to Streeth so that he could hear him above the noise of firing. 'Nick, he takes his time getting back up again. We should all be up on top as soon as the bomb goes off, trying to shoot the bastard as he gets behind the gun.'

'What about the sniper?' Streeth wasn't keen.

'Hell, he can't shoot all of us. And maybe we'll get a shot at him too.'

'That bloody machine gun could kill the lot of us.'

'That's why I'm saying we have to pour it on him. Everyone forget the trenches and just aim for the loop-hole. Stop him getting back behind the gun.'

'Yeah, but then what?' Streeth pressed his lips together and shook his head.

'Then Phil can see where he's throwing and maybe score a hit. Christ, like this we could be trying all day. You said yourself, they'll start chucking them back soon.'

'All right, *all right,*' Streeth held up his hand. 'Pass the word to start firing at the bugger when the bomb goes off. Except for you.' He pointed at Robert. 'You keep lighting bombs and passing them to Phil, fast as you can.'

The plan was repeated along the line. There weren't enough fire steps yet for everybody to get over the top, so some men arranged ammunition boxes or water cans to step up on. At the last moment, Streeth moved along the trench, pointing and saying repeatedly, 'He's over there somewhere, about forty yards or so. Look for the sandbags. Aim for the loop-hole, or the centre, if you can't see any gap.' He continued like this, making everyone twice as nervous, until there couldn't be a man who didn't know exactly what to do. Then he returned to Withers. 'You right, Phil?'

'Whenever you are.' Withers had a bomb in his hand. Robert held a match poised.

From further down the trench, Jonathon waited to see the bomb arc outwards. Too many men between prevented him from seeing Withers actually throw. When it came, it was a black shape flicking across the empty sky briefly before the trench parapet obscured the view. Moments later, the same cracking detonation echoed around the hills.

Before the sound faded, the Australians were heaving themselves out of the trench and into the open, their rifles thrust forward to shoot.

But something strange happened to Jonathon. An impulse took over and he obeyed it, before common sense might have stopped him. He suddenly realised there was enough time to cover the distance on foot to the enemy machine gun position.

He could *run* over to the Turkish emplacement and make sure of the job before they recovered from the bomb blast.

So instead of lying flat and firing, Jonathon held his rifle at his hip and sprinted towards the Turkish lines. The exhilaration of being out above ground, away from the narrow confines of the trench, gave him extra strength. It was too late to fix his bayonet, and he didn't fire. Behind him, he could hear yells of confusion and frustrated curses. Somebody called his name angrily, but these sounds were secondary to those of his boots pounding at the dirt, and the rush of blood and breath inside his head. Each footfall brought him nearer the chance of succeeding. In his madness, that's all Jonathon thought about. The need to reach his goal.

It nearly got him killed. With him running crazily towards the machine gun, none of the Australians back at their trench could fire safely. The two Turkish soldiers manning the gun had recovered and reached for the trigger. They looked up too late to see Jonathon bearing down on them. He was so close they couldn't elevate the heavy machine gun enough, but they struggled and tried, instead of aiming for his feet to bring him down.

He wasn't even looking at them. He could see a third man in the rear of the pit, clambering up from the floor where the sandbags had protected him from the bomb's shrapnel. At first, this Turk looked no different from the others.

The steel of his rifle gleamed in the sunshine with oil, and the wooden stock shone from constant polishing. This was a beautifully tended gun, a tool of trade.

This Turk was the sniper.

Jonathon sidestepped the final frantic efforts of the gun crew and kicked the barrel aside. He shot the sniper in the heart as he was desperately swinging his own weapon upwards. The two machine gunners had no other gun, and seeing their comrade killed, threw their hands high in the air. This was no time for taking prisoners and Jonathon deliberately reloaded and shot the nearest of them. The surviving gunner screeched out for mercy and Jonathon hesitated, before someone else's bullet hit the man in the face and punched him back against the sandbags.

Someone cannoned hard into Jonathon's back and sent him sprawling forward and down into the pit. A distinctly Australian string of curses stopped him from fighting off the body that smothered him. When he twisted around and untangled his limbs from the others—including the dead Turks—he found himself lying in the pit with two other Anzacs from his company. One was a man called Crowe, and the other was Jones, the young messenger.

Jones gabbled wildly, 'Jesus, who said to *charge*? I didn't hear anything! Were we supposed to? Didn't Sergeant Streeth say—'

'Shut up,' Crowe snapped. 'I just took off after *this* bastard!' He nodded angrily at Jonathon.

They all flinched as two more bodies slid violently into the pit, a private named Marsden and his constant partner, a man known to everyone as "Chopper" because he'd been a butcher in civilian life.

Recovering from the fall, Chopper brushed at a skinned knee and said tightly with a grin, 'Hell, I don't know if this was a good idea, boys.' He began to dismantle the breech mechanism from the machine gun. Then he held a piece towards them all. 'You know, what's the bloody point? They've probably got spares all over the place.'

'Can we smash it?' Crowe asked, knowing the answer.

'Not properly.'

'Then we'd better take it back with us,' Jonathon told them. 'Just the gun. Forget the ammo.'

No one needed reminding that the reckless dash across no-man's-land had been hazardous enough without being weighed down by a captured machine gun. A return trip with their prize could be suicidal.

Jonathon figured he'd better see what other trouble he'd caused. He carefully raised his head above the level of the sandbags and looked around. Their whole section of the front had come alive with firing and the Anzac trenches glittered with the muzzle blasts of Lee Enfields aimed their way. In response, the Turks had stirred themselves to shoot back. A furious crossfire filled the space between with a tremendous noise.

Incredibly, the enemy didn't seem to realise yet that there were Australians in their own lines. Jonathon knew it wouldn't be long before someone asked why the machine gun wasn't making a contribution.

'We have to go soon,' he yelled at the others. 'Now, before the bloody Turks figure out we're here.'

'We haven't got a hope.' Marsden sneaked a look and grimaced at the torrent of bullets being exchanged across no-man's-land.

'We're on the edge here. They're all too busy shooting at each other. If we head left and stick to the face of the cliff, we might be all right.'

'It's the same as standing against a wall and letting them shoot us.'

'You want to stay here instead?' Jonathon glared at him.

Marsden shook his head and grinned. 'Not on your life.'

'The lads will see us coming and help out. You blokes ready?' Jonathon checked the others. Chopper and Crowe had the machine gun held between them, one by the barrel and the other by the breech handle. Jones was strapping on three water bottles he'd taken from the dead Turks. Each man nodded at Jonathon nervously.

'Then let's go.'

Jonathon went out first. As he emerged above the sandbags, he felt a flash of guilt. After causing their dilemma, he wasn't carrying anything extra. It was too late now. The firing seemed louder out in the open and his skin crawled, expecting the agonising slam of a bullet at any moment. The Australian trenches looked impossibly far away, and he put his head down and ran as he'd never done before.

The sandy cliff beside him flicked with rounds, the yellow soil dancing upwards. He heard bullets snap past him and something tugged at his shirttail. An urge to turn and encourage the others would only slow him down, so he didn't. He could almost feel the intensity of the Turkish gunfire grow as the surprised enemy switched their attention their way. There was no point in ducking or weaving, just moving as fast as he could back to the Anzac lines.

At the very last moment, Jonathon twisted around to slide backwards to the edge of the trench. He tossed his rifle over the lip, freeing his hands to reach towards the others and help. This was his first look at them since leaving the Turkish gun pit and he was relieved to see everyone still up and running. In that instant he saw Chopper stumble and pitch forward, dropping his end of the machine gun and making Crowe stagger too. Jones leaped across them both and rolled over the parapet with a whoop. Chopper fell only a yard short of Jonathon, who crawled across the ground, grabbed him by the collar and dragged him closer to the trench. The last to arrive, Marsden stooped to grab the fallen end of the machine gun and literally threw it on top of Crowe as he fell to safety, juggling his grip on the gun because of the unexpected assistance. Then he took a handful of Chopper's clothing and with Jonathon's help, plus a dozen extra hands grasping from the parapet, the three men collapsed into the trench in a heap.

Chopper's face was inches away from Jonathon's. The wounded man was white with shock, his eyes wide. 'The bastards shot me in the arse,' he said hoarsely. 'Of all the places to get hit. Jesus, it *hurts.*'

Jonathon pushed himself upright to see Chopper's bloodied buttock. It was already covered in grit and swarming flies. Marsden was yelling for a stretcher. Jonathon said quietly, 'You'll be fine. It's not too bad, and you'll get to lie down for a bit.'

'But I can't sleep on my stomach, Jonno.' Chopper's weak smile trembled.

'Honest, you'll be right.' Jonathon touched him on the shoulder. 'At least you get to sleep. Grab it while you can. You'll be back in no time.'

'Keep an eye on Bob for us.' Chopper gestured at Marsden.

Jonathon nodded. 'He can look after himself, but I will.'

They rolled Chopper face-down onto a stretcher and took him away. Satisfied that he would be all right, Jonathon wearily pushed his way along the trench, hardly registering the storm of gunfire all around him, and found Robert balanced on an ammunition box so he could shoot at the Turks.

Robert paused only long enough to flash an angry look at him. 'What the hell did you do that for? Are you trying to getting yourself fucking killed?'

Jonathon drew back from his friend's rage. 'I didn't know what I was doing,' he said quietly. 'I just *did* it.'

Robert yanked at the breech of his rifle and shoved the next round in. For a moment, he was lost for an answer. Then he put the stock against his shoulder and took aim across no-man's-land. 'Yeah, well...' He squinted through the sights. 'Now look what you've bloody started.'

***

That night, the two of them crouched around a tiny fire in the trench, warming water for tea. The rest of the day had been used to widen the trench, make more fire steps and loop-holes, and generally turn the place into something more liveable. No one had been sniped at again, and the Turks had twice put a replacement machine gun into the pit, only to be bombed out each time by Withers who was getting good at this particular target. Robert hadn't mentioned his angry remarks, then he had another chance to comment after someone loomed out of the darkness to tap Jonathon on the shoulder.

'Willow wants to see you in his bunker.'

'Does he? Thanks, Bill.'

Robert had his nose over the pot, stirring tea into the water. He muttered, 'He probably wants to kick you up the arse too. For that stunt you pulled today.'

'You might be right,' Jonathon shrugged. 'Are you coming?'

'Better not. Streeth will have a fit, if he knows two of us have left the line.'

The fighting had died down to the normal night-time levels, the front trenches trading occasional rifle fire, the machine guns sweeping the open ground just in case. A bright, starry sky and half-moon gave enough light to watch no-man's-land, so neither side would be trying patrols.

First, Jonathon found Streeth and told him about the call to Willow's bunker. Then he made the journey back through the network of trenches. Under darkness, the trip was like walking in some subterranean landscape. With the near-black sky above, the trenches felt like tunnels. Further from the front lines, in places where a more permanent stay was expected, dugouts in the sides contained flickering candles and gaunt, curious faces that watched as he went by. The pin-prick glow of cigarettes was everywhere. Unseen, heard among the echoing rifle fire from the front line, came the noises of an army at night. The clank of metal cooking tins, a teaspoon rattling a mug, and the grinding of a blacksmith's stone wheel sharpening bayonets. And, always, the murmur of thousands of men talking.

Willow had his oil lamp burning to study a map across his table. He straightened and nodded a friendly greeting when Jonathon announced himself at the curtained doorway.

'Good evening, sir,' Jonathon didn't salute. Willow wasn't wearing his cap.

'Hello, White. Want a mug of tea?'

The question took Jonathon by surprise. 'Ah, no thank you, sir. I've just had one,' he added the lie, so that Willow wouldn't be offended.

'I've got a little something to lace it with.' Willow raised his eyebrows.

'In that case, sir, perhaps I will.'

Jonathon watched as he poured a generous serve of rum into two enamel mugs of tea, then he took the one offered. Silently they toasted each other. He was feeling uncomfortable. Relations between officers and enlisted men were generally informal in the Australian trenches, although not where Willow was concerned.

'That business with the machine gun today,' Willow began. 'Well done. My spies tell me it was your idea. You even captured it personally.'

'Not really. I was just the first to get there. I'm fast on my feet.' Jonathon shrugged. 'I couldn't have done it on my own.'

Willow wasn't about to be fooled by any false modesty. 'Nevertheless, I like to hear of men showing initiative. Leading by example. We need all the resourcefulness we can get.'

'Well, it was more spur-of-the-moment, sir,' Jonathon admitted. 'It wasn't really planned.'

'Acting on your instincts is often the best way.' He gave Jonathon a moment to understand this, lit a cigarette and offered a pack of ready-mades. Jonathon took one.

Willow went on, 'Anyway, the point is your unit needs a corporal since Streeth was promoted and I'm giving you the job. It's all above board and correct, the proper paperwork might take a while to come through, that's all. So you'll have to take my word for it.' Willow smiled at his own joke. 'Get some stripes, if you can. Ask the Master-at-Arms on the beach next time you're down there. He's usually prepared for this sort of thing.'

The unspoken message was that the army was always prepared to replace officers and NCOs killed in the field. The Master-at-Arms would carry spare badges of rank among his supplies. Still, it struck Jonathon as slightly macabre to anticipate men's deaths, even in a battle.

Otherwise, he was momentarily speechless at the promotion and not sure that he wanted it. As he lit his smoke, he thought fast and quickly figured that he didn't have much choice. Refusing it would put Willow offside, and it wasn't like they were trying to make him an officer. Just a corporal, and the extra pay could come in handy later.

'Thank you, sir,' he said, almost too late. 'I'll do my best.'

'Good man. I'll write a note for Sergeant Streeth. Which reminds me.' Willow clicked his fingers. 'Talking of letters, there's one here for you that's come through the command system. It's not normal mail.' He went to his desk, picked an envelope out of a wicker tray and handed it to him. It was a plain colour, with Jonathon's name and military address written in a tight, precise hand.

Jonathon glanced at the oil lamp. 'Do you mind if I read it here, sir?'

'Of course you can.' Willow's curiosity showed. 'I need a minute to write this note for Streeth anyway.'

Jonathon opened the envelope carefully. Everything about it was too neat to suffer just tearing the seal. Willow sat at his desk, his pen scratching across a memo pad.

The brief letter made Jonathon glad. This was good news indeed.

'It's from a nurse called Rose Preston aboard the *Gascon*, a hospital ship,' he told Willow. 'Actually, it's more a note from Tom Carter. His wound wasn't as bad as he'd thought, and the nurse says he can expect a full recovery. And the silly bugger wanted me to leave him behind in that shell hole.'

'Excellent,' Willow jumped up from his seat, holding out his note. 'I'm happy to hear it. We get precious little encouraging news at the moment.' He paused and turned, suddenly thinking. 'My mother was a nurse in South Africa during the Boer War, you know. A God-awful job that no one appreciates, but we all invariably start crying for our mothers when we take a bad knock. She damned near died of malaria herself and never really recovered.' He shook off the melancholy. 'Yes, that *is* good news. Now, take this and give it to Streeth. Your promotion is effective immediately and I'll be keeping an eye on your progress.'

The meeting was over. The mug of tea was only half finished, and with the rum, Jonathon wasn't going to waste it. He hastily gulped down the rest and burned his mouth.

'Thank you, sir,' he said again.

'Good luck, White.' Willow was already back at his desk, searching through some papers. Then he asked suddenly, 'What was her name again? The nurse?'

'Preston, sir. Rose Preston.' He checked the letter and spelled it out.

Willow wrote it on a scrap of paper. 'Thank you. Yes, good luck,' he said again.

'The same to you, sir.'

***

'You're a bloody corporal?' Robert said. Jonathon was back at the front line and had explained everything, including Carter's letter written by Rose. Robert had more pressing concerns on his mind. 'You're not going to tell *me* what to do, are you?'

'I can't show any favouritism,' Jonathon said, with a deadpan expression.

'What about all the shit jobs? Can't you sort of pass me over, when you're choosing blokes?'

'I dunno, Robert. I can't promise anything. You should know that.'

Robert sensed defeat and turned sly. 'I'd do it for you.'

'Hey, don't start with that...'

'Ah, bugger it.' Robert tossed him a can of bully beef which was still warm from the fire. 'Here, you've got to eat this. Streeth wants the tins for more bombs. They reckon the Turks are attacking.'

'Where?'

'Everywhere. One of the ship's seaplanes spotted them this afternoon. Thousands of the bastards all lined up behind their trenches, ready to attack.'

Jonathon stared out into the darkness and realised it was strangely quiet. Hardly a rifle shot or artillery round was being fired, when normally a steady, harassing rate would be exchanged between the opposing sides, even though it was close to midnight by now. The silence made him uneasy.

'Do you think they're coming tonight or in the morning?' he asked.

Robert looked at the sky. 'Maybe tonight, but they'll wait until the moon's gone.'

'Are you sure it isn't just a rumour? Willow didn't mention it.'

'Streeth is sure of it. But maybe you're right.' Robert shrugged.

Without warning, the night was transformed. A storm of rifle fire erupted from the Turkish trenches. It was as if all the enemy soldiers on the peninsula had, as one, turned their guns towards the Anzacs and started shooting. Bullets snapped and whined over the Australian trenches, the firing already so thick that a man raising his hand would be hit instantly. The noise was deafening. Startled, Robert cursed and stooped low. He put his face close to Jonathon's.

'They can't be coming now, surely? The silly bastards would be shooting themselves.'

'No, but when it stops, we'd better be ready,' Jonathon shouted back.

'Well, don't tell *me*. You're the bloody corporal. Go and tell everyone else.'

With a guilty start, Jonathon remembered. He was responsible for this sort of thing now. Men were pouring into the trenches from the rear support areas, cramming shoulder to shoulder in the narrow space, their moonlit faces urgent. Nobody could look over the parapet or try to return the Turks' fire. That was inviting instant death. So they spread out as far as they could, finding room along the trench wall, and watched the trench lip for any hint of the enemy.

Jonathon pushed past, warning everyone repeatedly as he went that an attack would most likely begin when the firing stopped. Working his way along, he watched for Streeth and found him near the far end of their section.

'Nick?'

Streeth turned from where he'd been trying to raise a periscope. The timber at its tip was splintered. A stream of tracer ripped above his head, sizzling the air. 'Jonno,' he nodded tersely, shouting to be heard. 'Looks like trouble's coming. So, did Willow give you a bollocking, or a medal?'

'He made me your bloody corporal.'

'Jesus, that's worse.' Streeth waited a second, then with a tight grin slapped Jonathon on the shoulder. 'Go back and take the other end of the line. Your guess is as good as mine what's going to happen. Willow should be here soon enough.'

It was easier for Jonathon to return. The men's initial rush to defend the front trench was over and they crowded the forward wall, leaving space behind to move. Many of them gazed upwards at the bullets passing above, the tracers of automatic fire stitching bright patterns in the air. Now it was a matter of staying calm and patient until the attack came. Most of the Anzacs found time to roll a cigarette. Few of them talked, apart from yelling encouragement or wry jokes. The roar of gunfire was too loud to bother. When Jonathon reached Robert, he signalled his presence with a touch on his friend's arm. Then he, too, took a place below the parapet and waited anxiously for the Turkish attack.

The night was torn apart for over half an hour. Finally the onslaught of bullets stopped almost as suddenly as it began. No one heard any orders or whistles from the Turkish side, but the firing along the entire front ceased within seconds, so it had to have been pre-arranged. Reacting to the tense silence, calls to "Stand to!" were passed urgently down the trenches and the rattle of rifle bolts being cocked ran along the line. Then bayonets were fixed. The men stood guard on the fire steps, watching the blackness of no-man's-land, or prepared to heave themselves into a firing position outside.

Nothing moved and the Anzac officers were puzzled. Surely the enemy would be attacking any moment?

After several minutes, it began to look like the whole thing had been an accident after all, a mistake by the Turks. It wouldn't be the first time a frenzied exchange of fire had been triggered by a nervous sentry jumping at shadows. The entire front could be panicked into loosing off a full day's ammunition in less than ten minutes. Perhaps the expected attack wasn't coming at all.

Nothing happened for nearly four hours.

***

'Rob, someone's seen something.' Jonathon shook his friend's shoulder. 'The Turks are coming.'

Without leaving the front trenches, the men had been told to stand down and rest. Cramped and uncomfortable, some like Robert still managed to sleep. Others kept watch. Now, dim in the starlight, a mass of shapes was moving through a gully towards the beach.

'Silly sods,' Robert whispered sleepily, rubbing at his eyes. 'What the hell do they think they're doing?'

'God knows,' Jonathon said, both fascinated and appalled at what he knew they were about to see.

The Australians held the high ground on either side. The Anzacs silently rose up and now it was their turn to fill the night with furious gunfire, shooting down into the gully at the trapped enemy. The muzzle blasts were like lightning flashing off the rocks. The Turks screeched in terror and tried to turn around. It was hopeless.

The skirmish was a signal for the whole front to break out into fighting again. This time, the Turks clambered out of their main trenches and advanced on the Anzac positions in an orderly charge. Their peculiar discordant bugles urged them on. Some of the enemy officers blew on their whistles like men possessed. In the near-darkness, the Turks simply rolled across no-man's-land.

In Jonathon's trench, the men couldn't reload and fire fast enough. They shot into the packed Turks savagely. For many, this was the first time they'd really had a chance to kill their enemy in numbers. Until now the Turks had sniped from the hills, or gunned the Anzacs from behind good cover.

The Turks wavered and collapsed. The last of them standing realised their fate too late and ran among their own dead like frightened rabbits, looking for somewhere to hide. The Anzac rifles hunted them down.

Another wave swelled out of their trenches again and advanced, doomed like the first.

'Be damned to this,' someone near to Jonathon said. A soldier scrambled out of the trench to sit comfortably on a sandbag in the open. Now he could shoot more easily, without being jostled by the men on either side. In moments, others had followed his example and left the trench, taking with them supplies of ammunition.

'Hey! *Hey*! Get the hell back down,' Jonathon yelled, but no one took any notice. Already their rifles were roaring, cutting down the Turks in their hundreds. Behind them, another line gathered above their defences. They weren't even waiting to see the fate of their predecessors.

Somewhere, Major Willow's strident piping voice cut through the noise. With half the men out of the trench, he was practically running through the section. 'Hold your fire! Hold your fire, men!'

Jonathon wasn't the only one confused, then Willow added, 'Wait until the bastards are out in the open. Give them time to form their line and you can kill the bloody lot of them.' He rushed on past, saying this again and again, and the Anzac troops lowered their weapons.

The Turks might have failed to sense the trap, or perhaps they chose to ignore it. With dumb obedience, they again formed a solid wall of men and began to jog across the open ground towards the Australians. This time, their movements were hindered by the countless bodies of the dead and wounded.

'*Fire at will,*' Willow screamed almost girlishly, his voice echoing from the furthest end of the trench. The Anzacs' Lee Enfields lifted and lashed out once more.

Jonathon had given in, climbed above the parapet, and he was lying on his stomach to fire. As he pumped bullets into the breech and shot into the wall of enemy soldiers, an odd sound made him turn.

With so many Anzacs firing at the Turks, two Australian soldiers had started a fistfight over a loop-hole that offered them a clear field of fire. And beyond them, Jonathon saw another man offering money to buy time at a sandbag.

'Cut it out, you stupid bastards,' he yelled. The scuffling men ignored him and rolled to the trench floor in a childish grapple.

The Turks had started to break ranks, ignoring the discipline of their officers, and now some of them were sprinting forward. A few reached the Anzac lines where they were utterly outnumbered and bayoneted.

In the distance, a fresh attack lifted itself from the Turkish lines, then wavered before the bugles, whistles and bellowing officers drove them across the killing ground. Without being told, again the Anzacs waited until the entire wave of men were beyond retreat and wiped them out with devastating fire.

The pattern repeated itself over and over until it seemed the Turkish army must run out of willing men, or the Anzacs had simply run out of bullets—which might have been the Turks' intent. Each wave of attackers approached with less fervour, beaten forward by their officers, and the Australians shot them down with the same enthusiasm. This was an opportunity not to be missed.

At dawn, the sun rose on an incredible, tragic scene. No-man's-land was covered with the Turkish dead and wounded, the latter pleading for help. Between the continuing attacks their pitiful cries filled the air and tore at the consciences of men on both sides. Help was impossible. The light restored some balance to the battle and Turkish snipers sent the Anzacs scurrying for cover down into the trenches again.

The carnage stopped at midday. Under a hot sun, over five thousand Turkish soldiers lay dead or dying. An equal number had somehow managed to return to their trenches. During the past night and early morning, the Turks had suffered more than ten thousand casualties either killed or wounded.

***

At Gallipoli, the men learned to live under extraordinary conditions. Enduring the constant sight and smell of death, knowing that some rotting mound nearby used to be a friend, became a part of surviving the war. Mostly, the dead were left out in the open because retrieving them was out of the question. The enemy would shoot you too. Worse, a wounded man crying out for help could unwittingly lure mates to their own death as they tried to bring him back to safety.

The unbearable stench of the corpses wasn't the only problem: there was the increased risk of disease.

'There's talk of an armistice to bury the dead,' Jonathon told Robert and several others. Streeth and Jonathon had come back from a midday meeting at Willow's bunker, where the idea of a cease-fire had been announced.

'Thank God for that,' Crowe replied morosely. 'This bloody stink is killing me.' He sat on the fire step, his shoulders hunched to protect his cigarette from the light rain that was falling.

There were just a few soldiers manning the parapet. The Turks were unlikely to attack after the disaster of the previous day and the Australians had sated their appetite for killing, at least for the moment. The change in weather had brought relief from the heat and temporarily slowed the awful process of decay. The open trenches began pooling with water and many sandbags, made heavier with the wet, collapsed and exposed the men. Soldiers who would have paid anything for a fresh drink the day before were already cursing the rain.

Robert looked at a stretcher leaning against the rear wall. 'If we could just get rid of the bastards nearby, it would help. Surely the Turks wouldn't shoot a stretcher-bearer going to their own men?'

'After the beating they've taken, they're going to shoot anyone,' Marsden said, and plucked the cigarette from Crowe's hand for a drag.

'We could raise a white flag first.'

'A *white* flag?' Crowe frowned at Robert. 'I don't bloody think so.'

'Well, a Red Cross flag, then.' Robert looked to Jonathon for support. 'What do you reckon?'

'I say we wait until the officers figure out this cease-fire.'

'That could take all day and never happen. We should try and get the wounded, if nothing else.'

Some of the Turks were still alive, calling out pitifully for mercy and affecting the morale of the Anzacs. Killing a man in battle was one thing. Letting him suffer a slow death unnecessarily was another.

'I don't like it any more than you do,' Jonathan said. 'But it's too risky.'

Robert could see he was weakening. 'If we could just stick our heads up and drag anyone close into the trench, it'd be better than nothing. Some of our blokes are out there too, don't forget.'

Jonathon thought about asking Streeth, then decided an experiment couldn't hurt. 'All right,' he gave in with a growl. 'See if you can find a flag, but make sure it's a Red Cross. We don't anyone to think we're surrendering, for Christ's sake.'

It didn't take long. The trenches were littered with plenty of flags for all sorts of reasons. They tied a Red Cross banner, made from the vests that stretcher-bearers wore, to one of the poles. Robert tried raising it and two shots rang out immediately. One of the bullets smashed the pole and brought it toppling down.

'Shit!' He dodged the falling wood and the others laughed.

'What'd I tell you?' Crowe said triumphantly. 'They'll shoot anyone.'

'The bastards.' Robert inspected the broken pole. 'They didn't even give it a chance.'

Crowe nodded. 'See? They just don't respect that sort of thing. They're bloody natives. Haven't got a clue.'

'Their officers must have half a brain—'

Suddenly a Turkish face appeared at the lip of their trench and stared anxiously down. It had dark skin and a black moustache and eyebrows, and the eyes were very white and nervous. The Australians were so shocked they simply stared right back.

'Please, we're very sorry,' the Turk said in heavily accented English. 'It was not meant to be.'

Jonathon recovered enough to blurt out, 'Tell your officers we want to collect the wounded. Your men, too. Before it's too late.'

The frightened eyes turned to him. 'We won't shoot the flag again. Very sorry.' Then the Turk vanished, scrambling backwards out of sight.

The Australians gaped at each other in disbelief.

'I'll be damned,' Jonathon said. 'He could have been killed.'

'But did he mean it?' Crowe said. 'It could be a trick.'

'It's a bloody mad thing to do, if they're just trying to trick us.'

'I agree. I reckon he's dinkum,' Robert offered.

Crowe looked at him. 'Are *you* going to go out there?'

'Sure, when I fix this.' He gestured with the broken flag.

Someone called, 'Hey, Jonno? Look at this.' It was a soldier nearby with a periscope rifle. His face still at the mirror, he used a free hand to wave them over. 'You're not going to believe this.'

Jonathon gazed out over no-man's-land. The glass was spotted with raindrops and flecks of mud, but he could still see. At the Turkish lines, three Red Crescent flags were waving slowly above the parapet. Then, as he watched, two men emerged cautiously. They were unarmed, and one of them carried a stretcher over his shoulder.

At the same time, all along their section of front line, the gunfire was dying away. An eerie silence replaced it.

Two more pairs of Turkish soldiers popped up, again with a stretcher between them.

'They're doing it,' Jonathon said urgently, dropping back down from the fire step. At the men's worried looks he added, 'Sending out stretcher-bearers, I mean. So off you go before someone figures it's a bad idea. Bob, go and find another stretcher. You and I will head out next.'

Marsden hurried away. Robert and Crowe clambered up and out into the open, slipping in the mud. They started to search among the nearest bodies, looking for anyone alive.

They brought back a wounded Turk, close to death from half a dozen bullets, his eyes still open in a desperate plea.

'Well done. Good thinking,' Jonathon told Robert. It was a show of faith, bringing back one of the enemy before any Australians.

They all went back out together. Jonathon's instincts rebelled at letting himself be such an easy target. It felt so *wrong*. He kept his mind on the task of treading between the corpses. There were so many that it took care.

'Over here,' Marsden said, leading the way to a Turk who was grasping feebly at the air. Gagging at the smell of his body, they heaved him onto their stretcher and carried him back to the lines.

By the time they'd finished three more trips, no-man's-land was dotted with many more stretcher-bearers from both sides, moving about unhindered, checking the thousands of bodies. Sometimes Australians and Turks would come close, and in unspoken agreement they manoeuvred to avoid each other. Then a group of officers from each side gathered in the middle and exchanged words, smoking and ignoring the corpses at their feet.

'Why couldn't they do that *before* we started shooting?' Robert grumbled over his shoulder to Jonathon. He'd managed to swap places with Marsden.

'And miss out on all this adventure?' Jonathon grunted at the weight of the man they were carrying.

The work went on for another half an hour. Then the officers' meeting broke up and they gestured emphatically to the soldiers as they returned.

'Everyone back to the lines. Back to your trenches.'

The word quickly spread that a proper armistice was being arranged for the next day and that the High Command was furious that men on the front line had taken matters into their own hands.

***

In the morning, it was still raining heavily and had turned bitterly cold as troops gathered, armed with shovels this time, and moved out onto no-man's-land to begin the task of mass burials. Red Cross and Red Crescent flags were flying everywhere, fluttering in the breeze with a macabre gaiety. A line of sentries stood in front of their respective forward trenches, tense and watchful. Officers were out in strength, organising teams to dig in different areas and supervising the taking of private belongings from the corpses and returning them to the proper side, which was almost always the Turks. This was a blatant excuse to inspect the enemy's defences up close and caused friction on both sides. Close to the Australian trenches, a bunch of Anzac staff officers stood on a high parapet made mostly of dead Turks and watched keenly.

Working side-by-side with the enemy, at first the Anzacs and Turks deliberately ignored each other. Then their nightmarish task led to a sort of bond forming. It started with trading cigarettes. The men smoked constantly, rather than breathe in the stink of the corpses. Everywhere, the soldiers would pause in their digging, take out a pack of ready-mades or a tin of tobacco and begin rolling. It was habit to offer the makings to the nearest man and soon, cautiously, soldiers from opposing sides stood beside each other and smoked.

Jonathon found himself watched by a thickset Turk probably twice his age. The man's shovel scraped half-heartedly at the ground after he spied the tobacco tin in Jonathon's hand.

'Smoke, Abdul?' Jonathon asked softly and offered the tin.

The Turk smiled, nodded gratefully, and took the tobacco. Jonathon watched his fingers as he teased the paper and brown leaf into shape, seeing they were callused and scarred, a worker's hands. It struck him that perhaps this man was a farmer as he was, and he wondered how he might ask. All around them were the grating sounds of shovels biting into the ground. Orders were given quietly, and the men talked in a hush.

'My brother,' the Turk suddenly said, startling Jonathon. He pointed down at the dead man before them, a Turk who had been nearly cut in half by rifle fire.

Jonathon was appalled. *By sheer coincidence, was he helping to bury this man's brother?* Then the enemy soldier looked sad and gestured at Jonathon.

'Your brother, too,' he said hesitantly. When Jonathon didn't understand, the Turk took in the entire battlefield with an expansive wave. 'Brothers together.' His smile came back, wistful now.

'Oh–yes, you're right.' Jonathon realised what he had meant. He added awkwardly, 'Perhaps if it were left up to us, we wouldn't be fighting.'

The Turk seemed to understand his tone. He shrugged and picked up the shovel again. A few minutes later, as their work began to separate them, the Turk paused and came over to him, offering something in his clenched fist.

It was a cap badge. A momento for the Australian to keep.

'Thank you,' Jonathon said, trying to think of something to give back. With a reluctance he didn't show, he took off his hat and removed the rising sun badge from the crown. The Turk accepted it with a bow and murmured gratitude. Then they went opposite ways.

They mostly dug long communal graves and carried the Turkish dead to them from wherever they'd fallen. It was simpler than digging individual holes. Any Australian bodies were taken back to behind the Anzac trenches. At one point the Turks asked, and were allowed, to remove some of their countrymen's corpses from another sandbag battlement that had been built chiefly with the dead men. In return, the Anzacs were able to fill the holes created with more sandbags, which otherwise wouldn't have been possible during the cease-fire.

The job was no easier to perform or accept as the day wore on, the corpses already shattered by gunfire, now made worse by time. The end wasn't in sight until mid-afternoon. Then, as some of the soldiers finished digging and began to drift from the area, all over no-man's-land the enemies shook hands and exchanged final souvenirs. When there was a common language, they wished each other luck in surviving the war.

At four o'clock, the last man out in the open, an Australian officer who had been negotiating directly with the Turks, dropped back into the Anzac trenches.

Fifteen minutes later a Turkish sniper fired from the hills. The round ricocheted off a steel drum with a loud *clang*. The Australian answered with an artillery gun aimed roughly in the right direction.

The entire front burst back into life with a deafening roar.

***

'They weren't bad blokes,' Robert called to Jonathon. 'Just like us really.'

With a laden stretcher between them, they were picking their way through the front lines to the beach. Jonathon was up front.

'Now you *like* them?'

'No, but I don't *hate* them. They're just a bunch of poor bastards doing a crap job, like we are. They're probably got wives and kids at home too.'

'Of course, they have. How do you think... wait, hang on.'

They were passing through a section where the opposing lines were only yards apart. In front of Jonathon a soldier was about to throw something into the Turkish trenches. His action blocked the way.

'Check this out,' he grinned at Jonathon, showing him the missile. It was a tin of unopened bully beef.

'What are you doing?'

'I'll show you.' He lobbed the tin skywards, yelling loudly, 'Hey Abdul? Try this, you bastard.' They could hear the thud of the tin dropping into the Turkish line. Before Jonathon could move on, the soldier stopped him again, holding up his flat hand.

'Wait for a tick,' he winked.

Puzzled and getting impatient, feeling the ache from the stretcher's weight on his arms, Jonathon stood and watched. A few seconds later something landed softly in the dirt at their feet. The soldier picked it up.

It was a bunch of ripe grapes. Some had split, but the soldier was still hugely pleased.

'A bargain,' he said, plucking one and offering it to Jonathon, who was too surprised to do anything except take it in his mouth. The sweet juice was an explosion of taste for someone deprived of any fruit for so long.

'I'll be buggered,' he said.

Further down the track, Robert said wryly, 'So instead of killing them, now we have to feed the bastards?'

Jonathon shook his head. 'Damned if I know.' He was still perplexed by the incident and the question expressed his mixed feelings perfectly.

'Well, don't worry. The Turks'll launch a full-scale attack the moment they taste that fucking bully beef. So they should, too.'

The evening gloom deepened as Major Willow divided the wounded into groups on the beach according to the severity of their injuries. Using an oil lamp to check the man on the stretcher, he suddenly realised that Jonathon was one of the bearers.

'Ah, it's you, Corporal White. I've been keeping an eye out for you.' Willow hastily dug a letter from his top pocket. 'I've written a note of appreciation to that nurse who wrote to you about Sergeant Carter. My mother would never forgive me, if I didn't thank her properly. That's the *Gascon* out there now, and these men are being ferried there in the next boat. There's a good chap. Hitch a ride with them and help out with the unloading, and see if you can't grab a moment to deliver the note, if she's still there.'

Jonathon was dumbfounded. It seemed odd, but Willow was known to be strongly compassionate in unexpected ways. At least Jonathon wouldn't be doing anything too out of the ordinary. Fully fit soldiers always travelled on the navy cutters to help unload the wounded at the other end.

'Do you think she will be, sir?' Jonathon blinked down at the letter in his hand.

'Perhaps not, but there'll be a nurse who can pass it on much more reliably than any of our people. Don't take long, though. Thornton? You come with me. I need your help over here.'

With a helpless look, Robert was led away as Jonathon was left to figure out how to get to the hospital ship. Then Robert's laughing voice floated out from the darkness, reminding Jonathon of a conversation weeks before. 'Don't forget, Jonno. If she's old and ugly, I don't want to know.'

To Cairo and Beyond

Even before she joined up, Rose had suspected that the rigid ideas of the army were going to annoy her. Travelling from Melbourne to New South Wales seemed unnecessary when there was recruiting all over the country, but apparently the nurses corps were being organised from Victoria Barracks in Sydney and nothing except presenting herself there would do.

So Rose took a cramped cargo steamer up the coast. It was privately owned with a dozen passengers' berths, and she endured a rolling, grey journey in poor weather. The low clouds and hissing whitecaps didn't come with a chill but with a humid, summer heat that chased Rose from her cabin as often as possible. She stayed on deck most of the day and read, struggling to hold her pages against the wind.

The crew took a liking to her. Meals were served in a dining room that was beautiful, though small and in contrast to the rest of the aging vessel. For the four days of the trip she was joined each evening by the captain and at least one other officer who obviously enjoyed her youthful female company, much to the annoyance of the few other passengers, who were looking on with ill-disguised envy.

Waiting on the dock in Sydney were friends of her father, a family called the Galstons. George and his wife Martha and their two children welcomed her as if she were a long-lost relative, and she felt completely at ease. Everything, it seemed, was working out just fine.

Until she reached the barracks and trouble came in the shape of Major Cromwell, a severe-looking man who peered at her suspiciously from behind his desk. The office was spartan, the green walls bare except for two frames, one, a certificate that Rose couldn't read because the writing was small and hopelessly florid, and the other a display of medals behind glass. Rose wondered whether the medals were his and immediately decided they weren't, since he would have been wearing them. His desk was neat beyond belief, the few papers shuffled into perfect alignment, the pencils lined up like ammunition ready to fire. The blotter was spotless.

Through the open window came the sounds of men parading out in the sunshine, shouting and stamping in unison.

'You're not a registered nurse, Miss Preston,' Cromwell observed from her letter of introduction, which he held in front of him in a precise manner, as if there were a correct military way to do this. 'In truth, you're not fully trained at all.' His trimmed moustache quivered as he spoke.

'I served in the Voluntary Aid Detachment in London for nearly six months,' Rose said, puzzled because it was written plainly for the major to see for himself. 'I expected that to be just as valuable as any formal training. Besides, I'm not offering my services as a regular nursing sister, but as an assistant with duties similar to those I had in England.'

'But we're talking about nursing wounded men close to the fighting itself. An entirely different thing, don't you think? There is some doubt whether it is a place for women at all.' The major sighed. 'After all, the army has men well-trained for nursing.'

'Oh, I see,' Rose said, catching on to his condemnation of anything female—at least, she guessed, when it came to the army. 'Don't you need all the men you can find for the fighting?'

His nostrils flared and he said tightly, 'The modern army is a team, Miss Preston. Every man has his place and does his duty.'

'Yes, and the modern *British* army has women nurses and VADs in casualty clearing stations only two thousand yards behind the front trenches. Close to the fighting, as you said yourself.'

Caught with no reply, Cromwell picked up a pencil and tapped it against the desktop. He reread the letter.

'You're rather young,' he said finally. 'Do you have your father's approval?'

'I don't need it, but it's signed on the next page.' Again, he must have already seen this for himself. Rose felt a flicker of anger.

'Still...' Cromwell inclined his head doubtfully. 'Most of the registered nurses we have serving are quite... ah... senior to yourself. Older women are expected to be steadier under duress, of course.'

Rose bent forward, her eyes suddenly cold as she stared into his.

She said with a mock sweetness, 'I'm old enough to cauterise the main arteries in a man's legs while the surgeon amputates them both. And I'll take away the dead limbs afterwards. Often it's not that hard because there isn't much to carry.' She leaned back again without dropping her gaze. 'Otherwise, they wouldn't need amputating, would they? You should hope, Major Cromwell, if you're ever in dire need of medical attention, that someone as experienced as I am is doing the job.'

Cromwell paled, then his neck reddened with either anger or embarrassment. He tossed her letter down and yanked open a drawer. For a heartbeat, she wondered whether he was going to accept her offer or dismiss her. Cromwell pulled out a sheet of letterhead and began scribbling on it, some of the ink spattering from the inkwell in his haste.

'The infirmary is the white building on the other side of the parade ground. Beside the officers' mess. Introduce yourself to Matron Lambert and ask for the appropriate papers.' He handed over the letter without blotting it. Rose put it in her bag carefully without reading it. Cromwell smiled unpleasantly. 'She may well still find you unsuitable, even if I can't find any reasonable fault to prevent your enlisting.'

'Thank you, sir.' Until then she felt neither obligated to address him properly, nor that this sour man deserved it. She didn't ask for the introductory letter back because she had a copy with her and he didn't offer it.

Back outside, she breathed deeply as she walked the perimeter of the tarmac parade ground. It was unwise to judge the entire establishment on just one man. Then again, everything around her spoke of *men* and all things male. She could feel the eyes of the marching soldiers sneak her way, despite a barked instruction by the drill sergeant not to let them do so, and their attention came for entirely different reasons. It seemed from a professional standpoint the army was a male bastion that no women should dare try to invade. Major Cromwell wouldn't be alone in his anti-female sentiments.

Matron Lambert was much more welcoming, although stern and concerned about Rose's age. She was tall and strong-looking, with a sharp face and piercing grey eyes that suggested a woman approaching fifty. Otherwise, there was little to judge her age by. Her full-length white uniform crackled with starch and she wore a blood-red, short cloak that fell to half-way down her back. The white veil, like a nun's, concealed her hair except for the tiniest wisps of silver at the temples.

Beside the matron's desk, through a wide internal window, Rose could see a small ward with a dozen empty beds. Each was precisely made, in perfectly alignment with the others, and accompanied by exactly the same bedside cabinet and wooden chair.

Matron Lambert, like the major before her, spoke as she studied Rose's documents. Her voice was quiet and utterly confident.

'Your experiences in London speak for themselves, Rose. As much as the regular, trained nurses would like to think themselves prepared for wartime service, I expect the reality will be an unpleasant shock. You could be an invaluable addition to our staff.'

'Is there a problem, Matron?' Rose frowned at the implications of "could be". *Had Major Cromwell written something derogatory?* She had resisted the urge to read his letter during the walk over. She assumed he hadn't scribbled long enough to say anything other than a brief approval of some kind.

'You're too young, Rose,' the matron explained, sounding undecided as she thought the matter over hard. 'The King's Regulations insist that nurses enlisted in the Australian Army Nursing Service be at least twenty-five years old.'

Rose didn't dare break the silence that followed.

'However, by simple omission they make no mention of Voluntary Aid Detachments, which might let me reconsider your offer...' That idea hung in the air while she fingered the second letter and pursed her lips thoughtfully. 'And Major Cromwell has given me his somewhat terse approval. Perhaps he is of the same opinion? Heaven forbid that he be mistaken.'

Seizing the chance, Rose put in earnestly, 'The major seemed most adamant that no women except the most eminently acceptable be allowed to enlist in the army. I'm sure he wouldn't have made a mistake.'

The matron allowed herself a brief, wry smile. 'No, I expect you're right. Major Cromwell's stand on such issues is well known and an error on his part is unthinkable. Anyhow, with the way events are occurring around here, I suspect you'll be on the other side of the world before anyone questions your eligibility.'

The decision made, she began filling in a form that she'd taken from a pile. Then her pen stopped, poised above the paper as she stared at Rose.

'Are you engaged, or considering marriage in the near future? You strike me as a girl who may have several suitors knocking on her father's door.'

Rose was taken by surprise and smiled. 'Goodness, no. I don't have anyone intimate right now.' She added awkwardly, 'I mean, I seem to scare men off quite quickly. My father can't understand it. Does it really matter?'

'Married women are definitely not allowed in the AANS, unless they have the misfortune to be widowed. If you marry during your service, you must resign immediately.'

'But that's ridiculous—' Rose began.

'Those are the rules, Rose and we must abide by them all. Occasionally even I'll admit to bending a few, but that is one in particular that we cannot ignore. Is that clear?'

Rose nodded, trying to read the other woman's expression to see whether it was hiding anything. As the matron continued filling out the form, and offered only her lowered head, Rose changed the subject. 'You mentioned travelling soon?'

'There's hardly anyone left here. The first two hundred girls sailed last month. I would have been with them, except my father took ill. My ship leaves in two weeks' time and I expect you to be ready. There will be another twenty reinforcements with us.'

The excitement took Rose's breath away for a second. Suddenly it was happening. She'd been given her first order before the enlistment papers were even finished.

'And you're our commanding officer?' Although she'd known Matron Lambert only a few minutes, Rose found she liked that idea.

'For the moment, I'm answerable to the medical officers, yes. The future is uncertain.' The matron glanced up to see Rose's enthusiasm falter. 'Rose, I'm always going to be part of the administrative structure, however you should understand that we are adrift upon a sea of hopeless, military bureaucracy. They can't quite agree on our proper status in the army, our ranks or even our rates of pay, which I should warn you are significantly lower than those of our British counterparts. You will even have to provide your own uniform. On the whole, we make our own decisions because no one will make them for us, despite the fact that we're not empowered to do so. So, to answer your question, yes I am your commanding officer. That could change at any moment on the whim of somebody like Major Cromwell or any of the medical officers.'

'I understand,' Rose said, not really sure. From the gleam of irritation in the matron's eye, it was obviously a sensitive subject. 'Then I suppose if we're sailing in two weeks, I'd better get a winter uniform. They're saying the cold in Europe is the worst for years. The snows might last until late March.'

Matron Lambert was writing again, her nib darting into the inkwell like a drinking sparrow. Without looking up, she said, 'You won't need too many woollens in Egypt, you know. We're setting up hospitals throughout Cairo and adjacent areas. Half the Australian army may not know where they're going, while *we* by the grace of God and the odd sympathetic ear in higher ranks, are aware that we're establishing ourselves in the Mediterranean. So I doubt you'll see much snow. Please keep that to yourself, for what it's worth. The army is fanatical about its secrets, even when everyone knows them.'

Rose considered this while the matron filled out the rest of the form. It was true that the army's location in Egypt was almost common knowledge now, but it was generally believed that their purpose was still to fight in Belgium, despite the unusual training conditions. Rumours of fighting in Africa had begun to surface, although no one took them seriously. Why waste an entire army on capturing mere colonies? Still, setting up hospitals in Cairo suggested that there might be some truth to the stories.

'Sign here,' Matron interrupted Rose's thoughts, spinning the paper around so she could read it. 'I'm afraid I've made a slight error in your date of birth,' she said easily. 'It's hardly worth rewriting the entire form just for that, do you think?'

'Oh, I'm not precious about my age,' Rose signed the paper quickly.

'No, at your time in life you can afford not to be.' She watched Rose carefully. The only sound was the nib scratching eagerly at the paper.

***

The ship was the *SS Kyarra* and it had already done one trip to Cairo with the original two hundred nurses squeezed among too many soldiers. The overcrowding on that voyage saw the ship stripped of most of the comforts from her previous existence to avoid similar problems. Rose was allotted an austere twin cabin in what used to be the ship's third class with another nurse, a girl in her mid-thirties called Julia Cornwell. After her tiny flat in London, Rose was at ease sharing such a small space. Julia was concerned about imposing on her. Even bumping into her between the bunks brought effusive apologies. So far it was only amusing, but Julia would need some straightening-out soon before she drove Rose mad.

Standing at the rail and watching the still-unfamiliar shoreline of Sydney slide past, Rose felt a presence nearby and turned to find Julia next to her. She was a plain-looking woman with an innocent smile and a strangely vulnerable nature. She wondered how Julia could be a nurse and not be hardened by some of the things they did.

Julia was gazing towards the land, too. 'Will you miss it, Rose? Are you sorry you decided to come?' She was really asking herself.

'I could hardly miss it, Julia. My feet haven't touched the ground since I got here. Sydney means nothing to me. I felt more sorry when I left Melbourne, where my family lives.'

'But what about Australia, I mean? You've already been overseas, I know. You should always feel a bit sad leaving your own country.'

'Oh, Australia will always be here waiting for us,' Rose said. 'We might not often have the chance to go overseas. To strange, foreign lands and all that.'

'Hmm, Egypt. It's a bit daunting.'

'It's a little piece of England, mostly. Except the natives have darker skin. There's even a Luna Park there, did you know?' Julia laughed and Rose added,

'No, really. Unless they've changed that into a hospital too.'

'God, how many hospitals will they need? Surely not that many?'

'Better to be safe than sorry, I suppose.'

Julia didn't answer that. Although Rose was by far the youngest of their group, and the only VAD, the other nurses regarded her as an equal. Rose was grateful and didn't ponder why it was so, only assuming that her status as a volunteer was appreciated. When she looked in a mirror, she didn't see the extra years in her eyes that her father had seen, put there by those harrowing months in London.

'Julia, you'll have to promise me something,' she said.

Julia looked alarmed. 'What? What's happened?'

'That you'll stop apologising,' Rose smiled. 'Or I'll have to strangle you, honestly. We've got weeks to spend in that cabin together and we're bound to get on each other's nerves. Don't worry about it too much.'

'I know,' Julia sighed. 'I'm just nervous about everything.'

'Well, don't be nervous about me. You'll have plenty of other things to worry about soon enough.'

'Yes, I suppose so.'

Rose bit her lip because it had been a rash thing to say. It was too late to take it back. 'Come on,' she said instead. 'We'd better check that Matron hasn't got a search party out looking for us. She'll have thought of something new to keep us busy by now.'

***

Already the nurses' presence on board was causing a predicament for the military men. Meals were cycled through the dining rooms in an awkward system allowing for rank, whether or not you were a member of the ship's crew, or in the army. Apparently it wasn't acceptable to have the women eating with the enlisted men, even though it was quite all right for the nurses to feed and even bathe these men once they were wounded. The officers weren't keen to be hosts to the women, although common sense suggested the girls' low numbers meant they could share a mealtime rather than have their own. So the nurses were told to dine alone after everyone else had finished.

This was one of many times that the nurses were made to feel they were a burden on the system. Major Cromwell had been left behind at Victoria Barracks, but his bigoted stance towards women in the army, even under their separate banner of the Australian Army Nursing Service, was shared by plenty of men. Clearly, the army had never expected women among their ranks. Most issues were headed off by Matron Lambert before the others got wind of them. It wasn't until months later that Rose and her companions learned how often the matron had been an outraged champion of their rights.

For the first three days, as the *Kyarra* sailed south, the nurses rotated in shifts to help the medical officers inoculate almost the entire passenger list against typhoid. Most of the troops were wary of the needle, waiting in a nervous line through the door and down the passageway. Some of them sweated and chatted loudly about anything to take their minds off it. The nurses teased some for being able to go off to war, and yet they couldn't face an injection.

When everyone was vaccinated there was little else to be done. Then the ship turned west without stopping in Melbourne and headed for the Great Australian Bight. The weather took a turn for the worse, as expected, with a long rolling swell coming up from the cold south. Seasickness ran through the ship like a disease, the smell of vomit more contagious than any germs. The nurses could only offer sympathy and plenty of water to the stream of men hoping for a cure. The medical officers didn't bother to examine them, preferring to leave this menial task to the nurses, many of whom were just as afflicted but couldn't show it.

Albany in the far south of Western Australia was the next port of call, a respite for the seasick men and their nurses alike. The *Kyarra* stayed long enough to re-provision and take on more soldiers, who were impossibly jammed into the lower decks, and several officers. When the ship sailed again, there was another brief period of inoculating before the nurses became restless with so much repetitive training and lecturing.

With time to waste, their dining room became a place they could gather and do personal things between meals, such as mend uniforms or read. They could dress more casually against the increasing heat.

Here, one afternoon with the last landfall days below the horizon, a medical officer burst in breathless. Rose guessed he was one of those who had embarked in Albany, a handsome man with a confident, easy manner. His brown hair was longer than regulations allowed and made him look as he was—a civilian new to his captain's uniform.

'Right, who's had the measles here?' he asked, surveying the group. It took everyone by surprise, not just the question, but his tone of voice. He sounded almost friendly, a rarity in the male officers. His eyes stayed on Rose and she felt compelled to reply.

'Yes, I have.'

'Good, then you'll do. Two others, please?'

Matron Lambert wasn't there. Otherwise, she might have pointed out that Rose wasn't a nurse and chosen someone else. They sorted out two more girls.

'To sick bay.' The officer waved them to follow. 'Or meet us there immediately, if you need anything.'

No one did. They hurried through the confines of the ship, struggling to keep up with him.

Rose was in the lead and she found a chance to call out. 'Why do you need three of us to deal with a case of measles?'

'I need three of you to deal with a *burst appendix,*' he said over his shoulder. 'In a lad who unfortunately has the measles as well.'

The officer was Doctor Mark Cohen, and he came from Perth. He'd put off enlisting until someone was found to take his place at the hospital, and if he were honest he welcomed the chance the war offered to use his medical skills. At the age of thirty-two, it seemed he had been moving inexorably towards a career in administering cough medicine and looking down the throats of spotty children in the public clinic. The chance to perform surgical procedures that were being mostly taken by the more senior doctors didn't come often. He had grown tired of waiting to be considered senior himself.

The appendectomy should have been simple. The added complication of measles and having to operate in the ship's small, basically equipped sick bay made it challenging. Mark worked with impressive calm, thanking the nurses for each task or asking politely if he wanted something done differently. The operation went smoothly, although they often got in each other's way and the air became stifling with the smell of chloroform and antiseptic, acrid in their throats. For a while, Matron Lambert stood in the doorway and watched. Mark merely nodded to her, that was all, and she soon disappeared.

After almost two hours he sighed and stepped back from the table.

'Thank you, everyone,' he said, taking off his cotton mask. 'Take him next door and have someone sit with him. I don't want him left alone for an instant.'

An unnecessary instruction, the women forgave him in return for his otherwise kind manner. Later, they might exchange wry observations on his inexperience.

The two nurses manoeuvred the wheeled stretcher from the sick bay and left Rose to clean up the mess. Mark watched her silently, sometimes moving to let her reach things. Rose carried out her jobs as if he weren't there.

'You can't have been a nurse very long,' he said eventually. 'But you're very good—you all were, of course,' he added quickly.

'I'm not a nurse,' she explained briskly. 'I'm a volunteer, a VAD.' She felt his mood go sour.

'What? But I thought you were all nurses? Why didn't someone tell me, for God's sake?'

Rose kept working and said calmly, 'Rosemary and Nellie are regular nurses. I'm the only VAD here on the ship.'

'You should have told me. What if something had gone wrong? There would have been hell to pay.' Her apparent lack of concern started to irritate him. 'Damn it, have you any idea what I'm talking about?'

Matron Lambert's voice cut through from the doorway. 'You'll mind your language in front of my staff, Doctor Cohen.'

Mark looked guilty for only a moment, then turned to face the matron. 'Sister Lambert, Rose just assisted me in a serious operation without informing me that she was only a VAD. There could have been serious repercussions if something had gone amiss.'

'Did anything go wrong, Doctor?'

'That is not the point.'

'All my staff are extremely competent. They wouldn't be here, otherwise.' Her tone was steely.

'It's not a question of whether—'

Rose cut him off. 'Perhaps it is my fault, Matron. I should have let the doctor know, although I assumed it wasn't an issue.'

The matron didn't take her eyes off the doctor. 'That doesn't excuse his language.'

'It didn't bother me,' Rose said truthfully.

'It bothers *me*. Perhaps, Doctor Cohen, we should continue this discussion somewhere else?' She turned on her heel and left, giving him no option but to follow.

Rose went back to cleaning and heard their voices in a room nearby. She idly guessed it wasn't just the doctor's harsh words or his behaviour that the matron didn't like. This was an opportunity for Matron Lambert to impress upon the new officer just who pulled the strings around the place, regardless of the real chain of command. Rose smiled to herself.

She saw neither of them until late in the afternoon when she was taking some fresh air on the upper deck. The sun hovered above the horizon, minutes away from vanishing, and she could still feel its warmth on her face. She closed her eyes, enjoying its touch. This would have been the promenade deck in the past and there was a walking circuit used by the officers in the evenings. The paint lines for games of shuffle and hopscotch were still there, the equipment locked away. Behind her, small groups of men in deep conversation, puffing on pipes and with their hands invariably behind their backs, strode past regularly. They rarely acknowledged Rose and she didn't care. She preferred this deck for watching the sun go down because the enlisted men weren't allowed here. Not that she wanted to segregate herself, but with so many soldiers it was impossible to be left alone. Someone always wanted to try chatting to her.

'Miss Preston? I'm glad I've found you.'

Sighing, Rose turned from the rail to see Mark Cohen walking towards her.

'Good evening, Doctor Cohen,' she said coolly. 'Is there something wrong?'

'No–no, not at all.' In his haste to reach her, he had to sidestep two officers strolling past. He excused himself and got a frown in return. He was still looking at them over his shoulder, puzzled by their unfriendliness, when he stopped in front of Rose.

She told him, 'You know, you should at least try and salute colonels. When you get in their way, at any rate.'

'Oh? Was that it?' He glanced after them again, then shrugged. 'I thought we weren't bothering with that sort of thing. Otherwise we'd be saluting each other like mad on this cramped little ship.'

'They're British colonels, hitching a ride to Egypt with us. Didn't you notice the different uniform? They're sticklers for protocol. Saluting, and all that.'

'Well, I wouldn't even recognise my own uniform,' he admitted ruefully.

There was an awkward silence.

'You were specifically looking for me, Doctor?'

'Oh–yes, I was hoping to apologise. For this morning, I mean.'

'I've heard much worse language. Really, I wasn't offended at all.'

'It wasn't that so much,' he pulled a wry face. 'Although Matron Lambert has made her views clear to me. I wanted to say sorry for suggesting you were not qualified to assist us. Matron has told me you've spent some months in London at the beginning of the war…' He shrugged again in a youthful way that nearly brought a smile to Rose's lips. 'It would have been a difficult time, and I can imagine you learned a lot that we're yet to see.'

'I was just one person caught up in a larger tragedy, Doctor Cohen. I'm no one special. Hundreds of women, nurses and volunteers alike, did exactly the same thing. In fact, they're still carrying on that work now.'

'But those first months of the war took everyone by surprise. The sheer scale of the casualties was unheard of. You were there to witness it firsthand.

I'd like to talk about it with you, if I may.'

Rose raised her eyebrows at his enthusiasm. 'I was only a volunteer. I've already told Matron Lambert as much as I can recall that might be helpful. She can probably turn my stories into something more scientifically useful, if you ask her—'

'It would better coming from the horse's mouth, so to speak,' he interrupted. 'I thought perhaps we could take a few turns around the deck while we chat? There's no rush. We've nearly a week of sailing still left.'

'Oh, I don't think so,' she said quickly, although the idea was unexpectedly attractive. 'It wouldn't be right.'

He frowned, sensing her real answer. 'Surely you don't need the army's consent for a stroll around the ship? Especially as I have a professional motive?' He smiled to make it sound less formal.

Rose looked along the deck towards two of her nursing colleagues who were standing close, talking. Men walked past them without offering any courtesy at all. The girls' white uniforms, changing to orange in the dying sun, billowed slightly in the wind of the ship's passage. There had been some talk of banning the nurses from the upper decks at night because their clothing might be seen by German submarines. Matron Lambert had already angrily claimed it would never happen.

Mark followed her gaze and guessed what was coming.

Rose said gently, 'I'm sorry, I meant it wouldn't be fair. Perhaps if you could take us all for a stroll?'

'I understand,' he said reluctantly. 'Though I think you're worrying needlessly. I'm sure your friends wouldn't begrudge you a simple walk with an officer.'

'Things have been difficult and I wouldn't be comfortable, Doctor Cohen.

That's my concern.'

'Then what about when we reach Cairo? When everything is a little more... let's say, anonymous? We could do some sightseeing together. The war can't be all work and no fun.'

She gave in with a slight smile. 'All right, if we see each other, ask me again.

Cairo is a big place. We might never cross paths.'

'We'll see.'

He didn't press her further and lingered for a while, chatting about their work. Then Rose excused herself to go and join the two nurses. When she reached them, she looked back to see if the doctor was still at the rail, just in time to see him disappear into a hatchway. It seemed he wasn't so keen on walking the decks alone.

***

The climate in Egypt was bearable. Most of the nurses had endured the worst summers in Australia, while some had worked in the arid outback under the burning southern sun. Constant heat and dry earth underfoot were nothing new.

No one was prepared for the bustling *strangeness* of Cairo with its choking smells coming from everywhere, the flies, and the hordes of people always pressing forward. The narrow streets where children begged because they'd already learned that white travellers from Europe were easy touches. Trinkets and souvenirs of the ancient pharaohs. A babble of voices claimed theirs to be genuine and cheap, the others to be fake and avoided. It was impossible, in some parts of the city, to walk down an alley without being solicited from every doorway.

This was Rose's introduction to Cairo. First, the nurses disembarked from the *Kyarra* and spent several uncomfortable hours waiting on the docks for transport. They were a low priority and Matron Lambert fumed with ever-shortening patience as one truck after another was loaded with military supplies and disappeared into the crowds, ignoring the clutch of white-garbed women. A steady stream of sulkies and horse-drawn carts came and went too, all piled high, but no one was interested in carrying the twenty-two nurses to their quarters. Finally the matron confronted an Australian army captain who was supervising the unloading of an artillery piece. They were using a derrick crane on the ship. The howitzer dangled precariously from a sling high above the unaware crowds. The derrick's cable quivered, as if it were stretched to the limit.

'When are we going to be transported to the hospital, Captain?' Matron Lambert demanded, tapping his shoulder and shouting to be heard above the noise.

He was annoyed at the interruption. 'What? It has nothing to do with me, Sister. I'm rather busy at the moment. Can't you see?'

'I can see you have some sort of authority over what leaves the docks. Can't you assign some lorries to take us?'

'I won't be using any more lorries. These pieces are horse-drawn. In fact, have you seen any new teams arriving? These damned Arabs can't be relied upon for anything.' He stared beyond her, completely oblivious of her problems.

'Captain?' Matron Lambert snapped, dragging his attention back. 'I don't care about your precious guns. I need to get my staff to the Heliopolis Palace Hotel immediately. Who *can* find me transport?'

He suddenly bellowed instructions at the derrick operator and the matron jumped. She knew he'd done it deliberately. Then he told her irritably, 'Why don't you all walk? It's not far. I'm sure your luggage will find you eventually.'

'Walk? Unescorted through these streets? And how in God's name will we find it?'

'Get some of these men to take you,' he gestured at a bunch of Australian soldiers lounging against the sheds. He added waspishly, 'They obviously have nothing better to do.'

The men watched Matron Lambert's approach warily. Some stamped out cigarettes. Their uniforms were faded and their faces were well browned. These were troops who had been in Egypt longer than most.

The matron picked out a corporal, the highest rank she could see. 'You there! I need someone to escort my nurses to the Heliopolis.'

He blinked and looked about, hoping for someone he could pass the problem on to. 'We're supposed to be here, ma'am,' he said uncertainly.

She fixed him with a glare. 'That captain over *there* gave me permission to find a detail from among yourselves. How many men do you have?'

'Half a dozen, only I don't think we're allowed to leave. He's not our—'

'Corporal!' she barked. 'Some of my girls are far too *young* to be walking these streets without proper protection. I will take full responsibility if you get into any trouble.'

'Are they, ma'am?' His eyebrows went up as he tried to see the nurses through the crowds. After a moment he offered, 'I suppose, if you say it's all right.' The other soldiers were gathering close, hoping that the nurses were not as imposing as Matron Lambert.

'Come on then, you lot,' the corporal told them unnecessarily. 'We've got a bit of escort duty to do.'

Distinctive in their white uniforms and with their armed escort around them, the nurses squeezed through the streets followed by an entourage of Arab children paid to carry personal luggage. Rose soon saw that the soldiers' presence was almost pointless. The locals had no interest in harming their visitors at all unless you counted haranguing them to death with offers of food, drink or souvenirs. The soldiers swaggered importantly and occasionally snarled a warning at someone who got too enthusiastic in pushing their wares.

'Don't buy anything,' one of the men told Rose, as a grubby urchin dared to break into their ranks and hold a carving high in her face. 'None of it's real.' He grabbed the child by the scruff of his clothing and hauled him unceremoniously to one side. The boy accepted this meekly, as if it were one of the perils of his trade.

'How do you know?' Rose was amused. 'Perhaps there's a real treasure here somewhere. Maybe the child himself doesn't know it.'

'No, it's all fake. Every bleedin' last bit of it—pardon my French, Sister,' he added quickly. 'Otherwise, they wouldn't be selling it on the streets, would they? You have to know where to look, if you want the genuine stuff.'

Rose didn't bother to correct his addressing her as "Sister". All the nurses were called that regularly, even Matron Lambert. It was a safe term used by most men, since the nurses' ranks and proper titles were still largely unknown. 'And where would that be?' she said.

'In the back streets. The bazaars and like. It's not a safe place for a pretty girl on her own. I could take you there sometime, if you want.'

Rose's smile widened, more at herself for having unwittingly solicited the invitation. It was best to remember that these men, starved of female companionship, would snatch at any chance.

'Thank you,' she said politely. 'I doubt we'd be allowed there in the first place, alone or otherwise. I have no idea what we can do, so it's not much use making any plans.'

The soldier accepted this with good grace and didn't press her.

'Fair enough. Perhaps later, hey?' he said, winking.

The Heliopolis Hotel, the nurses had been forewarned, was a magnificent building converted into a hospital and now called the Australian General Hospital No.1. As a hotel it had been famous. As a hospital, it left a lot to be desired. It offered a striking combination of British empirical grandeur and Egyptian finery. The imposing buildings were set among green lawns and flower-beds. Balconies and ornate awnings surrounded every window and door. Inside, the ceilings were high and chandeliers plunged down into the clear spaces. Most of the decorations were laced with gold, whether real or not Rose couldn't tell, so plentiful that it spoke of a country whose regard for the precious metal was always more aesthetic than monetary.

One jarring note in all the décor was the apparatus of a working hospital. The long dining rooms and spacious ballrooms had been converted into wards, with rows of white-sheeted beds lined up perfectly. Trolleys of instruments stood ready and racks of bedpans were tucked into corners. One room was filled with just wheelchairs.

The new nurses were given a tour by one of Matron Lambert's colleagues. The matron had been joyfully greeted by many of the women and it wasn't long before someone offered to show them all around.

'What are they going to do with all these beds?' Julia whispered to Rose, in yet another room lined with impeccably made cots.

'Use them, I'm afraid,' Rose sighed. It troubled her that Julia and many of the others still didn't seem to realise what they'd got themselves into. She had quietly estimated there were over five hundred beds in the Heliopolis, and larger hospitals were being readied elsewhere in Cairo. A massive invasion was being planned and to look at the preparations here at the Heliopolis, it wasn't far away either.

'All of them?' Julia was frowning. No one answered her and she looked around to discover she had been left behind. She hurried to catch up.

They were billeted in rooms all around the hospital, or in apartments close by. By now, Rose and Julia were close friends, so they organised a room for themselves above a rug vendor's store less than a minute's walk from the Heliopolis. Accommodation for the nurses must have been planned in advance, or a room so close by wouldn't have still been available.

It seemed to be the only consideration that the army offered the women. The obstructive and unreasonable manner of the male officers continued to make life difficult for the nurses. There were rumours of an intense rift between the army's commanding officer of hospitals and the principal matron in charge of all the AANS in Egypt over the men's poor attitude. Her complaints seemed to be falling on deaf ears.

***

The issues of unfair treatment often seemed petty, compared with the urgent need to get the hospitals ready. Stories of attacking Palestine, Africa and even the Western Front, as unlikely as that might be now, still circulated. Nobody took any of them seriously. Then again, nothing official was offered to prevent the wilder rumours. Beyond Cairo was a great tent city filled with expectant soldiers. Most of them were let loose every night. They flooded into the nightclubs and bars, buying prostitutes and fighting among themselves. Australian soldiers had the worst reputation for baiting the English and causing scuffles. They also had the highest incidence of venereal disease.

These were the only cases occupying just a fraction of the beds available in each hospital. Apart from the odd few instances of real sickness or accident, the nurses only had to contend with men wounded from battling each other, or becoming ill from an indiscreet moment with Cairo's whores.

For Rose, the weeks flew past. She saw nothing of Doctor Mark Cohen, which surprised her, considering his apparent interest on board the *Kyarra*. She didn't hear where he'd been posted and didn't ask. Like everyone else, Rose immersed herself in her preparations, intent that nothing should be left wanting when the real work began. With nothing actually happening, the efforts became repetitive and frustrating, but it was only a matter of time. The only recreation they had outside the hospital walls were carefully chaperoned visits to places of interest, like the pyramids and the Sphinx, and occasionally small, arranged dances which the men seemed to suffer more than enjoy.

Despite the lack of hard information, the sense of an impending invasion couldn't be ignored. It filled the air. The ranks of the soldiers were still swelling, their tents spread like a rash across the yellow sand beneath the pyramids. The hospitals continued to expand, and the nearby Luna Park was, as Rose had thought, converted into another part of the Australian General Hospital. Stores were stockpiled in every available space.

Rose walked through the Heliopolis and imagined with a heavy heart that soon the countless lines of empty beds would be filled with dying men. It was inevitable, and apparently what the army wanted. An attack would begin soon.

Then, late in April, she was told that she wouldn't be staying at the hospital after all. Matron Lambert had more important things in mind for Rose Preston.

***

The matron's office was a tiny area that had been a linen store. At least it had a window and plenty of shelf space. She cramped herself behind a desk that took up most of the room and invited Rose to sit down on a scratched wooden chair.

'They're asking for some of us to be seconded to hospital ships over the coming week, starting immediately. I've chosen you to go—' she stopped, sighed and pinched the bridge of her nose between two fingers. 'Oh, I can't be bothered with this foolish secrecy. I'm sure you can be trusted, and you must be prepared.'

Rose held her breath. Something big was coming.

'You're going to the SS *Gascon* immediately. The day after tomorrow, the men land somewhere in the Dardanelles. I can't tell you exactly where because I don't know. Nobody has any idea how bad the casualties will be, or how long the campaign will last. I'm spreading some of the girls over several hospital ships, and the rest must be ready here.'

'Am I going alone to this ship?' Rose tried to keep her voice firm.

'No, I need to choose someone else.' The matron frowned as she consulted a list.

'Then can it be Julia? We work together very well, and it would prevent her staying alone in our apartment.'

The matron's shrug was unusual gesture because she kept herself so disciplined. 'I don't see why not. Send her up to see me straightaway.'

'I'll tell her.' Rose hoped she hadn't done the wrong thing for Julia's sake, and the matron read her thoughts.

'Are you certain she'll want to go?'

'Yes, but I'll find her right now, in case I'm wrong.'

'Make sure you do. Both of you need to be packed and ready at the ship by midday today. Prepare yourselves for a long stay, just in case. Come back here before you leave and I'll have the papers ready.'

'Thank you, Matron.' Rose stood and lingered a moment in front of the desk. She felt moved to say, 'Really... thank you. This is what I came to do.'

Matron Lambert looked up at her, a slight smile on her lips. 'I have every faith in you, Rose. Be careful. We might not see each other for a while.'

Rose nodded and left. Beyond the door her step quickened, the urgency of getting ready overtaking her. First, she had to find Julia.

Now, finally, she was going back to the war.

Anzac Day aboard the *Gascon*

Nobody on the ship except the usual watch officers and crew needed to be awake before dawn on this day. The *Gascon* had no troops to disembark, or guns for bombarding the landing zones.

But they were all out of their bunks well before the sun came up. They gathered in groups on the deck, sipping tea or hot chocolate in the darkness. Around them on the quiet ocean the armada of the Gallipoli invasion fleet steamed slowly closer to the shore. Some of the pinpoint stern lights could be seen, lit to avoid collisions, although with the risk of being targeted by German submarines. Otherwise these last minutes of the night still concealed the vast number of ships advancing on the Dardanelles. Many were already drifting to a halt, preparing to drop their boats and load them with troops. Sometimes muted sounds came across the water. You could hear orders called out too loudly, and the clank of machinery lowering the larger motorised pinnaces which would be used to tow the rowboats closer to the beaches.

'It feels funny,' someone murmured among a clutch of seamen near Rose and Julia. 'Do you reckon the Turks haven't figured out we're coming?'

'Nah, they know all right,' another replied. 'They won't start shooting until they can see us.'

Rose felt Julia tense beside her and it made her own nerves tingle. She wasn't feeling too brave herself.

'Rose, they won't be shooting at *us*, will they?' Julia asked, keeping her voice low.

'No, we're a hospital ship. Even the Turks will respect that. Besides, I think we're too far off the shore.'

'Those poor boys, having to row all that way. They'll be exhausted before they even get near the beach.'

'The navy does all the rowing. The soldiers just have to sit tight until they get there.'

A sailor came past with a large kettle of tea and offered to top up their mugs. The two nurses accepted gratefully, if only to wrap their hands around the warm tin cups. The slight chill in the air crept under your clothing if you weren't busy, and standing at the rail like this, simply waiting and watching, let it in.

Time dragged. Below decks, everything was ready for the worst the day might bring. There was nothing further that anyone could do. Julia and Rose exchanged inexpert ideas on how events might unfurl. Always, their ignorance brought each conversation to an inconclusive halt. Under their feet, the ship vibrated slightly, the engine just turning over to keep the *Gascon's* position against a current.

'Look,' Julia pointed. 'It's like a row of ducklings following their mother.' They could see the silhouettes of four rowboats being tugged towards the distant line of hills rising from the sea. The pinnace in front chugged out black smoke.

'Oh...' Rose said, realising they could see the boats now. An orange glow was building behind the landfall. Dark shapes were becoming visible on the sea. 'It won't be long now, I suppose.'

A flare went up from the shoreline. It was tiny, given the distance, like a shooting star.

'That's one of theirs,' the same voice said grimly. 'Now it's on, for sure.'

The sun was suddenly approaching fast, the pre-dawn wash of colour turning pale. It threw long shadows down the cliff faces that the watchers could now make out behind the beaches. At any minute, the golden arc would appear above the jagged hills and turn the scene completely into a new day.

Like the crackle of distant fireworks, there was a barrage of rifle shots on land, then the stutter of one machine gun quickly followed by another. Aboard the *Gascon* it was too indistinct a sound to give an impression of what must have been occurring on the beaches. Rose concentrated, affected by a strange need to hear the men's crying out and make everything real and urgent, even though it would horrify her. Even the gunfire was sometimes lost in the slap of waves against the ship's hull, or the men beside her talking loudly. The invasion had started, but it felt so far away and somehow benign.

Everyone on deck jumped violently as a warship nearby opened up with a thunderous barrage, all its guns firing at once. It wreathed itself in brown smoke and Rose heard the shells tear through the air towards the hills. This was a signal for other ships to start bombarding too, and all along the gathered fleet the grey, men-of-war fired at the coastline. Geysers of dust erupted on the cliffs. It was impossible to tell if they were having any effect. The deafening roar of the warships' guns changed everyone's mood.

The men aboard the *Gascon* took heart from this display of firepower, cheering and shouting savage insults towards the Turks. When some of them turned to the nurses, inviting them to celebrate too, Rose offered a weak smile of encouragement. She remembered stories told to her by survivors of charges across no-man's-land in France, after bombardments that lasted for days, only to see that the enemy had crawled out of their holes to mow down their surprised attackers.

'Are you all right, Rose?' Julia shouted at her. 'You look very pale. Do you want to go below?'

'No, it's just the smell of the guns,' Rose lied. 'And goodness they're loud! I'll get used to it. At least we can watch something up here. I couldn't stand to wait below decks and not see anything at all.'

'It will be getting hot down there too,' Julia agreed absently, gazing at the shore again where the deadly flowers of high explosive blossomed everywhere.

She put her fingers in her ears and hugged her arms against her chest.

Half an hour later, a Bosun's Mate ran along the decks blowing his whistle. The men moved away quickly, recognising the command. Rose had to reach out and stop him as he passed.

'Excuse me, please tell us. What's going on?' As she spoke the ship rumbled under their feet.

'Everyone to their station, Sister,' he explained breathlessly. 'There's been heavy casualties ashore and we're going in closer to pick them up.'

'Thank you,' Rose nodded. He was already gone, blowing his whistle urgently.

The two women exchanged grim looks, then hurried towards their infirmary.

***

When the first boats arrived alongside they looked like beasts with broken limbs. Few had a full complement of rowers, the missing oars making them look crippled. Some of the seamen were injured themselves, and they rowed with bloody hands clutching the oars. Wounded soldiers sprawled haphazardly in the cutters, the white sides of the navy's boats stained red with their bleeding. Sailors from the *Gascon* swarmed down ropes to secure hoisting lines. Slowly, the first of the injured men were brought aboard. Other boats laden with casualties and recognising the hospital ship could be seen heading their way too.

The *Gascon* was much closer to the coast now. The soldiers on the beaches crawled like ants across the sand and up the cliffs. When Rose came up onto the decks to supervise, she flinched from the gunfire. She hadn't been ready for it, the constant rifle fire and the steady, awful hammering of machine guns, having been partly shielded from the noise below. At one point, Rose was watching the exact place on the beach where a Turkish shell landed, scattering broken-limbed men and shattered supplies aside. After that, she tried not to look again, but the dreadful scene kept dragging her eyes back.

The men she lay on the decks, wounded but not too badly, stayed quiet and even cheerful as she moved among them, offering water and checking their battle dressings. Occasionally she rolled a cigarette for them if they didn't have good use of their hands. It was the last thing any doctor would want his nurses to do, and the soldiers loved her for it. Blood was everywhere and made the flooring slippery. The hem of Rose's skirt was soaked bright red. The smoke of battle from the shore scratched her throat and stung her eyes. She moved from one end of the ship to the other, the journey each time taking at least half an hour as she examined or comforted each man, however briefly. In her head, she kept an accurate note of who needed to go below next for treatment. Often her planning would be changed by another, more seriously hurt man coming aboard.

The day wore on, never changing. Only the sound of the gunfire eased a little as the fighting moved away from the beach. The lines of boats bearing the wounded seemed endless. Rose never thought of herself for a moment, except to drink water. The weather was clouding over, but it was still warm, and she knew it was important to keep hydrated.

Finally, when Rose couldn't have guessed how long it had been since the first wounded appeared, a young midshipman blocked her path and held a plate out to her. It had a thick ham sandwich on it.

'You must eat, ma'am,' he told her. Rose vaguely noted he had to almost scream above the noise of gunfire. Some heavy shelling had begun again.

'What time is it?' she shouted back.

'Four o'clock in the afternoon, ma'am. The first officer says you've been out here all day without a rest.'

'I don't need a rest. There'll be time for that later.'

'He'll be watching from the bridge. Please eat the sandwich. He said to make sure you do, or I'll be for it.'

Rose glanced up to see a white face observing them from the ship's bridge. She went to take the sandwich and noticed her hands were filthy. Dried blood rimmed her fingernails.

'Wait a moment,' she said, going over to a bucket of sea water. She came back, shaking her hands dry, then began eating. Suddenly she was ravenous and gulped down pieces that stuck in her throat. Like a faithful servant, the midshipman stood and stared at her bloodstained uniform until she'd finished. She swallowed the last bit with an effort.

'Would you like a mug of tea, ma'am?'

'No, thank you. Water's fine.'

'It's no trouble, honestly.'

'Well, all right. Thank you, with milk and sugar. Please leave it on the hatch over there.'

He dashed away, eager to please this pretty nurse. When he returned with the tea, Rose was busy rolling a wounded man from a stretcher, so he left the mug on the hatch without disturbing her. Rose forgot about it anyway.

By nightfall it was raining, at once cleaning the deck and also making it uncomfortable for the soldiers lying out in the open. The ship was at full capacity, and the number of wounded coming aboard finally slowed as the opposing armies dug in for the night, and the battle eased. The firing continued, meant to be harassing more than anything, and the exhausted soldiers kept their heads down.

It was ten o'clock before Rose realised that she hadn't heard a boat come alongside for some time. Using a shaded oil lamp, she had been trying to supervise some sailors rigging tarpaulins to provide shelter. By now, she had to admit that every time she got down on her knees, it was difficult to get up. And closing her eyes to ease the grittiness was always a mistake because they didn't want to open again.

She was surprised by a white figure looming ghost-like out of the darkness. It was Julia, the first time Rose had seen her since early that morning.

The lamplight wasn't kind to her friend. Julia looked haggard, her whole body wilting with exhaustion. The white uniform was bloodstained and blackened by dirt. Rose was shocked by her appearance and about to say something when she saw a similar expression on Julia's face.

‘Hello, have you heard?’ Julia asked, her voice toneless from fatigue.

‘Heard what?’ Rose fought an urge to lean against a nearby davit.

‘We’re sailing. They’re going to unload these patients at Imbros and come straight back for more.’

‘Well, I suppose we need the room,’ Rose said absently, looking around at the men strewn across the decks.

‘The commanding officer says we must sleep. He’s ordered us. We’ll need our strength tomorrow.’

Rose nodded. ‘All right. I’ll be down in a moment.’

It was an hour before she could finally tear herself away from the wounded men on deck and Julia was already asleep in their cabin. Rose collapsed on her bunk without undressing and fell instantly into utter, dreamless dark.

***

After two weeks of constantly ferrying casualties, the nurses had seen and heard everything, and little surprised them anymore. The *Gascon* would sail into Anzac Cove, stay for nearly twelve hours while the wounded were loaded on, then move on to either Imbros Island or back to Alexandria to hand the patients over to the permanent hospitals. Rose didn’t focus beyond the next load of casualties. Her world was either the decks or the infirmary below. Nothing else. She even became used to the roaring gunfire that assailed her senses for the hours they anchored off the beachhead. The Turks often shelled ships in the bay, but thankfully—or by sheer coincidence—they never targeted the hospital ship.

Her best chance for sleep was during the journey back to Anzac when the ship was empty. On the voyage out, with the wards filled with men, she would move among them and offer any help she could. Often, they would ask her just to write for them, short letters assuring their families they'd survived despite the wounds. Rose was astonished at how much these men wrote, even if they were semi-literate. Many carried diaries and painstakingly recorded their own misfortunes and the stories of what happened to them and their friends. Letters to loved ones were always foremost.

However one man, a sergeant, surprised her.

'Sister?' he called out from the gloom of the ward. It was after dark and the *Gascon* was grinding towards Imbros again. The entire ship stank of antiseptic, unwashed bodies and in some parts the deadly sourness of gangrene. Everything was quiet. Most of the casualties slept or lay silent once they were aboard, the stress of getting there draining away and leaving them weak.

Rose hurried over to him. 'What's wrong?'

'Nothing—well, nothing bad, I mean. Have you got something I can write on?' His voice was weak.

Rose examined him, and he let her. He had a gunshot wound to the abdomen. It was a clean injury and hadn't done too much damage, so he seemed to have a good chance of surviving. Often they wanted to write some final words, if they felt their own life-force beginning to slip.

'Just a moment,' Rose told him, puzzled because he appeared strong. She found some paper and a pencil at a table the nurses used when they watched the ward.

'You want to write a letter?' she asked him.

'Just a note, yes.'

Rose knelt beside his cot and balanced the paper on her lap. 'I can write it for you, if you like.' She didn't volunteer this easily. Sometimes the words they wanted broke her heart, especially when it was obvious they wouldn't survive. But the sergeant seemed alert and not despairing, although frail.

'Would you?' He sighed, fighting off a spasm of pain. 'Maybe it would be better.'

'Who's it to? Your wife?' She smiled. Reminding them of family often helped strengthen their resolve to recover.

'No, the boys back in Anzac,' he replied.

'Really? You just saw them,' she joked.

'One of them pulled me back, when I told him I was as good as dead. I ordered him to leave me, but he didn't. I need him to know I'm all right. The stubborn bastard was right, and I owe him one.'

'Yes, I'd say you certainly do.' She pulled a face to make him smile. 'What's his name, do you know?'

'Jonathon White. He's a private in the Light Horse.'

He explained how to address the letter and Rose wrote down the details. Then he dictated a brief, stumbling thanks, adding, 'I don't know what else to say, Sister.' The effort had tired him immensely and he couldn't say more anyway.

'I'll put something,' Rose said. 'So he knows you're fine.'

She wrote on the bottom of the page, "Sergeant Carter is seriously wounded, but he is strong and I feel sure he will eventually recover completely. You need not worry about him. Signed, Rose Preston. V.A.D. on the SS *Gascon*."

He reached up shakily and grasped her arm. 'Can you pass it on to someone next time you're back at Anzac? It'll get to him for sure, that way.'

'Of course. I'll find somebody, I promise.' She got up stiffly from her awkward position. 'Now you need to rest.'

Like an obedient child his eyes closed. Rose was so startled by the instant transition that she again checked his life signs, thinking he had suddenly died. It wouldn't be the first time. He was only asleep. It was something she would eventually get used to—these men had learned the trick of sleeping the moment they could. In the trenches, every second of rest was precious.

***

She saw Carter again as he was being carried from the ship. He caught her eye and gave her a feeble wave. She patted her pocket in a gesture that meant she still had his letter, and it would be passed on to Private Jonathon White as best she could.

Blackboy Hill Training Camp

Blackboy Hill Training Camp was a far cry from the romance of joining the army, travelling to exotic places and waging a just fight against the Huns—or the Turks, for that matter. Joseph's first taste of army life began in a hastily erected encampment in bush land east of Perth. He'd been in a group of recruits transported by train, then abandoned by the accompanying soldiers as the carriages pulled away for the return journey. Other NCOs who appeared from the camp told them to find their own way to empty tents. That was all.

Here, the land was still dry from summer and too far from the coast to enjoy any sea breeze. Even in late autumn it was uncomfortably warm. Making things worse, hundreds of men had already passed through the camp on the way to their fateful morning on the Gallipoli Peninsula. Although the place was well established with cooking facilities and well-dug latrines, at the same time it looked worn out and stretched to the limit of its resources. The white, pinnacle-shaped tents all suffered rips and damaged stitching that let in the flies during the day and bloodthirsty mosquitoes at night. The paths between the tents were beaten to bare earth, any grass long since crushed under thousands of footsteps, and the fine dust got into clothing and belongings. Fresh water came from a river tributary nearby and at least the men could take comfort from bathing regularly or brewing endless billies of tea. Nobody had a uniform or any kit yet, except for those men who were the camp personnel and—it could only be guessed—were going to be responsible for training the newcomers. At first, they took little notice of the recruits apart from feeding them.

It took three days of lying around and waiting for something to happen before the army decided that enough men had arrived to begin training and matters abruptly turned serious. Until then, Joseph had been sharing a tent with one other man, a youth slightly older than himself who seemed awed and nervous about everything happening around him. His name was Ben Harding. Though Ben wasn't fat, he carried a fleshiness that slowed him down and left him puffing after the slightest exertion. His face was soft and wide like a child's, and he had fair hair that curled tighter on his scalp as it grew instead of getting longer. He sunburned easily and when the sun reddened his cheeks, he looked permanently out of breath. He recognised Joseph as someone less overwhelmed by his new life and soon he was taking his cues from him. Everything from getting a meal to having a bath, Ben would wait until Joseph started and then quickly join him. Joseph began to accept, whether he liked it or not, that he had a friend. He didn't mind. Ben wasn't so bad.

The tent was supposed to house four soldiers. George Poole arrived in the morning of the third day. George was a wiry, raw-boned man in his thirties, with thinning hair and skin browned almost to leather by a lifetime of working in the northern sun as a stockman.

'Why didn't you join the cavalry? The Light Horse?' Joseph asked him as they sat on a log beside the nearest campfire. There were hundreds of fire sites everywhere. A tin of water was boiling on theirs. Ben squatted on the ground and blinked at George uncertainly.

'No one's going to tell me how to ride a horse,' George answered in a slow, measured way, his attention mostly on rolling a cigarette one-handed. This done, and his cigarette lit, George leaned back far enough to pick a handful of tea leaves from a wooden chest and throw them into the water. Ben hastily moved to replace the lid on the chest. George didn't thank him other than to give a small, fatherly nod in his direction.

'No one's riding any horses anyway,' Joseph said. 'It's all trenches and digging.'

'The army pays better than a stockman. That's all I care about.'

It made Joseph's grand ideas of seeing the world seem trite. 'I'm going to join my brother,' he said, nonchalantly. 'He's already there. Landed on the twenty-fifth with everyone else.'

George squinted at him through the smoke. 'Have you heard from him since?'

'No, I expect it'll take a while for any letters to be passed on. From home, I mean.'

'Most likely,' George leaned forward, grunting with the effort, to stir the tea with a stick. Poised there, he suddenly asked Ben, 'What about you?'

Ben flinched. 'My–my dad said I should join up. Make a man of myself.'

'Your dad here too?'

'No, he's too old.'

'Yeah, right,' George snorted with a lop-sided grin.

The last place in their tent was filled by a younger volunteer called Dexter Bell. His name amused George and he repeated it several times. Dexter took in everything methodically, as if an ordered system would ensure that nothing went wrong. He was painfully thin and short in contrast to Ben and seemed more so, standing beside him. He had a pronounced narrow face.

'Does anyone know what we do now?' he asked in the evening gloom, after he'd carefully stored his few belongings in one corner of the tent. The others, back to sitting around the fire, were noisily scraping the last of a meal from enamel plates. During the day, the camp had slowly filled with more recruits, and countless campfires sent spirals of smoke up everywhere. The rumble of a hundred conversations mixed with the clicking of cicadas in the trees.

'Go and get something to eat, before the kitchen packs up,' Joseph told him. 'Then take it easy. Nobody seems to be in a hurry to get us to the war.'

***

That changed at dawn the next morning. A stentorian voice bellowing abuse and orders to "Wake up, get the hell out of those beds" came closer. Any grumbled complaints that came back were greeted with an even louder outraged command to do as they were told. Joseph was only just awake and groggily decided it would be best to meet this standing up.

'Hey, you blokes,' he half-whispered so he didn't startle them. 'We'd better get up. Something's going on.' He reached out to shove Ben, who wasn't moving. 'Come on, Ben. You can't sleep in around here.'

The four of them emerged stretching and yawning in the weak morning sunshine as the sergeant major appeared. His name was Beatty and he looked the epitome of the long-serving, professional NCO. His huge face glowed red with burst blood vessels from a lifetime of shouting and hard drinking. In his younger days, he had been short and powerfully built. Now his body sagged with the onset of middle age. All he needed to complete the picture was an aggressive swagger. Instead, he walked with a limp and usually carried a cane. He used it now, slapping at the tents he passed, making a loud, snapping noise as he smacked the canvas.

He wasn't impressed with the four recruits' efforts to be outside to greet him.

'Get the hell out of your beds,' he yelled at them regardless. Ben almost fell over backwards in fright. 'Everyone line up on the parade ground. *Quick smart* about it.' Without waiting to see the response, Beatty turned away to attack the next tent.

'Parade ground?' Ben asked meekly, screwing his eyes up in the glare.

'He must mean next to the kitchen,' Joseph said. 'Where the flagpole is.'

'Now things are going to get silly,' George murmured dourly. He ducked back into the tent and came out with his boots, hopping about to put them on. Magically, a lit cigarette was already in his mouth. The other three did the same with Dexter reappearing first, neatly clothed and his laces tied. Joseph and Ben had to rummage among their blankets and belongings for their own boots, matching socks and the best of their shirts.

They made their way towards the parade area with hundreds of others doing the same. Men materialised from tents everywhere to descend on the open ground near the kitchens.

'The whole army's here,' Dexter said, looking around.

'They're raising a new battalion,' Ben surprised them. 'Which is about a thousand men.'

'Is anyone going to be left at home?'

'It doesn't look like it, does it?'

Other voices like Beatty's were exhorting the new troops to form lines and stand at attention. Cigarettes were stamped out. Personal belongings were dumped in a growing pile. NCOs herded the new men into some semblance of parade ground formation in five long rows. The four new comrades-in-arms found themselves in the front row and Beatty returned to strut up and down before them, waiting impatiently for order and silence from everyone. Finally, the entire gathering went as quiet as it ever would. Men still coughed or shuffled their feet in the dirt. It was the best Beatty could expect at this point.

'Right, then,' he shouted, and noticed Ben jump. 'My name is Sergeant Major Beatty and you will address me as nothing *but* Sergeant Major Beatty, or if time is pressing I will *grudgingly* accept "Sergeant Major".' He let that sink in. The men were to soon learn that Beatty had a habit of speaking almost theatrically. 'As of today, you men are in the army proper. No more lying about in the shade swapping yarns and trading smokes. We've got a lot of work to be done and not much time to do it. This country's army, the Australian Imperial Force, is forming a new brigade of which you men are expected to be a battalion. I have the dubious *honour,'* he paused again for effect. 'Of making sure you are properly prepared to fight the Turks. Is that clear?'

A ragged cheer went up after they belatedly realised that one was expected.

Pulling a wry face, Beatty went on. His voice carried clearly on the morning air. 'You will be formed into separate companies, platoons and sections. Your first job today is *thoroughly* learning where you belong and who your officers and non-commissioned officers will be. And you will be issued uniforms.' He ran his eye disapprovingly over some of the men nearest in their civilian clothes. In the background, a few others tried cheering again, thinking it was required. Beatty glared them into silence.

'Just because you have been judged *medically* fit to join up and are now paid the princely sum of five shillings a day, don't believe you can't be kicked out on your arse just as fast. We will win the war without you, if you're guilty of drunkenness or disorderly conduct. And catching a dose of the clap from any of the willing young ladies around here will see you sent home to your mothers immediately too. That is *not* a joke.'

Still, it brought a chorus of laughter. It was difficult to imagine the isolated encampment offering much female company. The small town of Midland was four miles away.

'Of course, you can't all be rotten apples. God forbid, some of you may stay in the army long enough to achieve the rank of Kitchener himself.' Beatty suddenly rounded on Ben and said into his face, 'Could that be you, son?'

'No–no, I don't want to be a cook, Sergeant Major Beatty. I promised my dad I'd be a soldier.'

Beatty's eyes popped alarmingly while a few men dared to chuckle.

He choked, then thundered, 'I'm talking about Field Marshal *Lord* Kitchener, you fool. Have you never heard of him? Don't you read the newspapers?'

After an embarrassed pause, Ben said in a small voice, 'I can't read, Sergeant Major Beatty. Never learned.'

Beside him, Joseph's heart sank with sympathy. Of all the people Beatty chose to pick on, Ben was the least prepared to cope.

Beatty turned oddly quiet. 'Then we should do something about that, lad. It won't do, if you can't read letters from your dad at home, will it?'

'No, Sergeant Major,' Ben replied uncertainly. Joseph guessed it was likely his father couldn't read or write either, and Ben wasn't about to admit this.

Beatty stepped back and issued a string of orders that had NCOs moving busily among the men, splitting them into smaller groups, and again into sections of ten men each. The officers, watching from under a shady tree, began to come forward and take charge. Joseph managed to stay with his new friends in one section and the officer commanding their company, Captain Moore, arbitrarily chose George as an acting sergeant and a man called Robertson as his corporal. Both men, though pleased with the instant pay-rise, looked uncomfortable about the new responsibility. They were on a brief probation period and their ranks would be confirmed if they proved capable.

The rest of the day was spent in frustrating long lines while uniforms and equipment were issued. As more recruits rummaged among the piles of clothing for sizes that suited, so the mounds of trousers, shirts, underwear and jackets became impossibly mixed up. Then came an issue of boots, which were supposed to be chosen from one huge jumble of odd pairs, the mess caused by the men searching for matching sets and idly throwing aside rejected offerings. Finding hats was no easier.

At least the midday meal was better organised. Each company section was called forward by name to eat. However, some sections hadn't received their mess equipment yet, and that caused further chaos.

A final mass parade was called again as the sun set. Rather than being transformed into a new army, the men were by now a disgruntled mob in ill-fitting clothes, tired and annoyed, and sorely tempted by the smells coming from the kitchen because they hadn't yet been fed an evening meal. Everyone supposedly had his equipment, although rifles hadn't been issued. There weren't enough to go around, and an armoury would be handing weapons out as the training required, then taking them back ready for the next men. A supply of Lee Enfields was expected soon.

This time, the battalion commander himself addressed the men. He used grand sentences about the glory of fighting for king and country, and how much was expected of the soldiers.

No one really listened. Most of them were thinking about food, a cigarette or some rest. The new uniforms itched.

***

Joseph couldn't believe there were so many different ways to march. He would have thought getting from one place to the next would be done as quickly as possible, but no, the army had complex ways of marching diagonally or sidestepping, then changing formation so they could do it again. None of it seemed practical or likely to be useful in a fight. Avoiding obstacles had to be done together without breaking formation. In some exercises, they had to hold imaginary rifles. Later came differing speeds, strictly adhered to, which seemed even stranger to him. A "slow" march was seventy-five paces a minute with each step to be exactly thirty inches long. "Double time" was one hundred and eighty paces a minute at forty inches each step.

'Bugger this,' George muttered to Joseph one day, when there were no NCOs near. 'If anyone's trying to shoot me, I'm bloody running. I don't give a damn what the training manual says.'

'I think it's supposed to instil discipline,' Joseph told him, shrugging as they marched.

'Hell, I've been herding cattle all my life. Now some bastard's herding *me*.'

There was a correct way to salute and an extraordinary amount of time was spent practising, often under the watchful eye of Sergeant Major Beatty, who they'd come to accept as permanently loud and angry. At the same time, they were instructed who to salute and when—which seemed to be everybody, and at any time.

'He was wounded in the Boer War,' Dexter told them. Huddled in their leaking tent one rainy night, they were discussing Beatty. Outside, the fire was losing the fight against the rain. Winter had arrived and it was getting colder. Fortunately, army greatcoats had been issued.

'Why wasn't he pensioned off?' George asked. His weathered face looked twice as drawn in the lamplight.

'A career man, I guess. It meant a lot, back then.'

'It explains why he's here, instead of at Gallipoli,' Dexter said. 'He gets pretty unsteady after a while, even with the cane. He'd be no good during a fight.'

Joseph nodded. 'I'll bet it's killing him inside. A career soldier who misses out on the biggest war ever.'

'Yeah,' Ben said. 'And he takes it out on us.'

'It's what a sergeant major does,' Joseph told him.

George growled. 'All I know is *I'll* be ranting and raving soon if I don't get a drink. I haven't been this long without a whisky in my entire life.'

'Fat chance of that,' Joseph said. 'Beatty has the road to town watched like it's full of Germans. He catches a couple a blokes almost every night. And it's four miles each way. That's a bloody long way for a drink.'

George tapped the side of his nose and looked sly. 'Some of us know a better way.'

'Like, how?'

'Are you going to come?'

Joseph had tried strong liquor only once and hadn't been keen on the taste. But he was intrigued by George's secret. 'Probably not. Don't worry, I won't tell. Anyway, we've got our first gunnery practice tomorrow. You don't want to be doing that with a hangover.'

'Suit yourself.' George shrugged.

'I'll come,' Ben announced.

'You'll have a drink?'

'I used to pinch some of my old man's. I don't mind a bit.'

'I'll come too, if I can,' Dexter said.

George was suspicious. Joseph figured it was more bravado than any desire for a drink. Both Dexter and Ben saw George as a role model with his quiet confidence and no-nonsense ways. Inexpertly, Dexter had started smoking.

'I don't know if it's a great idea,' Joseph offered. 'I heard some of those AWOL blokes got kicked out, like Beatty said they would.'

'They were hopeless drunks,' George dismissed it with a wave. 'Not just

AWOL. Beatty would've been waiting for his chance.'

'Still... where is this place anyway?'

'It's a wagon from town. He parks on the east side, away from the road, and sells grog. No beer. Just wine and whisky.'

'Outside the camp? That's still absent without leave.'

'Not for long. Just enough to grab a bottle and come back. Everyone does it.

The bastard's making a fortune from soldiers dying of thirst out here.'

Joseph laughed. 'So he'll charge a king's ransom for a bottle of bad whisky.' He was hoping to discourage Ben and Dexter, but he could see they weren't put off. 'Well, you blokes can go. It's not for me.'

'When do we go?' Dexter asked eagerly.

George cocked his head and listened to the rain hitting the canvas. 'It's getting heavier. Soon even Beatty won't be out prowling in this. We'll go in about half an hour.'

Joseph watched as they readied themselves. Impatience got the better of them and less than ten minutes later the three of them were leaving. Ben tried to convince Joseph one last time.

'You sure you won't come? You don't have to drink. It's a bit of a lark, that's all.'

'In pouring rain? I don't think so. Be bloody careful. Beatty might figure this is the perfect time to catch fools like you.'

Beside Ben, Dexter only laughed. 'We won't be long.'

Minutes after they'd left, Joseph began to regret having stayed behind. Although he had no interest in finding a drink, it seemed a betrayal of their growing comradeship. It was something they should have been doing together, despite the risks. And while the cramped tents often had him wishing for some space of his own, now he felt lonely without them.

He had only a rough idea which way they were going, so trying to catch up was out of the question. He turned out the lamp and tried to get some sleep, and only found himself listening for his friends' return. Time crawled and there was no sign of them. The rain came and went in sweeping, heavy showers and he figured they had to be sheltering somewhere, or perhaps they'd stopped at another tent to drink so they wouldn't disturb him.

A couple of times he stirred and peered out from the tent flaps to see if he might spot them. All he got for his trouble was a wet face and, once, a trickle of freezing water down his neck. The last time he looked, almost all the campfires were out and each of the nearby tents was dark. It was getting late.

The next thing he knew was someone shaking his shoulder and whispering harshly in his ear.

'Joseph? *Joseph*. Wake up, we've got a problem.'

He opened his eyes and rolled over to be greeted by sickening, whisky-laden breath and a dark shape above him. It was George. Someone else moved unsteadily outside the tent.

'What?' Joseph groaned, sensing real trouble. 'Jesus, you stink like—' He couldn't think what. It was hard enough trying to wake up.

'We've bloody lost Ben. Can't find him.'

Sitting up suddenly, he almost head-butted George. 'What do you mean?'

'We sat around in this bloke's wagon having a drink because it was raining real hard. Ended up staying there for a while. Then Ben goes off for a slash and he doesn't come back. We went looking but couldn't find him.'

Joseph's stomach was looping. 'You mean he's lost in the bush somewhere?' 'Nah,' George shook his head and droplets flew from his hat. His voice was slurred, but he was sobering up fast. 'He was rotten drunk though. It hit him sudden-like. He'll be flaked out under a tree or something, for sure. We've got find him before morning and bring him back.'

'He could drown, if he's fallen in a puddle.'

This hadn't occurred to George. 'No, he'll be right,' he said unconvincingly.

'We've just got to find him.'

'Where's Dexter?'

'Outside. He's not much better.'

'Well, he's not staying here. He can search on his fucking hands and knees,' Joseph said with a flash of anger. 'Come on. Show me where this bloody wagon is.'

It was the dead of night by now, as cold as it could be and completely dark. They couldn't risk taking a lamp because any activity at this hour would raise suspicions. Without lights in the soldiers' tents, it was difficult to pick a safe route among them. The white, canvas shapes loomed too late out of the darkness. The three men kept tripping on guy ropes and pegs and kicked some out. Normally oil-lamps were kept burning all night, especially on the main tracks to the latrines. The weather had put out almost all of them. It was still raining in brief showers and the ground had turned to slick mud. Joseph's boots were quickly soaked through and his greatcoat got heavier by the minute. Before long the damp would seep through. At one point, Dexter stopped to throw up noisily.

It seemed to take ages before George announced, 'It was here.'

Joseph looked around. He could hardly see a thing. 'Where's the wagon?'

'He doesn't stick around.'

'Are you sure it was here?'

'Yeah...' George decided, after too long a pause.

Dexter began, 'We should have some sort of a system—'

'Don't start with that bullshit,' Joseph cut him off. He turned to look back towards the camp. He could only see two lit lamps, both probably marking latrines.

'Can you two remember where we are now?' he asked. 'By using those lamps?'

"Course, I can.' George was sober enough now to be offended. 'I found my way back to the tent, didn't I?'

'Dexter?'

'Probably.' He was less certain and hurt by Joseph's tone.

'Then just spread out and start looking. We'll all meet back here in about half an hour.' This was almost useless, as nobody had a watch. Joseph added sternly, 'Whatever happens, no one goes back to the tent without the rest of us. Otherwise, we'll all be looking for each other the whole bloody night.'

At that moment, their luck changed a little. The clouds above parted long enough to allow a half-moon to glow mistily through before being covered again. It wasn't much, but it helped. It let George spot the wagon's wheel marks in the mud.

'See? We're in the right place to start,' he said.

'Thank God for that,' Joseph muttered sourly.

George moved directly out into the bush, while Joseph searched to the right along the edge of the camp and Dexter went left. They called out to Ben, though quietly so it didn't carry. Within moments, the three lost contact with each other. The dark bushland closed in around Joseph and he was grateful for the occasional glimmer of the lamps from the latrines.

The ground was sandier than he'd thought, so he was less concerned with finding Ben drowned in a puddle of rainwater. Their biggest threat was not finding him at all. It would mean a major search in the morning and there would be hell to pay. The camp would rise at dawn, as always, and Ben would be found missing at role call—although as his sergeant, George might choose to hide his absence, though that would only compound the crimes. Besides, there *was* a chance Ben had stayed on his feet and got really lost in the bush. If that was the case, every minute counted. Rather than try and hide his disappearance, they'd have to tell Beatty and mount a proper search at first light.

The drama was building inside Joseph's head and he consciously pushed it away. The most likely turn of events was exactly as he figured now. Ben was fast asleep under a bush somewhere. They just had to find him and get him back to camp.

The moonlight faded in and out again, often enough for Joseph to quickly search the open areas. He concentrated on feeling around the base of large trees and kicking through bushes, sweeping his boot under the low branches. Now and then he called out, although that felt pointless. Joseph could picture in his mind Ben dead drunk and curled up on the ground, beyond hearing any calls. Looking for tracks was no good because the ground was covered with them. Troops trained out here all the time.

Despite his best hopes, Joseph was utterly surprised when his boot, probing under a thick shrub, struck something soft and heavy. He prodded again and got a low groan back.

'Ben?' He dropped to his hands and knees, and he could see only see a dark shape. A waft of whisky mixed with bile gave him a better clue.

'Oh *shit...'* he growled at the stink, turning his head away, then he groped around until he found a handful of coat collar and with all his strength dragged the body clear.

It was Ben all right. He was as totally drunk as Joseph feared he might be.

He shouted down at him, 'Ben? For Christ's sake, wake *up*. We've got to get you back to camp.'

Ben responded with a soft snore. Joseph swore, then an odd sound, like wind in the trees, caught his attention and he looked around, uselessly in the darkness until he realised what it was—the edge of a heavy rain shower moving through the bush towards him.

'Great, that's all we need,' he told the sky. 'Ben, *wake up*. We've got to get moving.'

The rain actually helped. It suddenly pounded down, cold and wet onto his back. It also stung Ben's face and made him groan. Joseph felt inspired and started slapping at his friend's cheeks.

'Come on, you stupid bastard. You've got to get on your feet.'

'Leave me alone...'

'No, *come on*.' Joseph kept slapping, maybe harder than he needed. It improved Joseph's mood anyway.

Trying feebly to fend Joseph off, Ben spluttered, 'Bloody *hell...*'

Joseph slapped, then pinched at his friend and yanked on his hair. Finally

Ben heaved himself muddily from the ground to sit upright, swaying. The first thing he did was lash out. Joseph dodged him easily.

'It's me! Joseph, you fool. We've got to get you back to camp.'

The rain was pelting down now and they were soaked through. Ben began to topple backwards.

'No, I'm going to stay here a while.'

'No, you don't.' Joseph grabbed his coat lapel with one hand and cuffed him over the ear with his other.

'Ow! Damn you,' Ben growled with a slur, then went still. A vague understanding of his situation was starting to get through. 'Shit...' he decided.

'Yes, shit. Exactly,' Joseph hissed. 'You've got to get to your feet, Ben. I can't carry you.'

'Oh, dear. You want me to stand up?'

'Good, *now* you're starting to see the problem. Come on, let's try and get you upright.'

With Ben at least trying to co-operate, it wasn't as hard, but his legs were weak and the dark world around him began spinning madly. He ended up leaning heavily on Joseph with his arm draped painfully across his shoulders.

'I think I'd better sit down again...'

'Like hell. You're up now.'

'Where's–where's my hat?'

'What? Oh, shit.'

It had to be under the bush. Like a trapeze artist in a balancing act, he edged carefully away from Ben and left him standing, lurching about on feet glued to the ground, his arms windmilling crazily. Joseph dived under the bush again and felt around, luckily finding the hat straight away. Then he ducked into Ben's body again and took the weight.

Those lamps through the trees were temptingly close, except Joseph had insisted everyone meet back where the wagon had been. At least, once he got there, George and Dexter could help him carry Ben.

'All right,' he said, taking a deep breath. 'We're going this way.'

They staggered off, Ben's feet dragging hopelessly. It was going to be a very slow journey and Joseph hoped the others didn't give up on him. Ben started to mumble apologies and Joseph snarled at him to save his breath. His clothing was saturated with mud and Ben's vomit. He couldn't imagine how he was going to make himself presentable by daybreak, which couldn't be too far away.

Someone appeared in front of him.

'Am I glad to see you,' Joseph groaned. 'I found him. Here, take the other side of this bugger. He weighs a ton—'

His words stopped when Joseph realised the shape was all wrong. It couldn't be George or Dexter. Besides, this person carried a covered oil-lamp.

‘Good morning, gentlemen.’ The cover was lifted from the lamp and Sergeant Major Beatty held it close to their faces. Both soldiers blinked unhappily in the glare. Beatty was wearing an oilskin coat with a hood. Even in the face of disaster, Joseph couldn’t help thinking the sergeant major would be completely dry underneath.

‘Private Harding, isn’t it? I didn’t think you’d take long to disappoint me.

And Private...?’ Beatty shifted the lamp, considering Joseph’s appearance.

‘White, Sergeant Major,’ Joseph obliged him miserably.

‘And Private *White*. What a sorry sight the two of you make. AWOL and drunk, for a start.’ Beatty spoke softly with a smug menace. ‘Be at Captain Moore’s tent first thing after morning parade. Tell your section sergeant I said so. Try to make yourselves look presentable, for what it’ll be worth.’ He smiled without any humour in his eyes. ‘Perhaps the navy will want you? The army certainly doesn’t.’

He abruptly turned on his heel and stalked away, leaving Joseph and Ben in utter darkness after the lamp had ruined their night-sight.

The enormity of what had just happened began to hit Joseph.

'I don't believe this,' he whispered. 'Sent packing before I even got to fire a gun.'

Beside him Ben slipped to his knees and began vomiting. Joseph stared down at his dark outline and didn't care.

***

The next morning, Joseph was out in the pre-dawn light trying to find the most acceptable combination of his uniforms. Everything was damp, and the gear he'd worn during the night was streaked with mud and yellow stains. The rain showers had eased by now to an occasional flurry, but the wood in the campfire was too wet to light, and anyway he couldn't afford the time to try and get it going. He resorted to wiping the mud from his clothes and hoping damp patches would be all right, considering the weather.

The night's episode had ended when George and Dexter, after seeing Joseph's confrontation with Beatty and hanging back out of sight, came forward to help carry Ben back to the tent once the sergeant major had definitely gone. Joseph had angrily refused to discuss the whole thing.

Now George came warily out of the tent and began brushing at the mud on his greatcoat too.

'I guess this is my fault,' he said reluctantly. 'It was my idea to go looking for a drink in the first place.'

Joseph said tightly, 'There's no point in blaming anyone. It's done, and that's that.'

'You don't know for sure that you'll be kicked out.'

'Beatty seemed positively happy to do it. He's a bitter bastard, I reckon. Because he can't go to the fighting himself, he takes pleasure in stopping others.'

George lit a cigarette and sent a plume of smoke furiously towards the ground. 'Damn it, I might go and tell him what happened. You were only trying to help find Ben. Hell, you didn't even have a drink.'

'No, don't.' Joseph glared at him. 'Jesus, you'll only get yourself into trouble and maybe thrown off camp as well.'

'Maybe.' George kicked at the damp soil. 'Let's see what happens to you. If it's bad, I'll speak up. It'll be Captain Moore, don't forget. Not Beatty.'

'Moore has to listen to Beatty. That's the way it works. Ben and I are gone, for sure.' Joseph refused to grasp at any hope.

Ben chose this moment to crawl out of the tent. He looked up at Joseph, his face screwed up in pain, and said, 'I'm going to be sick, I think.'

'Then piss off away from the tent,' Joseph said harshly. 'I already stink enough from your puke.'

'I'm sorry, Joseph. This is all my fault. I'll tell them too.'

‘I said no.’

Rebuffed by Joseph’s manner, Ben staggered to his feet and walked away with his head down. They heard him vomiting nearby in painful heaves.

Somebody cursed loudly and there was the metal clang of an empty food tin being thrown. Ben yelped.

‘It must have been a good shot,’ Joseph said, grimly pleased.

‘He should’ve gone a bit further away,’ George said. He was stirring the dead fire, trying to clear out the wettest ashes.

‘Can you light that? I could do with a tea.’

‘Maybe. I’ve still got a few tricks from my stockman days.’ George made it sound as if it were years ago when they’d only been in the army less than a month.

‘Joseph?’

Joseph turned to see Dexter offering him a clean shirt.

‘I want you to use this, when you see Captain Moore. It might make a difference.’ He pulled a face. ‘I can’t help Ben. He’s too big. We’ve only been given two shirts anyway.’

‘Don’t bother. You need it.’

Dexter’s uniform was just as stained and muddy,. ‘Yes, but I’m not fronting the company captain.’

‘Really—thanks, but it’s all right. What’s a clean shirt going to do when everything else is filthy?’ Joseph jerked a thumb at the tents surrounding them. 'It's been raining solid for two days. Everyone's in the same boat. I don't think it'll make much difference.'

***

In the end, it seemed Joseph was right. The entire battalion gathered for the usual parade after breakfast, when they were told what training was set for the day, and they were a sorry-looking bunch. The wet weather made a mess of clothing, boots and the men themselves. The river was a muddy torrent and didn't encourage bathing. Even the tea they brewed tasted of clay.

From a large clipboard, Beatty announced the training schedules. George's section and two others were due for their first visit to the firing range. They were told to report at the armoury to draw weapons. Before Beatty dismissed them, he walked over to Joseph, who closed his eyes.

'Privates White and Harding,' Beatty growled. 'Captain Moore is indisposed this morning. You will report to his tent after range practice, before the midday meal. Meet me there at twelve noon, sharp. Understand?'

'Yes, Sergeant Major Beatty!' Joseph barked, holding himself rigidly at attention. Inside, he was groaning in despair. The whole rotten business was going to be dragged out for another few hours. He wished it were over with. Beside him, Ben echoed his words in a soft voice and winced at the effort.

The three sections, thirty men in all, marched off to the armoury. There a disgruntled-looking master sergeant, who must have been close to retirement, eyed them all suspiciously. Reluctantly he handed out rifles and fifty rounds of ammunition to each man.

'Treat these weapons like they're your own mother,' he told them. 'And bring 'em back in the same condition you got them.'

'Hey, I shot my mother, sarge,' someone said from the background.

'As long as you cleaned the barrel afterwards, I don't give a damn,' he rasped back.

The countryside around the camp was hilly and it was a hard march to the rifle range that was a safe distance away from everything else. The bush smelled of the night's downpours and the men brushed against wet overhanging leaves that soaked them just as much as any rain. This was the first time they'd travelled any real distance with rifles and the weight became a burden. George was given command of all three sections for the journey. He had been told to march them in formation at "shoulder arms", just for the experience, rather than carry the rifles slung by their straps. Within a few minutes, arms and hands started to ache and more than a few of the men turned imploring eyes towards him once they'd left the camp well behind.

'Oh, all right, you useless bastards,' he gave in, after Dexter stumbled and nearly fell. 'March at ease. Be ready to get back into formation bloody quick, when we get near the range.'

There were groans of relief as the rifles were slung and just about everyone lit up a smoke.

The rifle range was run by a master gunner called Sergeant Handle. Like Beatty, he was a gruff, old-school soldier who'd begun his career during the Boer War. Handle wasn't happy with this wartime system of rushing raw recruits through training, nor could he get used to dealing with civilians from all walks of life, many of them knowing absolutely nothing about guns. He regarded everyone as a complete novice and constantly harped on about safety rules.

'Do not point a gun at anyone, unless you intend to shoot and kill them,' he said flatly, bringing the truth home to some of the men. 'Not in jest, or to demonstrate your prowess, or to practise. If I see any man aim his rifle at anything other than the clouds or the range targets, I will personally punch him in the nose.'

Joseph was preoccupied by the imminent meeting with Captain Moore and endured the basic weapons training with sour impatience. It took him only a few seconds to become familiar with the Lee Enfield. Other men needed painstaking explanations of the breech mechanism, the magazine and the safety catch—a feature Handle really laboured. Finally, the sergeant ordered the first ten men to lie prone on the mound and take aim at the targets one hundred yards away. Joseph wasn't among them. He stood back with the others and watched.

Before allowing anyone to shoot, Handle walked along the line and kicked at the men's legs or nudged their elbows with the toe of his boot into the correct army position for firing a rifle.

'On my command, fire five rounds at will into your targets,' he called, stepping back. 'All right, open fire.'

A ragged volley crashed off the hills, then the shooting became uncoordinated as the men worked the bolts with varying proficiency. Ahead of them, the targets were mostly untouched. Made from a square of timber with a head and torso roughly painted in black, they kicked backwards when they were struck. It rarely happened. Rounds that missed wide or went high disappeared into the hill further back. The last shot rang out very late, fired by a young soldier struggling with the breech action.

'Cease fire! Clear your weapons!' Handle shouted, then went to each soldier and ensured his rifle was safe. Satisfied, he took a green flag from a holder and waved it slowly so the colour was clearly unfurled. Down-range, a group of soldiers crept cautiously from a trench and inspected the targets. They didn't need long and returned the green signal without making any changes. Handle was watching through binoculars and lowered them with a dismayed growl. 'Same again,' he told the shooters. 'Make yourselves ready.'

The results this time weren't any better. Some good-natured abuse came from the watchers now, who'd realised that if the targets weren't moving, the shooters had missed.

'Next section,' he bawled, thoroughly disgusted. The men on the ground looked up at him puzzled because they still had forty rounds each left. 'Don't worry, you'll get another chance—at something a bit *closer*,' he added dryly.

Joseph was in the following group. He was still angry at the way things had gone wrong. It made him look forward to shooting the hell out of something— anything. He flopped down and lay as Handle had shown them. Still, the master gunner tapped the insides of his boots to make him spread his legs further apart.

'You want to be rock steady, son. Don't be shy.'

Joseph didn't reply.

'On my command, fire five rounds at will into your targets,' Handle repeated, before taking one last look along the line. 'Steady... open fire.'

Joseph ignored the crashing of the other rifles around him. He found working the bolt action easy because he wasn't holding spare bullets between his fingers as he had to at home. He kept his cheek against the stock and fired rapidly without bothering to wait until the target stopped moving after each hit. With the last round a chunk of timber the size of a saucer was punched out of the painted head. Without moving, he waited for the order to cease fire and clear weapons. When it came, it sounded odd. Joseph felt another tap at his ankle.

'Have you done this before, son?' Handle asked sarcastically.

'I shoot rabbits at home, Sergeant.'

'Rabbits? Are there any left?'

'Sorry, Sergeant?'

'Never mind.'

Handle waved the green flag and watched as the range crew came out to wonder at Joseph's target. Handle suddenly shouted at the top of his voice, startling everyone.

'*Leave it*. Back to your trench.'

They scuttled away, one of them hastily flapping their own flag.

'Aim for the heart area,' Handle said.

Joseph calmly put all five bullets into the black torso and didn't think about the fact that he was pretending to kill a man.

His mood appreciated the kick of the rifle against his shoulder, and the savage noise of the gunfire.

'Next section,' Handle roared, when it was over.

As they gathered to watch the last ten men take their positions on the firing mound, half of Joseph's section stood around him.

'Where the hell did you learn to do that?' George asked for them all.

'At home,' Joseph shrugged. 'It's nothing special. The target's not moving, and the rifles are good.'

'Jesus, you could still do it if the target was moving?' Dexter asked. He suspected that none of his ten bullets had hit a thing. Luckily, Handle was too interested in Joseph's results to notice.

'It'd be a big rabbit.' Joseph shrugged again. 'Hard to miss.'

For the next hour, each section took turns firing ten rounds. They stood, crouched on one knee, then fired from a trench in front of the mound, and finally prone again, which was Handle's method of demonstrating the best way to aim a gun. He explained about aiming and allowing for the wind and shooting downhill. By the time this last chance came, most of the men were hitting the targets with half their bullets. Joseph's skill was regarded with a mixture of awe and jealousy, neither of which he seemed to notice.

Finally the sergeant told them to line up in formation, and he stood in front of Joseph.

'What's your name, Private?'

'White, Sergeant!' Joseph said smartly. 'Joseph White.'

'And who is your section sergeant?'

'George, Sergeant—ah, Acting Sergeant Poole, I mean.'

George stepped forward to identify himself and snapped to attention. Handle moved to him.

'I want Private White back here at 1800 hours with his rifle and fifty rounds of ammunition,' Handle told him, taking a notepad from his shirt pocket. 'I'll write you a note for your company commander. If the armoury sergeant has a problem, return your rifle and tell him White needs to redraw it shortly before he return.' Handle was already scribbling with a pencil, but he stopped. 'Do you understand?'

'Private White has to see Captain Moore at midday. Sergeant Major Beatty found him AWOL outside the camp last night.'

Handle glared at Joseph. 'You were caught at the grog wagon?'

George answered before Joseph could speak. 'I know for a fact he wasn't drinking, Sergeant. Joseph was trying to help a mate back to camp, that's all.'

'And Sergeant Major Beatty knows this?'

'No, he didn't ask.'

'You seem to know a lot, Sergeant Poole. Were you there too?'

'Ah, no, but Joseph told me everything. As his section sergeant, of course.'

'Of course.' Handle studied him. With a sigh he finished writing, tore the note off, and gave it to George. Then he wrote another, folding this one before he handed it over. 'Make sure Sergeant Major Beatty gets this before the meeting with Captain Moore. If you can't do that, give it to the captain yourself. Is that clear?'

'Clear as day, Sergeant.'

'March these men back to camp. And for God's sake, make sure you shoulder arms *well* before you get there.'

'Yes, Sergeant.' George nodded with a guilty look.

***

Just before noon, Joseph and Ben stood outside Captain Moore's tent. George had passed on Handle's note. Beatty didn't read it in front of him and no one knew what it said.

'What do you think's going to happen?' Ben asked miserably.

'Sergeant Handle liked my shooting,' Joseph said. 'He wants me to have a second chance.'

'That's what I figured. That won't help me. I didn't hit a damned thing.'

'It won't help me, either. I can't see Beatty letting someone else overrule his decisions.'

Ben perked up, oddly encouraged that the two of them might still share the same fate. The tent flap opened and Beatty stuck his head out. 'You two, in here *now*.'

They shuffled inside and stood awkwardly in the small space. The tent was larger than most, but with a desk and the two men already in there, it was full. Captain Moore was seated. That didn't hide his tall, gaunt frame and the habitual stoop he affected. His thick, greying hair was swept backwards and he had a kind face with a heavy moustache. Beatty stood beside him and loudly announced the privates' names and the charges.

'So, you were both drunk and beyond the camp limits?' Moore had heard it all before. 'Sergeant Major Beatty here takes a dim view of that sort of behaviour.'

Ben surprised Joseph by speaking up first, his voice trembling. 'Joseph wasn't drunk, sir. He was trying to help me back to our tent.'

'But you *had* been drinking, White?'

'No, sir. I only went out to help Ben back.'

Moore frowned at Ben. 'You intended to get so drunk, you couldn't walk back alone? You asked White to go with you and get you back safely?'

'No, sir. It was an accident. Joseph came out later to find me.'

'How did you know he needed finding?' Moore turned curious eyes back to Joseph, who saw the trap.

'I just guessed he was in trouble, sir. When he took too long to come back.'

'I see,' Moore murmured, fingering a note on his desk. 'Very loyal of you. Did you know that Sergeant Handle insists you're too valuable to let go to the navy? What *would* you do, by the way, if I discharged you now?'

'Re-enlist somewhere else, sir.' Joseph shrugged before he could stop himself. 'Adelaide, if I couldn't do it here again.'

'And you, Harding?'

'The same, sir. I wouldn't even go home first. My dad would kill me.'

'Really? I trust he would be upset if the Turks achieved that in his place?' Ben didn't answer. 'Anyway, it makes my discharging you a waste of time, if you are being honest,' Moore said, glancing at Beatty. 'Besides, Sergeant Handle's note is quite insistent. He fancies you'd make an excellent sniper. Are you satisfied, if I simply reprimand these men, Sergeant Major Beatty?'

'Of course, sir. Whatever you think fit.' Beatty glared at them. 'Naturally, I will be watching them both very closely.'

'Then the matter's settled.' Moore tapped his desk once with his finger, like a judge rapping a gavel. 'After basic training, you will all be afforded ample leave before we embark for the journey to Egypt. Until then, resist the temptations of Mr Wright's booze wagon. Is that clear?'

'Yes, sir,' they both echoed, with Ben adding, 'I won't be drinking ever again, sir.'

'I doubt that,' Moore murmured. 'You're probably just starting to get a taste for it. You're both dismissed.'

As Joseph and Ben turned and flipped the tent flap aside to leave, Moore called out.

'Private White, your appointment with Sergeant Handle still stands at

1800. He'll be expecting you.'

'Yes, sir. Thank you, sir.'

***

'A sniper? Is that good?' Dexter asked that evening as they sat around their campfire.

Joseph had spent an hour with Sergeant Handle shooting at smaller targets, and at greater distances, all in the fading light of dusk. The sergeant could barely contain his enthusiasm at the results, while Joseph still didn't quite grasp what all the fuss was about. He'd always assumed everyone could shoot as well as he. It felt natural.

'Good?' George said, stabbing at the fire with a stick. 'Depends on your point of view. They'll think you're valuable and won't waste your life on frontal attacks, stuff like that. But no one likes a sniper. Our boys hunt them down like mad dogs.'

'What do you reckon, Joseph?'

Joseph was finishing his mug of tea and he threw the dregs onto the ground. 'It's kept me in the army, so I'm not complaining. Anyway, I'll always have you blokes to look after me, right?'

'That's right, we'll be there,' Dexter said sombrely, nodding and taking him seriously. 'All the time.'

Father and Son

It felt strange to Jonathon to be truly safe for the first time in weeks. The Turks hadn't tried to shell any supply ships since just after the landings and they never targeted the hospital ship. So as the boatload of wounded men, with Jonathon standing in the stern, pulled well clear of the beach, the chances of his being hurt diminished more with every oar-stroke. By the time he was surrounded by a black ocean, with the lights of Anzac Cove only visible from water behind him like some enormous celebration, a weight had lifted from his shoulders. A constant tension he never realised was there eased away. It was almost peaceful out on the sea.

The SS *Gascon* loomed out of the night as a wall of steel. A swell slapped noisily back from the ship and made attaching the derrick ropes difficult. Then with a soft order from above the boat was lifted from the water.

The scene on deck was slowly revealed to Jonathon as the boat was raised higher. Men lay everywhere, most under blankets, although some were well enough to shrug them off and prop themselves up on an elbow as they smoked. They talked to each other in low voices. A string of lights was rigged haphazardly, tied to anything that allowed that part of the deck to be lit. The ocean swell made it swing in slow arcs. A smell of disinfectant lingered despite a breeze and a dozen of the ship's crew in white square-collared shirts moved towards Jonathon's boat with stretchers ready. He felt useless as they bustled around him, securing the falls and chocking the keel steady. Only when they started lifting the wounded men out could he offer help. Some of the serious cases were sent directly below by a young nurse, while each man Jonathon carried was found a place on the open deck. It didn't take long to empty the boat.

'When are you going back?' he asked the midshipman who had been in command.

He couldn't have been more than fifteen, but the boy spoke with authority. His fresh face was lined with strain and lack of sleep. 'I'll get the lads to hose out the mess while I have a cuppa.' He nodded at the bloodied timbers in the boat. 'I've been going all day. About ten minutes? How long do you need?'

'That should do. Don't leave without me.'

'Then don't go missing. My captain will have a fit if he sees me hanging about for no good reason.'

Jonathon thanked him with a nod. He decided to ask the young nurse who organised the casualties, since she was closest. He had to walk the length of the ship before he found her attending a wounded soldier near the bow. He waited until she stood away from the man and stepped in her path.

'Excuse me, Sister,' he said quickly. 'I know you're busy...'

She held up a lantern and squinted at him in the flickering light. 'Yes?' She sounded puzzled.

'No, I'm not hurt. I'm trying to find someone. A nurse called Rose Preston. Do you know her?'

She was taken aback, then replied carefully, 'I'm Rose Preston. How can I help you?'

Jonathon was surprised at finding her so easily, and this attractive young girl was the last thing he'd expected.

'Are you? Oh, well... I–I have a letter for you,' he said, fumbling at his shirt pocket.

'A letter? Who from?'

'One of our battalion officers, Major Willow.'

She frowned as she took the note. 'I can't remember any Major Willow.'

'You might recall Tom Carter. He was a sergeant—our section sergeant. You wrote a letter for him telling us he'd be all right.'

'Tom Carter...'

Jonathon noticed how exhausted she looked and how difficult it appeared to be for her to think of anything except the job at hand. He didn't know that staying focused was what got her through the long days. Then her tired expression brightened as she remembered.

‘Of course, he was the one who needed the letter addressed back to Anzac. That hadn’t happened before.’

‘It was nice of you to let us know Tom’s all right. Major Willow wanted to thank you... ’ Jonathon stopped, nodding at the note still in her hand and adding awkwardly, ‘But you’ll read that for yourself, of course.’

‘Yes, thank you, anyway.’ She looked at him quizzically and tucked the note into her apron. ‘Do you want a mug of tea? And something to eat, before you go back? I’ve got a ham sandwich I can share with you... it’s somewhere close, I’m sure. It’s the only type of sandwich they seem to make around here. I’ve eaten hundreds in the last few weeks.’

His time on board was already getting short and he hesitated just a moment, then said lightly, ‘I won’t steal any of your tea, but I’d give anything for a taste of fresh ham. I don’t have long, though.’

Rose laughed softly. ‘I doubt whether it’s still fresh, and you’re quite welcome. I forget where I put them half the time. I can’t dally about too much myself. My patients are waiting.’ She waved a hand at the crowded decks.

She took him to a hatch cover where a large urn and a selection of mugs, plus some tins of milk, stood ready for anyone who needed them. A large sandwich cut in half was on a plate and she offered it to him.

'I'm surprised no one's pinched it,' she said. 'So grab it while you can.'

While Jonathon wolfed down the sandwich, savouring every morsel of the meat, Rose poured two mugs of tea anyway, putting plenty of milk in one to cool it.

'You might as well,' she said, putting it in front of him. 'You don't have to drink it all.'

'You're very kind,' Jonathon managed to say, choking down the last lump of bread.

'It's the least we can do.'

They stood side-by-side in the shadows of the swaying lights, both of them suddenly at a loss for something to say, so they sipped their teas. Then Rose tilted her face at the shoreline sparkling in front of them.

'Did you land on the twenty-fifth?'

'Third wave. It wasn't so hard, by then.'

'I was right here watching,' she reprimanded him gently. 'I know exactly what it was like.'

'Well, the lads who went in first definitely got the worst of it.'

'And now?'

He shrugged. 'If you keep your head down, it's not too bad.'

Rose looked pointedly at the blanketed shapes around them, then raised her eyebrows. 'So I see,' she said.

He quickly changed the subject. 'Do you write for many of the men?'

'A lot, I don't mind. Some of them are too hurt to do it themselves. Some can't read or write anyway.'

'Do they write to you? Later, I mean. To thank you.'

That made her smile. 'Now, there's a funny thing. No, I've never had a letter from anyone I've nursed. Of course, some of them might not have...' she didn't finish, her expression turning sombre.

'Well, apart from Major Willow,' he tried to cheer her up again. 'Doesn't he count?' He was glad to see the smile half returning.

'Yes, of course. Now I have Major Willow's letter.'

'I could write to you too.' The words came out before he could think about them and he felt instantly embarrassed. He went on awkwardly, 'You know, just to let you know what's happening over there. Then again, I suppose you don't need to hear it.'

After a silence, she said, 'Of course you can write, if you like.'

'Really? You don't have to, if you... I mean, would you write back?'

'I can't promise too much. Just a short note perhaps, now and then. I'm very busy, or I'm too tired.'

'Anything would be wonderful. All the blokes just live for mail from home.'

'I know. That's why I don't mind writing.'

'You could tell me what you're doing.'

'It's hardly the stuff of cheerful letters,' she said, quietly amused.

'No, I'd like to know. Honest.'

Beyond Rose, Jonathon spotted the midshipman staring and searching along the deck. Although he was sorry to leave the company of this beautiful girl, he figured it wouldn't hurt to retreat while he was well ahead.

'I have to go,' he told her, pulling a sad face. 'I can see the navy's looking for me. Has Major Willow put our company address on his letter?'

Rose pulled the single page from the envelope and peered at it in the poor light. 'Yes,' she said finally.

'I can write to you first, anyway. Do I address it to this ship?' Jonathon thought he was gabbling and hated himself for it. He was edging away too, suddenly anxious not to upset the midshipman. He might need a ride again, sometime in the future.

'That will do,' Rose smothered a sudden laugh. 'It would help if I knew your name.'

'Bloody hell... oh, sorry. It's Jonathon–Jonathon White. Will you remember?'

'I'll try.' She waved.

Jonathon waved back and jogged towards the lifeboats, calling an apology to the midshipman as he did.

***

On the makeshift jetty, Robert had been watching each boat as it returned, looking for Jonathon. He was relieved to see him get back.

'You were right, Robert,' Jonathon told him cheerfully as he stepped ashore. 'She is absolutely beautiful. Like an angel, just as you said.'

'You bastard.'

'She might even be the most beautiful girl I've ever met.'

'Not that you've met many. You're still a bastard.'

'She said I could write, and she'll write back.'

'You *bastard.*'

Robert pestered him as they began the climb back to the trenches. Bursting bombs on a ridge above them lit their way.

'So, how old is she?' he called above the noise.

'Don't know. Young, though,' Jonathon answered over his shoulder.

'How young?'

'I don't *know*. She's young, and yet looks sort of older.'

'That's flattering. Did you tell her that?'

'Of course not. She gave me half her ham sandwich.'

This made Robert silent a moment, then he snarled, 'A *real* a bastard.'

***

The next morning was quiet in their sector, although the Turks were attacking loudly somewhere nearby. In the reserve trenches, crouched in a sandbagged dugout that they shared with other men in turns, Jonathon and Robert could hear the crack of Turkish hand-bombs and the yelling of the Australians as they counter-attacked in a bayonet charge. There was a machine gun firing, but it was difficult to tell whose. The Australians had captured some of the German Spandaus and used them until the ammunition ran out. The dugout had no roof and during the day it was wise to stay close to the walls so Turkish snipers in the hills above weren't tempted to shoot. The ceiling today was an absolutely clear blue sky.

'Someone's getting a rude wake-up call,' Robert said, listening. 'I hope they keep it on their side of the fence. I haven't had my breakfast yet.' Both of them held mugs of black tea.

Robert was dunking a hard biscuit to soften it enough to eat. The biscuits could break teeth otherwise.

'We'll find out soon enough,' Jonathon murmured, lighting a cigarette. His mood, so high the night before after meeting Rose, had dropped to a quiet brooding.

'Cheer up, mate,' Robert said, half-guessing. 'You'll get to see her again.'

'Not before some smart-arse officer does, I'll bet. It's all a bit pointless, don't you think? We don't stand a chance against all those blokes strutting around High Command with their clean uniforms and polished boots.' An artillery shell landed close enough to shake the ground and they ducked instinctively. A fine dust drifted down and Robert cursed, covering his tea with one hand. Jonathon gestured at the noise and mess around them, 'Besides, I might get bowled over before the end of the day. Where's the future in that?'

'Christ, you're Mister bloody Cheerful, aren't you?'

'I'm just trying to be realistic, that's all.'

'She only said she'd write you a letter. You didn't ask her to get married, right?'

'No, I know.'

'Then try dreaming instead. Like, the war will be over in a year, and we'll all be home. You and what's-her-name will have ten kids before you're thirty. There, what do you think of that?'

'Ten kids? Shit.' He grimaced and ground out his cigarette. 'I hope the Germans can put up a better fight than that.'

A private called Appleton stuck his head around the opening. 'There's fresh meat at the top of the communications trench, lads,' he said cheerfully. 'For those who want it.'

'Hey... *hey*,' Robert stopped him disappearing. 'How fresh?'

'Well, you know. The usual.'

'Have you seen it?'

'No, I'm just passing the message. I'm told there's a couple of blokes guarding it, to make sure everyone gets a fair share.'

'Come on, Jonno,' Robert was suddenly interested. 'That's a good sign. It might be worth checking out.'

'I'll believe it when I see it,' Jonathon grumbled, getting up to follow.

The only fresh meat the Anzacs ever saw came as sides of beef, frozen and carried up from the beach so they could carve chunks off for stew or share the bones for soup. The meat hardly ever survived the journey from the boat's freezer. Supplies always stayed on the beach for some time, waiting their turn like everything else. Then the beef was hauled by men up the dirt tracks and through the trenches, exposed to the open air and the countless flies that had been gorging themselves on the rotting corpses everywhere.

The meat deteriorated rapidly and turned green, a process hastened by the flies' attention. So it could rarely be eaten by the time it reached the men it was meant for.

The two friends worked their way along the trenches. Men on the fire step offered morning greetings or ribald comments. Jonathon still had to think twice sometimes when the men called him "corporal", reminding himself that they meant him.

'What's it like, Smithy?' Robert asked another of their section who was pushing past in the opposite direction, on his way back from inspecting the meat. Smith grunted and kept going.

'What'd I tell you?' Jonathon said from behind.

'You never know. We'll still have a look. Maybe he was trying to put us off?

Get more for himself.'

'Yeah, right.'

They rounded a corner into an intersection of trenches where there was slightly more room. A side of beef leaned against the dirt wall. The soldiers guarding it were keeping their distance, smoking and eyeing the newcomers doubtfully. At first,

Jonathon thought the beef had turned black. Then he realised it was the mass of flies that covered every inch of it.

'For God's sake,' he said. 'Why the hell do they bother?'

'Wait a minute. Don't be so quick to give up. It might be all right if you cut through the top layer,' Robert said, trying to wave the flies away. He could scoop them aside with his hand, glutted and sticky. Hundreds instantly took their place.

'That's what everyone says,' one of the guards said dryly. 'It's fucked, believe me. It was before it even left the beach.'

Jonathon asked, 'Then why are you still guarding it? No one's going to steal the bloody thing.'

'We're trying to work out what to do,' the other admitted. 'Major Willow told us to stay until it was fairly shared out. He doesn't like his orders disobeyed, no matter what.'

'Then *I'll* tell you to get rid of it,' Jonathon said, tapping his new stripes with a finger. He was angry about the false hope. Other men would hear of the meat, and like Robert, believe that for once it might be worth eating, only to have their hopes dashed.

'What will we do, Corporal? Carry it back?' The soldier was trying to be helpful.

'Of course not. Just chuck it over the top.'

They all looked at each other.

Robert backed away with his hands in the air. 'I'll leave that up to you blokes,' he said, smiling humourlessly.

The two soldiers put down their weapons and each of them reluctantly picked up an end of the beef. The flies rose up, clouding around their faces and getting into their eyes, ears and mouths. The men spat and cursed angrily, then with a hurried count of three tossed the rotting meat high and out into no-man's-land. It landed with a heavy thud.

Immediately the air above came alive with Turkish rifle rounds. The bullets zipped overhead or gouged into the lip of the trench. Some could be heard smacking into the carcass. The firing only lasted about fifteen seconds, and then silence. Next, laughter and an excited babble floated over from the Turkish lines.

'That's cheered them up no end,' Robert told Jonathon. 'Good on you.'

Jonathon sighed. His rank was only one small step above the others, but he'd discovered it made every decision he took, no matter how small, open to judgment even from his friends.

'We'd better get back,' he said, turning back to the others. 'Tell Major Willow that Corporal White ordered you to throw the carcass to the Turks in the hope that we might poison some of them—no, never mind.' He waved a hand.

wearily. 'Just tell him it was my decision if he gets pissed off.'

Back in their own part of the line, two new faces were waiting. One man was clearly older with a wizened expression and drooping, grey moustache. His companion was half his age, similar in build and clean-shaven. He looked eager to please anyone he could.

'We're after Sergeant Streeth,' The older man said, looking at Jonathon's stripes. 'We've been posted to his section.'

A burst of machine gun fire raked the trench, and he hardly flinched. The younger man bobbed his head and swore loudly.

'Anyone seen Nick?' Jonathon called out, staring around.

A voice answered from further up the line. 'At the latrines. He's got the shits, real bad. Been there half the night and all morning.'

'He'll get himself killed if he's not careful.' Robert said, only half-joking, The Turks regularly dropped artillery into the latrine area knowing there was a good chance that men were in there.

'Anyway, that's our mob,' Jonathon explained, introducing himself and Robert. 'I'm your section corporal. Glad to see you. We were down to six men.'

'I'm Paul Strand,' the older man shook his hand. He had an old-world style and spoke carefully, as if making sure that he said each word correctly.

'Albert,' his companion added. 'Albert Strand.' He waited for a reaction, obviously used to getting one. Jonathon obliged them with a puzzled frown.

'What's the story, then?'

'He's my dad.'

'Bullshit, how old are you?'

'Nineteen.'

'And you?' Jonathon turned to Paul.

'Forty-one, last March.' Paul held himself taller. 'Fit as a fiddle, don't you worry.'

'You both signed up together?' Robert asked, amazed.

'Someone's got to look after the lad—'

'I can bloody look after myself,' Albert said quickly. Plainly, they'd had this conversation before.

'So who's looking after Mrs Strand?' Robert winked at Jonathon.

'She's been beyond any looking after for five years gone. Pneumonia, in the winter of 1910. There's only the two of us, so we might as well keep each other company.'

Robert was already muttering an apology, his attempt at humour having backfired badly. Saying something about making tea for him and Jonathon, he headed for the dugout.

'All right,' Jonathon said, aware of his youth compared to Paul's years. As the section corporal, he was expected to tell the older man what to do. 'We're in reserve here, in case things get too bad at the front line. They often do, so don't get too comfortable. Chances are we'll have to rush up and give them a hand for a while, then come back. It can go on like that all day.'

'Are the Turks attacking?' Albert asked nervously.

'The Turks are *always* attacking.' This wasn't quite true. In fact, things had quietened down noticeably since the brief ceasefire, at least when it came to large offensives. Jonathon didn't want Albert getting the wrong idea. 'Be ready. Can you read?' He pointed at a nearby sign warning about a sniper. 'None of these are for fun. The blokes are always cracking jokes about all sorts of things. Never think the signs aren't for real.'

Albert nodded with short, jerking movements. His father took out a pipe and calmly lit it.

'Get some rest while you can,' Jonathon added finally. 'Make yourselves a brew. I'll introduce you to Nick, when he comes back—if he comes back.'

He meant that Streeth's complaining bowels might keep him away. Albert looked anxious, thinking about Robert's comment on the risks of going to the latrine too often. Albert had no illusions about being a hero, but figured he didn't want to get shot going to the toilet either.

In the dugout, Robert was pensive, cautiously stirring tea into some boiling water. Enough fresh drinking water had arrived overnight to allow this small luxury. It wasn't something to be taken lightly and he made sure that not a drop was spilled.

'What's wrong with you?' Jonathon asked.

What do you reckon? Do you think it's a good idea having a father and son fighting side-by-side?'

'It took me by surprise. I suppose it's no different from two brothers, or even good mates.'

Robert shook his head. 'I don't know. The old man's going to be so preoccupied watching out for his kid that he won't be paying attention to the job. That's what worries me.'

Jonathon considered this. 'Well, there's nothing we can do about it. Let's see what Nick says. I reckon he'll just be glad of the reinforcements.'

'If he doesn't shit himself to death first.'

'Don't laugh. We're all eating the same grub, just about. And drinking the same water. You might find yourself running to the latrines with him before the day ends.'

Robert pulled a face. 'There you go again. Always looking on the bright side of things. That poor girl's going to be miserable after reading your bloody letters.'

***

Their comparative calm was broken halfway through the morning, just when it seemed that they were going to have an easy day. Willow thrust his face into Jonathon's dugout.

'Where the hell's Sergeant Streeth?' he demanded, red-faced.

'Probably in the latrine, sir,' Jonathon guessed. 'He's been sick all day, really bad.'

'Then don't bother about him. Get your section to Quinn's Post straightaway. Someone's spotted a band of Turks making their way through the gully into an attacking position.'

Jonathon and Robert scrambled for their rifles and gear, including spare ammunition and water bottles. Willow had already gone.

'Right then, B section on the double, follow me!' Jonathon called urgently.

As the word was passed on, Jonathon found himself in front of Paul and Albert Strand. The two newcomers stared at him, panicked by the sudden rush. He reached out and tore the pack from Albert's shoulder.

Forget all that shit,' he said. 'We're not going to set up camp. You just need your rifle and ammo, and some water. Have you got those?' Albert nodded wordlessly. Behind him, Paul was calmly shedding his extra equipment. 'Stay close and listen to the other blokes if you can't see me. We'll look after you.'

Robert ran up, followed by more members of their section. 'Can't find Billy either,' he said breathlessly. 'They say he's helping Nick. Will we go and get him?'

'No, there's no time. Damn it, that makes just six of us again—lucky you fellows turned up,' he said to the Strands. 'Let's get moving everyone.'

They trotted through the trench system, pausing only at the hazards that were scattered everywhere. At one corner, a Turkish sniper was known to have a perfect set shot on anyone passing, although he was slow and the opportunity brief. Dashing past one at a time was safe. In another place, a machine gun could strafe just ten exposed yards of the trench. Again, moving quickly cheated the enemy.

When they reached Quinn's Post, they found the line crowded with soldiers. Other reserve sections were called up to strengthen the defences. Bullets from the Turkish lines snapped overhead, the enemy aware of the large target. The trench was deep enough to provide plenty of cover from rifle fire, at least.

'We're jammed in like bloody sardines,' Robert said anxiously. 'If they lob a bomb in here, we'll all cop it.'

'Then keep your eyes peeled,' Jonathon said sharply. 'What's going on, sir?'

This he asked of a lieutenant nearby, squinting through a makeshift periscope. The officer replied without taking his eye away from the mirror.

'I can see the rotten beggars amassing in their old front line. The one we bombed them out of last week. They can't be meaning to reoccupy it, surely? We'll just do the same again. I think they're going to attack and try to push us out of this line.'

'What do you want us to do?'

'Tell your men to fix bayonets. We'll wait until they rise out of their trench and go out to meet them. Fight the bastards hand-to-hand. We must wait until they move first. The Turks have got a machine gun enfilading this parapet. It'll cut us to pieces if we show our hand too soon.'

Jonathon swore softly. Fighting hand-to-hand was brutal and terrifying, and so far he'd managed to avoid using his bayonet. There would be no choice this time. It was going to be a shocking introduction to the war for these new recruits. He gathered his men close.

'All right, this is going to be nasty,' he said grimly. 'We're going to charge them as soon as they're out in the open. So fix your bayonets, and forget the bloody rules about unloading your rifles. Have one up the spout and shoot the bastards, if you get the chance.' He looked pointedly at Paul and Albert Strand. They would have been taught that bayonet charges were done with an empty breech, in case you accidentally shot one of your own troops in front of you.

The lieutenant pushed past, calling out to everyone. 'Do *not* attempt to take their trenches, men. It is an untenable position. Understand? Beat the hell out of them and come back to this line. Is that understood?' He moved on, repeating himself.

Robert tapped Jonathon on the shoulder. 'Does that mean this is all going to be a waste of time?'

'Something like that,' he growled. 'They don't really want to attack us, and we don't really need to fight them off.'

'Good,' Robert nodded, then spat out a shred of tobacco. 'As long as it's worth getting killed for.'

Jonathon shot him a look, then said to everyone, 'The important thing is to get the hell back here when the time is right. The Turks will open up with that machine gun even if their own blokes are still out there, if they think the fight's been lost. If you hear anyone order a retreat, don't muck around. Turn tail and run like hell. Got it?'

They murmured agreement and there was the clicking of bayonets being clipped to rifles. Jonathon wanted to tell Albert Strand something more— something that might give him a better chance of surviving this first battle, but there were no tricks. No secrets to staying alive other than to fight like a madman. The older man, Paul, seemed philosophical, standing calmly with his head lowered and puffing comfortably on his pipe.

Curious, Jonathon watched him. *Perhaps he was considering his best options? Should he hang back and try to shoot the enemy point-blank, or move close and rely on sheer savagery?* Something Robert had said occurred to him. *Would the father take his eye off the fight for just a moment, looking for the wellbeing of his only son, and pay the price?* Jonathon suddenly felt he had to say something.

'Paul, watch out for yourself,' he said quietly, so no one could hear. 'You'll get a Turkish bayonet in your own back if all you think of is running after Albert.'

Paul nodded slowly. 'It'll be every man for himself, I know,' he said. Something in his manner told Jonathon that the message wasn't being heeded.

'Stand to, men,' someone called, and Jonathon made sure his men got ready. The enemy rifle fire had almost stopped. They were about to attack.

It began with the strange bugling that warbled over the landscape, prompting fierce cries from the enemy trenches. Whistles blew and suddenly a brown mass of men, their faces contorted in screams of defiance, rose out of the dirt and ran at the Anzac line.

'Steady...' the call came again. '*Steady,* boys.'

They could see the Turks had a hesitancy about them. By now an Australian machine gun should have opened up, or at least the front-line troops would be shooting a barrage of rifle fire. It was disconcerting, even in the heat of a charge, for neither to happening.

Then there were strident Australian whistles.

'Out at them, lads! Get out there!' This was the officers.

The NCOs used more earthy language. 'Come on, you bastards. Get the hell out there. Go! Go!'

The Anzacs scrambled over the parapet and ran, their rifles thrust forward, bayonets wicked with their purpose. They yelled out incoherent savage sounds to give themselves strength. Jonathon was close to the front with Robert beside him. Both fired as they ran and saw two Turks fall. Awkwardly, Jonathon reloaded, hauling on the breech bolt without letting his pace slacken.

The opposing lines of soldiers came together in a mess of frightened cries and clashing weapons, beginning a desperate, dreadful fight in the bright sunshine. In this small personal battle the only way to survive was to kill the man in front of you. The steel bayonets grated on the rifle barrels as men parried blows, polished stocks smacked loudly, wood splintered. Some men fired the precious bullet they had in the breech, the shots close and shocking. Within the first few seconds, men fell screaming with pain, only to be kicked and trodden on by the victors as they turned to face the next threat.

Jonathon was lucky. The first Turk he confronted aimed for Robert and it was easy to sidestep his rifle, the alarm and despair clear on the man's face as he realised his mistake before Jonathon's bayonet sank into his chest and broke bone. He felt it snap, as if he'd shoved the bayonet into a pile of dry twigs. He even felt the muzzle punch against the man's breast and pushed him backwards. Jonathon lifted his boot high and kicked the Turk off his blade, which came out slick and red with blood. Then it was kill the next man before *he* was killed.

He saw a moment of safety, so he clubbed his rifle sideways into the head of a Turk grappling with Robert, who stabbed the dazed man in the neck as he staggered to his knees. A young Turk holding back from the fight was desperately cocking the trigger on his rifle. Jonathon shot him in the head. Another screeched out of nowhere, hurling himself at Jonathon with a bloodied bayonet aimed at his face. Robert fired point-blank and dropped the man so abruptly that it was unreal.

Jonathon's senses were heightened. His hands on the stock of his rifle were greasy with sweat, and he could feel the grit on his palms. The smell of fresh blood scoured the back of his throat. Next it was the stench of a man's bowels loosening in pain or death. His ears rang with high-pitched screams and rifle shots right beside him. The muscles in his shoulders ached as he raised the butt of his weapon and smashed it into a Turk's cheekbone, the man about to lunge downward at an Anzac sprawled at his feet. Jonathon reversed his rifle and bayoneted him under the ribs.

Then he found himself alone, ignored among the frenzied fighting. The Turks were trying to retreat, fighting a way out of each struggle so they could run. He saw at once that he could be the only man still standing with any rank.

'Pull back,' he yelled frantically. 'Get the hell back to the lines, before that fucking machine gun starts up.'

The dreaded staccato hammering suddenly burst from a Turkish position. Rounds zipped past. Two Turks screamed, their legs shot out from under them by their own gun, and they collapsed writhing to the dirt. The Australians were echoing Jonathon's call and urging each other to retreat. The fight abandoned, the men scurried to reach the trenches. Many of them paused to grab a handful of clothing on a fallen mate, hauling him across the broken ground to safety.

The machine gun's arc of fire passed within only yards of the Anzacs. Some, including Jonathon and Robert, knew it was coming and threw themselves forward to roll over the parapet and drop into cover. Three who lingered in the open, trying to help the wounded, were hit and fell. Two were killed. One was dragged fast into the trench, his hands clutching in agony at the red stain spreading across his lower back.

Devoid of targets, the machine gun stopped. The silence was filled with the crying of the wounded. Jonathon lay with his back to the trench wall, his eyes shut tight and mouth open, gasping for breath like a long-distance runner at the end of a race. Blood pounded in his ears. Beside him, Robert was swearing a mindless mantra to calm himself and regain his own ragged breathing. Jonathon opened his eyes when someone shook his arm roughly. Paul Strand crouched in front of him, his expression deeply pained.

'Albert's still out there,' he said hoarsely. 'My boy's still out there. He was running back next to me, then he just disappeared. Dropped without a sound, when I wasn't looking. I was...' He faltered.

Jonathon forced back his own weariness to reach forward and squeeze the older man's arm. 'Shit, all right, Paul. Stay calm.' He pushed himself upright. 'He might be lying doggo if he's not hurt bad.' It sounded false even to him.

Most men who fell silently were already dead.

He called, 'Anyone got a periscope? Or a mirror?'

A sergeant he didn't recognise shouldered his way along the trench, a makeshift periscope cradled in his arms. He was a gruff, weathered man with a thick beard. A streak of bright blood ran across his forehead. 'Dave Madison. How many we lose?' he asked Jonathon, glancing at his stripes. He looked for himself without waiting for an answer, pushing his cap back on his head and hoisting the periscope. 'Christ,' he muttered. 'There's half a dozen out there.'

'Anyone close?' Jonathon said.

'Two, but not close enough.' After a pause Madison added, 'One dead, the other wounded pretty bad. Anyone you know?' He passed the periscope over.

Jonathon steadied it and peered into the mirror. It took a few seconds to get his bearings, then he centred it on the first of the Anzacs nearest to them. It was the dead man, and it wasn't Albert or anyone else from his section. The injured soldier a few yards further out *was* Albert Strand, squirming feebly and curled into a ball.

There was nothing they could do. The Turks would have seen him moving and were just waiting for someone to try a rescue. He brought down the periscope and handed it back.

Paul Strand stood close, confronting him again.

'Can you see him?'

'He's wounded,' Jonathon nodded. 'I can't see how bad, but it doesn't look good.'

Paul's eyes went to the parapet. Jonathon was expecting it and grabbed his arm. 'Don't even think about it, Paul. You won't last a second. They're just waiting for someone to try.'

'We can't just leave him out there, for God's sake.'

'*Listen* to me. If you go over, you'll be dead before you even get close to Albert. Is that going to help him?'

Paul screwed his face up and with a trembling sigh asked, 'So what do we do?'

The other Anzacs close by in the trench watched uncomfortably, some of them knowing the answer. No one else would say it.

Jonathon told him grimly, 'We have to wait. Until nightfall, and a while after that too. They'll expect us to do something as soon as it's dark.'

Paul was aghast. 'Are you fucking mad? He won't last that long. All day, out in the sun?'

'He might—he's got a chance. That's all we can do. If you rush out there and gct hit, you might get someone else killed trying to save *you*. Understand?'

'What about a white flag? A truce? They did it before.'

'We can't do that without an officer,' Jonathon said impatiently, and a little angrily. Strand needed to obey his judgment and orders, despite the circumstances. 'And an officer won't do it just for one man. Besides, the Turks won't be interested in a truce. We've just bayoneted half their blokes to death.'

He turned away abruptly, cursing the luck that made him face the father's grieving, hopeless expression. A guarded look at some of the nearest men ordered them to watch Paul carefully. They nodded back discreetly. He wished there was something else they could try. There was nothing. Albert Strand would have to survive by himself until dark.

Robert followed Jonathon to a fire step and offered a cigarette, which he took gratefully. They lit up, then Robert said cautiously, 'That was a bit of bad luck. Bound to happen though, like I said, right? Why didn't they split them up? Put them in different sections?'

'It wouldn't make any difference.' Jonathon shook his head. 'They'd get together somehow.'

Suddenly, Major Willow pushed his way along the line and stopped in front of Jonathon. 'Corporal, have you seen Sergeant Streeth yet?'

'No, sir.' Jonathon didn't bother rising. 'He might be here. We just got back in.'

Willow went quiet. 'Many casualties?'

'We did pretty well. Drove the bastards back. But yeah, we lost a few, and there's some wounded we can't get to. The Turks are waiting for us to try.'

'Damn them.' Willow fingered his pistol and gazed upwards out of the trench. 'Well, you'd better keep your section here in case they try something again. Our sector's very slow for business. I'll send for you if things hot up.'

'I'd like to stay until dark, sir.' Jonathon stood up. 'We'll have a go at getting our wounded in then.'

'Very well, don't take any stupid chances.' The major turned and moved off.

Then he was nearly killed.

In front of him, a Turkish hand-bomb landed on the soil, somehow dropping perfectly between the men and equipment scattered everywhere. It rolled around, innocent yet deadly. A private screamed a warning, dropped his rifle and pounced on the missile with amazing speed. With a deft flick he threw the bomb back into the open where it exploded with a deafening crack. Willow had frozen mid-step, everything happening too fast for him to react any better.

'Well done, man,' he managed to say calmly. 'You're as quick as a bloody cat.'

The soldier stared at him, his face pale. 'That's the fourth one this morning, sir. I'm getting the knack for it.'

Willow nodded his thanks, then walked past. Jonathon and Robert allowed themselves to breathe again.

'He's a bloody cool customer, isn't he?' Robert said.

'Better than most,' Jonathon agreed shakily. The bomb might have killed them all, although the major would have taken the brunt of the explosion.

An hour later, Albert Strand began to call out weakly for his father. The Turks hadn't attempted to attack, and they were keeping an eye on the wounded man. Any movement in the trench near him immediately brought a raking burst from the machine gun. They were mindful not to hit him, though.

Paul was frantic with his boy dying in the sun only yards away. Hearing him call out was almost too much to bear.

There was always noise—rifle fire, and the blast of hand-bombs, and Albert's plaintive cry too over the top of them. '*Dad... Dad, are you there*?'

'Oh no,' Jonathon groaned. He was standing against the rear of the trench, watching for hand-bombs. 'Christ, that's all we need. Where's Paul? Someone hang on to him, for God's sake.'

Too late, Paul Strand was bouncing impatiently just below the parapet and trying to make his voice heard. 'Hang on, son!' he yelled desperately. 'You'll be all right. I'm coming to get you.'

'Like hell you are,' Jonathon growled. Robert was firing from the fire step and quickly used his rifle to block Paul's way.

'Stay where you are,' he snapped. The two men locked eyes, Paul judging whether he could force a way past. Another call came from above.

'*Dad, for Christ's sake... where are you*?'

'Dear God,' Paul whispered.

'You can't help him,' Robert said grimly. 'Not now.'

Midday passed and the afternoon wore on. It was one of the quietest days they'd had, the attack that morning the only real threat. The men in the front line could almost have relaxed except that Albert Strand would call out pitifully just when they believed he'd spoken his last. He asked for his father and sometimes for water. Once he called for his mother.

Paul Strand sat with his head buried in his hands and took no part in any shooting. He stayed like that all day and Jonathon allowed it. It was easier for everyone. Paul only began to move again when the sky turned orange. Even the dusk dragged itself out.

‘All right,’ Jonathon finally whispered in the gloom, when it seemed too cruel to make Paul wait any longer. The Turks hadn’t thrown any flares and were either being very cautious, keeping their night sight, or they’d got tired of the game. Or it was possible that they were having a meal.

In one long, nerve-wracking minute Jonathon and Paul clambered over the top and crawled to where Albert lay. They didn’t waste time checking him out in the open, dragging him back by the shoulders. Willing hands caught him as he fell into the trench.

He was dead. Two bullets had hit him in the back, one puncturing his lung, the other lower and smashing vital organs. It was incredible that he had lasted so long and had the breath to call out for most of the day. Jonathon looked across at Sergeant Madison. Albert would never have lived into the next day, no matter when they’d rescued him.

Of course, Paul Strand would never believe that.

Lemnos Island

4th August 1915

Dear Jonathon,

I hope, as always, this letter finds you well and in good spirits. I got your last note during the week and I must admit it made me smile, which doesn't happen often these days. Your friend Robert certainly sounds like a handful! Please give him my regards. With luck we will meet one day.

I only have a few minutes to write this before the ship weighs anchor and the last lighter is sent away. Otherwise I will have to post this in Cairo, which means it might take ages to reach you. I'm afraid our chances of meeting again in the near future have taken a bit of a blow. Matron Lambert has had both myself and Julia transferred back to her command and I'll be leaving the *Gascon* at the end of this voyage. I'll be re-joining the main group and setting up camp on Lemnos Island, where a lot of the less serious casualties will be cared for. This should free the hospitals in Cairo for the badly wounded, I think.

Please continue to write. My new address is below in full. I'll send you some more news when I've settled into my new home!

Kind regards, Rose Preston.

Rose had been treated well aboard the *Gascon*. The wounded soldiers, of course, appreciated everything she could do for them, and the crew admired her stamina and dedication. It had been a happy, satisfying time—aside from the trauma of their grisly work.

So it came as a bit of a shock for her and Julia to find themselves cloistered once again in the difficult conditions the other nurses still endured at the hands of their own military. Matron Lambert continued her one-woman stand against the male bureaucracy. Little had improved for her "girls".

The two of them were a part of a second group of nurses to reach Lemnos Island, the first women including the matron herself having arrived the day before. As Rose and her companions clambered from the boats, the long skirts of their uniforms not helping, they saw a small reception committee gathering on the beach. An officer glared at them and the soldier beside him obviously wasn't glad to be there. Beyond them the sandy, dry landscape of the island didn't look too inviting either.

'My God,' Nellie said aloud to everyone. 'Is that man carrying bagpipes?'

Most of the nurses were too absorbed in avoiding the wet, clinging sand to have noticed. Nellie's amused tone made them all pause. The officer waved an imperious hand at them.

He bellowed against the hiss of the surf, 'Come on, ladies. Form up in four equal ranks here.' He dropped his hand to point at the ground in front of him.

A ripple of disbelief went through the women. Someone said, 'He can't be serious.'

Colonel Fischer was absolutely serious. He was nothing if not a military man who would gladden the heart of Major Cromwell back at Victoria Barracks. Fischer's official title was commanding officer of the Third Australian General Hospital on Lemnos Island.

Another officer, a Lieutenant Colonel Drake, appeared strutting across the sand to join him. Drake was second-in-command. It seemed the nurses were worth quite a welcome. Unfortunately, it wasn't to be any more civil than they were used to from men in officers' uniform.

'Yes, come on ladies,' Drake barked with Fischer's approval. 'We don't want to stand around in the sun all day, do we?'

'Oh dear,' muttered a nurse named Yvonne. 'It appears we're still in the army after all.' She was a small, cheerful girl with a ready quip to make the others laugh. Those who heard her chuckled now and Fischer's frown deepened.

'Quickly, quickly,' he snapped, and made some comment under his breath to Drake, who nodded sombrely.

The nurses shuffled into some sort of a marching column. It all seemed so silly, but there was little else they could do. Their belongings were strewn about the beach above the high-water mark to be collected by some enlisted men later.

Matron Lambert arrived late, puffing from having to walk on the sand. She stopped abruptly, surveyed the scene with dismay, then came to stand tight-lipped at the head of the column. A few of the nurses near her looked askance, and she ignored them. The piper made some experimental noises on his bagpipes as he prepared to play. The odd peeps and squawks made some of the women giggle.

Colonel Fischer had apparently already given up on getting any real soldiering out of these girls. Still, he wasn't going to let them off easily. Gruffly, he gave the order to start marching and barked at the piper to play. When it came to proper marching, everyone had done some basic training back in Australia, but it had long been forgotten. At the first warbling notes of the bagpipes, the nurses exchanged funny looks, then all began moving at once in a most unsoldierly fashion that caused more laughter.

Fischer glared over his shoulder. Meeting Matron's angry gaze, he kept quiet.

The fun had gone out of it by the time the nurses had covered the two miles to the hospital. The summer sun was hot on their backs, made worse by the heavy cloth of their uniforms. Wounded soldiers cheered as they arrived and several dogs barked. The women were too exhausted to offer anything but weak smiles in return.

'Welcome to the Third Australian General Hospital,' Colonel Fischer announced, making them linger in formation a moment longer. Their worn expressions seemed to satisfy him. 'Matron Lambert is familiar with everything here already. I will leave you in her capable hands.' He flipped a salute at them and marched away. Lieutenant Colonel Drake hurried after him.

***

'There's no beds! Not even a mattress,' Julia exclaimed, staring around the inside of their cramped tent. The canvas smelled of years of exposure to the elements, a smoky and unpleasant odour. Their tent was one of a type for housing two occupants. Others held four, but Rose and Julia had chosen to continue bunking with just each other, despite the lack of space, each being long comfortable with the other's habits by now.

'Did you see those patients?' Rose said angrily. 'They haven't been given any shelter at all. They're expected just to lie out on the open ground. We must get out and do something.'

'Matron Lambert has been here a day longer than us, don't forget,' Julia told her mildly. 'I'm sure things wouldn't be like this if she had any choice.' She dropped her valise beside a rolled-up blanket. Rose took the other side of the tent and threw her bags down.

'Exactly, I doubt whether those two fools who marched us from the beach will be giving her any choice. Bagpipes, for God's sake. Who does he think we are, the Coldstream Guards?'

'Look, we have to think of those poor boys who have been hurt, not waste our energies on anyone else.'

Hearing Julia's calm acceptance, Rose sighed, 'You always look on the bright side of things, Julia. I wish I could do that.'

Julia pulled a face. 'And I wish I knew how to sleep on the ground! To think I used to complain about the narrowness of my bunk on the *Gascon*.' She gestured helplessly at the dirt floor and stopped in surprise. 'My God, what's that?'

The two of them bent and peered at the ground. A centipede over four inches long was worming its way through the soil, having emerged from under Julia's baggage. Rose quickly stamped on it and they both recoiled in horror.

'Ugh,' she said, feeling the fat body crush under her shoe. 'How are we expected to get any sleep knowing that those things are crawling into our blankets with us?'

'They'll have beds for us shortly, don't you think?' Julia had suddenly lost her positive outlook.

'I wouldn't bet on this army doing anything in a hurry.' Rose was hobbling through the tent flaps to scrape the remains of the insect off her sole.

She was right to be doubtful. Later that morning, at a meeting of all the nurses, Matron Lambert revealed that all their equipment was still coming from England and wasn't expected for at least another ten days. Until then, it was a matter of making do.

'I'm afraid we have another shipload of wounded arriving tonight,' she added, bringing groans of frustration from many of them. 'All the available fresh water is to be used on the patients and even then, you must be extremely frugal. Water is in *very* short supply. Colonel Fischer has promised to do something about that as soon as he can.' This brought more groans and few derisive laughs. The commanding officer's reputation was well established already.

Matron offered them half a smile. 'Do your best.'

***

All the good intentions in the world couldn't have prepared the nurses for their work that night.

A hospital ship arrived with over four hundred casualties, many of them badly wounded during fresh landings at Suvla Bay by the British Army. In the dark, a grim procession of oil lamps marked the progress of ambulances, horse-drawn carriages and stretcher-bearers on foot—all carrying the stricken soldiers from the makeshift harbour to the hospital. Many didn't make this last part of the journey, their bodies left beside the track to be collected later. There was little point in carrying a dead man the whole way, when survivors were still waiting back at the ship.

At the hospital site itself there wasn't much more hope of help or comfort. Surgeons operated in crowded tents with minimal supplies, trying to squeeze the last use out of everything they had. Outside, the nurses tended the wounded who still had to lie in the open. Straight away the women had resorted to ripping up their own spare clothes for makeshift bandages. Men who died had their dressings removed, washed in the ocean and used again. There was not enough fresh water to boil them properly.

Again, it was Rose's job to identify which of the wounded needed the earliest attention. Carrying an oil lamp, she walked up and down the long lines of men on the ground. When she found somebody had died, she removed part of their clothing and covered the corpse's face so that other medical staff wouldn't waste any time on them. The stars glittering gaily in an ink-black sky made a mockery of the misery gathered below in neat, bleeding rows. A breeze helped those who were working hard, while it chilled the wounded. Some soldiers softly cried or groaned with their pain. The harshest sound came from the motorised ambulances grinding through the sand to deliver the latest batch of wounded from the ship. Horses pulling the carriages snuffled faintly now and again, as if aware of the tragic moment, while their harnesses jingled. With the animals, the hospital staff and the many wounded men, there was never enough water to drink, so everyone was thirsty.

Worse than the hard decking of the *Gascon* ever did, the rough ground was taking its toll on Rose's knees. Sharp stones cut through the material of her skirt and she was sure they were bleeding, but didn't bother checking such a trivial injury. At one point as she sank to the ground, wincing, and she allowed herself a moment to recover before examining the man in front of her. He was young—too young—and curled tight in a foetal position, clutching at his stomach. Nothing she could do coaxed him to straighten out and let her see. She saw another nurse passing behind her.

'Grace, would you please help?'

The two of them managed to pull his knees away and while Grace clamped them down with her own weight and held the lamp, Rose cut away the youth's sodden shirt and saw a bullet hole below his ribs. He whimpered at her gently probing fingers.

'A stomach wound?' Grace asked in a whisper.

'I'm not sure,' Rose frowned. 'It might have just missed. Is there a doctor nearby?'

'I'll find one.'

Grace disappeared into the gloom, leaving her with this young soldier closing up like flower. She couldn't prevent it. Grace returned in minutes with a medical officer following. The nurses rearranged themselves to lever the boy's legs down once more and the doctor pushed himself close against Rose to see properly in the poor light of the lamp. Something about the officer struck her as familiar and when he spoke, she recognised him. Rose wasn't sure whether she wanted to say anything.

'Yes, I'd say this poor devil has had his stomach wall ruptured,' the doctor said heavily. 'You were wise to ask.'

'I'll mark him as a serious case, then,' she said, keeping her voice neutral. It didn't work. The doctor lifted the lamp higher and stared into her face.

'Rose? Rose Preston? Is that you?'

'Hello, Doctor Cohen. Yes, it's me.'

'Goodness, how good to see you again...' he faltered, hearing how inappropriate it sounded under the circumstances. 'Well, you know what I mean. How long have you been here?'

His face was drawn and pale with weariness, dark shadows over his cheekbones from lack of sleep. There was still a sparkle of boyish charm in his eyes.

'We arrived this morning,' she said.

'Among those girls who marched from the beach? I didn't see it myself, but

I'm appalled that–'

'Please, Doctor.' She interrupted him. 'We don't have the time for chat.'

'No, of course not.' He looked embarrassed. 'It's just such a pleasant surprise to see you. We must get together...' He stood abruptly, almost knocking Grace aside, and spoke in a rush. 'Anyway, I'd better carry on. Well done with this man. We'll get to him as soon as we can.'

'Yes, I know you will,' Rose frowned. He was already striding away.

'An old friend of yours?' Grace asked, busying herself with the wound.

'He likes to think so.'

'Don't complain too quickly. A *male* friend among the doctors might come in handy.'

They exchanged a knowing look over the dying boy.

***

The next day, tents began to arrive. Men erected them over the wounded where they lay, although many still remained in the open or, at best, were shaded by staying close to the white canvas walls. At least the weather remained kind with a strong breeze that kept the flies and heat at bay, while it proved a bit of a hindrance in erecting the tents. Water was still a severe problem. By midday, Rose had drunk only a cup since the night before. Oddly, at the noon meal, a mug of tea was provided. It seemed the army could never make enough water available for drinking, yet managed to supply endless cups of tea. The heat in the brew stopped Rose from gulping it down. She ran each drop over her dry lips, before swallowing.

She caught glimpses of Mark Cohen during the day, carefully keeping her distance, although she still didn't understand exactly why. The extra tents made it easy to avoid anyone as they blossomed in their hundreds like huge dirty mushrooms across the landscape.

After a lunch of hard biscuits, tinned meat and the cup of tea, she went towards a section of the wounded who had been in the sun too long. She wanted to check on them and perhaps wipe them down with a damp rag soaked in sea water. Anything to ease their suffering.

Matron Lambert stopped her. She looked as exhausted as everyone else, her white headband stained dark by sweat, dust and blood on her face. The once-immaculate uniform was a mess.

'I want you to get some rest, Rose.' Her voice was husky. 'Go to your tent and lie down.'

Rose was taken aback. It sounded like she was in trouble. At the same time, she felt a stab of guilt because the idea sounded so attractive. 'We're all tired,' she said softly with a meaningful look at Matron's own clothing. 'There's still work to do.'

'More than you think. Another boat arrives tonight with about the same number of wounded. I want you on duty when it docks. I'm insisting some of us get rest now or we'll all drop in exhaustion together. I know it's hard to ignore the suffering of these poor boys, but others are coming and we can't help them if we're dead on our feet.'

While it made sense, Rose was reluctant, especially knowing that Matron Lambert wasn't about to give herself a break. 'I want to check on some of the men first, then I'll see how I feel.'

'I'm not asking your *opinion* on this, Rose,' Matron almost snapped. They could hear the grating of shovels from the cemetery close by. It was nothing more than an allotted square of land where it had been decided to bury any dead. Already, Colonel Fischer had ordered the area tripled in size.

Matron visibly sagged. She had no energy for arguing after needing to confront Fischer and his second-in-command, Drake, almost constantly. 'Rose, we are going to need your youth and strength more as the days go by,' she said wearily. 'Some of our sisters never imagined they would be working under these sorts of conditions. Many of them are more than twice your age. Gwen Hampshire would have retired next month, if it weren't for this war.' She paused with a trace of a smile, probably thinking of her own position had the war not come. 'I need you to rest while the older women can carry on, because later in the week you'll be carrying more of the burden. We need to think ahead and plan.'

Rose held up her hand in defeat. 'All right, I'll sleep for a few hours.' She explained about the men she was going to check and the matron offered to do it. Then with the promise of rest making her feet drag in anticipation, Rose headed for her tent.

***

It had collapsed. Rose stood helpless in front of the heap of canvas and suddenly felt like crying. She hated that, too. But exhaustion, thirst and hunger were weakening her resolve.

'Is this your place?' a voice asked behind her.

She took a moment to compose herself and turned around. Mark Cohen stood watching her. The sunshine wasn't any kinder to his appearance than the lamplight had been. There were still black rings under his eyes and the wind made his fair hair appear thin.

'What's left of it,' she said dully. 'I'm supposed to be getting some rest. Matron Lambert ordered me to.'

He looked around. Several of the nurses' tents had fallen. One still held an occupant, the sleeping form oblivious of the canvas piled over her like a shroud.

'Do you think she'll be all right?' He almost smiled.

'That's Joanne,' Rose said absently. To have sleep stolen away like this felt so unfair, now that she was expecting it. 'She's tough as nails and won't appreciate being woken.'

'I'll tell you what.' He moved closer. His uniform was faded and had some permanent, ugly marks. 'Come to the officers' mess and have a cup of tea. On the way, I'll find some men to fix your tent. It won't take long.' Seeing her hesitate, he added, 'Really, by the time you've had some tea, the tent will be like new. You can get some rest.'

Rose had a bad feeling about this. To the nurses, only half in jest, the male officers were as much the enemy as the Turks. She didn't like the idea of going anywhere near their Mess, which was supposed to be out-of-bounds to her anyway. Despite herself, the image of a huge mug of tea appealed to her and she nodded. 'Thank you, that's very kind, Doctor Cohen. As long as you're sure someone can repair my tent quickly. Otherwise I'd better just crawl into someone else's.'

'It's as good as done.' He offered his arm, then quickly dropped it again with an apologetic look, and gestured instead. 'This way, then.'

They walked side-by-side through the growing camp. No one took any notice of just another doctor and nurse going about their business. Rose worried that Matron Lambert might see them and she'd have to explain. True to his word, Mark stopped at a party of men digging a latrine and ordered two of them to go and re-erect the nurses' tents immediately. They seemed glad of an excuse to escape the shovelling.

The officers' mess was one of the largest tents, the same size used for the operating theatres, and seemed somehow luxurious compared with what Rose and her companions slept in, although it was still just a tent after all. Their own nurses' mess was only half as big and had no tables or chairs, only a collection of packing crates for anyone who wanted to sit. There weren't enough for everyone of course, so most of the women sat on the ground to eat.

The mess here had two long tables covered in white cloths and a line of matching chairs down each side. In one corner, a third trestle carried a tall urn of boiling water surrounded by teapots, a selection of tin mugs and bowls of sugar. A plate was piled high with biscuits.

With lunch recently finished, most of the officers had returned to their tasks, so there were less than half a dozen men still around. Rose's entrance seemed to cause both irritation and suspicion, but with Mark there nobody challenged her.

'No milk, I'm afraid,' he said as a joke, pulling out a chair for her right at the end of the table, well away from the others.

'Of course,' she answered. With that urn full of water she could have offered a drink to perhaps fifty men during the night. And the tablecloths would have provided countless bandages. Mark had gone for the teas. Only one thing stopped her walking straight back out in disgust. She needed that drink, even if it was tea.

He returned and immediately her plan to swallow the tea and leave was thwarted. It was too hot. She sat there and sipped as fast as she dared without burning herself. Neither of them spoke at first, while around them the canvas creaked and rippled in the wind. Finally, Mark tried to make conversation.

'I heard you were on a hospital ship?'

'The *Gascon*.' She nodded. 'Since the first day of the landings.'

'That's tough luck.'

She looked at him over the rim of her mug. 'No, that's what I came here to do.'

'Well, of course.' He shrugged. 'They sent me to the Luna Park Hospital at first. I was hoping to see you again in Cairo. But, as you said, our paths didn't seem to cross. It *is* a big place after all.'

Rose needed a second to remember their last conversation. It seemed such a long time ago.

'Yes, and we were all so busy,' she murmured into her tea.

'It can be quite a gay place—Cairo, I mean. If you know where to go.'

'We weren't allowed to go far without being chaperoned, and that didn't appeal to me.'

'I could have taken you.' He tried an encouraging smile.

'You could have *asked*.'

He accepted her rebuff with a sigh. 'You're not very pleased about things, are you?'

She stared at him. 'Do you know we have nothing like this?'

'Like what?' He looked confused, but something in his eyes told her that he knew exactly what she was talking about.

'This mess—the tent. The *tablecloth*.' Her voice turned harsh. 'How much water sits in that urn all day? We've got nothing like this and we wouldn't keep it if we did.'

'Steady on,' Mark hushed her with a hand. 'We've been here a bit longer, that's all. I'm sure the nurses' facilities will be fully equipped soon.'

‘I’m not talking about *facilities,*’ she almost hissed. ‘I’m talking about drinking water and bandages for the wounded. My God, we’ve torn up most of our own clothing.’ He looked lost for an answer and she went on, ‘Besides, what’s stopping Colonel Fischer from offering us the use of this mess?’

‘I’ll admit the colonel makes no secret of the fact he isn’t... pleased with having women in his charge. He’s an old Boer War soldier and has different ideas—’

‘The colonel’s a prat!’ Rose said. She gulped down the last of her tea and slammed her mug on the table. It had burned her throat. Some of the other officers looked their way. One seemed on the brink of coming over.

‘Wait,’ he put his hand on her arm. ‘You won’t help matters by putting on a scene here.’ Rose’s eyes widened in anger. ‘Please, calm down a little,’ he said.

She sat back in the chair and pulled her arm away.

Mark said quietly, ‘These are the only tablecloths we still have, I believe. And the urn is expected to last the entire day between all the officers and isn’t refilled.’

‘One biscuit each?’ Rose asked primly.

‘Rose, don’t be like that. It’s not my fault.’

It occurred to her that she hadn't invited him to use her first name. She thought about reprimanding him, and stood up instead.

'My tent will be repaired. I must go back and get some rest.'

'I'll walk with you.'

'No, please don't. I'd prefer to walk back alone. Thank you for your help and the tea.' She couldn't keep the bite out of her voice.

Mark stood as well. 'If there's anything else I can do to help, don't hesitate to ask.'

Again she was tempted to be curt, then recalled Grace's comment about having male friends in the right places. It was true he might come in handy not just for herself, but her companions as well. So it would be foolish to alienate him too much.

'Thank you, I'll keep that in mind.' She gave him a tight smile.

'You know, I wish we'd met in better circumstances. Even spending some time together in Cairo.'

'We missed the chance. These are difficult times,' she agreed reluctantly.

Mark stood at the entrance to the mess and watched Rose wind her way through the tents until she disappeared. He felt someone behind him and turned to find one of the other officers.

'A very pretty girl, Cohen,' he said with a false smile. 'Very pretty indeed. I doubt that excludes her from the rules. I wouldn't bring her back here again, if I were you. The colonel will have a fit, if he finds out.'

'Then don't tell him,' Mark said sharply, turning his back on him.

***

The tent had been put back up and Rose found Julia inside. She'd only just arrived because she wasn't yet asleep. She said drowsily, 'Hello, Rose. Thank God our tent didn't blow down. Lots of others have.'

'Yes, thank God.' Rose didn't bother explaining. 'Did Matron Lambert send you to rest?'

'Most emphatically, and I'm not complaining. She's sending someone to wake us when the new wounded start arriving.' Julia's speech got slower as she fell asleep with her last word.

Rose didn't disturb her further. She inspected the ground briefly for centipedes, spread her single blanket, and without undressing, lay down, using her bag as a pillow. She expected to find herself staring at the canvas above, her mind too consumed by anger and frustrations. She fell into a deep and dreamless sleep within a minute.

***

Mark knew it was none of his business, but his curiosity about what might be possible took him to the hospital's adjutant, Major Miller.

Rather than commandeer a tent, Miller had built a shelter for himself and his desk by stacking empty crates in a large square and roofing it with pieces of timber and iron. It looked unstable, piled high enough for room to stand. The structure squeaked and groaned alarmingly with the wind, and sand rattled against the wood.

The major was a short, busy man with a bristling moustache. A lifetime in the army had kept him trim and muscled. 'No one's having a very good time here, Doctor Cohen,' he said. 'If we transferred everyone who preferred to work in Cairo back there, there'd be nobody left on this bloody island.'

'I realise that, and I'm not asking for my own benefit,' Mark said. 'It's just that without any real facilities I'm being wasted here. We're simply patching up the worst cases and sending them on to Cairo anyway. Anyone can do that. The real work of operating on these men and giving them a chance to recover fully needs to be done in a proper theatre, and that's where I should be working. I'm a surgeon. I should go back to Cairo even if it were just until better equipment is available here.'

'That might be so,' Miller said carefully. 'I can discuss it with Colonel Fischer, but I doubt he'll do anything. I won't make any promises.'

'I think it's worth considering. It might save lives.'

'I *understand* you, Doctor.' Miller held up an impatient hand and glanced at the paperwork waiting on his desk.

'There's something else.' Mark knew he was taking a risk. 'One of the nurses here has proved to be an excellent assistant. She's a VAD actually. I'd like to take her with me.'

Now Miller sprawled back in his chair. 'That makes things a little different,

Captain. Not to mention a bit obvious, don't you think?'

'You're assuming too much, Major Miller.'

'Perhaps. Maybe I've just been in this army too long. I get suspicious about everything.' Miller held his gaze a moment. 'What's her name? I'll see what I can do.'

'Rose Preston. She's a VAD in Matron Lambert's charge.'

Miller wrote this down on a scrap of paper. 'All right, we'll see,' he said by way of a dismissal. When Mark had thanked him and was halfway out the door, Miller called out. 'Do you drink scotch, Captain Cohen?'

'Yes, I'll admit I like a good single malt.'

'So do I, Doctor. And I drink a *lot* of it.'

Mark got the message and deliberately echoed Miller's words. 'All right, we'll see.'

***

That evening, many of the wounded died as they lay on the ground around the hospital, waiting to be seen by the doctors. The British invasion at Suvla Bay had met even fiercer resistance from the defenders and most of the casualties were gunshot wounds from extra machine guns the Turks had brought in during the day. Many Australians were among the injured too. The Anzac troops were mounting diversionary attacks to try and draw the Turks back from Suvla again.

At least more tents had arrived and were erected over the men where they lay, and bandages had come from Cairo. However, even with the doctors working furiously, the backlog of patients grew and men were dying.

By early morning, Rose was utterly exhausted, still doing rounds and comforting as many men as she could with her own face blank and feet that felt impossibly leaden. A dull roar sounded in her head all the time and she didn't dare close her eyes for a second. She was pulled up abruptly by Sister Grace, who didn't look in any better condition. Rose understood her own appearance had to be much the same.

'Nellie's just told me one of the wounded is asking for you,' Grace explained wearily. 'Jonathon White. Do you know him?'

Rose couldn't have imagined herself feeling worse, but the blood drained from her face. 'Yes, we write,' she said, suddenly hoarse. 'Where is he?'

'One of the last to arrive, over there. He hasn't been given a tent yet.'

'Thanks, Grace. I'll go and see him now.'

'Do you want me to come with you?'

'No, that's not necessary. Thank you all the same.'

As she walked across Rose felt a coldness grip her heart. She'd only met Jonathon the once and they'd exchanged half a dozen letters, but his face and voice had stayed with her, even though she'd met hundreds of young men since. Perhaps it had been his letters, although she wrote to many others too. Maybe it was because he'd come looking for her personally while being fit and healthy, not shattered by a bullet or shellfire.

She worried about what he looked like, where had he'd been wounded, and how badly. Coming off the ship last, he might have been delayed until the more serious cases reached the hospital. That made sense, but Rose didn't dare allow herself to think so optimistically. The opposite might be true, that he'd been injured so terribly they hadn't expected him to survive moving across the island. So the sight of him now was going to be dreadful. She might not even recognise him.

She did, relief flooding through her at the first sight of him. The men on either side were asleep or unconscious, both with head wounds. Jonathon was lying on his back, eyes closed beneath the brim of his cap, with a cigarette between his fingers. A wide bandage spread across his chest, the bright red splash beside his right shoulder showing the exact position of his wound. Another dressing covered his right thigh. Rose knelt down quietly beside him.

'Jonathon? It's Rose Preston.'

His eyes flicked open immediately. 'Hello,' he said, trying to sit up. 'I asked if you were around, but didn't hold out much hope. I thought you might be a bit busy too.'

Rose pushed him back gently and he let her. 'Well, we are,' she said, confident now that he wasn't badly hurt. 'With the likes of *you*. Has someone had a look?'

'Not since I got on the ship. I can nearly look after myself.'

'That's what everyone says. You'd better let me see, so you will have to sit up after all.'

She helped him get his shirt off, then carefully unwound the bandage from his chest. The bullet had entered under his armpit and come out cleanly through the pectoral muscle. The blackened, dried blood around the wound looked worse than it was. He saw her glance at his leg and reach for the dressing there. He gently grabbed her wrist.

'Bayonet wound, and it's a cut, not a stab. It isn't too bad.'

'So now you're a doctor?'

'No, but there's other blokes worse off. It can wait.'

'Let me be the judge of that, Private White.'

He grinned weakly at her tone. 'It's Corporal White, I'll have you know. My damned tailor hasn't sewn on the stripes.'

Unimpressed, she said, 'Wait here while I get some water.'

She came back a minute later with a bucket and a cloth.

'It's sea water and it's going to sting quite a bit,' she told him, as he cupped his hand for a drink. 'I'll get you a drink soon.'

He didn't make a sound as she washed the wound, although she noticed him gritting his teeth tightly. Fearing the worst, she asked, 'How is your friend, Robert? Was he in the attacks too?'

'He carried me back, whingeing about it all the way. God knows how much trouble he'll get into without me to look after him. He's all right for the moment. I got your last letter the same day I was bowled over, by the way. Here, see? That's how I knew to ask for you.' With one hand he opened the flap of the shirt pocket beside him and pulled out a wad of paper. Rose was touched to see all her letters together.

'I'm sure Robert will cope,' she murmured.

She dressed his wound with the same bandage and checked the cut on his thigh. He was right. It was a long, shallow wound that would heal quickly. Rose cleaned this too, and again replaced the old bandage. Last, she put his shirt back on.

He stayed sitting up, smoking as he watched her work on the men beside him. Both had suffered shrapnel wounds, their heads and faces peppered with it. One man had lost an eye.

When she finished, Rose stood at Jonathon's feet, unaware of swaying slightly as she looked down on him.

'That's all I can do for the moment. You'll get a tent soon before it gets too hot, with any luck.'

'Will you come back to see me?' He gave her a crooked smile.

'When I get a chance, but I won't have many. I have to sleep first. And there'll be another boat tonight.'

'Sleep...' he said softly. 'That's all I'm going to do. It's going to be wonderful, sleeping without having to worry about what might happen while you do.'

'I can imagine.'

'You have the nicest smile,' he surprised her, then changed the subject. 'How will you find me?' He gestured at the hundreds of tents all around.

'Don't worry. You're not going anywhere. They'll pitch the tent right over the top of you. I'll find you.'

'I'll look forward to it.' He gave her a small wave. 'Thanks for everything.'

Rose walked for a few minutes before she remembered the drink she'd promised him. Rather than go back and spoil a moment she thought they'd shared, she stopped another nurse and asked her take some water to Jonathon straight away.

***

The British attack subsided into a stalemate like the rest of the battles along the Gallipoli Peninsula and the Anzac offensives were scaled back. The war in this part of the world returned to its steady attrition of casualties on both sides, the men in the trenches fighting daily with little in mind but killing as many of the enemy as they could.

With the number of daily wounded reduced to a manageable rate, the hospitals had some chance of consolidating and recovering from the flood of men they'd experienced during the first weeks of August 1915. The nurses' baptism of fire close to the fighting had been sudden and alarming, but they'd coped with the lack of equipment and supplies, and all with so little rest. Even when the workload eased, their personal living conditions hardly changed. The cycle of working, eating poor rations and collapsing into sleep never altered. Having severely restricted access to fresh water, as always, was a constant privation to the wounded and nurses alike. None of the women had bathed since arriving and their clothes were washed in sea water, so they were stiff and itching. The promised beds never arrived. Every day, a tent blew down and the owner's meagre belongings were scattered across the landscape. It seemed that nothing could be done to protect the tents from the unceasing wind.

And at any time there were nearly a thousand injured soldiers to care for.

Rose could see Jonathon once a day without impinging on her other duties. She enjoyed his company. Their contact until now had hardly been cause for them to call each other a friend, but she liked his quick smile and polite manner. No matter what they talked about, he took her away from their grim surroundings. Even discussing the war and what she'd done during the night was like a release that helped her shake off the horror of some of the things she'd seen. She often felt guilty about the extra time she offered him and warned Jonathon early on that there could be no favours. He was mildly offended and chided her with a smile.

One morning, ten days after he arrived, he emerged from his tent as Rose approached up the laneway.

'Good morning,' she said. The dullness of exhaustion was ever-present in her voice now and she had lost more weight too. These things were being accepted as normal and on average, Rose was in better shape than most, as Matron Lambert had predicted. 'Are you all right?'

'Fit as a bull,' he said.

'Well, a wounded bull.' She nodded at his right arm in its dirty sling. The chest bandages were hidden by his shirt. 'Where are you going?' She guessed the latrines and wondered if he'd ask for help.

'With you,' he announced firmly.

'What?'

'I'm bloody sick of lying around in this tent all day. I can do something useful with my good arm. Take me with you.'

Rose was nonplussed, although the idea wasn't unusual. Every soldier who recovered sufficiently to help out was soon drafted into work. But she couldn't expect Jonathon to tag along behind her all day.

'You wouldn't be able to keep up,' she said, trying to imagine it. 'Besides, you need to stay off that leg if you want it to heal quickly.'

'It goes stiff when I don't use it,' he replied stubbornly. 'I'd rather be walking around.'

She sighed. 'Come on, then. I'll find you something to do. You won't be with me all the time.'

Rose slowed her pace so Jonathon could stay close, dodging through the throng of soldiers and medical staff as they moved between the tents.

'Where are we going?' he asked her, gladly.

'The new wounded last night, about thirty of them. Matron Lambert asked me to check their dressings and get them some water—you can do that. They arrived on a luxury yacht, did you hear? Everyone's been pulled in to help get the casualties off the peninsula.'

They arrived at the main area of the hospital and Rose headed for the tents they now used exclusively for new arrivals. As she was about to crouch past the first opening, she noticed a line of a dozen corpses on the ground behind, awaiting a burial party. Blankets had been used to cover their upper bodies. The wind had struck again, and some of the faces were exposed.

'Would you fix those?' Rose asked Jonathon gently. He nodded and left her. She went into the tent and quickly examined three men, all of them with bullet wounds that weren't life-threatening. The smell was awful, but she was used to that. When she came back out, Rose saw Jonathon standing absolutely still by one of the corpses.

She went over, and he spoke first.

'It's Nick Streeth,' he said flatly. 'The sergeant from my section. Shot in the head, by the looks of it.'

Rose didn't know what to say. She watched as he checked each corpse in turn, carefully lifting the makeshift shrouds to see the faces and making sure the wind wouldn't remove any again. He came back to her with an odd expression, a mixture of relief and sadness.

'Must have been a sniper,' he said. 'None of the other blokes are from my lot.

It doesn't look like they were in any attack.'

'I'm sorry for your friend,' Rose said.

'Yeah, well... he should have kept his stupid head down.' Jonathon tried to shrug it away.

She understood his callousness. 'We've got work to do,' she told him quietly, tugging at his sleeve. 'Someone else will take care of him. You can't help here with only one hand.'

She kept him busy all day carrying buckets of sea water from storage tanks to wherever she was working. It was still used for rinsing bandages, dressings and most of the initial cleaning of the filth around wounds. They only stopped for lunch, which was the usual mug of tea and a few biscuits each, which they ate out of desperation.

Jonathon hadn't realised how much his own injuries had weakened him and he was grateful after many long hours to limp back to his tent and let Rose ease him down onto his blanket. Groaning with the relief, he looked up at her.

Against the darkening sky outside, he couldn't see her face.

'Come and get me tomorrow?' he asked.

'Haven't you learned your lesson?'

'I'm happier doing something. Helping you.'

'I'll come and see you in the morning and you can make up your mind then.'

She lingered for an instant, an odd feeling in her mind. Then she turned and left the tent. Behind her, she heard Jonathon groan again.

***

She found Julia sitting on a packing crate in their tent. An oil lamp was propped high on another, and she twisted her head around to check herself in a small mirror that she was holding in one hand.

'Thank goodness you're back,' she said, brandishing a pair of scissors at Rose. 'You can do this for me instead.'

'What?' Rose asked. Most of the women were constantly repairing their uniforms, especially after ripping spare garments into bandages on the first day.

'My hair,' Julia said firmly. 'I'm going to cut it all off.'

'Are you mad? It will take years to grow back that long.'

Julia pulled a face. 'This morning I woke with a centipede tangled in my hair, and it only got worse as I tried to pull it out. I nearly died.'

'I'm sorry,' Rose told her, meaning she had already left and hadn't been close enough to help.

'It's not your fault. If it's not insects, it's grass seeds or burrs and God knows what else. This isn't hair anyway,' Julia flicked it with her free hand. 'It's a horse's tail. I haven't washed it for a month.'

Rose couldn't agree more. Her own hair was a mess, but the veil concealed everything. Even so, every day she needed to spend more time brushing out the knots, and as Julia said, all sorts of foreign things. 'I wouldn't have the first clue how to give you a decent haircut,' she admitted.

'Who cares, as long as it's short.'

'Are you sure?' Rose was terrified it would look awful afterwards. 'Really, someone else must have a better idea than me.'

'No, let's do it now, while we have the chance. I trust you.' Julia held the scissors out.

'You're mad,' Rose decided. 'Let's move outside. Maybe one of the other girls will hold the lamp better.'

It caused quite a commotion, with several of the nurses gathering around to watch and offer unhelpful advice that made them all laugh. Everyone stood close to stop the lamp flickering. Rose squinted in the bad light, at first feeling appalled at the long tresses dropping to the ground and whipped away by the wind to be lost forever. In the end she did a surprisingly good job, achieving a short and boyish cut. Running her fingers through Julia's remaining hair, Rose felt a flash of envy. Even before she'd finished, two other nurses were lining up for the same treatment. And although she was tired, she obliged, buoyed by the novelty and her audience's good spirits. Finally, she sat on the crate herself and held the scissors high.

'My turn,' she called with a laugh. 'I don't care who does it.'

It was Grace who took the challenge, frowning with concentration while the others encouraged her. When she announced that it was done, Rose was already feeling quite strange. The sensation of having short hair was so unfamiliar. The joy of having no knots or tangles to contend with more than made up for it.

'It looks fine,' Julia told her.

'Liar. You can't see a damned thing,' Rose replied. Grace was already having a go at someone else and had commandeered the lamp again.

'No, really. It suits you.'

'You're just saying that—'

'Miss Preston, can I have a word with you?' It was Matron Lambert standing apart from the other women.

Rose raised an eyebrow at Julia before walking over.

'Good evening, Matron.'

Matron nodded and led her even further away into the shadows.

'I must say I'm disappointed in you, Rose,' she said curtly. 'After our discussion last week, when I explained to you that we'd need your strength more as the days went by.'

Rose was surprised. It seemed such a trivial thing, staying up and cutting the girls' hair. She waved towards her tent. 'I'll be retiring soon, Matron. I've had some good sleep over the past few nights.'

'I'm not talking about getting your rest, Rose. I mean this transfer back to Cairo.' She brandished a piece of paper.

Rose was stunned. 'Why are you transferring me? What have I done wrong?'

'Don't be ridiculous, girl! I'm not transferring you anywhere. I *know* you've requested it yourself. Did you think by going behind my back to Major Miller that I wouldn't find out?'

As always, Rose's anger was quick to rise. 'I have no idea what you're talking about. What do you mean?'

'You have *asked* for a transfer back to Cairo.'

'I have done *no* such thing.'

The matron paused and noticed the other girls looking their way. She asked more calmly, 'Then where has this come from? Do you have relatives back there? Someone who might be requesting on your behalf?'

'Not that I know of...' A suspicion came to Rose. It didn't dispel her anger, but at least it turned it in another direction. 'Matron, can you make it go away? Tear the damned thing up?'

While Matron Lambert was relieved, she tried to make herself sound disapproving. 'Tearing up official documents is hardly the correct procedure for making things go away, Rose. I can simply refuse to release you, if you're sure that's what you want. I take it nobody will pursue the matter hard, if you yourself are unwilling to leave?'

'Of course it's what I want,' she gestured back at the others. One of the nurses was still halfway through her haircut with Grace poised beside her, scissors in hand. 'I want to stay here with Julia and the rest—and yourself, of course,' she added hastily. 'This is where the important work's being done.'

'All right, I hear you. This must have been some sort of mistake.' There was no reply and she went on, 'Or whatever. The request is denied and I'll see to it.

Your hair looks very nice, by the way.'

'Thank you. Good night, Matron.'

'Good night, Rose.'

Rose waited until the matron headed for her own tent, then she rounded on her heel and stalked back to the others.

'Is everything all right?' Grace asked carefully for them all.

'It's fine now, thank you.' She forced a smile to reassure them. 'I'm just going to see someone. I won't be long.'

Do you want company?' Julia called.

'No, I'll be back quite soon.' Rose walked away without bothering to replace her veil.

The officers' mess was brightly lit, an oasis of light surrounded by the dim, now empty tents that served as offices for various regimental departments. A hubbub of noise came out, as if it were a bar, and indeed the men were serving themselves liquor, although whether they were paying for it or sharing each other's private supplies Rose couldn't tell. She stood right in the entrance waiting for someone to notice. It didn't take long. An officer came over, smiling solicitously, his concern not reaching his eyes.

He was about Rose's age. 'Young lady,' he said. 'I'm afraid you can't come in here. This is a gentlemen's mess and—'

Rose cut him off after a pointed look at his lieutenant's tab. 'We are equal in rank and you will address me accordingly, sir,' she rasped. 'You may call me Sister.' Which, with her VAD status wasn't true. She was gambling that he didn't know that.

He looked slightly shocked and took a step back. He said tightly, 'I'm sorry, Sister. Is there something I can do for you?'

'I'm looking for Doctor Mark Cohen. I need to speak with him immediately. Is he here? He's a captain.'

'Captain Cohen... Captain Mark Cohen,' he repeated vaguely. Rose suspected the delay was deliberate. 'I'll have to ask. Please wait *here*.' It was a less-than subtle reminder that she wasn't allowed inside.

'Don't worry,' she snapped. 'I have no desire at all to follow you.'

From her position, Rose couldn't see the entire mess, but it wasn't large enough to hide Mark's presence completely. It seemed that the lieutenant really didn't know Mark, however, because he went and whispered in the ear of an officer seated nearby. He in turn stood for a moment, looked around and shook his head, while others she could see were passing comments and glancing her way, many with almost lewd smiles. She glared at anyone who dared meet her eye. Then the young lieutenant returned.

'He's not here, Sister. Someone has suggested the second operating theatre. He may be working late.'

'Thank you,' Rose nodded once. 'I'll let you return to your *party*.' She turned and left.

Behind her, the lieutenant called out in an affronted tone, 'It's not a party. We're entitled to some relaxation, don't you think?'

Rose wasn't going to bother answering, then something changed her mind. 'And so are we, *don't you think*?' she mimicked him, then went on before he could reply. 'But no, you don't, according to your *gentlemen's* rules. Enjoy your fine officers' mess. Good night, lieutenant.'

She found the operating theatre easily enough in the dark. The canvas glowed with lamplight from inside and silhouettes moved across it. No one else was close. Rose had little idea what she wanted to do or say to Mark, and the idea that he was in the middle of a surgical procedure was the last thing she expected, so she baulked near the entrance. Then there was a glowing cigarette and a voice next to her.

'Can I help you?'

'Doctor Cohen?' Rose recognised him. 'It's Rose Preston. I need to speak to you.' Her anger was quickly rekindling and her chest felt tight.

'Rose? How nice to see you.' He emerged from the shadows. He still had a white gown over his uniform. Its stains looked black in the gloom.

Rose snapped before he came close, 'Did you attempt to have me transferred to Cairo? The both of us?'

'What? I'm sorry...' he stalled. He was exhausted and not prepared for an argument. At least his instincts warned him to be careful. It looked like events had transpired faster than he had expected. Major Miller hadn't even been in contact.

'Did you, or did you *not*, try to have me transferred back to Egypt?'

'No–no, but I admit I was trying to arrange a small break. Like a holiday. As a surprise for you.' He lied desperately. 'Not a permanent transfer as such.'

'So it *was* you. How dare you!'

He closed his eyes a moment. He'd missed the opportunity to deny everything. Then he noticed her appearance. 'My God, what have you done to your hair?'

'Never mind my hair, Doctor Cohen. Just who do you think you are?'

'Please, Rose. You're over-reacting. I was only trying to help. Get you some time in Cairo, that's all.'

'With you?'

'I put in an application for myself at the same time, yes. It's not what you're thinking.'

'It's *exactly* what I'm thinking.' She was shaking with rage.

'No, it's not. Rose, please calm down.'

'Be damned to calming down! How dare you interfere in my personal affairs?'

'That sort of language is not going to help matters.'

'I will use any language I like.'

'I was only trying to help, Rose. Honestly.' Mark knew he'd made a serious mistake and doubted there was a way out.

'I don't *need* your help, Doctor. Kindly desist from offering it again, especially when I haven't asked for it. Matron Lambert has thankfully refused the transfer request. I hope yours is successful and takes you well away from here.'

She felt like lashing out, perhaps slapping him. To remove the temptation, she turned her back and stormed off.

He called out after her. 'Rose, I was trying to help. That's all.'

She vanished into the night.

Mark stared at the emptiness for a long time until he felt the cigarette burning his fingers. He threw the butt down and stamped it into the dirt.

***

Jonathon knew that his feelings for Rose were unrealistic. He was infatuated, although with his limited experience of women that was a new idea. His tiny home town hadn't offered much opportunity in the way of personal relationships and he'd lost his virginity to the whores in Cairo, like many of the young soldiers passing through.

Rose lingered in his mind day and night. She had done so ever since he met her on the *Gascon*. Now, having spent time with her and having got to know her a little, the fantasies were replaced with more likely dreams. She liked him, he could tell that. She spent time with him and laughed at his jokes. There were hundreds of men needing attention on the island, and yet she always found a chance to visit him and lately had allowed him to help her at work.

But she struck him as so worldly-wise and he had no idea what to do next.

She wouldn't appreciate him trying anything. He was, after all, just a farm boy from the Western Australian bush and Rose had travelled the world. She'd mentioned living in London and some of her childhood stories in Melbourne, a place so far removed from Jonathon's home. They had little in common aside from the circumstances they shared now.

Not surprisingly, he had no clue how to handle Rose's foul mood the morning after her confrontation with Mark Cohen.

'Jonathon, are you sure you want to help today?' She sounded discouraging.

'Of course,' he said. As he got up, he made sure he didn't wince at the pain in his leg. 'I feel fine after a good night's sleep.'

Which was more than Rose could claim. The tent had collapsed again during the night and she had lain awake for hours beforehand, listening to the canvas snap and groan threateningly above her. Fuming about Mark hadn't helped.

'All right, we have a lot to do.'

'That's fine.'

The nurses always had a lot to do. As usual, overnight a fresh batch of wounded arrived, but nothing like the numbers after the early August battles. In two days' time Rose would go back to greeting the night-time arrivals again. Everyone took turns unless casualties were high, in which case all of them were on.

Jonathon endured the morning silently doing everything Rose asked after his first attempts to be cheerful had met with a gruff response. Otherwise she hardly spoke at all. They were bathing a gunner's leg wounds when she curtly announced that they would find some sort of lunch afterwards. The man they were treating had been hit by a Turkish shell near his gun, the artillery piece shielding his upper body from harm. Both his legs had been slashed by shrapnel. He lay propped up, smoking and watching Rose carefully wash away the blood and grime.

'Why don't we take some mugs of tea and go for a stroll up there?' Jonathon asked her. He nodded towards a knoll that offered a view of the camp and the sea beyond. It was a popular place for getting away from the hospital.

'You wouldn't make it,' she said shortly.

I could get halfway, I reckon.'

'And I'd have to carry you back.'

'Come on, be a sport. It's better than sitting in the mess tent trying to eat those biscuits.'

That reminded her of the officers' mess the night before and she suddenly didn't want to sit in the nurses' tent either. Besides, many of her colleagues knew she'd had some sort of argument during the evening, and she didn't want to face their curiosity yet.

'All right.' She knew she was behaving badly and needed to get it out of her system. She didn't have the heart to disappoint him.

'Can I come too?' the gunner asked her. She laughed briefly for the first time that day, and pointed at his ruined legs.

'I don't think so. I'll bring you back a flower.'

It wasn't long before Jonathon was regretting the idea. What looked like a slight incline up to the knoll soon took its toll on his injured leg. He tried not to show it. At the mess tent, Rose had borrowed a water bottle and poured their allotted tea into it, then carried the two empty mugs. They clinked together as she walked beside him. The landscape was dotted by walking wounded all doing the same thing, getting away from the confines of the camp. Rose's mood lifted a little, relieved from the endless tents, the urgent bustle of hospital staff and the pleas of men who couldn't help themselves.

Finally, Jonathon gave up. 'Can we sit for a while?' he asked.

Rose resisted an urge to say, "I told you so." She turned him towards a small tree with a patch of shade. 'Let's go over here.'

They had to sit close because the shade hardly offered enough shelter for both of them. She placed the mugs on the ground, poured the tea and gave one to him.

They drank silently until Jonathon dared to mention her mood.

'You're not very cheerful today, Rose.'

'I'm sorry. I had a bad night.'

'Are you not well?'

She let out a small humourless noise. None of the girls considered themselves in the peak of condition anymore. The harsh rations and poor conditions made sure of that.

'I'm fine,' she said. 'I had an argument with someone. It upset me.' She

shrugged. 'I keep these things bottled up for too long. Ask my father, he'll tell you. I'm sorry if I've been taking it out on you.'

'You haven't really. Was it one of the other nurses?'

'No, a doctor.'

'Oh, I see.' He scuffed the dirt with his good foot. The way she had said it gave away most of the truth. The disagreement had been a personal one and that probably meant all sorts of things that he wouldn't like to hear.

Rose picked up on his reaction. 'It's not like that,' she told him.

'Like what?'

'You know, so don't pretend. This doctor was hoping to get a bit more... intimate, I suppose.' She added with her anger returning, 'He didn't think to ask me about it before he started making plans.'

'Have you known him long?'

'I hardly know him at all. It was presumptuous of him.' Suddenly the tension in Rose began to lift just from talking to

Jonathon. 'I told him exactly what to do with his advances. I'm afraid I wasn't very lady-like.'

He cringed inwardly. It was a stab of jealousy, but he didn't know that, and it gave him the courage to be impulsive.

'So what would you say, if I did the same?' he asked uncertainly. It came out all wrong and he regretted it immediately.

'You don't have to do anything on my account, it's not necessary,' she said absently. 'I think he got the message.'

'No, I meant tried to be more intimate. With you.'

'Oh...' She had been propositioned by a lot of men since she'd matured into a young woman and thought she could tell everything from the look on their faces at that moment. Most men were already half imagining her in the bedroom. With Jonathon, all she saw was a simple anxiety over what he'd said and what her answer might be. It was touchingly genuine. She said softly, 'I'd say it might be a foolish thing to do, Jonathon.'

'Fair enough,' he nodded, and looked down.

'No, you don't understand.' She put a hand on his arm. She felt her heart warm with a fondness at his instant acceptance. Most men wouldn't take no for an answer so readily. 'I like you, Jonathon. You're very sweet and I really enjoy your companionship. Would we be together here now, if I didn't?

Don't take this the wrong way. Heaven knows what I'd say in a different place, in another time.' She paused, thinking about this herself.

'What if we were back home?' He was only slightly mollified. 'And I asked you to a dance?'

'Can you dance?'

'No, we don't even have a town hall.'

She laughed, then quickly stifled it in case he thought she was making fun of him. 'See? You make me laugh. Not many people do.'

He still couldn't look her in the eye and wished he'd said nothing. Her hand on his arm squeezed gently.

'In a few weeks your wounds will have healed. You'll go back to Anzac and your battalion...' she hesitated before going on. Many of the soldiers were deeply superstitious and wouldn't appreciate what she said next. 'You might be killed the moment you step on the beach.'

He picked up a pebble and flicked it down the slope. Then he sighed and finally looked at her. 'No, it wouldn't be fair, would it?'

She shook her head slowly. 'The war changes everything. It makes me put my feelings aside for the time being. The future is so uncertain.'

Rose felt a small alarm inside. She was actually torn between encouraging him just a little more, keeping a spark of something alive, and obeying her own common sense. She *did* like him. It was like a natural attraction she'd never experienced before. The short time she'd known Jonathon didn't matter. But getting close to a man who fought in the trenches was inviting grief and heartache.

'Look, can you forget I asked?' he said.

'Certainly not.' She feigned annoyance. 'I'm glad you think so highly of me.'

'But now I've spoiled things.'

'No, we must remain the best of friends—the *best*. I'd be very sad if we weren't. I don't think badly of you for saying anything. Keep writing when you go back. Who knows what might be happening by this time next year?'

'I'll be here for a while yet,' he reminded her, still feeling awkward.

'Yes, and let's enjoy ourselves while we can.' She was treading a thin emotional line.

The thought came loud and clear, *For God's sake, don't start falling in love with a frontline soldier*. The very idea of loving anyone was so unexpected that she shied away from it and stood up quickly.

'Come on, we'd better be getting back.'

'Yes, I suppose so.' Jonathon got up with difficulty and took a moment to steady himself. She quickly put an arm around his waist to help.

The close contact felt different. It had another meaning. Suddenly she kissed him on the cheek, surprising herself again. It had seemed the right thing to do, and she didn't know what to say afterwards. There was a fleeting taste of salty flesh on her dry lips. Jonathon looked startled, then smiled gratefully.

'Thank you. I don't feel such a fool after all,' he said.

'I thought it might cheer you up.'

'Did you do the same for your doctor last night?'

'Hardly! I don't think I'll ever be kissing Doctor Cohen, that's for certain.'

He couldn't help himself filing away the name for future reference. Rose kept her arm around him as they stumbled back down the hill to camp. His leg had reacted badly to the stress of climbing.

After a few hundred yards, Rose puffed, 'This was a silly idea, don't you think?'

Jonathon was quick to answer. 'No, not at all.'

In Cold Blood

'My father's got a car,' Ben told Joseph doubtfully. 'And it doesn't always go very well. In fact, it breaks down quite a lot, but we just get out and walk home.' He nodded at the contraption in front of them. 'So what do you do when that buggers up? Jump out and flap your arms like a pigeon?'

Joseph wasn't easily discouraged. To him, the frail aeroplane looked a marvel of modern engineering. It was a Maurice Farman, an ungainly two-seater with the "pusher" motor behind the crew's cockpits. There was nothing aerodynamic about it. It was an over-complex kite with an engine stuck on. The cockpit section looked like a bathtub suspended between wings.

'I guess it would float down like a leaf,' he said. 'It wouldn't just drop.'

They were sitting in the shade of a date palm on a slight rise and looking down at the plane. The makeshift airfield was on the edge of Cairo near Camp Mena, where Joseph's battalion had done their final training. Occasionally they'd seen the aeroplane stuttering down out of the sky to land and Joseph had become fascinated, and keen to have a closer look. Today they'd found the airstrip, which was just compacted sand, glaring white in the sunshine. The Farman was parked beside a pile of drums and scattered, wooden crates. Two dirty tents pitched side-by-side apparently completed the airbase.

'No, it would *drop*,' Ben said confidently. 'A kite drops if there's no wind. When that motor stops, this thing doesn't have any wind either.'

Joseph didn't argue. Around them, Egypt stretched out in all its glory exactly as he had imagined and he never tired of watching it. The pyramids were behind them, majestic in their size and dominating the landscape. Everywhere the scene was dotted with something exotic. An Arab riding his camel or the dark women walking with loads balanced on their heads. Even the green palms were exhilarating.

Then there were the brown figures of Dominion troops. British, French and Australian soldiers wandered everywhere, sightseeing or buying fruit and souvenirs. For many men, like Joseph and Ben, these were the last days before they embarked and everyone was making the most of them. Nothing official had been said, for the sake of security. The hints had been dropped, and in a certain giveaway, plenty of leave was being granted.

A noise attracted Joseph's attention and he stared around the sky, excited.

'Look, there's another one,' he said, pointing at a black shape sliding down the blue towards the airfield. 'I thought there was more than one.'

It took a few minutes to come close. The two young men held their breath as the plane wobbled and skidded through the air, aiming for the end of the strip. The motor ran in ragged surges, the pilot riding the throttle. They could see his head bobbing up and down as he tried to see the ground better. The observer's seat in the nose of the nacelle was empty. The aircraft thudded down in a cloud of white dust and the engine roared, safely taxiing in the direction of the tents.

'Come on,' Joseph cried. 'Let's go and have a closer look.' He didn't wait for Ben and began running down the slope.

'Hey! Not so bloody fast.' Ben struggled to his feet. Despite the hard training and army rations he was still a big lad and didn't move quickly.

They reached the parking area as the plane coasted to a stop. The engine was deafening and kicked up a swirl of dust that had Joseph shielding his face. He glimpsed the goggled pilot looking his way as if he were going to warn him about the spinning propeller and Joseph gave him a reassuring wave. Abruptly the motor clattered to a stop. In the silence, hot metal clinked and ticked. Joseph felt the heat washing off the exhaust.

'Hello,' the pilot called cheerfully, pulling off his leather helmet and goggles in one piece. He was in his thirties, with thick fair hair and a handlebar moustache. Joseph played it safe and assumed that he was an officer.

'Good afternoon, sir,' he half-saluted, not sure if he should. 'This is a fine-looking machine.' Startled, behind him Ben stumbled to a halt and saluted too. It hadn't occurred to him that they were rushing to confront an officer.

'Yes, she's not a bad old girl,' the pilot patted the side of the aircraft like a horse. 'I've just been for a test-ride. The mechanic's been tinkering with the carburettors or some damned thing.' He started to lift himself from the cockpit and stopped halfway. 'I say, you wouldn't like to go for a quick hop, would you? I need the extra weight, you see—not too much, I'm afraid,' he added hastily, eyeing Ben.

'Are you serious?' Joseph blinked. 'Would it be all right?'

'As long as you don't fall out,' the pilot said straight-faced. 'That'd be hell to explain, especially if you hit someone. I really *do* want the ballast in the other seat.' He looked at Ben again and said unconvincingly, 'Perhaps next time for you, all right?'

'Don't worry, sir,' Ben shook his head. 'I'll keep my feet on the ground, thank you.'

'How do I get in?' Joseph was scanning the plane for a way to climb up.

'Not so fast,' the pilot said, pleased at his enthusiasm.

He got out and introduced himself as Lieutenant Duffield. He ducked inside the tents to confirm that no one else was around, cheerfully shrugged, and he got the two soldiers to help turn the aircraft around and face the open strip.

Then he instructed Ben on how to swing the propeller to start the engine.

'Don't forget to step back,' he told him. 'Or you'll get a hell of a haircut.'

Next, they installed Joseph in the front observer's cockpit and found a spare helmet, but no goggles. By now he was trembling with the thrill of what was happening and he kept glancing around, worried that some senior officer might suddenly arrive and stop them.

'Where is everyone?' he asked as Duffield climbed aboard.

'At the docks, I expect. Another three aircraft should be arriving all crated up. It's a bit of a job getting them back here. It needs all hands on deck—that sort of thing.'

'Why don't they fly them here?'

Duffield laughed. 'From England? Too hard. These kites don't get much more than sixty miles before we run out of petrol.'

'Have you got enough now?' Joseph couldn't help visions of putting Ben's argument to the test. What *did* happen when the motor stopped mid-air?

'Plenty for a spin around the town.' Duffield was preoccupied fiddling with switches in his cockpit. 'Contact, Private Harding!'

If for nothing else, Ben's extra bulk was well suited to swinging the propeller. He gave it a lusty heave and the engine caught immediately, roaring to life and sending Ben scampering for cover. Duffield leaned over, clapping Joseph on the shoulder and shouting something encouraging. The Farman lurched forward.

Every moment was intensely exciting for Joseph. When the engine roared, the entire frame shuddered. Everything groaned and squeaked alarmingly as the plane picked up speed over the rough ground. He could hear the wheels rumbling and felt the vibrations in his feet. The earth sped towards him, then with a swoop and change of all the sounds around him they were airborne. The white sand dropped away and took Joseph's breath with it. The sensation was incredible. He stifled a savage whoop of joy, thinking that Duffield might panic if he heard him.

As the Farman climbed over Cairo, Joseph was given a view straight from his daydreaming on the hill behind his family's farm. The higher they went, the more he lost the sensation of moving forward at any speed, then Duffield began to bank, dropping the wings and letting Joseph stare sideways down to the spinning earth. Twisting around he saw the other aircraft behind like a toy on the sand with a speck beside it. It was Ben, just where they'd left him, no doubt anxiously watching.

They circled the pyramids closely, the broken stonework rushing past the wingtips. Soldiers climbing them paused and waved at the plane. Joseph returned the gestures with a dignified salute, hoping to appear the seasoned flyer. Next, Duffield flew along the Nile and followed its sedate turns. Arab dhows with their dirty sails littered the brown water, the sailors staring upwards as the Farman passed overhead. Joseph couldn't decide from which side of the aircraft he wanted to see most. He kept turning from one to the other, then stretching forward to peer directly over the front. He didn't notice the wind tearing at face and making his eyes water. Once, though, he put his hand out sideways to catch the blast of it between his spread fingers.

It was over all too soon, and there was the city again before him with the wide band of the landing strip coming closer. He had a sinking feeling in his stomach as the Farman lost altitude.

Touching down gave him his only moment of panic. The earth leapt up alarmingly as Duffield dropped the last few feet in a hurry. The plane hit the sand with a thud that snapped his teeth together, but the instant of fear was gone as he knew they were down safely. The aircraft bumped towards the tents and Ben emerged from the shade under the other plane's wings. They stopped almost perfectly, parked in line with the first Farman, and the motor wheezed to a halt. Joseph was already ripping his helmet off and twisting around to shake Duffield's hand.

'That was incredible!' he blurted out. 'Absolutely brilliant!'

'Sorry about the landing,' Duffield smiled. 'All this heat and sand can be a devil. Updrafts, then downdrafts... God knows what will happen.'

'I thought it was a perfect landing,' Joseph said, as if he'd know, and Duffield accepted it with a wink.

'Anything you walk away from,' he said. 'That's a good landing. That's what we say, anyway.'

They climbed to the ground. 'You've got to give it a try,' Joseph cried at Ben, the adrenalin still racing through him.

'Not on your life,' Ben told him dryly. 'Besides, I weigh more than the whole thing. That can't be good.'

Duffield laughed, relieved that he hadn't hurt Ben by refusing him a joyride.

'How do you join your unit, sir?' Joseph asked. He didn't see the dismay on Ben's face.

Duffield scratched his head. 'You could ask for a transfer and retraining, I suppose. It's pretty simple and I could put a word in for you, if you like. I doubt you'll have much luck. You blokes will be pushing off within a day or so. They won't look too kindly on anyone trying to get out now.'

'I'm not trying to dodge the fighting,' Joseph began, before hearing the sense in Duffield's words. He was briefly despondent until a new thought struck him. 'What about in a few months? We're bound to have beaten the Turks by then.'

Duffield gave him a strange look. 'Come into the tent and I'll take down some details. I'll give you mine too. If you do get the chance, by all means give me a yell and I'll see what I can do. We're always looking for keen fellows.'

His generosity was genuine and Joseph was obviously eager to try flying as a career. The pilot was also comfortable making offers to help, because where these two boys were going he knew there was a good chance he wouldn't have to make good his promise. From what he'd heard, they would be lucky to still be alive in a few months' time.

***

Four days later, Joseph and Ben and the rest of their battalion joined the war.

An early morning sun showed the Anzac beachhead in stark relief, the piles of stores and sandbagged bunkers throwing long shadows down to the water. The sand appeared golden. From five hundred yards out the place seemed a chaotic, crowded holiday camp. Then something began plopping into the blue water around the approaching boats. George frowned at this, and nodded over the gunwale at the splashes.

'Some bastard's shooting at us,' he nudged Joseph. 'Look.'

'No, it's not...' Joseph began absently, captivated by the sight of Anzac Cove. He was immune to the tension in the men around him. About sixty soldiers were crowded between the gunwales.

'It *is* shooting,' Dexter jerked, staring in alarm. Rifle fire and machine guns echoed down from the hills and he looked up that way, as if he might see the barrels aimed in their direction.

'Don't worry,' George told him quickly. 'We're too far out. They're spent rounds not even meant for us.'

Dexter didn't look convinced but stayed quiet. George was a man who was supposed to know these things, not just because he was older and more worldly-wise. He'd kept his sergeant's stripes after basic training and was expected by youths like Dexter to have all the answers now. George wasn't so sure about that, but felt the other men at least respected him.

An artillery round burst in the water, well clear of their craft and doing little except drenching some men on the beach. Joseph could hear cursing and almost laughed as others in the boat hunched down.

'Steady,' Sergeant Major Beatty called from the stern. He was standing up, ramrod straight and sniffing the air like an old warhorse returning to glorious battle. Despite his old injuries and often needing a cane to walk, he had somehow convinced the authorities to allow him at the fighting.

‘If one of those shells lands in the fucking boat, we’ll all be goners,’ someone said morosely.

‘Christ, give it up. They can’t even hit the bloody beach,’ someone replied. It caused a ripple of laughter that eased the mood.

The small jetty was crowded with lighters taking on the wounded, so their own boat ran into the sand. The men could have disembarked over the bow and not got wet. Most were too nervous to wait. They jumped over the sides, splashing messily into the water and hurrying forward. They didn’t need Beatty’s urging.

‘Get to the base of the dunes, men,’ he shouted.

Soldiers on the shore watched with amusement as the newcomers scurried for cover. Three more boats arrived quickly flooding the beach with reinforcements. Hundreds of men gathered in tense disarray and waited for further orders. Their sergeants moved among them checking equipment and numbers. Captain Moore was conferring closely with Beatty, their heads bent together.

Another officer, his uniform faded from months of wear at Anzac, wandered slowly over to them and offered a slapdash salute.

'You'll be sorely tempting Big Bertha, sir,' he told Captain Moore, who stared at him uncomprehendingly. 'If you take your men up that path, you'll find the brigadier's headquarters near the top. A big bunker with a cookhouse right behind.' He pointed at a track leading up the dunes. 'Keep your heads down and obey the signs, and you'll be right... sir,' he added as an afterthought.

'Thank you... Major?' Moore squinted at the filthy tabs on the man's shoulders. The major was already turning back to his tasks on the beach.

They did as he'd suggested, filing up the narrow path and finding themselves in the maze of bunkers, trenches and makeshift shelters where the men lived. Their clean informs and clanking extra equipment labelled them as fresh from the training camps of Cairo. Men called out good-naturedly to them as they passed.

'Did you blokes bring any decent grub?'

'You going to win the war for us?'

'Don't let Johnny Turk put a hole in them nice, new hats.'

The soldiers of Joseph's battalion answered nervously, uncertain at the gallows humour. After a brief wait for Captain

Moore to take orders from the brigadier, they were shown to a rough, rock-strewn gully filled with supplies and working soldiers. The sounds of firing and bursting bombs came from all around, although this was an area relatively safe, or so it appeared. George returned from a meeting with the company officers.

'Home sweet home for a few days,' he announced with a shrug. 'Until we get used to the place. Everyone finds somewhere to put his head down. Watch for snipers, they say. And the Turks'll drop a shell in here every now and then.'

'Find somewhere to sleep?' Ben asked, staring around at the hard, open ground.

'Dig a hole, if you like,' a passing soldier said, a veteran of the beachhead, judging by his ragged appearance. 'You'll save us the trouble later on.'

***

The next day, sooner than expected, the battalion was moved into the reserve trenches. The first casualties came from a Turkish hand-bomb that trickled over the edge and exploded before anyone had a chance to move. Three men, all from the recent arrivals, were killed. Stretcher-bearers took the corpses away as the newcomers watched wide-eyed. Some of the experienced men bickered casually among themselves. One was accused of eating too many of the hard biscuits and getting so fat that he couldn't move fast enough to dispose of the bomb. The argument ended in laughter.

Everyone took turns on the fire step and loopholes, snatching shots at the Turkish lines. There was nothing definite to aim at, but it gave the men a familiarity with shooting at a real enemy. It also got them used to exposing themselves, however briefly. Bullets slamming into the dirt nearby moments later let them know the Turks were unforgiving, given the slightest opportunity to kill them. The fear of further hand-bombs made everyone vigilant.

Joseph was surprised by a tap on his shoulder as he crouched, about to take a peek over the parapet. He jumped nervously and twisted around, a rebuke on his mind, and he found himself staring at Sergeant Major Beatty.

Beatty said in a kind voice, 'Have you been looking for your brother, son? Jonathon, isn't it? In the eleventh battalion?'

Joseph felt a coldness in his gut. 'Yes, Sar'nt Major. I was thinking I might go and find him last night, but we were posted here.'

'He was wounded two weeks ago. Nothing too serious. He's been shipped to Lemnos Island for recovery and he should be back here within a month or so.

Try to stay in one piece yourself and you'll get to see him.'

'That's good news. Thank you, Sergeant Major.'

Beatty nodded. 'Now come with me. The captain wants to see what you can do.'

Puzzled, Joseph followed, his departure watched by the curious eyes of Dexter and Ben. Beatty took him along the zigzagging trench until they came to a heavily sandbagged position at the end. The protection had been built up until a man at the loop-hole could raise himself above the parapet. The loophole itself was covered by a thick steel plate drawn aside by a length of twine.

'Purpose-built for sniping,' Beatty explained. 'Not for much longer. The

Turks are getting wise to it.'

Captain Moore was there, waiting with another officer, who Joseph guessed was the commander of the unit sharing their section of the line. He didn't salute either man. It wasn't done in the front trenches because it might identify officers to the enemy. A third person, a private introduced as Wilson, was peering through a periscope at the Turkish lines.

'Private White,' Moore said quietly. 'Here's a chance to see how good you are.' Instead of explaining, he tapped Wilson on the arm. 'Anything more?'

Wilson didn't take his face from the periscope. 'There's a sandbag collapsed near a machine gun site and the Turks haven't noticed it yet. Either that, or they're not game to try fixing it until after dark. One of their mob keeps wandering into the gap showing us his stupid noggin', like he doesn't know. I reckon he might be the gunner and we see him when he bends down, checking over his sights for any targets.'

'All right,' Joseph said, trying to be calm, his insides churning. They wanted him to shoot an unsuspecting enemy in cold blood. A deliberate, measured kill. That's what snipers did and Joseph was here, now, because these men were told he had the skills. It saved his enlistment back at training camp. Joseph wasn't sure what to feel about the killing, but he was aware of an urge to do well in front of the officers. He cranked a round into his rifle. 'What do we do?'

'When he comes back, I'll give the word. You be ready at the loophole. Sar'nt Major, can you pull on the string? Don't take too long.'

As Beatty took hold of the string and Joseph got ready behind the loop-hole, Wilson said, 'The site's just to our left. Look about three yards this way near the top and you'll see the gap. If his head's still there, it kind of blends in with the sandbags because he's wearing a turban. You can still spot it.'

'All right,' Joseph said, and resisted an impulse to apologise for repeating himself. He tried to think of something else to say, then Wilson hissed suddenly.

'He's back. All right, have a go. Quick now!'

Beatty yanked the string and through a small hole Joseph could see the dreadful space of no-man's-land with its litter of decaying bodies. An instant later his rifle cracked twice, Joseph's hand a blur of movement on the bolt action, and he dropped backwards, so Beatty would know to close the loophole.

'Too quick, lad,' the other officer said, mildly. 'You should have used the time to take one good shot and make sure. Once your first bullet's missed, you've blown it.'

'No, sir. I got them both.' Joseph shook his head. His face was pale and his eyes blank. He was seeing the turban splatter red as it kicked away from the sandbags, revealing for a fraction of a moment a second, shocked Turk who Joseph instinctively shot in the forehead.

'I'll be damned,' Wilson said, letting the periscope drop and staring at the officers. He got *two*, sir. This bloke's a fucking killer. I never seen anything like that.'

'Are you sure?' Moore frowned.

'Saw it clear as day. Bloody hell!'

'All right, Wilson. We get the point.'

When Moore congratulated Joseph, he accepted it calmly, keeping his face neutral.

The captain said cheerfully, 'We need to get you a spotter of your own. Make a team. Shooting skills like that shouldn't be wasted hanging around the front line waiting for something to happen.'

'I'll see to it, sir,' Beatty snapped. 'Straight away.'

The act of killing two men was shocking, but not upsetting. They were the enemy and all Joseph's training to this point had been to prepare him for doing just that. And they had been a machine gun crew, possibly responsible for killing hundreds of Australians. They might have even wounded Jonathon.

He'd done his job well, that was all. If it would help win the war, that was fine by him.

Jonathon Leaves Lemnos

'The doctor asked me when I want to go back,' Jonathon told Rose.

They were walking along a cliff face, watching the sea crash onto the rocks below. In the last few weeks, rest camps had been set up on the island for all the allied troops to give them respite from the shocking conditions on Gallipoli. Now some of the small villages on Lemnos were making opportunities from the friendly invasion of soldiers, sending carriages to transport men and sometimes selling goat's milk cheese and sour bread. Rose and Jonathon had paid for a ride to the southern side of Lemnos to trek these cliffs in comparative privacy. The fact that Jonathon could make the journey at all was proof that he was healing well.

'What did you say to him?' Rose pulled her cloak closer. The hint of winter approaching made her shiver. Some of her sudden discomfort came from knowing that he was leaving soon.

'What could I say? I've got to go back—I *want* to.' He smiled and risked saying, 'Seeing you is the only reason I can think of for staying here.'

'That didn't answer my question.'

Jonathon hesitated. 'Tomorrow night. I said I'd go back with the next ship that was returning to Anzac Cove, and that's tomorrow.'

Rose stopped abruptly and sat down on a large boulder, staring out to sea. Jonathon could only stand nearby. There wasn't enough room to sit beside her.

'You will look after yourself, won't you?' she said in a small voice. 'What do the men say? "Keep your bloody head down".'

'Close enough,' he said with a wry laugh. 'It doesn't sound the same coming from you.' He moved in front of Rose and took her hands in his. 'You'll write often, won't you? You won't forget about me?'

There was more to this and they both knew it, but there was a line they'd agreed not to cross. The two of them had talked again several times on the futility of having any closer relationship, but all this common sense sometimes drove Jonathon to despair. He suspected Rose didn't feel much different. In the end, Jonathon agreed it was unfair to ask of Rose anything of her except friendship.

'Don't be silly. Of course I won't forget you. I'll write as often as I can. And you must do the same, even if it's just a card.'

The moment threatened to get maudlin, so he pulled Rose to her feet. 'Come on, let's not get too worried. The lads might be storming the Turks right now and the war will be over by tomorrow night.'

'Fat chance.' She gave him a wan smile. 'I'm cold. Do you mind if we go back?'

'In time for some tea and that lovely tinned meat? I can't wait.'

***

The next evening, Rose was moving the new wounded straight to the usual tents near the surgical wards. She kept an eye on the rate they were arriving. She watched the line of lights crawl across the night landscape from the beaches. Jonathon hung around and did the same, helping when he could. Both of them were trying to identify the last transport to take back to Mudros Harbour. Rose planned to go with him and see him off at the ship. The ride would be their last time together until God knew when, if ever.

The casualties were light and mostly English, coming from the southern end of the peninsula where the British army were just as impossibly stalemated against the Turkish defenders. The work at the hospital would finish early and then Rose could slip away for the few hours she'd need. If things had been dreadfully busy her conscience might have kept her back.

Jonathon arranged for a lift in a horse-drawn carriage. He chose this deliberately, figuring it would take longer and wouldn't be as uncomfortable as the noisy, stinking motorised ambulances. He told Rose and she looked around, checking the darkness. Things were quietening down.

'Grace said I could borrow her coat while she slept,' she told him. 'She should have left it on my blanket. I'm just going to slip back to the tent and pick it up.'

'Do you want me to come with you?'

'No, please stay here, in case anyone asks where I am.'

She walked quickly through the dark camp and was surprised to find Julia wrapped up and curled into a ball under her blankets. She was awake and offered Rose a weak greeting.

'What are you doing here?' Rose asked. 'Aren't you on roster?'

'I've been sent away to rest,' Julia groaned, her voice muffled. 'I must admit, I feel rather dreadful.'

'You're sick? Have you told anyone?' She knelt beside Julia and felt the wash of sickly warmth coming from her. 'My God, you've got a fever.'

'I must have Lemnositis.' Julia tried to joke. It was a name everyone used for any malady the nurses suffered, from exhaustion to a real illness.

'It must be quite serious. You're burning up. Have you taken anything for it?'

'Only the worst cases get aspirin,' Julia reminded her. 'I'm not that bad, really.'

'Rubbish. I'll go and find you some straight away.'

A hand came out of the blanket and grabbed Rose's skirt. 'You're seeing Jonathon off. Do that. Don't worry about me.'

'He can go on his own. There was always a good chance he might have to.'

'No, please go with him. I'd never forgive myself if I stopped you.'

'He's just a good *friend*, Julia,' Rose said firmly.

A soft laugh came from the blanket, then Julia said, 'I want to sleep, that's all. I'll tell you what, see if you can get some aspirin when you come back. Don't worry if you can't.'

'I'll certainly get something. I'll find Matron Lambert if there's any problems.'

'Say goodbye to Jonathon for me.'

Rose lingered for a moment and heard Julia's breathing turn rhythmic, as if she were already sleeping, though there was no way of knowing. In the end, she decided on doing as Julia insisted. She could look for some aspirin when she returned. At least she would have something to offer her in the morning if she wasn't any better.

She took Grace's coat from her blanket and left, a guilty feeling whispering in her mind.

Jonathon was waiting for her beside the carriage. The driver was an older private recovering from a foot wound. His bandage was a pale lump in the darkness.

'We'd better get going, Jonno,' he said. Rose guessed they'd been sharing a smoke and a chat for him to be so familiar. 'Or someone will stop me heading back at all. The ship might be empty as it is.'

'You'll miss your ride,' Rose joked weakly, letting Jonathon help her onto the flat tray behind the seat.

'There's another hour before it sails. So I'm told. Maybe it's something to do with the tides.'

They sat close together on a pile of stinking blankets. They could have sat bunched together beside the driver, only Jonathon didn't want to share these last minutes with anyone but Rose. The driver had turned the lamp low to conserve oil and give his passengers the privacy of darkness. Above them the stars swayed and tilted with the wheel ruts, and at one point the ride got so rough that Jonathon put an arm around Rose's waist to steady her. He left it there and she didn't complain.

'How do you feel?' she asked him softly. 'About going back?'

'I can't remember how it feels to be scared,' he said. '*Really* scared to death, I mean. Maybe that's why I'm not too worried. It's like pain. You can recall being hurt, but it's hard to remember what the pain actually felt like.' He let out a quiet laugh. 'I'm not sure if I'm looking forward to the rations or not. Sometimes I think we got fed better than you.'

'Well, you can send *me* a parcel.' Rose smiled in the gloom.

'I don't want leave you,' he said, suddenly earnest. 'I don't like it at all.'

'Don't... please,' she said gently. 'We've talked about this too much already. We don't have a future here. They wouldn't let you stay and might send you anywhere if you wait too long. At least this way you're going back to your own battalion. Perhaps you'll get sent back to Lemnos for a rest period, like the others?'

'That would be funny,' he said. 'Getting sent straight back here for a holiday, just after I return.'

She leaned her head on his shoulder and they spoke quietly about other things. After a while, she stopped answering and Jonathon realised that she'd fallen asleep. In a way, he liked that. It let him hold her close, so the rocking of the cart wouldn't wake her, and he enjoyed the feel of her body against his.

The dim harbour lights came out of the night too quickly and the driver pulled to a halt at the end of a makeshift pier. There was the hospital ship. It was after midnight and her tragic cargo was all gone. The crew must have been taking a break before setting sail once more.

Rose sat up, stirred by the lack of movement. 'I fell asleep,' she said guiltily. 'You shouldn't have let me.'

'You need it,' Jonathon said. 'I don't mind. Stay here. There's no need to get down.'

'No, I want to stretch my legs anyway.' She leaned over and touched the driver's arm. 'Will you wait five minutes, while I walk the pier?'

'Take your time, Sister. Give 'em hell for me, Jonno.'

'I will, Dick.'

They walked arm-in-arm slowly down the pier. The wind coming across the sea was even colder and Rose pulled her coat tight, tucking herself in against Jonathon for warmth until the ship offered shelter. At the foot of the gangplank they stood close, facing each other. Above them a midshipman on guard turned away politely.

'We've run out of excuses now,' Jonathon said. 'You shouldn't come aboard.'

She took both his hands and kissed him on the lips for a long second, which took him by surprise and he didn't know what to do.

She felt tears coming and whispered, 'I want you to come back. That's all I can say. I can't offer anything more. It wouldn't be fair. For God's sake, be careful.'

'I'll keep my bloody head down,' he grinned.

She tried to match his tone. 'Go straight below decks now. I don't want to be waving over my shoulder the whole length of the damned pier.' It suddenly struck Rose that it was like *she* was leaving, not Jonathon. Saying goodbye on the shore would have been better.

'All right,' he said. It didn't sound as if he would.

She kissed him again and this time he was ready for it, wrapping his arms around her waist and pulling her to him. She had to break away, pushing gently against his chest.

'That's just to give you something to think about,' she half-teased. 'To *make* you be careful. Now go. This is turning into the longest goodbye I've ever had.'

'Goodbye, Rose.'

She watched until he reached the top of the gangplank, where he murmured his name to the midshipman before waving down to her.

'I'll write soon,' his voice echoed from the shadowy steel of the ship.

Rose lifted a hand and turned for the shore. She walked the entire pier without looking back, then faced the ship again. A dim movement, the waving of a hand, came from near the bow.

'You rotten thing,' she managed, laughing sadly to herself and waving back, certain it was him.

She had intended to keep the driver company. He cheerfully insisted she lie down in the back and get some rest. She didn't need much convincing. In the dark, Rose started to cry for the first time in years. She wouldn't ask herself why, fearing the answer would come quickly and too easily. It helped to let the tears flow and she wiped her nose on the filthy blanket until she fell asleep again.

When she reached the hospital, Rose found Nellie still working the night shift, who fetched her some powders for Julia from one of the surgical wards.

Back in the tent Julia was sleeping fitfully, the air filled with the sourness of her illness, and Rose decided to wait until morning to give her the medication.

***

At first light, although she was desperately tired, Rose woke and crawled over to check Julia. What she saw frightened her. Julia was so hot her skin glowed red. Her breathing was shallow, and she hardly stirred at Rose's touch. With the back of her fingers she examined Julia's lips, but she didn't need the contact to see they were cracked and dry. She had dehydrated badly during the night.

'Dear God, I'll get you some water,' Rose said, doubting Julia could hear.

Rose hadn't undressed that night. Exhausted emotionally and physically by Jonathon's departure, she'd collapsed onto her blanket in her clothes. Now she emerged from the tent rumpled and half-asleep, disoriented by the sudden transition. With the thousands of men sick and wounded all over the island, the dawn light showed the endless nursing still going on. She saw Yvonne, who was always cheerful and ready with a joke, struggling along with a bucket of water. Rose prayed it was fresh for drinking and hurried over.

'Yvonne, Julia's very ill. She needs water—'

'Oh... hello, Rose. Julia? Well, here...' Clearly, she'd been working all night. 'Do you need the cup?' she said vaguely, looking down at the tin mug in one hand and the bucket in the other. Rose gently took them both.

'Why don't you sit down for a minute until I bring these back?'

'That's my tent over there, actually. You know, I think I might lie down a bit.'

'That's a good idea.' Through her worry for Julia, Rose could still feel sympathy for Yvonne. She looked exhausted.

Back beside Julia, she lifted her friend's head and let a dribble of water run over the parched lips. Julia moved and her tongue licked eagerly, so Rose made her sit up. Her eyelids were gummed together with a yellow secretion.

The heat coming from her flesh was truly startling.

'Julia, it's Rose. How are you feeling?'

With an effort she cracked open her eyes and looked groggily at Rose. Her voice was barely audible.

'Terrible, I must say. I–I don't what's wrong with me.'

'You've got a fever, that's for certain. I've brought you some aspirin, but I think I should fetch a doctor or Matron Lambert first.'

Julia protested feebly. 'No, they're busy enough with the wounded. We can look after ourselves. Can I have some more water?'

Rose made her drink the entire mug, a luxury not so long ago. Even now drinking water was still scarce and somewhere, thirsty men would be waiting for the ration Yvonne should have been bringing.

'Sleep again,' Rose said firmly, letting Julia fall back easily. 'I'm going to find one of the doctors.'

Rose hurried between the tents, seeing nurses and orderlies everywhere, and none of the doctors. When she saw Mark Cohen ducking out from behind a tent flap, she hesitated. They hadn't spoken since she'd confronted him, and things seemed best that way.

This was no time to be selfish about her own feelings.

'Doctor Cohen?' she called, stepping into his path. 'Would you have a spare moment?'

'Hello, Rose.' He smiled uncertainly. 'I didn't think you'd ever talk to me again. How are you?'

'I'm fine, thank you. One of my friends is very ill and I'd be grateful if you could—'

He interrupted, 'The private with the chest wound? I thought he was going back soon.'

'One of the *nurses*, Doctor. It's Julia. She has a dreadful fever.'

'Oh? Well, of course.' He looked around as if to ensure that it was all right to go. When he turned back, she had already gone.

His manner turned grim the moment he got inside the tent. Rose crowded in beside him.

'Oh dear, you *are* under the weather,' he said with a forced lightness. Julia woke again, but she couldn't move. He said to Rose, 'Come on, help me undress her. I need a closer look.'

Somehow Rose couldn't consider any young woman being undressed in front of a man like this, doctor or not, no matter how ill. They were in a tent, open to anyone who chose to look inside. Normally the nurses worked together and took elaborate measures to protect each other's privacy, when the need arose—which wasn't often. Some of them still hadn't bathed since arriving over a month before. Suddenly, Mark Cohen wasn't her idea of a suitable doctor.

'Rose?' he said, frowning.

'I'm sorry, you took me by surprise,' she admitted, then bent to the task of removing Julia's clothing. She was glad to see him tie the flap closed.

Rose felt embarrassed for her friend. Not for Julia's nakedness, but because of the discoloured underwear and crude repairs to her private things. Her slips were greyed from perspiration and the knickers yellow from being boiled in sea water. Everyone suffered the same, the lack of spare clothes, clean water and laundry soap taking their toll on the women's belongings.

Mark didn't appear to notice and didn't completely disrobe Julia.

'Look,' he said softly, with a glance at Julia's closed eyes to see if she was listening. He pointed at red marks blossoming on her breasts and across her stomach. 'I think they're rose spots.'

'Typhoid?' Rose breathed. Rose spots were the name for the disease's distinctive rash.

'There's a lot of it here, all over the island,' he said, pulling the blanket up to Julia's chin. 'I'm surprised more of you girls haven't caught it before now.'

'Oh God,' Rose touched Julia's face. One of the Canadian nurses had died from it recently and sent shockwaves through the women on the island. Despite everything around them, the nurses expected to be immune.

'We have to keep her isolated until we can get her to Cairo. Choubra Hospital has been set aside for enteric diseases—'

'No, Doctor.' Rose grabbed his arm urgently. 'We can't send her away.'

'She must go to a proper hospital.'

'And be with hundreds, maybe thousands of other cases, mostly men? We can look after her better here. I'm sure Matron Lambert would agree.'

He shook his head. 'Colonel Fischer won't allow it now. Not after that poor girl died. He's insisting all cases of typhoid fever be sent immediately to Cairo.'

'Then don't tell him,' she pleaded. 'We really wish to look after our own, Doctor Cohen. I'd never forgive myself if we sent Julia away and–and she didn't survive.' She choked the last words out. It was unthinkable, and a possibility they couldn't ignore.

With a deep sigh, Mark sat back. 'She's going to get worse, you know. Helpless as an infant. You'll need to keep her absolutely clean and get rid of anything that comes into contact with her. Give her all the water we can spare. That alone will be hard enough.'

'So, you won't report her to Colonel Fischer? She can stay here?'

'On her *own*, Rose,' he said firmly. 'You'll need to find somewhere else to sleep.'

'That's easy. I'll move into the tent next door.'

He sighed again. 'I'll try to see her every day, at least until the worst of the fever passes. I should be able to bring her aspirin. Supplies aren't too desperate right now.' He stood up and looked down at Julia, a doubtful expression on his face. Rose couldn't tell if it was about her friend's health, or his decision to keep it a secret. 'You ladies will have to do the rest. Especially the water. She's going to lose a lot of fluids.'

'Thank you, Doctor. I understand. I'm very grateful.'

'For God's sake, can't you call me Mark?' he asked irritably.

'All right, Mark,' Rose said. A whisper of unease touched her. Although the circumstances demanded it without doubt, she owed him something now and she didn't like that.

'I'll try and pop back at midday,' he said. 'You'd better warn the other girls I'm not doing anything improper with Julia, creeping in and out of her tent like this.'

'I'm sure they'll understand,' Rose gave him a smile.

***

And so, through Julia's illness, Rose saw Mark Cohen almost every day for the next month.

He didn't ever press for a renewed friendship with Rose or try to use the favours as an excuse to wipe out his errors in the past. She slowly warmed to him anyway, seeing he genuinely cared for others under his charge. Perhaps his attempts to get them both transferred to Cairo had been more innocent than she'd believed? He didn't seem so capable of deceit anymore, except for his hiding of Julia's situation, of course. His daily visits even went some way to filling the void Jonathon's absence had created. He was someone different to talk to who wasn't a nurse or a wounded soldier needing attention.

Jonathon's letters came regularly with cheerful anecdotes and only good news. Rose knew from other sources that conditions at Anzac were still terrible, but his chances of surviving were better because the offensives had slackened off. She deeply appreciated his positive words, being surrounded herself by the many wounded and Julia's sickness.

Still, Rose had a shock one day when Julia was strong enough to ask about things other than her own misery.

'What's the latest news from Jonathon?' she whispered.

'The same,' Rose said. 'You'd think they were all on some holiday camp, if you only read his letters.'

'Who do you think is more handsome, Rose? Jonathon or Doctor Cohen?'

'Julia! I can't believe you're even asking such a question. You must be feeling better.' Rose wagged a finger at her.

'Oh, I'm only teasing.'

Teasing aside, Rose felt some alarm in her heart because she'd unconsciously compared the two men and found she couldn't decide. Putting Mark in the same thoughts as Jonathon felt somehow unfaithful.

What did that mean? Her feelings for Jonathon were stronger than she dared admit? Or that Doctor Mark Cohen was getting under her skin too?

Two Brothers Together

Jonathon couldn't affect the nonchalance of everyone else on the beach, ignoring the bullets that flicked the sand and pecked the wooden crates. He wasn't used to it anymore and thought everyone was foolish to dismiss the dangers so lightly. In the ocean, a bunch of naked men were swimming noisily, playing a kind of tag, heedless that Big Bertha had lobbed three shells into the bay in the last half-hour.

The sun was warm and an easterly breeze brought the stench of the battlefields down to the cove along with thick swarms of flies. The rattle of gunfire and sounds of bursting bombs came too.

He found a stores dump and requisitioned a rifle, a full allowance of ammunition and all the other paraphernalia such as a water bottle, mess tin and blanket. The gear he drew was all used, the previous owners no longer requiring them. He'd been told his company held exactly the same position in the line. Nothing had changed tactically except for the heroic capture of Lone Pine in August. That didn't affect their sector.

He reported to Major Willow's bunker.

'Jonathon?' Willow greeted him, looking up from his desk and surprising him with both his enthusiasm and his first name. The bunker was dark, compared with the bright sunshine outside. 'Good to see you back. Excellent, in fact. How are you?' He stood and shook hands.

'Fine, thank you... Major,' Jonathon said. 'Fit as a fiddle.'

In truth, Jonathon couldn't raise his arm very high or quickly. An artillery shell landed close by and he flinched. Willow didn't even blink.

'The lads will be glad to see you back too. Just in time to solve a problem for me,' Willow said.

Jonathon was tempted to ask, *who was left*? The thought had been nagging him since he'd stepped on the beach. He had kept infrequently in touch from Lemnos, meeting wounded who were mutual friends, but Robert might have been dead a week or more and he wouldn't know. Any of his section could have been killed. Or even all of them.

'Problem, sir?' he asked instead.

'I'm afraid Nick Streeth got bowled over by a sniper about three weeks back.'

'Yes, I know. They brought him to Lemnos. He was dead by the time he got there.'

Willow pulled a grim face. 'No, I didn't think the poor beggar would last long.' He brightened again and turned away to rummage in a drawer. 'I haven't been able to replace him, either, with you gone as well. Now I can.' He held a pair of sergeant's stripes. Jonathon's shirt was bare of his corporal's insignia after he'd acquired new clothing on Lemnos. Willow tossed the stripes at him and he caught them.

'Here, get those sewn on and I'll have the paperwork done today.'

Jonathon stared doubtfully at them and Willow mistook his hesitation.

'It's quite all right and above board.'

'But I'm not sure I'm ready for this, sir,' Jonathon admitted. 'I've been away for weeks. It's all a bit new to me again.'

'Nonsense. The others will see you straight. Thornton is your corporal. He's a good man.'

'Robert's a corporal?'

'A reluctant one, but he does the job. He's been running things since Streeth went south. Your section is in reserve. Same place. Nothing much happening, so you should have a quiet day to settle in.'

Jonathon nodded his thanks. Walking along the trenches to the reserve lines brought him back to the reality of Anzac. The closer he got, the more he saw the mad things they'd all come to accept as normal. Turkish corpses were used as sandbags, their limbs sometimes protruding from the surrounding dirt and seeming to grasp at passers-by. Other bodies lined the edge of the parapet, useful where they lay rather than being dragged in for burial.

He found half his section huddled around a small fire trying to coax a billy of tea to boil. Robert, Dougie Hanson, Marsden, Appleton, Crowe and the young soldier Jones. They were arguing about how much tea to put in. Robert glanced over his shoulder.

'Well, I'll be fucked,' he said, and the others turned to look. 'The stupid bastard came back. I told you he was a bloody idiot.'

He and Jonathon shook hands and embraced roughly. The rest did the same, each commenting on his return as if he'd had a choice. Only Jones welcomed him back shyly.

'Someone's got to look after you bastards,' Jonathon said, finally getting a word in.

'Yeah, well Nick took a bullet,' Robert shrugged.

'A sniper. Willow told me, but I already knew.'

'It wasn't really Nick's fault because it was a bloody good shot—but hey!' Robert stabbed a finger at him. 'We've got someone better.'

'Who?' Jonathon grinned, indulging him, expecting it to be somebody he knew that would be funny.

'Your brother, Joseph. Bloody Joseph, can you believe it?' They're calling him The Assassin. He's a legend.'

'Joseph? He's here already? And he's a sniper?'

'The damned best. His score is up to 112—'

'*Thirteen*,' Appleton corrected him. 'I heard it's 113.'

Jonathon turned on him. 'They're keeping score?'

Robert explained, unaware that Jonathon was more shocked than impressed. 'They say a kill's got to be confirmed by a sergeant and no less, so it's probably more. But the official tally…' he gestured at Appleton.

'That's bullshit,' Crowe growled. 'As long as his spotter sees a shot, that's good enough.'

Robert didn't argue. He looked annoyed that Crowe had spoilt the story.

Jonathon sat back against the trench wall, still trying to take it all in.

'Jesus,' he said to himself. 'I wonder if Mum knows?'

'She'll know when he gets a medal,' Robert said.

Again, Crowe ruined it. 'He's not going to get a bloody medal. Christ, the man's only doing his job.'

Joseph a "man"? It was just his little brother, not a man. 'Where is he?' Jonathon asked.

'Somewhere around Chatham's Post. I got to see him once for a minute, on his way to the beach for fatigues. He said they were at Chatham's mostly.'

'I'd better go and see him.' Now was probably a good time, before he settled back in.

'I wouldn't bother,' Robert said. 'He'll be out on his blind and no one goes near him, in case they give his spot away. He won't come in until after dark.' He tugged at Jonathon's bare sleeves. 'Did you lose your stripes? Look, they gave 'em to me. You can have the bastards back, if you like.'

'No, they made me a sergeant—*your* sergeant, so don't give me the shits.'

***

When Jonathon managed to get away that evening and see Joseph, he found that his brother was almost a stranger. The grown-up Joseph was confident and even seemed to stand taller, although the harsh rations had whittled away the last of his boyish flesh.

In turn, Joseph greeted a man with a tired look in his eyes and a drooping shoulder, as if a part of him had aged. Jonathon was more wiry too, and when he moved close to a shaded lamp Joseph saw his brother's skin had become a deep brown.

They exchanged a hug, which was unusual for them and awkward, then Joseph waved at a fire step and they sat down. Ben came over, introduced himself, and joined them.

'So, you came out here,' Jonathon said, taking a cigarette from a packet of ready-mades he brought from Lemnos. Joseph reached over and plucked one for himself and Ben.

'What'd you expect?' Joseph lit both the smokes, offered the match to his brother, and grinned at him in the darkness as he gave Ben his and waited for Jonathon to say something about it.

'I was hoping you'd stay at home and look after things there,' Jonathon said.

'Dad's more than capable of running his own farm, you know. Will drops over every day. They help each other out.'

'Actually, I wanted one of us to stay out of *this*. Just in case.'

'What? So you'd get all the glory?'

'I don't give a damn about glory. I want one of us to stay in one piece.'

A Turkish machine gun opened up briefly and someone called, 'Give it a break, Abdul. We're trying to get some bloody sleep over here!' The machine gun stopped and an officer used a periscope to check no-man's-land for any raiding party. No one bothered to shoot back.

The two brothers watched this in silence until Jonathon said, 'It's been pretty quiet?'

'So they say. We haven't seen any real attacks.'

'You're lucky. Sometimes they sent us over the top just to make some bloody officer look good.'

'We've heard the stories, haven't we, Ben?'

Ben grunted.

'What's this about you being a hero already? What do they call you? The Assassin?' Jonathon said.

'Nothing heroic about it,' Joseph laughed. 'I can shoot straight, that's all.'

'Some blokes are keeping score. It's 113 Turks, I'm told. Do you keep score yourself?'

'Well, 118 after today.'

'You haven't written home about it?'

'No, of course not. I don't think they'd understand.'

'No, you're right.' He couldn't keep the relief out of his voice.

They talked for a while about their parents and the farm, comparing the letters they got. There was little they didn't both know. So Joseph told him about Sergeant Major Beatty and Ben chipped in with the story of their getting caught drunk outside Blackboy Hill camp.

'I wasn't drunk, you were,' Joseph interrupted him.

'That's what I meant.'

'I like your story better,' Jonathon turned to Ben with a wink. He told them he was a sergeant, with Robert as his corporal. They laughed at how unlikely this should be. Ben too, although he didn't know either of them. The conversation was drying up, despite the months of separation and thousands of miles they'd both travelled, and Jonathon felt guilty about it and racked his brain for something new to say.

'What was it like being wounded?' Joseph asked. Oddly, he hadn't remembered until this moment.

'You don't know much about it. Suddenly everything hurts like hell and you're lying on the ground. It's not like you see the bullet coming and have a chance to worry.'

'Was it bad?' Ben said anxiously.

'No, otherwise I wouldn't be back here so soon. Anyway, I'd better be heading back. We're in the reserve trenches and you never know.'

Joseph shook his hand solemnly. 'We're pulling out for our rest tomorrow. I'm hoping to catch a swim at the beach. Can you come down?'

They both knew the answer. 'No, it wouldn't be fair since I've had such a break away,' Jonathon said. 'We'll make an effort to stay in touch, right?'

With tens of thousands of men from many units, all doing different tasks, it wouldn't be that simple. Just finding each other's companies in the maze of trenches would be hard enough.

Jonathon paused and said reluctantly, 'I could ask about getting you transferred to our mob, if you like.' He couldn't decide if he would worry more or less, having Joseph under his command.

'I wouldn't want to go,' Joseph said. 'My mates are all here.' Behind him, Ben nodded enthusiastically. 'Besides, it's probably better we stay split up.'

With a wave, Jonathon set off on the trip back through the trenches. He was planning to write to his parents that night and tell them he'd finally re-united with Joseph. He wished the story was bigger, their meeting more passionate, but they couldn't be blamed for the circumstances that prevented it. Still, by the time he returned to Robert and the others, he had decided to be upbeat in the letter and add a few white lies. Make it more like his parents expected. It was easier than trying to explain the truth.

'How's Joseph?' Robert asked, as soon as he saw him.

'Same as ever, the cocky little bastard,' he said.

Robert looked puzzled. 'You reckon?'

***

In the morning, George Poole took his entire section, including Ben and Joseph, down to the shoreline to unload a consignment of bully beef. Sometimes Joseph would be excused these duties in exchange for more sniping, along with another member of their section needed for spotting. Captain Moore allowed it, like letting a prize team player get extra practice. The entire battalion was basking in Joseph's reputation.

Today, Joseph wanted a swim, even if it meant carrying a few hundred cases of tinned meat first.

On the trip down to the beach, walking in single file through the trenches and paths, the men chatted cheerfully. It was a relief to be away from the front line. Already they were veterans, casually heeding the warnings along the way that told of Turkish snipers and enemy machine gun enfilades. Some signs just announced company headquarters or first aid stations, but on one broken plank some wit had scrawled in thick chalk, "How many times have I got to tell you?".

It was for a short gap in the sandbags and each man rushed through at odd intervals.

The shipment of bully beef was one of many such cargoes that reached Anzac Cove every day. Things weren't as organised as the officers thought, and it was likely that George's section would be given another job. For once, they trooped along the jetty to a barge loaded high with boxes of the tinned meat. There was also jam and flour for making bread—extra unloading work that brought a grumble from the section. The first job was transferring it all to shore and under some sort of cover because Big Bertha didn't particularly mind what she shelled. Supplies of any sort would do.

The day was pleasantly warm, which soon had everyone sweating freely. Joseph wasn't the only one eyeing a group of swimmers off the beach enviously. Four times the big, Turkish gun landed a shell in the cove, the last bursting in a geyser of pale sand. Nobody stopped their labours anywhere along the shore. It was a part of life here. Men were killed frequently, but that was no reason to shirk your duty. The chances of being blown to pieces were just as good cowering in one of the bunkers, as standing in the open.

They rested for a lunch of tea, biscuits and not surprisingly bully beef, which they ate cold straight from the tins. George stopped them from taking a quick dip, thinking that once they got in the water it would be impossible to bring them back out. The job had to be done first. It took them another hour while a second barge was emptied, and he finally told them it was time to beat a hasty retreat before someone found a new job. As it was, they were expected to carry ammunition back into the front lines on the return trip.

'You blokes can have a dip off the beach,' he said. This was away from the jetty where an officer might drag them into further work.

Eagerly they jogged down the sand to where the last shell had fallen from Big Bertha. Superstition insisted lightning couldn't strike twice. The men stacked their rifles upright together and stripped naked, piling clothes haphazardly everywhere. With whoops of joy, everyone rushed into the ocean and started fighting and splashing each other like children. Ben, as always in these situations, used his size to good advantage. He wrestled the others to submission and whipped the waves to drive his opponents back. Dexter held up his hands in surrender, spluttering in the deluge that hit his face.

'Hey, hey! Hang on a second, Ben. Look.'

Ben stopped and turned around. Beside him Joseph did the same. They saw George sitting on the sand watching them all, his rifle cradled in his lap.

'George, what the hell are you doing?' Joseph called. 'Come on in.'

'Watching for sharks,' George shouted back morosely.

'What bloody sharks?'

'What do you think, with all the stuff in the water?'

Corpses washed ashore all the time, stirred from whatever depths they were trapped in by currents or the wash of boats. No one had ever seen any sharks.

‘She’ll be right, George,’ someone said. ‘You wouldn’t be able to hit the bastard anyway. You’ll more likely shoot one of *us*.’ Everyone laughed and a spray of water went towards the beach.

‘I’m happier here,’ he waved. ‘Don’t worry about me. You bastards enjoy yourselves while you can.’

The others didn’t need any urging and happily resumed their horseplay.

Only Dexter was about to argue. Joseph touched him on the shoulder.

‘Leave him be.’

‘Jesus, there won’t be any *sharks*, Joseph.’

Joseph lowered his voice. ‘I don’t think George can swim. He doesn’t like the water.’

‘But you don’t have to!’ Dexter raised his hands to show they were standing on the sandy bottom.

‘It doesn’t matter. He’s not used to it, that’s all.’

To end the discussion, Joseph shot a jet of water at Dexter and a fight was suddenly back on, George’s lonely figure on the beach forgotten.

The men stood unashamedly on the sand until they dried before dressing. They had learned in the past weeks that rinsing their stinking clothes in the ocean provided temporary relief, but they paid for it with stiffness later. One man got a burning sting from a spent bullet hitting his calf, and there jokes about worse places he might have been hit.

'All right,' George announced loudly. 'Everyone get dressed. A box of ammo between you and we'll head back.'

The metal chests of ammunition could be carried by a man on his own, except not up the steep tracks into the main trenches. Only Ben prided himself on carrying a box by himself, balanced on one shoulder with his rifle slung from the other. As he forged ahead, he called back cheerful insults about them all being too slow and weak.

Within minutes, the joy of swimming and feeling clean had gone.

Joseph and Dexter were the third pair carrying a load with Joseph taking the lead. Bent over with the effort, he mostly saw the stooped back and kicking boots of the man in front, spraying soil back into his face. Into the headlands and among the first trenches the trip got easier, the gradient flattening slightly, although the soldiers were tiring. Joseph gritted his teeth and ignored the aching muscles. He concentrated on the need to keep going and get the task finished.

A warning inside his head came late—maybe too late.

'Jesus... *Ben,*' he breathed, dropping his end of the case. Dexter stumbled and swore at the sudden stop. Joseph ignored him. He was already pushing past the men in front, shoving them roughly aside.

'Ben? Wait! Wait on!'

They were coming to the gap in the sandbags with the elaborate, chalked warning sign.

Words Ben couldn't read.

'George, stop Ben!' Joseph called, seeing George above him on the track paired with their corporal, Robertson, and much further ahead, Ben's large and shambling figure. George twisted around awkwardly to give Joseph a puzzled look.

Joseph shouted urgently. 'Stop, Ben! *Jesus...* for Christ's sake, Ben! Wait for us!'

Ben heard him and turned around without stopping, walking backwards and grinning down at him in triumph with the shouldered ammunition box nestling against his cheek. He was happy. This was his moment when he was the best. The strongest and fittest, better than them all. He moved into the gap unaware.

Joseph later believed that he heard among the battlefield's gunfire the single shot that was aimed at Ben. There came a metallic clang, a bullet striking the chest he carried, and for a moment Joseph thought the sniper had missed. Then he saw blood running down Ben's neck as he collapsed slowly to the ground.

Joseph scrambled frantically past George, who too late understood the danger and called out a belated warning. The two of them let out anguished snarls of rage and frustration when they saw Ben fall. Joseph kept rushing forward. George had the presence of mind to grab his clothing and haul him back.

'*No, Joseph*!' He fought him to a halt. 'Wait, fuck you. Or you'll get the next one.'

'Ben! Shit, *Ben,*' Joseph called desperately, slapping away George's hands.

'Ben, are you all right?'

Ben didn't move. He lay on his side and stared at them with glazed eyes. He gave no sign that he'd even heard. A dark stain spread through the soil under his face. On the far side of the gap some soldiers sharing a cigarette looked on impassively.

The rest of the section quickly bunched up behind Joseph and George, their own cases dropped and forgotten. Someone cursed loudly and Dexter made a crying sound.

George kept his voice flat and purposeful.

'He's closer to the other side. We'd be better off trying to get him there, all right?' When Joseph started to move, immediately George stopped him again. 'Wait until I say. You grab his right shoulder, I'll get his left. Don't worry about hurting him. Just get him behind the sandbags.'

George took a moment longer. Either the sniper was waiting for just such a rescue attempt to give him another target, or Ben's low profile had robbed the Turk of a second shot.

'Now,' he snapped.

They ran forward in a crouch and each scooped a grip under Ben's arms. Even though they were prepared for it, Ben's weight surprised them. They expected to feel a bullet at any moment. The crack of a rifle came but nobody cried out. The load got suddenly easier and Joseph looked back to see that Dexter had run with them and picked up Ben's legs. The few seconds of extreme danger felt like an hour until they all tumbled behind the opposite sandbags in a tangle of limbs and flaying boots.

One of the smoking soldiers said, 'It wasn't worth the risk, you blokes.'

Joseph ignored him, crawling around to lift Ben's head. A mess of blood spilled over his lap. He let out a cry seeing the bullet had entered behind the ear and passed through Ben's skull before hitting the ammunition box on his opposite shoulder. A perfect shot.

Ben wasn't breathing. The sniper's second round had struck him too. Below his ribs, but most likely he was already dead.

***

'It wasn't your fault,' George told Joseph quietly, not for the first time. Before now, Joseph hadn't answered this, even though it was nightfall and Ben had been buried half the day. The two of them were hunched over in a dugout, smoking one cigarette after another in the darkness. Dexter was asleep curled up on the ground, his face pale from crying.

'He couldn't read that bloody sign,' Joseph said bitterly. 'With so many words, he probably figured it pointed to a divisional headquarters or some fucking thing. He knew the simple warnings. I taught him.'

'He couldn't read it because he had the bloody ammunition box on his shoulder,' George insisted. 'He couldn't *see* it, the fool.'

'That's right,' Joseph gave him a stricken look. 'And that box protected his head. If I hadn't called out and made him turn around, the sniper wouldn't have had a shot.'

'So he would've copped it in the heart,' George threw down his cigarette. 'He was that good. You should know.' After a pause he added, 'It might have been Abdul the Terrible.'

A Turk with a reputation as a deadly shot similar to Joseph's. A legendary enemy that the Anzac troops had dubbed with a name.

Joseph stood up. 'I'm off to tell Captain Moore I'm going out tomorrow. Do you want to spot for me?'

'We're having a break, remember? You'll be back in the line soon enough.'

'You don't have to come.'

George swore and lit another cigarette, waving the match out. 'I can't,' he said. 'I can let you take Dexter. I'm sure he'll be glad to find some Turks for you to shoot.'

A Taste of Winter

November 1915

'I don't believe this,' George muttered, shivering against a small fire. The trench sheltered the flame, but no warmth came from it. A howling wind across the parapet acted as a draw, sucking the air up and away. Their section was resting about 400 yards behind the reserve trenches at Chatham's Post.

'It's going to piss down again,' Joseph eyed the scudding clouds above. It hadn't rained recently—he was talking about the violent storms a month before. Two fierce gales partially destroyed the piers at all three landing beaches. The soldiers, who had no idea of any plans to withdraw other than wild stories no one believed, rebuilt them. The runoff of rainwater had caused havoc, flooding trenches and collapsing sandbag emplacements. Corpses had washed down the hills and gullies like leaves caught in a gutter. It could have been a military disaster for the invaders except that the Turks suffered just as much and didn't get a chance to take any advantage.

'At least it keeps the flies away,' Dexter offered, shoving his hands almost into the flames. One fingerless glove smoked and he pulled it back hastily.

The three of them wore a ridiculous assortment of clothing. Anything that helped keep them warm, like extra shirts, socks and makeshift scarves around their necks made from rags. All filthy, all taken from the dead and wounded, the latter often happily on their way to hospital and glad to help out. The rumours of an evacuation had achieved just one certain result—the supply corps had sent back to Egypt the only shipment of winter clothing, believing the army wouldn't be there for the cold weather.

Surprisingly, Dexter was in the best health. He'd caught dysentery and suffered malnutrition like everyone, and yet he shook these things off quickly. George, on the other hand, never seemed to entirely lose the diarrhoea and a sallow skin appearance. Joseph wasn't much better. He wasn't out sniping today because his muscles started trembling whenever he tried to stay still, taking the weight of the rifle on his forearms. He knew from past experience that the condition would go away in a few days. His score was up over 200.

The men continued to keep count and applauded the mounting tally. Joseph the "Assassin" was a celebrity.

It was still dangerous to show any part of your body to the enemy. The Turks threw bombs and the Australians now had proper grenades to toss back in retaliation. The daily requirement of killing each other went on. However, every soldier on both sides was sick of the pointless battles. They achieved nothing.

Jonathon walked into the trench, followed by Robert.

'Hello, little brother,' Jonathon said, shaking hands with Joseph. They always did this, regardless of long it had been since they'd last seen each other.

Robert took a friendly swipe at Joseph's ears, which he ducked, grinning.

'We're looking for some help,' Jonathon said, blowing on his cold fingers. 'They said grab anyone I want not in the front line. Just one section. You blokes want to go for a walk to the beach?'

As sergeant, it was George's place to answer. 'What for?' he said suspiciously.

'Unloading barges, what else? Before a storm front gets here. Nothing special. Some beef and ammo.'

George raised an eyebrow, unimpressed. They didn't need the beef. Migrating ducks had taken an unfortunate flight path directly over the peninsula and thousands had been brought down in a hail of gunfire.

Jonathon added slyly, 'And fresh bread from Imbros. I can probably get you a loaf each for the job.'

'Sounds good to me,' Dexter said instantly. 'Let's go.'

George asked, 'Are the barges at the pier or on the beach?'

'At the pier. It's too rough to run aground and expect to get off again.'

Unloading goods from beached boats could get wet and cold as the surf swirled up the sand and caught a man unawares. The pier offered a chance to stay drier. Joseph knew George preferred the beach. The piers moved and twisted with the swells, and it was common to lose your footing completely.

'We'll be all right, George,' he said easily. 'In fact, I'll do your bit if you give me your loaf,' he added with a wink.

George wasn't open to any deals. Neither could he deny his men a chance at the fresh bread. He said reluctantly, 'No, I'll do my share. Dexter, go and round up the rest of the lads. And tell Sar'nt Major Beatty where we're going. Tell him he can have hot toast for dinner.'

Jonathon's section had already gone ahead. As they came in view of the beach, it was obvious what the fuss was about. A line of almost unnaturally black cloud was advancing on the cove from the north. Lightning leapt down to the ocean regularly and a freezing wind touched their faces.

'This is going to be bad again,' Joseph said.

'You're right about that,' Jonathon nodded grimly. The harbour heaved with a choppy swell and small breakers crashed onto the beach. 'I reckon the sooner we get this done, the better.'

Sand whipped at them as they crossed the beach. The pier was like a carnival ride, twisting and groaning under their feet like a live thing. Two barges at the end kept slamming against the timbers with each wave. Some soldiers tried hard to fend off the worst blows, but it was almost impossible. It was going to make the job of passing crates and ammunition boxes over the gunwales to the pier extremely hazardous. The black water between seemed to be reaching up hungrily for any unwary soldiers.

They worked for two hours without a break to empty the first barge. Joseph could see that George was very uncomfortable. It was too late now and the only thing to do was finish the job. George's pride wouldn't let him stay on the beach. Each time he dropped a load on the sand at the base of the dunes, he came back eyeing the shifting jetty like a nervous animal. It didn't help that rain began to pour heavily, surprising the men because the black cloud still hadn't reached the cove.

'Fat lot of good this will be,' Joseph shouted to his brother, holding up a sodden sack of bread. Jonathon gestured helplessly at the sky.

The wind picked up and a wave swept across the pier without warning, bringing curses from the soldiers as it soaked their boots and spurted icily up their legs. Worse, the larger swell made the jetty tilt alarmingly. The second barge still had half a load of ammunition, the only supply they couldn't abandon. The terrible bully beef could sink to the bottom of the harbour any day, but not precious bombs and bullets. Grimly the men went on unloading. Joseph watched George carefully and finally couldn't stand it any longer. He stopped him halfway along the pier. George was returning to the barge for the next crate while Joseph was heading for the shore, sharing an ammunition case with Dexter.

'George, you can't swim,' he called above the sounds of wind, sea and rain. 'It's getting too dangerous. Why don't you team up with Dexter and take the stuff off us at the end of the pier? You two carry it over the beach.'

George was about to refuse. Then he nodded, his face streaming with water. 'One more, and I'll stay on the beach,' he agreed. 'I'm shitting myself every time this fucking pier moves.'

Joseph grinned and used his free hand to give him a slap on the shoulder. 'So am I, but at least I can swim to the beach if the bloody thing tips me off.'

Dexter and Joseph dumped their load at the dunes and turned around. Dexter stopped at the end of the jetty to wait for George, who they could see coming back holding the rear handles of a case.

The first warning of the wave for Joseph was a hissing noise. He stared around anxiously, at first thinking it was a Turkish shell about to land close. They hadn't fired all day. Instead, he saw a high swell of black water with a frothing whitecap, bearing down on the pier. It was twice as big as any before. Just about the entire working party was actually on the pier, either making the journey or gathered around the barges. Like George, most of the men had their heads bent against the weather.

'*Look out*!' Joseph screamed uselessly into the wind. He pointed frantically. A few of the soldiers heard his warning and looked up, some habitually towards the sky. As Joseph had, they expected an incoming artillery shell. Few of them saw the wave.

It crashed into the pier, breaking waist-high on the men caught in the open. Everyone fell and disappeared into the boiling foam. Those soldiers around the barge were carried into the vessel, which foundered then slowly emerged floating again with water pouring from the decks. The men surfaced with it, lying sprawled across the remaining cargo.

A second wave followed, not as bad, but it nearly took Joseph's running feet away as he rushed down the jetty. A dozen heads bobbed in the open water, arms flailing. Nobody was left on the pier, although some men clung to the edge. Joseph's thoughts were for George, who had vanished like the rest. Jonathon, he knew, was a good swimmer.

'George? *George!*' Joseph yelled frantically at the men in the foam. 'Where are you?' Again a wave nearly carried him into the sea, hitting him from behind as he searched the water. In the last moment, before one of the struggling heads sank below the surface he recognised George's pale, terrified face imploring him. He was less than ten yards out.

He ripped off his boots, flung them aside and dived into the sea, striking out for the spot where George had gone down. His clothing dragged heavily and the water was a thin mass of roaring bubbles around his head. It was cold, clutching at his chest. He felt himself lifted, then dumped into a trough. After thrashing for a dozen strokes he twisted around, then he dived and kicked towards the bottom.

On the warm, sunny days when they swam for pleasure the Aegean had been clear. You could see for some distance under the water. Now it was dark and murky. Joseph could hardly see his own fingers in front of his face and didn't know if he was really making any progress into the depths. In desperation, he reached out around him, hoping to feel George, but found nothing and soon had to return to the surface.

He ducked downwards again, thrusting with his legs to get deep faster.

This time, as his lungs were about to burst, he felt a limb brush against his. It was an arm and he managed to grasp the hand as it was about to float away. Desperate for air again he struggled upwards, pulling the other man with him. Something was wrong and he felt a dreadful, snapping sensation. The hand came away. Gasping, he broke into the open air and stared in shock at what he held. It *was* a hand, now severed at the wrist and trailing grey tendrils. It must have belonged to an old corpse trapped below the jetty and now freed by the heavy weather. With a cry of disgust he hurled it away. He was preparing to go under again, when a voice called his name.

Jonathon stood beside Dexter on the pier. Blood poured down his cheek from a cut above his eye. He was reaching towards Joseph and although his words couldn't be heard, it was clear he wanted him to come back.

'No!' Joseph shouted, choking on sea water. He dived and as he groped around, he couldn't help thinking what else might be sharing the water with him. More corpses, some that been submerged since the April landings.

This time he found nothing.

Twice more he tried and on the last attempt admitted that he barely had the strength to get back to the surface. His clothes felt like lead. George would be deep below him now and beyond saving.

Joseph used his last reserves to swim back to the jetty. Dexter and Jonathon hauled him onto the pier, and the waves kept washing over him. So they dragged him to the shore where he lay face down in the sand, sobbing with rage and grief.

***

For two days the rain caused much damage, then it stopped—though not for better weather. It got colder.

And the rain turned to snow.

The novelty for the Australian troops faded quickly. Icicles as hard as iron formed in the dugouts. Clean drinking water, so precious even after the pouring rain, turned to useless ice. Driven by an incessant wind, the snow caused deep drifts in the trenches that hid everything, the men tripping on all manner of things under it. Then constant traffic created a freezing slush, soaking them from the waist down. Beyond the trenches, Gallipoli took on a Christmas-like innocence, with the blanket of white burying the corpses and their stench.

Beneath the snow living soldiers were freezing. Neither side was prepared for the sudden, plummeting temperatures. An unspoken truce took over as enemies met scrounging for wood to burn. Few rifles could fire anyway, the oil in the mechanisms locking into solid ice. Major Willow, personally inspecting the sentry outposts, found a man still standing and gazing through his loop-hole at the Turks. He had frozen to death.

Joseph had stopped sniping. When he worked, it was vital not to move at all. Right now, that would mean freezing to death like the sentry.

On the third day of winds and snow he was poking at a tin of bully beef in the fire. The contents seemed to sizzle through holes poked in the steel, but it was only on the outside. He knew the middle of the beef would still be frozen solid.

'They've sent Beatty away,' Dexter told him, sitting down heavily beside him and rubbing his hands together furiously. 'He's got bad frostbite on his crook leg. They say he didn't think the numbness was anything different. The old bastard must be mad as a cut snake. First he survives the boiling heat of South Africa, then this bloody place in summer, only to get kicked out of the army with frostbite.'

'They won't kick him out, while he can lift a rifle and fire it,' Joseph said dully. 'We're losing too many blokes.'

'Yeah, well he won't be leading any bayonet charges either.'

Dexter looked around at the thick snow. A rim of ice hung along the parapet.

'Do you think we'll be staying all winter? Everyone's talking about a retreat.' 'Which way? Back out to sea?'

At first, Dexter didn't reply. The cove was an impassable mess, strewn with storm wreckage from the past three days. The piers were all damaged and several boats had sunk.

'Well, we can't just *give in.*' he said, finally.

‘Hell, I don’t know about giving in,’ Joseph shrugged. ‘I can’t see us going anywhere, that’s all. A storm like this and the whole bloody army would drown, if the Turks even let us get into the boats.’

Nobody wanted to admit defeat and leave, although all the stories of a possible evacuation had a ring of hope. They ignored the harsh reality that tens of thousands of men might be condemned to death or surrender in the process.

‘Something’s got to happen,’ Dexter said stubbornly. ‘Christ, we deserve better than this.’

***

"Something" came the next day, when the sun shone weakly from a clearing sky. The killing wind had finally gone and men emerged from dugouts blinking in the light, like animals coming out of hibernation. Word passed around that over 1000 soldiers suffered from frostbite and 200 had drowned in the sea or in their own flooded bunkers.

The job of rebuilding began, mindful that the bad weather had been premature and winter was still a month away. After only three days of freezing snows they’d sustained serious casualties. How could they possibly survive the entire season?

As if to taunt them all into staying, the fine conditions prevailed and gave the Anzacs their best chance to establish a permanent position. The snows and the stinking mud were soon forgotten. Longer nights allowed plenty of rest and even the Turks didn't bother them much. Shelling dropped to a minimum.

The future was uncertain, and for the moment things were almost comfortable. For the first time since the April landings, plenty of water was available.

Captain Moore broke the news to Joseph's section. Only seven of them were left. His face frightened everyone as he confronted them huddled together in a sheltered gully. With a sinking heart, Joseph guessed a final attack would be mounted while the weather held good.

'We're going, boys,' Moore said. 'We're leaving. The top brass have decided to evacuate and the army's pulling out completely.' Moore coughed into his hand and added unconvincingly, 'We're going to live and fight another day.'

There was a shocked silence, then Dexter blurted out, 'But we haven't given it our best shot, sir! We can't leave now.'

'Nobody wants to shirk the fight, Private Bell. Grand tactics are what count. The powers-that-be know what they're doing.'

'Since fucking when?' someone else snarled.

'That's enough of that,' Moore snapped, judiciously avoiding identifying the speaker. 'Corporal Robertson, you are to report at Battalion Headquarters at 1300 sharp for special instructions. The rest of you, carry on as usual and don't do anything foolish. You'll all be needed in France now, I expect.'

As he turned away, his shoulders seemed to sag with disappointment.

Dexter realised Joseph had gone too, walking in the opposite direction.

'Where are you going?' he called after him.

'Come along, if you like.'

After a while they stopped at a line of graves, the rough wooden crosses leaning in all directions since the flooding. Ben's was directly in front of them. George had never been recovered from the sea.

'I can't believe we're going,' Joseph whispered. Dexter nearly answered him, then realised he was talking to the broken ground. 'It's all been a waste if we leave now.'

Joseph tried to straighten the cross. It refused to stay upright in the loose soil. He seemed at a loss what to do. Dexter found some rocks and silently packed them around the base. Joseph helped and when it was finished they sat for a minute, staring at the grave. There was a rattling noise from above and Joseph looked up at a seaplane flying high over the beach.

He said quietly, 'If we get out of here alive, that's where I'm going. No more of these bloody trenches. Want to come with me, Dex? Learn to fly?'

Dexter pulled a face. 'I can't even ride a horse,' he reminded Joseph unhappily.

Time to Go: Anzac Cove

In the end, the evacuation was the best planned and executed manoeuvre the invaders had attempted. It began with a puzzling pattern of behaviour. On some nights not a single shot was fired at the Turks, or any bombs thrown or even insults shouted. The Australian front line was held in utter silence.

Soldiers began to leave in the dead of night with sacks tied to their boots to deaden the sound of marching, especially on the timber jetties. The flotillas that collected them vanished over the horizon before the sun rose. Still, a daily load of stores, ammunition and reinforcements arrived at the cove. The Turks didn't know they were the same empty boxes that had come the day before, reloaded in the dark, and the same men marching up the sand. Other ruses, not so elaborate, were carried out all over the front line. The men moved constantly during the day, firing from different positions to give the illusion of greater numbers. Someone came up with the clever idea of tins, one weighted with water and dripping into another, as timing devices to fire rifles automatically. Hundreds were set up all over the front line. Extra campfires were lit. They even staged a cricket match in full view of the Turks, beyond the snipers' range to show that everything was normal.

Each night, the Anzac force dwindled in size and it got very dangerous for the men who stayed, mostly volunteers from the original landings who didn't want to leave until the last moment. The greatest risk was a Turkish attack during this final phase.

***

Joseph insisted on being among the last to go, arguing that the Turks might be suspicious if the "Assassin" seemed to be absent. It was a thin excuse, but Captain Moore accepted it and allowed Dexter to remain as spotter too. The two of them went in search of Jonathon to tell him.

The trenches felt eerily empty as they moved through the beachhead, although the fire-steps were still manned at wide intervals.

'I hope the Turks don't get bored and come have a look,' Dexter said nervously to Joseph in front of him.

'This is madness,' Joseph agreed. He didn't feel too safe either.

They found Jonathon and Robert hunched beside a tunnel, inspecting the opening anxiously. Looking up at Joseph's arrival, Robert offered a too-cheerful greeting.

'Just the blokes we need,' he slapped Dexter on the shoulder.

Joseph was immediately wary. 'Why? What do you want me for?'

'Not you—him,' Robert nodded at Dexter, who gave Joseph a helpless look.

From beside the tunnel, Jonathon said, 'One of the sappers has put the mother of all mines right under the Turk's trench. There's a ton of explosive at the other end of this tunnel, but some bloody fool kicked the fuse wire and we don't know for sure it's still in place. We need somebody small to go have a look.'

'Oh now, come on...' Dexter held up his hands. 'I hate small places. I couldn't hide in cupboards as a kid or anything—'

'It's not *that* small, and it's perfectly safe,' Robert told him, shoving a torch into his hand. 'Just crawl down and make sure the fuse is still buried in the powder. And don't hang about for a smoke,' he added with a wink.

'Oh Christ,' Dexter moaned. He shrugged off his jacket and knelt down beside the hole. He hesitated for a moment with a last, despairing glance at Joseph, who encouraged him with a thumbs-up.

They watched his boots disappear into the darkness.

'Are you sure it's safe?' Joseph asked Robert.

'Nope. He's a bloody idiot,' Robert waved at the tunnel. 'You wouldn't get me down there for a hundred quid.'

'Nor me,' Jonathon said with a grin.

'Great. I think you should have told him.'

The tunnel was shored up by timbers, expertly placed by men who had been miners in civilian life. It wasn't as bad as Dexter expected, but it was still awful. He crawled on his hands and knees, sometimes sinking into mud still soft from the rains, and he had to shake off the creeping sensation of all the dirt above him, a sense of the weight trying to crush down. And images of a cave-in, burying him alive. Instead, he concentrated on the black wire on the floor and prayed he would reach its end soon. It seemed to take forever.

He was glad to find a large chamber had been dug to accommodate the explosives, also giving him space to turn around. The trip was worth it, because the end of the fuse lay two feet from the nearest charge. Dexter carefully replaced it, then stacked a second satchel on top to prevent it happening again.

As he twisted around to start the return journey, a noise made him go still.

It was voices, distant but unmistakable. He couldn't understand them, and it needed a second to figure it was the Turks above him. The enemy moving around their own trenches, oblivious to the huge mound of death under their very feet. Despite the earth between them, Dexter gave a shudder at being so close. What if he coughed or sneezed, and they heard him? Nobody had warned him about *that*, the bastards.

That gave Dexter enough anger to return along the tunnel without so many misgivings. He emerged smeared with mud from head to foot and made a comical sight.

'Why didn't you tell me I'd be right under the bloody Turks' arses?' was the first thing he snapped at Robert.

'What are you talking about?' Robert hid a smirk at Dexter's appearance.

'I could hear them. Yabbering to each other. I was right under their damned feet.'

'What'd you expect? That's good,' Jonathon said calmly. 'Then the sappers did a fine job. Is the fuse all right?'

'Yes, the bloody fuse is all right *now*.' Still annoyed, Dexter looked around for his jacket. Joseph was holding it for him.

'You're a bloody hero, Dex,' Joseph said sincerely. 'No doubt about it.'

***

The last night on the peninsula, the men filed silently and without smoking down to the beaches and the final boats. Booby traps were laid, fuses were lit, and festoons of barbed wire hauled into place to hinder any pursuit. Behind them in the front lines the automatic rifles fired regularly, the triggers pulled by the leaking tins.

It took every hour of darkness they had for these remaining troops, nearly 5000 of them, to get into the boats. The only alarm for Jonathon and his section was when Private Jones went missing.

'Where the hell's Jonesy?' someone asked. They were sitting in a boat still tied to the pier.

'For Christ's sake, who saw him last?' Jonathon snapped. No one answered. 'Oh shit,' he breathed, looking back up towards the deserted front lines.

Then Jones appeared, running along the jetty until he tumbled frantically in among them.

'Where the hell have you been?' Jonathon snarled.

'I–I fell asleep. I woke up suddenly, and you were all *gone.*' Jones looked terrified.

Jonathon could hardly believe it and was lost for words.

Robert reached forward and gave Jones a clip over the ear, making him yelp. 'You bloody fool.'

In the pre-dawn light, piles of stores left on the beach were set on fire and the boats pushed away from the pier. With perfect timing, a mine detonated with a tremendous roar and sent a tower of smoke and debris into the brightening sky. The Turks responded with a furious barrage of rifle fire, unaware that they were shooting at empty trenches. By the time they stopped, puzzled at the lack of response, the last Anzacs were well off the beach and had left it all behind.

In the quiet splashing of the oars, someone in Joseph's boat summed it up for all of them.

'Well, that was all a fucking waste of time, wasn't it?'

Time to Go: Lemnos Island

On Lemnos, despite suffering the same freezing winds, the snowstorms, the lack of proper clothing and rations, and the usual disdain from the officers, the nurses stayed cheerful and performed their tasks as best they could. Even Julia recovered enough to help with light duties, although it would be some time before she might be properly rostered.

Then a small miracle happened. A new officer arrived, flanked by Colonel Fischer and his second in command, Lieutenant Colonel Drake. He stood among the nurses' tents and scowled at everything. While the women made a point of keeping their distance, Rose with her mind on other matters managed to pass in front of the three men without really noticing them.

'Sister? Excuse me, do you have a moment?'

The officer wasn't asking. It was a command. His name was Lieutenant General Freemason and he considerably outranked his two companions. Startled out of her reverie, Rose sighed at the inevitable and silently cursed herself for walking into the trap.

'Good morning, gentlemen,' she said with the barest civility.

Freemason looked her over slowly. 'Where is your uniform, Sister?'

'I'm wearing my only uniform, sir,' she explained wearily. 'The weather hasn't encouraged washing it of late.' She waited for a nonsensical reprimand. It was the army's way.

Freemason turned on Fischer. 'Colonel, this young lady is nursing our troops back to health, and she is dressed in *rags*?'

Fischer looked uncomfortable. 'As the sister says, things haven't been very favourable lately, sir.'

'I fail to see the relevance, when she has nothing to wash,' Freemason said dryly, then asked Rose, 'May we inspect your hut? As long as it doesn't inconvenience anyone, of course.'

Listening carefully, Rose had already detected a change in fortune and her instincts were prickling, warning her. This still took her by surprise and she nearly laughed out loud.

'We're billeted in tents, like everyone else,' she said, giving in to a smile.

Again, Freemason rounded on Fischer. 'They're *all* in tents?'

'Oh, didn't I say that, sir?' Fischer turned to Drake. 'Did we ever look at housing the nurses in huts, Drake? I thought we did.'

Drake was momentarily wide-eyed. 'Ah, I think we did, sir. But things got difficult, as you say.'

'Then can we look at your *tent*, Sister?' Freemason said to Rose with forced patience.

'Certainly, sir. It's just over here.'

Rose led them to her tent and drew aside the flap. Things inside hadn't changed since their arrival, except for extra blankets that had been made into beds on the ground. A wooden crate served as a table for both her and Julia, with a single oil lamp. Personal luggage was stacked in a corner.

She said cheerfully, 'We don't collect much, sir. It all gets blown to kingdom come, when the tent collapses with the wind, which is just about every night.' Freemason was obviously furious.

'No huts, Colonel Fischer? No proper bathroom—not even any damned beds, man? How are the nurses supposed to carry out their work under such wretched conditions?'

'The men aren't faring any better,' Fischer tried.

Freemason snapped, 'Your officers live in comparative luxury, for God's sake!'

Fischer's eyes flicked to Rose, mutely complaining about being spoken to like this in front of a junior. Freemason acknowledged this with a noise of disgust before thanking Rose kindly for her time. Then he strode angrily away towards the officers' mess fully expecting Fischer and Drake to follow.

Rose watched them go until she was surprised by someone touching her arm.

'What was all that about?' Matron Lambert asked.

'I think that was our knight in shining armour, Matron,' she said. 'At last.'

***

The nurses were issued with beds and extra clothing—an odd assortment of riding jodhpurs and wet-weather gear, but clothing all the same. A hut with a real bath was built and they were given proper facilities at their mess tent. Other huts for billeting were promised as well, although that would take time.

All this was tempered by the news of the Gallipoli evacuation. A pall of disappointment and frustration fell over everyone. It had all been for nothing.

The battle was over.

It was soon announced that the hospital on Lemnos would be abandoned too. All the wounded still on Lemnos would be transferred to Cairo, and the nursing staff would be reallocated as necessary.

***

Things came to an end quickly.

On a cold January morning, Rose, Julia and all their colleagues were huddled together on the pier at Mudros Harbour waiting for a lighter to take them aboard a troopship. Bags and suitcases were piled around them.

'It feels like we've lost the war,' Julia said to Rose. They were perched back-to-back on a bollard.

'Not at all.' Rose sniffed morosely into a handkerchief. She felt a head cold coming. 'I doubt it ever mattered. The real war is in France—always has been. This was a sideshow. Isn't that what they called it?'

'Surely not. All those men died for something, for God's sake. Anyway, I hope this damned boat arrives soon. I'm freezing.'

'It'll come. The army won't forget us.'

Matron Lambert and her nurses were entitled to expect that at least they might leave the island in a better manner than they'd arrived, but it wasn't to be. Colonel Fischer's methods haunted them one last time. They waited in vain all the rest of the day. At nightfall, Matron surrendered her last hope and ordered everyone to walk the miles back to the hospital. There, with the place mostly dismantled, they were forced to sleep without blankets and on the ground, crowded into the few remaining tents.

The next day was more successful, though they waited in the open for hours before eventually boarding a ship for Egypt. They were among the last to leave.

Like the soldiers at Anzac, they left behind only the dead in vast cemeteries.

The War in Europe

We imagine the Western Front as a vast, monochrome panorama of destruction. Photographs and silent movies were taken in black and white, so everything is seen in various shades of neutral grey. It's hard to envisage the battleground with any colour at all. Only paintings and some very rare photography can offer different hues.

In reality, in 1916 the war was very colourful. It's important to fill in those imagined greys with scenes of what it was truly like. Early French soldiers wore blue jackets and bright red trousers in an almost Napoleonic tradition of blatantly announcing yourself to the enemy. At the beginning of the conflict, during that week when over 40,000 Frenchmen were killed, under a clear blue sky their bodies littered the green fields like thousands of fallen flags.

By the time the stalemated Western Front was established ("Western" refers to the western-most limit of the German's advance in relation to their own country. Thus their attacks on Russia were known as the "Eastern" front) the area of no-man's-land varied from between half a mile to, in extreme cases, twenty yards. Mostly the shelling from both sides carried into or beyond the opposing trenches and no-man's-land remained largely untouched. So between the trenches a green and lush vegetation grew unchecked, often flowering beautifully, fertilised by the rotting corpses of past battles. Add to this the tattered uniforms in all styles, the myriad of lost equipment and material, and yes—it was a colourful place. The trenches of the Western Front were a blight against a perfect, French countryside in all its glory. There was nothing black and white about it at all. Only later in the war, when massive bombardments were "marched" for a week at a time across no-man's-land in front of impending infantry advances, was the ground churned into a universal, black mud, the trees turned to broken, blackened stumps.

When the Australians first arrived at the front, spring was pushing winter back, blooming in all its beauty, spreading wildflowers among the corpses and carpeting the land with fresh, green grass. No one knew that winter would return within weeks at a terrible cost.

At Verdun, the French were being slaughtered in their thousands again. The British High Command were planning to mount their own offensive in the Somme Valley to distract the Germans and ultimately, they hoped, win the entire armed conflict. The Australian troops, it was decided, would need "blooding" against a significant target to teach them the art of war in France.

London, February 1916

Piccadilly Circus was a mass of people all hurrying around Jonathon as if he were a stone in the middle of a stream. It was five o'clock on a winter evening and nearly night. Travellers tried to find their way while the last daylight persisted. Blackout conditions meant the city went dark with the sunset.

He leaned back against a mailbox, smoking and trying to appear calm, unaware that he raised himself repeatedly on tiptoe to look across the top of the crowds. Rose was ten minutes late, and that was enough to worry him that she wasn't coming at all.

'You look like you're trying to see the king!' Her voice came from behind him.

Jonathon spun round and there she was, a long, black dress and matching coat, with a dark scarf protecting her hair. It struck him as unusual until he realised it was always the white nurse's pinafore that he expected to see.

'Hello,' he said with a wide, nervous smile. He didn't know if he should kiss her, or take her hand—or do anything. Three months felt like a lifetime. 'God, it's good to see you again,' he said finally without touching her.

'And don't *you* look well.' She stretched up to kiss him briefly on the cheek. He tried to respond, but made awkward, embarrassed moves and the moment was lost. They were left holding hands. Without letting go, Rose stepped back and inspected him.

'The good life suits you,' she said.

'It's just a new uniform and three meals a day,' he said. It was true. The heavier, winter uniform with its bulky overcoat made him appear well fed and two months regular rations since he'd left Gallipoli had made a difference.

'Not to mention some decent sleep,' she added for him.

He decided not to tell her that he *wasn't* sleeping well. At night, his mind still filled with the horror of the last nine months, while his body lay tense, ready to fight.

'Enough about me. You look beautiful.'

I doubt you can see me at all,' she laughed, gesturing at her clothes. 'Thank you anyway. You're very gallant. Where are we going?'

She took his arm and they strolled along the footpath. He said, 'To supper, then a show.'

'Are we meeting Robert?'

'Ah... no. Robert has gone with some lads to... well, another show. But he's dying to meet you. He said he'd wait until we were sure you're here.'

'Oh?' Rose arched a knowing eyebrow. 'And supper? How did you book that, since you couldn't be sure I was arriving?'

'I made an arrangement with a restaurateur,' he said grandly.

He'd received a note from Rose saying her ship was berthing in Southampton any time during the week, but nothing was certain. Replying to the address she gave him, Jonathon promised to wait in Piccadilly Circus every evening for an hour until she got there. This had been the third night, and for the previous two he had waited in the freezing cold long after he'd promised until the last tram to his barracks just before ten o'clock. 'And the show?' she asked slyly. 'Is it the same one Robert is seeing?'

'Certainly not,' he grinned.

The cafes and restaurants all had thick curtains across their windows, though discreet gaps indicated they were open, and some had coloured lanterns in the doorways. Jonathon and Rose used the faint lights to find their way along the streets.

'Here we are.' He guided her into a low-ceilinged room. The restaurant was dark and filled with couples, servicemen in uniform with young women. The air was thick with cigarette smoke and candle fumes. A waiter led them to a setting for two under some stairs.

'Business is obviously booming,' Jonathon said to Rose, feeling disappointed in the place now. It had been hard to find anywhere willing to reserve a table for consecutive days without insisting he pay each night.

'Then the food must good,' she reassured him, sensing his dismay.

'Are you hungry?'

'Starving. Besides, I doubt I'll ever refuse the opportunity to eat a proper meal again.'

They had a supper of watery soup, followed by a casserole with rather suspect traces of meat. It was supposed to be beef. Jonathon reckoned it was horsemeat. There was also crusty bread, and Jonathon had ordered a red wine.

'So I don't get to meet your brother either?' Rose asked and caught him watching her.

'No, he's gone absolutely bonkers, I'd say.'

'Sounds exciting.'

'Flying aeroplanes over the desert? I can't believe he wanted to stay in

Egypt. I thought Joseph would jump at the chance to see London.'

'And the Western Front?'

He shook his head. 'I offered again to get him a transfer to our unit, but he was set on joining the flying corps. He lost a few good friends at Anzac and things weren't the same after that. With a bit of luck, it'll take him so long to learn flying, the war will be over first.'

She looked around the restaurant. 'I'd say the soldiers are the only ones who want the fighting to stop,' she said softly.

'They might as well spend their wages while they can,' he said. 'Who knows what tomorrow will bring?' That came too close to their own unhappy dilemma, and he changed the subject.

'So, what is this place where you're staying? How come you're not billeted with the rest of your company?'

'It's the same flat I lived in before I left for Australia. The girls are still there and said it was okay for me to bunk on the floor. Matron Lambert's having a pickle of a time getting everyone bedded down somewhere, so it'll help until something better comes along. What about you?'

'We've got barracks at Battersea. It's a bit crowded, but we're used to that. We can do what we like. Everyone treats us like we're going to win the war for them.'

Rose pulled a grim face. 'How long before they send you over the Channel?'

'No one seems to know, or they're not telling us. Spies are everywhere, remember.' He winked. 'It won't be long.'

'Then I'll see you over there, I expect.'

'You're going to France?'

'We all volunteered to work in the Casualty Clearing Stations. The hospitals here can do without us.'

'A Clearing Station? I've heard they're just behind the lines, in range of the German artillery.'

'We didn't come all this way to live the high life in London.'

'Still, it's—' Jonathon stopped himself and took a different tack. 'Does your father know?'

'No, and he *doesn't* need to find out. Not until I want him to.'

'How would I tell him?' He raised his hands in surrender. 'He's never heard of me.'

'I've mentioned you several times in my letters.'

Jonathon found that encouraging and stored it away. He looked the clock.

'Bloody hell, we'll miss our show.'

They quickly finished their drinks and left.

The play was a typical English farce with lots of jokes at the Kaiser's expense and cheerful sing-a-longs about the poor rations and wartime conditions. Jonathon was happy just to have Rose sitting beside him, their shoulders touching and fingers entwined. Every time she moved, he feared it would be to pull away, but she was only laughing at the actors or joining in with the audience to boo at the villains.

Afterwards he accompanied her all the way home, which meant that their goodbyes at her front gate were hurried so that he could catch a return tram.

'When can I see you again?' He had hold of her hands and didn't want to let go. 'Tomorrow?'

Her hesitation alarmed him. 'I promised Julia we could go out somewhere. I hate to disappoint her.'

'She could come with us.'

'I suppose so. Could you bring someone nice to partner her? What about your friend Robert?'

'Definitely. He'd love to. I'll make sure he has a proper bath and everything.' Jonathon hoped he sounded more confident than he felt, and that he wasn't making any rash promises. Robert was meeting different women almost each night, or so he claimed. 'We'll come and pick you up,' he said.

She smiled at his eagerness. 'No, it's quicker if we meet like this evening.

Besides, I have to get Julia first, remember?'

They kissed and hugged, which turned into a tight, shivering embrace to fight off the cold. Then he hurried off to catch his tram. His footsteps were light, as if he were walking on air.

Rose went inside feeling just as happy, although their relationship was again becoming closer than they'd agreed was wise. Things just *happened*, like the kissing and hugging, despite their intentions.

She was smiling ruefully to herself when she walked into the parlour. The lights were still lit and turned low, she assumed, to guide her. Then she went still with shock seeing Matron Lambert in one of the chairs. Her face was grave and she offered no greeting, but stood up slowly, a piece of paper clasped in her hand.

Rose's heart turned to ice.

'Who is it?' she asked softly. 'My father or Donald?'

'Your brother, Donald,' she whispered. 'I'm sorry, Rose. He's been killed in Palestine.'

***

The next day, Donald's death weighed like a dulling black pall on her mind, but Rose went to the hospital for training as usual. There was nothing better to do, and she needed to keep herself occupied. There was an emptiness inside her too, and an odd feeling that she had missed or forgotten something. Later, she would realise that it was the rest of Donald's life. The many, many things he would have said or done, all a part of her world in some way. Now they would never happen.

There was no question of returning to Australia to be with her father. If she could have stepped into his embrace right now, it would have had meaning. Common sense said that the six-week journey by sea would ease the pain and turn it to pangs of guilt that she'd abandoned her important work here with the army. Besides, since the Germans had sunk the American liner *Lusitania*, no one was safe on the oceans and her father would worry himself sick.

And last, Donald was already buried in Palestine. It wasn't a case of accompanying his remains back to Australia. He'd been dead over two weeks.

You really should go home,' Julia said, her own heart breaking at the sight of Rose's suffering.

'No, I couldn't stand to be just sitting around, thinking about things.'

Julia sighed, at a loss for any better argument.

All morning the other sisters from Rose's unit offered their condolences. Everyone had something kind to say and Rose thanked them sincerely, but by lunchtime she needed to get away. Her cheeks felt hot and flushed the whole time and she yearned for fresh air. She and Julia went for a walk on a nearby common.

It had snowed lightly during the night, powdering the grass and trees. They walked slowly, their breath clouding around them, and it was a long time before either of them spoke. Rose was deep in thought and Julia didn't want to disturb her.

'Oh, I forgot to tell you about tomorrow night,' Rose said finally, with a forced cheerfulness.

'Goodness, don't bother about it now,' Julia said. 'There'll be plenty of time for that sort of thing later. You haven't had a chance to tell me about Jonathon. Is he well?'

'Yes, very well. And we *must* bother with tomorrow night. I told Jonathon I'd see him and you're coming too.'

'Can't you get a message to him?'

'I don't want to.'

Julia was flustered. 'Well, if that's the case, perhaps I should leave you alone. If you just want to see Jonathon, I mean.'

'No, you don't understand. He's bringing his friend Robert to meet you. We're all going out together.'

'What? You arranged a partner for me? I don't know about *that...*' She panicked. Then her anxiety faded. An easy excuse was available. 'Well, never mind. It's hardly proper we should do anything like that under the circumstances—'

'Rubbish,' Rose cut her off impatiently. 'The circumstances are exactly why we should carry on as normal. I can't believe Donald would want me sitting around mourning. This war is stealing everything away. So much is being *lost* every single minute.' Her tears threatened to come back and she swiped at her eyes.

'I–I don't understand,' Julia said quietly.

'Don't you see? I'm not crying about the past, or the memories. It's Donald's future I won't see, like him meeting a girl and getting married. His first child... everything that should have happened. What if Jonathon were killed tomorrow? Would I be glad we didn't become lovers, or would I regret our not seizing the chance when we had it?'

'Rose!' Julia was horrified.

'Oh, I'm not talking about throwing myself into a bed. I just mean, perhaps we should live our lives to the full and not be afraid of the consequences...'

Julia groaned and gestured helplessly. 'I can see it's going to be such a cheery night out with all this soul searching and Donald's death.'

'It'll be all right. Things might be uncomfortable for a few minutes, that's all. We're all grown up, aren't we?'

They were interrupted by a small dog that ran up to them, leaving a trail of green holes across the snow. Rose bent down and patted it before an elderly man called it away, tipping his hat to the two nurses. Julia gave him a wave.

'It's all right for you, Rose,' she went on. 'You always know what you're *doing*.'

'I don't, actually. I really don't.'

'What if this Robert fellow is horrid? What am I supposed to do?'

'If he's a close friend of Jonathon's, I'm sure he'll be very nice.'

Julia pulled a face, then made a doubtful noise when Rose didn't see it.

***

'What if this Julia's a bit... well, you know... a bit plain?' Robert asked anxiously, squinting at the crowds through the falling snow.

'For Christ's sake, don't examine her like a horse,' Jonathon grumbled. 'I told you, she's quite attractive. Just your type. I saw her almost every day on

Lemnos.'

'Well, of course, you *would* say that. How else would you get me here?'

'You make it sound like I'm trying to trick you. She's wonderful, believe me.' 'So is Alice.'

'But you have to *pay* for Alice, Robert.'

'Perhaps not. I think she's starting to really like me.'

Jonathon was saved from answering when he saw Rose among the hordes on the footpath. A second later, he picked out Julia beside her. Grabbing Robert's arm, Jonathon went forward to meet them. As they all came face to face, he could see something was wrong.

'Hello, is everything all right?' he asked.

Rose touched his arm with a gloved hand. 'Hello. Can you introduce us?'

'Of course. I'm sorry. Ah, Rose Preston and Julia...' Jonathon didn't know her surname and faltered. 'Well, anyway, this is Robert Thornton.'

When they all shook hands, Jonathon gave Julia a quick peck on the cheek and she blushed. 'Nice to see you again, Julia. You're looking well.'

'Yes, thanks to Doctor Cohen. Otherwise I'd probably still be bed-ridden in Cairo somewhere.' Julia surprised Jonathon by turning to Robert and saying, 'Mr Thornton, may I have a quiet word?' She led a puzzled Robert away until they stood under a doorway. Jonathon frowned at Rose.

'It's my brother, Donald,' she explained, before he could ask. 'He's been killed in action and Julia is giving me an opportunity to tell you in private.'

'Damn it, I'm sorry, Rose.' He felt a strong urge to take her in his arms. Her stoic manner stopped him. 'Would you like me to take you home?'

'I'd hardly make an effort to come out in the freezing weather, if I just wanted you to take us back again.'

'No, I suppose not.'

'I'm afraid I won't be the best company, but I'd like to celebrate Donald's life, not mourn his death.' When Jonathon still seemed uncomfortable with this, Rose slipped her arm through his and began walking.

'I thought about this half of last night, Jonathon. I know I should be wearing black and still crying a river of tears, but Donald wouldn't like it. He'd like me to toast his memory and remember what a good brother he was to me.'

It was the same attitude the soldiers had towards losing mates in the trenches, so Jonathon understood some of it. It was just a little strange coming from a woman, and about her own family too.

'I think you're being very brave and strong,' he said, wondering if that was the right thing to say.

'Is that what it is?' Rose laughed sadly.

Robert and Julia fell in behind them. She had taken his arm too, in the most proper manner, and Robert looked quite pleased with himself.

A music theatre show seemed disrespectful, so after dinner the four of them walked the streets with little idea what to do. They discovered a dance hall with a small, inexpert orchestra providing music. Peeking through the door, Rose saw couples gliding around the floor in formal steps.

'Come on, let's go in here,' she said, pulling Jonathon past the blackout curtain. It was a tuppence each to enter and while Jonathon searched his pockets for the change, eyeing the scene doubtfully, Robert hissed in his ear.

'I can't bloody dance like this, you idiot. Why'd you bring us in here?'

'Steady on, mate. Neither can I.'

'Liar. Your mother tried to teach you. We all heard about it at school from

Joseph.'

'Did you now? Look, there's a bar over there. That's all we need.'

Rose and Julia had other ideas. What could have been a disaster turned into a lot of fun as the two girls instructed the shuffling soldiers how to dance. Some of the other couples seemed annoyed at the intrusion, while most smiled as they whirled past and even offered encouragement. The night slipped past quickly. Still, Rose asked Jonathon to take her home earlier than he'd expected.

Julia and Robert were attempting another circuit of the dance floor.

'It's all right,' Rose told him. 'Robert has already offered to escort Julia back to her billet. She was going to stay with me, but this will be better for her in the morning.'

Jonathon worried about this arrangement. He didn't get a chance to say anything to Robert and just had to hope his friend would behave himself properly to the end.

This time, as Rose and Jonathon reached her doorstep in gently falling snow, she invited him inside. There was half an hour before he needed to catch the tram. Jonathon was glad, although her mood had been subdued on the journey home and that wasn't a good sign.

She took him to the parlour, which was empty, and offered to make him tea. He accepted and perched uncomfortably on the edge of a chair, listening to a ticking clock as if it were a doomsday countdown.

I wanted to ask you something,' Rose said, just as the silence became unbearable.

'Anything you like.'

'I might change my mind about you and me spending time together. What would you say, if I wanted that? We've talked so much and now I'm making up my own mind without you. It's not very fair.'

Disappointed, he said finally, 'I'll do whatever you think is best.'

'I know it's rather outrageous for a single woman to ask a man for intimacy, but with Donald's death I'm suddenly aware of wasting opportunities. Does that sound wrong? I mean, what if something were to happen to either of us, Jonathon? Would we regret having kept our distance like we have? Or be glad that we behaved sensibly?' When he didn't answer straight away, she added, 'Well, I've decided it would be a great shame, since we are already so close.'

His mind was spinning after hearing the opposite to what he'd been expecting. 'I thought you were going to send me packing.'

She glanced at the clock. 'Well, I am, actually. You've got less than ten minutes before you'd better leave to catch your tram.'

He almost dropped his teacup, hurrying to wrap his arms around her and draw her face against his chest. She slipped her hands behind him and hugged him back. It was a clumsy embrace. He wanted to kiss her, that was the only certainty, but he was almost afraid to move and break the spell. Then he felt

Rose shaking and he instinctively held her harder. She was crying.

The last time Rose had felt the rough wool of a clean uniform against her cheek, she had been greeting Donald back home in their garden at St Kilda. The memories came rushing, releasing emotions she'd held back for two days. She had cried for Donald before, and mourned too, but in Jonathon's arms it felt for the first time truly safe to let go.

***

They had less than two months together, and even this time was broken by Jonathon being sent into the country to train for fighting the Germans, as if battling the Turks didn't count.

'They haven't learned a thing,' he told Rose on his first evening of leave. They were having tea in a café near Waterloo Station 'We all line up in a fake trench, the officers blow whistles and we walk across the open ground to the German lines. We're supposed to stay in formation and keep going. It's like something out of the last century, facing up to bloody muskets and swords, not machine guns.' He noticed that Rose had gone pale and added quickly, 'I'm sure it won't happen like that at the Front. It's all about discipline and doing as you're told, which the diggers aren't very good at. They're trying to lick us into proper military shape.' He'd affected an English accent and got a glare from a British lieutenant nearby. Jonathon stared the officer down, then winked at Rose. 'When we're in the real thing, it'll be common sense. They can't march us straight into the enemy guns again, like they did at Anzac. The boys won't let them.'

'Mutiny, Sergeant White?' she said with a weak smile. 'You'll get shot for that, instead.'

'No, we'll be all right.' He reached for her hand. 'Really. We don't take any of that rubbish. Even our officers won't commit suicide.'

If not for the war, things could have been perfect. Exciting London was all around them and buzzed with people enjoying themselves. Everyone was getting a wage and was prepared to spend it, in case of the unspoken possibility that there was no tomorrow. Robert and Julia had struck up a friendship and the four of them often went out together. You just needed to forget the real reason that everyone was there.

When Jonathon got a twenty-four-hour pass, he and Rose would stay in a hotel and treat themselves to a late night and privacy. They always rented separate rooms and Jonathon would eventually go to his own after they'd made love then talked until the early hours, lying with his head in her lap or snuggled close under the blankets against the winter cold.

The first time he'd shared her bed, he could hardly believe it as she beckoned him nervously and whispered that she was ready. She didn't want to wait until everyone else thought it proper. While the entire world was robbed of its innocence, Rose willingly gave hers to him.

When it became plain that his battalion would be shipped to France within a week, he bought the best ring he could afford and asked her to marry him.

She was taken completely by surprise. It was in the evening and they were in their favourite café sitting close to a coal fire. Outside it was raining, a thin drizzle that seemed to bring the smog of London down with it, dirtying everything rather than washing it clean.

'Oh, Jonathon,' she said with a dismay that frightened him. 'Don't you think it's a bit soon? We hardly know each other really. It's been such fun these last weeks, but to get married?'

'I love you,' he said. 'There, I've said it.'

'You told me before, but you were drunk.'

'I *do* love you, and I want you to be my wife.' He looked at her anxiously.

She took her time, so that what she'd say next wouldn't be regretted for the rest of her life. Rose had to be certain that she *wanted* to say it too.

'And I love you, Jonathon,' she whispered. 'As much as I know about these things. I'm not much of an expert.' She saw him start to smile and cut him off. 'But I can't marry you.'

'What?' The hand holding the ring froze in mid-air. 'I don't understand. If you say you love me—'

'It's not so simple. The Nursing Corps won't allow married women. I'll be ordered to resign immediately. I don't know if they even allow women to be engaged.'

It was the last reason he'd have imagined she would say no, and by far the best. He respected her dedication and knew better than to ask her to give it up for a life of sitting at home somewhere, waiting and praying for her husband to survive.

He didn't know what to say.

She solved the problem by gently taking the ring from him. 'Let's do this,' she said softly.

Taking a silver necklace from around her neck, she slipped the chain through the band, then refastened the link. The ring sat on her breast, the cheap stones glinting in the candlelight.

'I'll have to hide it under my uniform,' she told him. 'No one else must know we're engaged. We can get married later, when we know it's *safer*. Please, Jonathon. I can't do it any other way.'

'All right,' he nodded slowly and kissed her fingers. 'As long as I know you're waiting for me.'

'I'm wearing it. Not quite where I should be but wearing it all the same.'

He sat back, overcome with relief. 'God, I was so worried what you'd say. Can

I tell Robert, at least?'

'Only if you swear him to absolute secrecy.'

'And you'll tell Julia, right?'

'Probably. She can keep a secret, I think...'

They both laughed as they imagined Julia bursting with a delicious knowledge that she wasn't allowed to share.

He pointed at the door. 'Come on. Let's find some champagne to celebrate.'

***

The next day, Jonathon's battalion was told they were leaving for France the following morning, earlier than expected. They were all given a final evening of leave, and had to be back in their barracks by ten o'clock at night. Major Willow knew that many of the soldiers had found lovers, girlfriends and even wives in the past two months in London. He warned that anyone attempting to stay out all night for *any* reason would risk being mistaken for deserters, with grave consequences.

'Don't ever take it off,' Jonathon said, pressing his hand to Rose's blouse and the ring against her skin underneath. They were standing in the dark outside her flat.

'I'll wait for you to put in on my finger yourself,' she promised, kissing him one last time.

As he walked away down the footpath, he heard her voice come from the open doorway. 'Keep your bloody head down, Sergeant.'

He spun around and waved once, unsure that she could even see him. Then, turning his collar up against a sudden shower, he began to hurry in case he missed the last tram.

The Western Front

June 1916

The journey to the front line is like a descent into hell. First, the villages, still thriving and busy with people who profit from the vast army up the road, and ignoring the distant roar of artillery as if it were thunder. Almost every house has turned part of itself into a restaurant or drinking establishment of some sort, called an estaminet, the owners becoming instant publicans. Prostitutes linger in doorways. The children offer services such as laundering or polishing boots. Even the least opportunistic of the villagers can't avoid the weary soldiers who come looking for a bottle of wine, a meal or just some company.

Past the villages are the huge piles of stores and the industry needed to move it forward to the trenches. This is by men and horses mostly, although trucks are replacing animals. On the outskirts of these enormous depots are camped the troops resting from the lines. They need delousing and some decent food, and look towards the villages hungrily for things that can't be satisfied by a full stomach. The artillery is closer, a percussive pounding that makes the air shiver.

Next come the big guns themselves, large pieces that aren't moved, if it can be avoided, set in lines across the open pastures. They're surrounded by high, neat piles of shells on one side and tumbling mounds of discarded brass casings on the other. These guns fire all day long at the enemy, sometimes steadily, at others intermittently to conserve ammunition, yet never give the Germans any peace. Here the ground trembles with their firing and among the shattering noise is the yelling of orders.

The generals' headquarters are nearby. For many of the officers, this is the closest they'll ever get to the real war, although they're responsible for the day-to-day running of the battles and the issuing of most commands. Here, too, are the Casualty Clearing Stations staffed by doctors and volunteer nurses. It's the first chance of trained medical aid for the wounded, and near each station the stricken men in bloodied bandages are lying on stretchers or blankets out in the open, patiently waiting their turn while the surgeons do their work. Somewhere close will be a row of corpses awaiting burial, the wounded who couldn't hang on to life. Also a large hole for the amputated limbs and other waste.

All around these command centres and the clearing stations are the beginnings of shell craters, the furthest reach of the

German guns. At times, the shelling is dangerous and people are killed, but that doesn't happen often.

Then there's the field artillery. These are guns moved constantly, hauled by horses into strategic positions to fire at targets identified by observation balloons or aircraft. In turn, the Germans can see the field guns with their own observers and try to destroy them. Oddly, the infantry on both sides despise their own artillerymen, because while the field guns are hastily limbered to the horses and withdrawn before the enemy's response drops out of the sky, any foot soldiers camped nearby suffer the vengeful barrage.

Now anyone moving into the true front line goes underground, into communication trenches linking the rear areas with the forward positions. The Germans' heavy guns probe here often, and the landscape quickly turns into a mess of interlinked shell craters. The continuous exploding of shells loosens the soil and any normally benign rainfall, even a summer storm, turns it into a deep, clinging mire. Littered everywhere, half-buried in mud, are destroyed equipment, the remains of horses killed earlier in the war, and sometimes a pile of shredded clothing that might have been a man, but too far gone now to bother retrieving, especially if it's an enemy. Occasionally a rise in the ground will let the communication trench become a path in the open with wooden duckboards to mark the way. These are like upside-down railway tracks with the sleepers on top and the rails beneath holding them together. In places during winter downpours, it's possible for exhausted soldiers to slip from the duckboards and drown in the mud.

Finally, the men reach the forward trenches, three of four in succession with the rearmost for the reserves. This is the real front line with only no-man's-land beyond. These trenches are better established and deeper with timber retaining walls and hundreds of bunkers like small rooms. The tons of soil removed for the dugouts is put in countless sandbags for shoring up the sides. The trenches never extend for more than ten yards or so before taking a sharp turn in a sawtooth pattern. From above they appear as an untidy zigzag, so that the blast and shrapnel of any artillery shell landing directly in the trench can't carry further than that section.

It is a surreal world that only the soldiers themselves understand. The stench of corpses in no-man's-land should be unbearable, but they get used to it, eating and sleeping with it. Sometimes a near-miss by an artillery shell will unearth an old corpse. The human pieces will be flung out into the open where they belong. The risk of being killed is constant, yet such a matter of fate is not worth contemplating for long.

Maintaining the Western Front is an everyday business understood by the enemy too. Unless the gallant officers in the rear decide on an offensive, or even just a trench raid, it's possible to survive by obeying the rules. The greatest threat comes from random shells or bombs. It makes the soldiers very superstitious and even the most educated of them dependant on lucky charms or rituals.

Despite all the evidence around them, most men believe they will live to see the end of the war.

***

'Christ, it's a home away from home,' Robert said morosely, looking at the neat timber of the trench walls. Mud seeped between the logs, and beneath his feet the duckboards only just sat above the brown water covering the floor. The rain kept falling. Everyone was cold and their greatcoats were dead weights of sodden wool. The men wore steel helmets now instead of all the different hats and caps they'd had in Turkey. Although it was the beginning of summer, the torrential rain had been pouring for a month.

After eight months at Gallipoli, then recuperating and training in England for nearly half of 1916, the Anzacs finally arrived at what many believed was the real war—the fight against the Germans. Their battalion was among the first to arrive. Other Australian divisions were expected over the following four weeks.

They were in the far north of France, near Pozieres. To the south, the British armies were preparing for a huge offensive to relieve the French troops being destroyed at Verdun. They believed it might even end the war. Such grand designs didn't matter to Jonathon and his men. They just wanted somewhere dry to sleep before nightfall.

'Check the dugouts and see if the Poms have left us anything worthwhile,' Jonathon told Robert. 'Blacky? You take first sentry duty. See if the Huns have heard we're here.' This was to Crowe, who asked around for their periscope, then without complaining took up a position at a heavily sandbagged part of the fire-step.

Jonathon called louder, 'The rest of you, store your kit and make yourselves comfortable.'

There was an empty laugh.

Major Willow came splashing along the trench. Like all the Australians, he looked odd in the bulky uniform for colder climates when most of the Gallipoli campaign had been fought in shorts and ragged shirts. Even stranger were the bits of equipment hanging from him. Gas mask, ammunition pouches, binoculars and a water bottle among others, and he rattled as he walked. He spotted Jonathon and came over.

'They do quite well for themselves, don't they?' he said easily, nodding at the craftsmanship of the earthworks.

'I suppose they've been here for two years, sir. Nothing better to do.'

'Hmm, perhaps you're right.' Willow took off his helmet, ran a hand through his hair, and replaced it after he'd shaken the water off. 'A British sapper is going to come looking for you. He's heading out tonight to cut the wire, ready for a trench raid tomorrow night. I thought you should go too. It'd be good to have an experienced person to show us the ropes, so to speak. Take half a dozen lads with you. It's only to cut the damned stuff and mark it for the raiders to find. Nothing too serious.'

Everything was serious, and Jonathon would have preferred staying in the line at least this first night. The Germans were probably aware of a fresh unit, new to the front, holding this section of the line and could be tempted them into a raid. He was spared any argument. A shell ripped out of the sky and slapped an explosion nearby, showering mud and clods of green turf.

Everyone hunched over, cursing.

When Jonathon straightened up, clumps of soil fell off his back.

'What time, sir?' he asked, as if nothing had happened.

'Eightish, I was told.' Willow removed his helmet again and frowned at the muddied crown. He tried to wipe it with his sleeve. 'Sergeant Sinclair's his name. You'll be in charge, for what it's worth.'

'I can hardly tell him what to do. I won't have a clue myself.'

'No, I suppose not. Still, you'll work it out. Come and tell me all about it, when you get back. My bunker is in with D section.'

He gave Jonathon a pat on the shoulder and left, greeting everyone who caught his eye, as he moved along the trench. The major was a popular officer who had kept his reputation for not risking lives unnecessarily.

Jonathon turned to find Robert waiting patiently.

'I've found us a beaut' bunker,' Robert said. 'Come and look.'

It was about fifteen-foot square with a floor of duckboards, and several more stacked either side as beds. The walls were solid sandbags, the roof sheets of corrugated iron. Robert had already hung their rations on hooks in the middle of the ceiling to discourage the rats that roamed in great numbers. Some of them were twice the normal size, well fed on the rotting meat of the corpses in no-man's-land. The soldiers hunted them enthusiastically with bayonets.

'Is the entire British army made up of dwarves?' Jonathon said, stooping under the roof.

'Don't you like it?'

'It's all right, I suppose. Did you hear what Willow wanted?'

'Yeah. I'll come along. I want to have a look out there too.'

'You *want* to have a look?'

Robert shrugged. 'It will help to know what we're facing.'

Jonathon knew it was just Robert trying to look after him again. He often did the same back. They never admitted it to each other.

This time Jonathon had other ideas. 'What if I want you to stay here? It might be good to have an NCO stay back, in case the Huns try to jump us.'

'Nah, they won't.' Robert lit a cigarette and offered him one. Both men smoked ready-mades now, rather than rolling tobacco. Packets of Woodbines were the second currency among the soldiers. Robert carefully put the packet into a waterproof tin. 'Not now that they know the Aussies are here. The bastards are probably retreating already,' he said.

'Shit scared, you reckon?'

'Too right.'

***

Sergeant Sinclair was a short, wiry man with a permanent frown on his pale face. He had a habit of rolling the dirt from the pores of his cheeks, rubbing at the flesh as he spoke. Everything else he did almost angrily, mashing out his cigarettes and hurling the dregs of his tea. His broad Yorkshire accent was peppered with so much profanity that even the Australians were impressed.

'Fuck 'em,' he told Jonathon and Robert, when asked why no officers were coming. They were all standing close together in the bunker. 'Don't want the bastards.'

'Is it far to the wire?'

'Too fucking far. About a hundred yards. We'll have to run like bastards, if things fuck up.'

Robert was puzzled. 'Is it ours, or theirs? We're going to cut a way through our *own* wire?'

'Who knows?' Sinclair struck a match with such ferocity it nearly broke. His cigarette lit, he waved the flame out with harsh, jerky movements. 'We put more out on this side, and the Huns add more on theirs, then poor bloody sods like us have to go and cut a path through the fucking lot. It's a bloody great briar patch. Get hung up, and you're there to stay until the Huns shoot you in the morning, make no mistake.' He glared at Robert from under his eyebrows to make his point.

'Can we tunnel under it?' Jonathon asked.

'Tried that once. Then it fucking rained cats and bloody dogs and the tunnel collapsed with six blokes in it. Never saw 'em again. You want to give it another go?'

Jonathon wasn't sure if he was serious. 'No, we're not sappers. It was just a thought.'

'And a shite one at that.' His frown deepening, Sinclair nodded this opinion to himself. 'But tell your men to bring the fucking shovels anyway,' he added.

'Just in case?'

'To kill the bloody Germans with. They're better than a bayonet. You can't fucking *hit* a Hun with a knife, but you can cut the bastards with the edge of a spade *and* bash the pricks to death too.' He took a trenching tool from his belt and showed them. 'When there's a chance, get your blokes to do this.' One side of it had been serrated and sharpened to a wicked edge. It glinted in the candlelight. Robert swore softly at the sight of it.

'Tell 'em to chuck the bastard away quick smart, if they get captured,' Sinclair said. 'The fucking Huns get right pissed off if they find you carrying one.'

'Right,' Robert said quietly.

The other four men in the party were Crowe, Jones, Tanner and Marsden. With Sinclair in the lead, at 2030 hours precisely, the seven of them crept over the parapet and crawled on hands and knees through the damp long grass towards the German lines. A thin moon, suffused to almost nothing by the clouds, let them see less than a few feet in front. It was still raining and in places the men's hands sank to the wrists in cold mud.

The conditions were deplorable—and they couldn't have wished for better. The night and the weather concealed them from the German sentries, yet still provided enough light to work by when they reached the wire.

The hardest part for Jonathon was maintaining his orientation in the dark. Sinclair seemed to know exactly where he was going, detouring around clusters of rotting bodies and at one point following the remains of a hedge. Several times he turned to Jonathon behind him and whispered, 'Remember this.' It would be a broken fence post or a twist in a ditch. Once, the ground had been pastureland and quite flat. The few trees that hadn't been cleared before had long been swept away by gunfire. There were no memorable features really, but Jonathon didn't say this.

The men bunched close for a brief rest against a shattered stone fence, hardly high enough to give them cover. They pressed themselves into it anyway. Jonathon saw Sinclair peer carefully towards the enemy trenches and raised himself to do the same. A ripple of artillery fire showed them a fleeting silhouette of the barbed wire, an impenetrable mess of coils and splintered timber about twenty yards further on. Nearby, a body hung with outstretched arms, dripping water.

'That's a mate of mine,' Sinclair murmured. 'They used him for target practice long after he was dead. Some of our blokes do too. There's not as much left of him as you might think.'

Robert leaned close to Jonathon and hissed in his ear, 'Bloody hell. No wonder he's so fucking pissed off all the time.'

Jonathon was thinking that, oddly, Sinclair hadn't uttered any blasphemy as he explained the fate of his friend.

If Sinclair had heard Robert, he didn't show it. With a last, careful look over the scattered stones, he said, 'Come on, then. Let's get this over and fucking done with.'

He led them close to the hanging corpse. The barbed coils were festooned with empty cans and pieces of chain—anything that would make a noise if the wire was disturbed and alert the sentries. Tonight, they tinkled musically with leaking rainwater. The ground was a bog, since both sides frequently tried to cut the wire with artillery shells. Bodies were everywhere, mostly decomposed beyond recognition. On this side, the corpses were all British or Scots, the latter in their kilts seeming indecent in death with their naked legs pale against the black mud.

The Anzacs felt exposed and looked at each other anxiously. *Surely the Germans would watch the wire more than anything? That's what it was for*. Not just to be a barrier, but to force any raiding party into action of some kind. The darkness didn't seem so black anymore, the night brightly split too often by falling shells. They were about due for a regular flare from the enemy too.

Sinclair didn't appear bothered. He gathered them around and showed them how to cut the wire.

'You're not trying to fucking get rid of it, right?' he said in a stage whisper. 'The stuff's so bloody tangled we can cut a tunnel through it. We go under, like a fucking badger going through a hedge, got it? You blokes got badgers where you come from?'

The question was so incongruous that no one answered for a moment.

Finally Jones said, 'I dunno. Do we, sarge?'

Robert groaned quietly, 'For God's sake, who cares?'

Sinclair shrugged. 'Someone hold the wire either side of where you're cutting. Holding it fucking *tight*, so the rest doesn't shake and give us away. Take out one piece at a time. Don't do the last bit. Leave it to mask the hole. The raiders will do that as they go.'

He made Jonathon grip the rusting steel while he began to snip each strand. Jonathon stared nervously at the tins, waiting for them to chime.

'Watch where I'm fucking working,' Sinclair said softly.

'Yeah—right. Sorry.'

They took turns to help him, moving deeper into the rusting, vicious web. Sinclair had taken off his helmet in case it clattered against the coils and replaced it with a beret. Unprepared, the Australians working with him in the wire had to stay bareheaded. The pair doing the cutting needed to stay close, the men lying like lovers in the mud to keep the tunnel small so it wouldn't be noticed the next day.

It seemed luck was on their side. In the hour they needed to force a gap within reach of the open ground beyond, there was no sweep of machine gun fire and no flares.

'That'll do,' Sinclair said, crawling out of the wire backwards after Tanner, who had helped last. Jonathon didn't realise how anxiously he'd been waiting to hear this until he caught himself letting out a long, pent-up breath as if he'd held it the entire time. He caught a glimpse of Sinclair, totally covered in mud.

Even the beret and his eyebrows were caked.

'You'll have to lead the way back.'

'Then pay fucking attention. My mob's already having a rest and I want to join 'em. I only stayed behind to show you this. You'll be bringing the raiding party to the wire tomorrow night.'

Jonathon stifled an exclamation. No one had told him that before. *Did Willow know?*

Sinclair had collected his rifle and helmet, and he started back on his hands and knees for the Allied lines. Jonathon growled an order for everyone to stay close, hurried to catch up, and in the dark he nearly crawled over the top of Sinclair. He'd suddenly stopped, motioning urgently for the others to stay quiet. Slowly, like an animal stalking its prey, he flattened himself into the mud. The others did the same.

In the dark, two shapes crawled across the ground. A flash of shell fire revealed a coal-scuttle helmet, the style worn by the enemy.

The faintest movement was Sinclair's fingers in front of Jonathon's face, telling him to kill the second man. Sinclair would deal with the first.

The Germans came impossibly close before Sinclair moved, remarkably not seeing the seven men in their path. Perhaps they'd been concentrating on the wire, looking for a break. Sinclair slithered forward with surprising speed. Jonathon had his bayonet ready and had to half-jump to attack at the same time and lost his footing in the slime, before swinging the knife down hard into the back of the second man. It ricocheted off something metal and got caught in cloth. The German cried out and twisted underneath him to fight back, nearly ripping the bayonet from his grasp. His chest was exposed and Jonathon struck again, punching the blade into the man's heart. The German went instantly still beneath him.

Jonathon turned his head away to avoid staring into the dead man's face.

Beside him, Sinclair smashed at his opponent with his shovel. The German grunted with each blow. Then Sinclair reached out, tore his helmet away, and with a last deliberate strike brought the shovel down on the German's bare skull. It made an awful cracking noise, like an egg breaking. With a satisfied snarl, Sinclair shoved the body away and lay there panting.

Everyone watched him with eyes wide in the gloom.

'That bayonet was a waste of fucking time, wasn't it?' Sinclair said hoarsely. 'I told you, get a fucking shovel.'

'I was thinking we could have taken them prisoner. Saved the trouble of a raid tomorrow,' Jonathon said.

'Bullshit.' Sinclair spat into the mud. 'They're just a couple of fools lost on the wrong side of the wire. They might have screamed blue fucking murder all night giving us away and all the hard work we've just done.'

Jonathon couldn't argue with that. After Marsden checked the pockets of the dead men and found little of any importance, the patrol continued its slow progress back to their own lines. Jonathon strained to see the landmarks he'd need the following night. It took his mind off his own brutal actions. Back at the front trenches, welcoming hands hauled them over the parapet.

Sinclair didn't stay around.

'Good luck,' he said gruffly. He didn't shake hands, only offering a wave to them all before he disappeared.

The patrol were given tea and stood around in a group and smoked. Robert said after a few minutes, 'I don't know about that shovel. You going to get one, Jonno?'

'Never,' Jonathon said curtly. 'I'll stick to the one I've got and use it for digging, that's all.' He shivered in the dark, so no one saw it. 'Christ, I couldn't kill a man like that.'

'No, nor me,' Robert nodded grimly.

***

Robert started screaming. His blanket thrashed to the floor. The noise woke Jonathon and sent him stumbling across the darkened bunker to shake him.

'Hey! Wake up! You're having a bad dream. What are you trying to do? Scare me to death?'

Robert came round slowly and raised himself on his elbows, moaning and passing one hand over his face.

'You want me to light a candle?' Jonathon said.

'No–no, it'll be all right.' Robert's voice trembled. 'Christ, that was horrible. We were all being buried alive. Just our hands, coming out of the ground...'

'I thought you said this bunker was just the ticket?' Jonathon tried to smile, although he couldn't help a nervous glance at the roof.

'I don't know where I was. Not here. Nowhere, probably. You know.'

Jonathon picked up the fallen blanket and handed it to him. 'It's just a dream, remember?'

'What time is it?'

'Must be close to stand-to.' Jonathon went over, stuck his head out the entrance and Robert heard him whisper to somebody outside. Then he returned. 'Only ten minutes to go. I'm wide awake. Might as well stay up.'

Robert gripped his arm. 'Jonno, send someone else to guide that raiding party tonight. You can do that, can't you?'

'What are you talking about? I'll be fine. You can stay behind, if you like.'

'No, I'll go—instead of you, I mean.'

'For God's sake, what's the problem? Willow's expecting me to go now. He was pissed off about it, but... well... besides, I'm the only one who took any real notice of *where* to go.'

'I've got a bad feeling after that dream. You weren't in it. I couldn't see you anywhere.' He fell silent, knowing it wasn't good to say such things, even though Jonathon was the least superstitious of them all. 'Maybe you should stay low for a few days, that's all.'

'A few days? Then what? Can you promise the war will be over?' Jonathon teased him. 'Don't worry about me. I'll take my chances like everyone else.'

Someone put his head around the sacking in the entrance. 'Stand-to in five minutes, Jonno, Robert. You blokes awake in there?'

'Coming, Smithy,' Jonathon said over his shoulder.

'Don't forget. Morning hate will be on its way soon too. If they don't attack.'

'The first time for us. I can't wait.'

Morning hate was the ritual bombardment the Germans dropped on the front lines every day. There was another, usually in the afternoon. The shelling lasted about ten minutes and caused few casualties because the men were prepared and hiding deep in the bunkers. The Allied artillery did exactly the same thing to the German lines. It was an almost civil arrangement. 'Come on,' Jonathon said. 'It's time to defend king and country again.'

'Not our bloody country,' Robert grumbled.

Outside, it had stopped raining, but the sky gradually revealed itself, still overcast. The sun appeared briefly, a weak orange ball below a sheet of grey, before climbing into obscurity.

Somewhere above the clouds a single aeroplane sputtered towards the east.

No-man's-land was empty. They saw only the tall grass and in the distance the endless coils of barbed wire.

Then came a sound like the gods were ripping the heavens apart.

'Take cover,' someone yelled and they dived for the bunkers as the first shells landed on the trenches.

The Anzacs had been shelled before at Gallipoli. This was their first morning on the Western Front. The ground literally jumped beneath their feet with each explosion and sent men staggering to their knees. The noise was incredible, a physical assault that made them cry out without realising it.

All they could do was crouch down, cover their ears and eyes, and wait for it to finish. The ten minutes felt like hours.

The barrage stopped as abruptly as it had begun and the silence after it seemed total. Of course, it wasn't. Stunned, the Australians came warily out of the bunkers to check for damage and casualties. They shook themselves and stretched their limbs, as if making sure that they were actually still alive. Some direct hits had collapsed the walls and shattered the timbering—things that would be repaired by midday. One bunker took a shell, and the three men inside had been killed. Otherwise, the tremendous energy of the shelling had achieved little.

'That's one hell of an alarm clock,' Robert said shakily to Jonathon, his morbid concern at the nightmare apparently forgotten. 'Can't we just tell them we're awake?'

***

The raiding party that night was from Jonathon's own battalion, but he didn't recognise hardly any of them. So many new faces had arrived since they'd come to Europe. The sergeant leading them looked familiar. Then Jonathon remembered Sergeant Madison, the man who had been in charge of the trenches at Quinn's Post the day Albert Strand had been killed.

'Good to see it's you blokes,' Madison said, shaking his hand, then Robert's.

'I thought some Tommies would be taking us out.'

'We thought the same,' Jonathon said.

'Got the orders this morning and a bunch of trench maps, whatever good they'll be,' Madison turned grim. 'Haven't even had time to find the bloody latrines here and the bastards are sending us into the German trenches.' He had over a dozen men gathered round, all of them waiting to go. He called aloud, 'Everyone set?' Then he turned to Jonathon. 'Just the two of you?'

'I'm supposed to be your guide. Robert here can't get enough excitement and he's coming too.'

'Jon's afraid of the dark,' Robert said quickly.

Madison was in no mood for jokes. He nodded. 'Then let's get going.'

As they moved through no-man's-land, Jonathon concentrated fiercely on anything that might confirm they were heading in the right direction. The broken fence posts and piles of corpses all looked the same. At one point he hesitated.

'You all right, Jonno?' Robert whispered.

'I'm fine, but we might be fucking lost.' Jonathon was annoyed with himself.

'We must be close. If we keep going towards the Huns, we should strike that collapsed stone wall. Then we just have to figure out which way, left or right.'

Madison pulled next to them and hissed, 'What's the problem?'

'Just checking my bearings.'

'Are we nearly there?'

'Almost,' Jonathon said confidently with a glance at Robert. 'I think.'

Suddenly a shell burst revealed Sinclair's dead friend still draped over the wire about fifty yards to their left. Jonathon had brought them closer than he'd realised.

He explained that the last few feet of the tunnel still needed to be cut. 'We'll wait here,' he said. 'To help you get back to the trenches.'

'Have you got a torch?' Madison asked.

'No.'

Madison took one from his pack. 'When all hell breaks loose and you see us running, flash this, will you? We won't have time to search for the break in the wire and I don't want to be caught going up and down like bloody sheep looking for it.'

Jonathon felt that flashing a torch might be a sure way to bring all hell down on *them* too.

As Madison's raiders disappeared one by one into the coils of wire, he and Robert retreated back to the broken wall, huddled in its meagre cover and waited. Robert couldn't stop looking out at the German lines every few seconds.

'I don't like this,' he muttered. 'I've still got that bad feeling. I wish you'd stayed behind.'

'Don't start that shit again. We'll be all right. We're on this side of the wire, remember?'

'Doesn't mean much.'

'Neither do dreams.'

All around them the night grumbled and flashed like a summer storm, as it always did. That would change when the

Germans discovered Madison and his men in their trenches. It started to rain. Rivulets of water ran down off the wall to pool under their prone bodies.

'How long do you reckon they'll be?' Robert said.

'Who knows what's on the other side of the wire?'

'They've got maps.'

'Yeah, and the Huns update them for us every week.'

'You're a funny bastard.'

Robert kept peering out anxiously.

'They'll see *you* and knock your block off, if you're not careful,' Jonathon told him.

'They must be there by now.'

'We'll hear it.'

A minute later, a section of the German lines ahead erupted with rapid firing and the crack of hand-bombs. The shooting quickly spread and there were screams and yelling. Jonathon snatched a look over the wall.

'Here they come,' Robert snapped, seeing a row of figures silhouetted for a moment. They were crouched and running.

'Christ, why don't they get down?' Jonathon whispered. 'They can't stay on their feet the whole way.'

It appeared Madison and his men knew different, for each new flash showed them still up and sprinting awkwardly over the treacherous ground. One of them was being half-carried. Rifle fire sparked behind them. Within seconds, Jonathon could tell they were going to miss the break in the wire by a hundred yards. Clearly, they would have no idea which way to turn for the tunnel. He pictured Madison and his men trapped against the wire, killed and hung up like the man already there, and used for rifle practice by bored troops in the days to come. Without thinking, he leapt to his feet and waved the torch madly at them.

'Over here! To your left. Over *this way.*' He stood in the open, ignoring the bullets zipping around him. He thrust the torch high, swinging it in a wide arc.

Someone hit his legs and sent him sprawling forward.

'What the fuck do you think you're doing?' Robert snarled.

'Let go, you stupid bastard. We have to show them which way to come.'

Robert swore and snatched the torch from Jonathon's hand. Then he quickly twisted its strap over the barrel of his rifle and used it to hold the beam up. He swayed it back and forth, the weight difficult to manage with his clumsy grip.

'Like *this,*' he said, glaring at Jonathon, who rolled onto his stomach to watch the wire.

Madison's group had taken heavy casualties and about half of them were returning. They saw the waving torch, changed direction and headed for the tunnel. Jonathon and Robert crawled out and as the raiders emerged from the wire they hauled them clear.

The first one through was a German. He stared up at them from the mud, his face white with terror. Madison was right behind.

'Meet the Kaiser,' he shouted, digging his pistol into the man to make him move forward. 'At least, he's a full colonel. The Huns will do anything to get him back.'

It explained the desperate running across no-man's-land from the enemy trenches. Before Jonathon could say a thing, the night sky exploded all around them. The ground lifted and shook. He heard Madison laughing crazily.

'And now they're trying to kill him.'

'We have to get out of here.'

Three men were still wriggling frantically through the wire, the last one caught up and dragging coils after him. They closed around him like a spider's web. The more he tried to move forward, the more the wire bunched and tangled round him.

'Here, watch him,' Madison said to Jonathon and jabbed his pistol at the German. Whipping out the wire cutters, he waited until he could thrust himself back into the tunnel, cutting every strand he could find. Watching him and guarding the colonel,

Jonathon was uncomfortably reminded of the last time he'd guarded a German like this.

Another salvo slammed down, the earth heaved, and a man fell screaming. Another slid over to check and immediately rolled away, seeing that his comrade was already dead. It was extremely dangerous to linger, but none of them would run back to their own lines while Madison was still struggling with the wire. Though their luck against the shelling couldn't hold much longer.

'Grab his feet,' Jonathon yelled, not daring to give the German a moment to escape. He'd cost them enough lives.

Robert and another soldier each took one of Madison's boots, and in turn he grasped the shoulders of the man in front of him. With a desperate heave they dragged both clear of the wire except for some last strands, which Robert tore out of the soldier's clothing.

Now they didn't need an order to run. They nearly picked the German up, hauling him with them, his feet barely touching the ground. A third salvo exploded close behind them. Nobody bothered to look how they might have fared if they'd stayed longer.

The survivors made it back to the trenches with ribbons of tracer fire searching the night all around them, so intense that it seemed a miracle anyone had made it back at all.

In the bottom of the trench, Jonathon found Robert on his haunches, gasping for breath and holding his head.

'Are you all right?' he asked hoarsely, then dropped down in exhaustion beside him.

Robert spoke through his fingers, sounding utterly beaten. 'That was part of my dream. Out there in the mud, caught in the open with all those bloody shells falling among us. I thought we were gone. Both of us.'

Jonathon put a shaking hand on his shoulder. 'So did I. Thanks for dragging me down, by the way. I wasn't thinking.'

'Is that what you call it? Fucking silly, if you ask me.' They both recovered enough to pull out a cigarette and then Robert said quietly, 'After this morning with the barrage, and now that. Out there in the middle of all those shells? Jesus, could it get any worse? Because I don't think I could stand it. I nearly went mad. I could *feel* it building up inside my head like—like... I don't know. Is that how you go crazy?'

'We're all the same, Robert,' Jonathon nodded slowly. 'All of us. Don't worry, you're not going mad.'

***

Next morning, the Australians were woken and took their places at the fire step for stand-to. As usual, they waited tensely, staring out into the mist that thinned as the sun rose. On any day the drifting fog might be filled with the shadows of German infantry advancing towards them.

Not this time, except there was a strange roaring noise and some men thought the ritual morning hate was coming early. These guns were to their right, to the south, thousands of them firing at the same time. The ground trembled and the mist seemed to shiver.

'What the hell is that?' Jonathon asked aloud. 'The end of the world?'

Major Willow was inspecting the trenches nearby and heard him. 'No, it's the end of the war,' he said proudly. 'The Big Push is on at last. It won't be long now.'

Everyone stared after him as he walked away.

***

The great Allied offensive in the Somme had started. Jonathon and his men listened for a week to the British artillery bombarding the German front lines, sending over more shells in seven days than had been fired in the entire war so far. The plan was to completely destroy the enemy defences by shelling, then let the infantry walk across unhindered. It might have been working, for the routine hates no longer happened. Rumours said the Germans were in disarray and retreating all along the front. Some of the men started to talk about being home by Christmas—not for the first time.

Then the rain came, torrential downpours flooding everything, the heaviest falls in recorded history. The more experienced soldiers looked out over no-man's-land and saw an impassable sea of mud. Even with severely weakened defences on the other side, how were men supposed to cross this, survive and have the energy to fight?

The answer came within hours of the first British troops going over the top to attack the German lines. After a week of such intense bombardment, the enemy were expected to be defeated already—those left alive. But they crawled out of their deepest bunkers, manned the machine guns and slaughtered the Tommies as they staggered through the mud. Twenty thousand were killed in a single day. As many again were wounded.

It was a disaster, but the offensive went on.

***

'So we've had a bit of a drubbing at Fromelles too,' Major Willow told Jonathon, standing respectfully beside his tiny desk. Jonathon wondered why he was being made privy to such opinions. He and Willow had chatted often, however this sounded more significant. Adding to the woes at the Somme, an Australian push at Fromelles just north of their own positions had failed with high casualties. Nearly 1200 men were dead. Worse somehow, 400 Anzacs had reached the German trenches successfully, only to be taken prisoner, the men surrendering when it was clear no one else was coming behind them.

'It was a complete cock-up, really,' Willow added with a sigh.

'So what do we do now, sir? Are we going up there to try?'

'No, we're going to have our turn right here.' His attempt at enthusiasm didn't quite carry. 'We're being ordered to attack Pozieres and capture it at all costs, as they always say. That's not to expect us to throw men's lives away needlessly again, but undoubtedly the High Command is eager for some good results.'

'We can do it, sir. The lads are sick of sitting around getting shot at. They'll be keen to have a go.'

It was true. Despite all the bad reports coming from the south, the Anzacs were frustrated at the lack of real action and wanted to get into the fight. There were no more rumours of being home for Christmas, and the men were complaining that they would never get back to Australia by simply waiting in a trench.

'Yes, I've heard some talk,' Willow said. 'We move out of here tomorrow morning, after the Canadians take over. We'll re-join the rest of our division and the attack is two days later. Not much rest for us, I'm afraid. The generals are in a hurry. Pass the word, will you?'

Jonathon flicked a salute and left. Outside the major's bunker, which had a doorway with a high sill of sandbags, the trench held six inches of water. It was the same everywhere, even though the sun was shining and had been for days. Draining the run-off from weeks of rain was proving difficult, and above the trenches the change to fine weather came too late to save the offensive at the Somme, but in perfect time to reveal the Australian troops crossing the open fields at Fromelles.

The news of the battalion moving and the impending attack travelled fast.

'About bloody time,' Paul Strand said to Jonathon. He was only half-joking. He had become a passionate fighter. Twenty years older than many of his comrades, he worked with savage determination, always volunteering for raiding parties or patrols into no-man's-land. Some of the men told stories that Strand crept out on his own, late at night, and roamed around until he found Germans to kill. The wilder versions claimed he had his own secret paths through the barbed wire and regularly sniped directly into the German trenches.

'You'll get your chance, Paul,' Jonathon said. 'More than you're hoping for, I'd say.'

'I doubt that,' Strand said with an odd look.

The next day, they made the unreal journey out of the strange world of the front trenches back into civilization. The "rear", as it was known, a place where men could walk in the open without fear, bathe every day and drink clean water. Jonathon could see his men looking around with a kind of wonder and distrust, reluctantly adjusting to the safer surroundings. There was no leave and they grumbled about that. All the officers and NCOs were told to be vigilant during the night for men sneaking away to have a quick gutful of wine at the closest village, though Jonathon knew that even the threat of being charged with desertion wouldn't stop some of them.

Most of the day was spent with delousing, getting fresh uniforms and real meals. The delousing was done in long rows of makeshifts baths made from animal troughs. Hot water, mixed with something foul-smelling and chemical, was constantly poured in and the men lined up naked, unabashed, to wait their turn. They looked bizarre, with their heads, necks and hands deeply stained by the grime of the front, and their chests and abdomens sickly pale by comparison.

Their old uniforms were put in a huge pile and prisoners from the guard compound sorted through them, choosing items to be washed and saved, and throwing the rest on a burning heap nearby. They were replaced with an assortment of new garments, and some that had been recycled from previous delousings.

There was nothing special about the midday meal except the act of eating it in relative comfort. It was a thick stew with fresh bread. There was no butter, but plenty of sweet jam. In the afternoon, they were allowed to relax in the sun on an open field. Most wrote letters while they could. A lot of tea was brewed on the many fires scattered around. For the NCOs, it was a simple way of keeping their charges corralled, like restless cattle in a pen, and in a space where they could be watched carefully.

Finally, they were assigned tents for sleeping that night, again another luxury after the muddy, stinking bunkers of the front line. The plan for the following day required a six-mile march to the place where the attack would be launched. The soldiers of Jonathon's battalion mostly retired early and slept like the dead. Some men dreamed, others had nightmares like Robert. His urgent cries left Jonathon staring at the white canvas overhead for a long time before he could sleep again.

Pozieres, July 1916

Tanner was dead, shot in the face by a machine gun that now had them pinned down. Killed, too, was Paul Strand lying beside him. He had been hit by an artillery shell. Since rushing one German stronghold after another, daring his luck beyond reason and always avoiding a fatal bullet or bayonet, Strand had been caught by a shell falling directly into the crater he was sheltering in. The force of the explosion had thrown his body out neatly beside Tanner's.

Jonathon had little idea how many of his section were left. Some of the men had just disappeared during the fierce fighting, wounded or dead, he didn't know. Robert was there, a bandage wrapped untidily around his head to cover the missing top of his right ear. Crowe, Jones, Appleton and Marsden cowered in the shallow trench too. These were the old soldiers, survivors of Gallipoli and still alive, though whether it was through sheer luck or experience, no one could guess. At that moment a German gunner was trying hard to change that. The rounds buzzed angrily overhead or chewed into the soil close by in what seemed like an endless supply of ammunition. The Australians had either to kneel or walk on their haunches, the trench was so shallow, and they were feeling cramped and muscle-sore on top of everything else.

The Germans were desperate. The Anzacs had fought to within sight of their objective, a line of enemy trenches surrounding the remains of a farmhouse. They wanted to take the positions before dusk, so they would have shelter for the night. The men were exhausted, many of them carrying small wounds and needing water, which was best stolen from the dead at great risk.

'We'll never get this bastard,' Marsden muttered, loud enough to be heard above the firing. 'Not without poor bloody Paul here to throw at 'em.'

'His luck ran out at the wrong time,' Appleton said, trying to light a smoke. 'He could've waited and rushed these sods before getting himself knocked.'

He doesn't give a damn,' Robert said. 'He's back with his son and wife, which is what he's wanted since Alfred copped it at Quinn's.' He held out his hand for a smoke.

'Have you run out?' Appleton said.

'What do you fucking think?'

Robert took the packet, lit up and tossed them back onto Appleton's chest.

Then everybody froze as the machine gun stopped.

'Reloading?' Crowe breathed.

Jonathon shrugged. 'Dunno. Wait a bit.'

A long thirty seconds went by, easily time enough for any gunner to put in a fresh belt. The firing didn't start again.

'Someone's got him, or he's scarpered, sarge,' Jones offered hopefully.

'Don't be in such a hurry to get yourself shot.'

'It could be jammed,' Marsden said reluctantly. 'Maybe we're wasting our best chance to take him.'

Jonathon knew he had to make a decision, and he'd been feeling the pressure all day. Making the right choices in a heated battle like this was nothing like organising men for meal-time, or ensuring the sentries stayed alert, which was the day-to-day work of a sergeant. Bad judgment here got your friends killed.

'Christ, wait a minute,' he said, nerving himself for a quick glance over the parapet. With a deep breath he jerked himself up, expecting a hail of bullets. All he saw were khaki figures running across the space in front.

'They got him.' He scrambled out of the trench. 'Come on, before the bastards set up again.'

The others were almost taken by surprise, falling over themselves to grab their rifles and follow. No one looked back at the two corpses left behind.

In contrast, the trenches around the farmhouse were deep and well-built with familiar German efficiency. The enemy's positions were always much better constructed than anything on the Allied side. Now they were filling with Anzacs as men appeared from ditches and craters all over the field. The Germans had to be retreating, since it would have been impossible to dislodge them from such good fortifications.

'Seen any officers?' Jonathon called loudly above the excited chattering and the rattle of weapons being tended. When nobody offered a reply he asked, 'What about Major Willow? Anyone seen him?'

'He went to the south,' someone called close by.

'Damn it, he's been with us from the beginning—'

'No, *to the south*, you stupid bastard. He tried to get around their flank. Haven't seen him since, though.'

'Oh, right.' Jonathon felt embarrassed and relieved at the same time. 'Jonesy, go back the way we came. Don't cut the corner, understand? See if you can find Willow and tell him where we are.'

'Right, Jonno.' Jones dashed away, always glad to be singled out for something special.

Over the next five minutes, the mood was anti-climactic. If the Germans were going to counter-attack, they'd most likely do it before dark, and each passing second without any action suggested it wouldn't be happening today. The Anzacs would be holding their positions until morning. Which meant, having advanced significantly and being without the security of friendly forces to either side, it would be a sleepless night. The attack had been too successful. Their own commanders weren't sure what to do next, and the battalion would be on its own.

In the lull, the order was passed to eat whatever rations were available and find water. The bodies covering the ground behind them were searched for both, plus any ammunition. The enemy front line—what used to be their reserve trenches—was now 200 yards away across more open space and they weren't putting up much of a fight. Snipers' rifles cracked and kept the Anzacs down, that was all. Advancing further towards the enemy wasn't an option for the rest of that day. They felt exposed enough and their objectives had been met.

Major Willow slide over the parapet.

'Well done, lads,' he said, slapping shoulders and shaking hands. Willow didn't look in much better condition than his men. 'Hello, Jonathon,' he said.

'Good to see you made it through.'

'We lost a few on the way, sir.'

'I know, I know... Now we have to make sure it wasn't all for nothing. We have to hold these positions until the rest of the line can catch up.'

'When can we expect that?'

'God knows. Your guess is as good as mine. I imagine the brass hats back at headquarters have run out of little flags to pin on their maps. They'll have no idea. All the communications have been blown to hell and the runners keep getting shot. In the meantime, expect the Germans to throw everything they can at us. The Huns won't like this bulge in their line at all.'

Jonathon gestured at the enemy trenches. 'I'm surprised they've waited this long. I wonder what they have in mind?'

'We'll find out soon enough. Good luck.' He nodded a farewell and moved on.

As the sun set behind them, the Australians found out. A tremendous ripple of light danced across the eastern horizon, then an ominous roar drowned out all other noise as heavy artillery rained down on the new Anzac positions.

Hundreds of shells fired into one area with a fury they hadn't seen before.

***

It didn't stop. When it became clear that this barrage was going to last longer than the usual ten minutes, they tried to adapt. After an hour, some men began to slip into an almost catatonic state, crouching at the bottom of the trenches, shielding themselves against the constant deluge of mud and the deafening noise. It was impossible to talk or to share the suffering. By now it was night and they couldn't see the towering mounds of debris before they toppled back to the ground and onto the soldiers. Only the searing flashes as they landed.

Casualties mounted, the worst coming from the trenches collapsing and burying people alive. Others around them had to dig madly, exposing themselves to blast and shrapnel. Some soldiers were smothered more than once.

By midnight, no one knew what he was doing. Instincts kept them moving, automatically going through the actions of digging out friends and ducking for shelter, if they had the chance. Everyone was deafened and in shock and stared blindly at each other when they needed to communicate. It seemed to each of them only a matter of time before the fatal shell would land.

Jonathon squatted in the bottom of a trench, beside a man who'd had an arm cut clean off by shrapnel, and tried to staunch the blood gushing from a severed artery. He could see it every time a shell exploded close by, a flash of red pumping out. He couldn't decide what to do. Nothing made sense. His own head hurt terribly and when he stuck his fingers inside his ears to try and ease the pain, they came away slick with blood.

Another explosion came close enough for him to feel his insides shift with the concussion and taste the bile rising in his throat. It was just one more shell among hundreds and made no difference.

Then everything shifted strangely, and Jonathon vaguely understood that the walls of the trench with its timber logging were falling on top of him. He was too tired to move and try and save himself. As he fell backwards under the weight of damp earth he saw someone reaching for him.

Robert was screaming his name, though neither man could hear it. He flung himself at a white hand disappearing under the soil and broken wood, and caught it just in time, crushing Jonathon's fingers in his. Then with another shell the whole world heaved upwards before something struck the base of Robert's skull with agonising pain. He started to black out, and felt death flutter eagerly at the edges of his consciousness until he managed to push it away—for how long he couldn't tell. Suddenly, trying to get out alive seemed pointless. Weakened by the blow and pinned by broken timber and earth, he lay there and waited to die, holding onto Jonathon's lifeless hand for comfort.

***

Two days later, three Australian sappers, one of them a corporal, were sheltering in a crater behind the captured German trenches. The shells were still falling, though not as intensely, and all contact had been lost with the forward companies. None of the officers at Headquarters had thought it worthwhile to try and find out what had happened. The ferocity of the bombardment told them all they needed to know.

The sappers were trying to eat lunch, almost oblivious of the explosions all around them.

'Jesus Christ, look at that,' one of them whispered suddenly.

A naked man had just walked past their shell hole, simply strolling along.

For a moment, the private had feared it was a ghost.

Hey! Hey, wait up!'

'Bloody hell, what's wrong with him?'

The corporal threw down his tin of bully beef in disgust, annoyed at the risk he was about to take. 'Shit, wait here,' he told the others.

He dashed out of the crater and tackled the naked man to the ground. He seemed to collapse without any protest and allowed the corporal to drag him back to safety without a struggle. They thrust him deep into the bottom of the hole, in case he tried to get up, and examined him. He lay there meekly without a sound.

'Who the hell is he?'

‘How should I know?’ The corporal gestured helplessly at the man’s bare chest. He wasn’t even wearing any identification tags.

‘Is he German?’

‘I bloody hope not. I wouldn’t want to have risked my neck for a fucking Hun.’ The corporal squinted down at him. ‘Nah, I reckon he’s one of our blokes. What’s your name, matey?’ He leaned closer. ‘Who are you? Can you tell us your name?’

The man’s blank expression didn’t change. Just as the corporal was about to give up, his lips began to move and the corporal put his ear to the man’s mouth.

‘What’d he say, Lenny? Did you hear?’

‘I’m not sure.’ The corporal shook his head. ‘I think it sounded like "Robert".’

He got up and took a cautious peep at the German lines, thinking.

‘You know what?’ he said. ‘I reckon he’s come from those Hun trenches we captured the other day. There must be some of our blokes still in there, holding onto them. Christ, we’d better let someone know.’

Rose in France

There were times Rose feared she was losing her compassion. How could any normal person stand here, sipping a mug of tea and enjoy feeling the warmth of the sun against her face, when she was surrounded by dead and dying men? It felt as if her heart had hardened. It had to, so she could get through each day and do her job. But to ignore the stretchers with their miserable loads scattered around the tents of the Casualty Clearing Station, just to give herself a moment's peace—was that right?

She stared towards the east and felt sick about what she knew. The front line was an unimaginable mess after that week of constant bombardment, followed by the enemy's month-long attempt to dislodge the Anzacs from the gains they'd made at Pozieres. That was how long, too, Rose had kept the letter she had written to Jonathon in her breast pocket. The envelope that had returned marked "Missing Believed Killed", the only notification a woman like her could expect. There were no official telegrams for lovers. Most sweethearts learned the worst news from the casualty lists in newspapers. She had been fortunate to find out relatively quickly and avoid a time when she might have been thinking fondly of a man no longer alive. That would have been awful.

She had accepted the fact that Jonathon was dead. The army's terminology, or at least the opinion of whoever scrawled the words across his name and address, wasn't supposed to offer hope of any miracles. "Missing" only meant that his remains were strewn across the landscape in unrecognisable pieces, or buried deep in the mud. It was an image that tortured her when she let it.

Jonathon's shattered body lying somewhere, alone and forgotten.

She shook her head now and shuddered, trying to chase the picture away. The surrounding French countryside was a brilliant green in the summer sunshine and full of life, legacy of the rain that had destroyed the Somme offensive. Behind the CCS the heavy artillery fired at the German trenches, making the canvas tents shiver with the tremendous noise.

The British were still trying, the generals refusing to admit that the plan had failed. They ordered more attacks every day. These intelligent men with their grand responsibilities were alone in their blind expectations. Everyone else agreed that the German line wasn't going to be breached. Worse, the enormous build-up and subsequent exhaustion of the British army's reserves now meant that the war would continue for another year. Regardless of what the Germans had in mind for the future, the Allies didn't have the strength to win it for another twelve months.

Mark Cohen spoke behind her. 'It's bloody awful, don't you think?'

Which part are you talking about?' she asked without turning round. 'It's *all* awful, isn't it?'

'That's what I meant.' He stood next to her and looked out at the dirty smear on the horizon, the perpetual cloud of smoke and dust hanging above the Western Front. His white surgical gown was stained with blood. A mask hung around his neck and he looked very tired.

'All this effort, Rose, all this industry, just to wage war on each other. Imagine what might be achieved if we tried as hard to do something worthwhile.'

'The Germans must be defeated, Mark. Isn't that worthwhile?'

'Yes, I suppose so.' He lit a cigarette and inhaled deeply. 'Alexander sent me out here. Insisted I take ten minutes off.' Squinting through the smoke, he held his hands up in front of him, the fingers spread wide. They trembled only slightly. 'Not bad,' he said. 'Nothing that a bit of sleep won't fix.'

'I can't believe I'm sleeping so well,' she said. 'All this racket going on, and I sleep like the dead.'

He looked uncomfortable. 'I–ah, heard your fellow's gone missing. I'm sorry to hear that.'

'Missing out there means he's been killed. I have no illusions about that. Dozens of men just vanish every day. Hit by a bomb or buried in the mud.'

'You shouldn't be so certain. He could be a prisoner.' He wanted to stop her tormenting herself

'The Germans didn't take any prisoners. Not that day. Anyway, *we* were attacking *them*. Even I know enough about the damned business to understand how that works.'

'That's not what happened at Fromelles.'

She turned and looked him in the eye. 'He's dead, Mark. His best friend is hospitalised in London and I've written to him asking for any details he might have. I don't know how ill he is or even whether he can reply at all. But I *am* sure that if there was any chance Jonathon was still alive, Robert would have told me somehow. He would have been there at the end.'

He gave in. 'I imagine you must feel quite hopeless.'

'I prefer to keep going, like I did after Donald was killed. We don't have the time to grieve for long. I have to believe Jonathon is at peace, the same as my brother.' Her tone was dull.

'And we're left to carry on.'

'Yes, to *carry on*.' She allowed some bitterness to creep in.

'Will you be going to visit this friend? In London?'

'Julia has gone and I'm covering for her. Matron Lambert was very understanding when she didn't need to be. You know what the Nursing Corps is like about women getting too close to their male acquaintances. Julia and Robert became quite close, when we were all in London together. Any hint of that and we're out on our ears.'

'Strange attitude.' He finished his cigarette and flicked it away. 'We need all the help we can get, married or not. So you won't be having any leave at all?'

'Not for a week or so.' She shrugged. 'I don't want it. There's nowhere to go.'

'Amiens still has some civilised parts, I'm told. Not exactly the romance of Paris, but the restaurants and theatres are still operating. You can get there in a few hours, if the traffic's all right.'

She gave him a long look, measuring his intent, then gave him the benefit of the doubt. 'Perhaps, one day,' she said unconvincingly. 'A group of us girls might go for a decent meal—if, as you say, there's still a good restaurant to be found.'

Mark sensed her becoming suspicious, so he squashed the subject. 'Can you help me with my next patient? Alexander dragged Grace away with him.'

Rose made a small, amused noise. ‘He has an eye for Grace and does little to hide it. I wonder what his poor wife would think, waiting patiently back home? Grace thinks he’s only being *nice*. Doctor Alexander isn’t being entirely honest, do you think?’

‘He’s a bit of a rogue, yes. But a good administrator, given the circumstances.’

Rose tossed the dregs of her tea away. ‘I’ll wash my hands and be there in a moment.’

***

Julia was back after four days and found Rose in their tent. Most of the nurses had billets in a nearby village: tiny rooms rented from the locals that weren’t much better, according to Rose, than living in a cupboard. And the landlords unashamedly demanded payment from the soldiers and women who risked their lives daily to keep them free from the Germans. The tents were almost more spacious and anyway were closer to the wounded, should there be an emergency. Rose had an arrangement with the ever-cheerful Yvonne, who did live in the village, to borrow her bathing facilities once a week.

It was evening and she was trying to read by the light of an oil lamp when Julia came in. Her friend’s expression was a mixture of hope and sadness. Rose hugged her and made her sit opposite on one of the two rickety chairs they'd stolen from the officers' mess.

'Well, tell me all about it,' she said with forced cheerfulness. 'How's Robert?'

'He's better than I expected,' Julia inclined her head. 'Wounds across his back and legs where he was hit by the timber. And he had a serious whack on the back of his head. No one's quite sure about that one, but he insists he's fine now.'

'Now?'

Julia hesitated. 'He–he doesn't remember much. In fact, he doesn't even recall being taken from the front line back to safety. He woke up in a clearing station and thinks it was about three days after he was hurt.'

'Oh,' Rose bit her lip. 'So he doesn't know much about Jonathon?'

There were tears in Julia's eyes. 'He remembers he was trying to save Jonathon, when the shell got him too. He feels dreadful, absolutely dreadful about it. Like he had a chance of saving Jonathon somehow.'

Rose sat there a long time, staring down at the packed earth between her feet. She said quietly, 'He shouldn't blame himself. God knows it can't be his fault.'

'He doesn't feel that way. Almost all the men in his section were killed during the bombardment, but he feels responsible for Jonathon.'

'They were close, that's all,' Rose murmured. 'At least he's safe. I must write again and thank him. With luck, he'll recover completely.'

Julia shook her head. 'He's already talking about going back.'

'To Australia? Perhaps he'll stay a while, if you ask him.' She guessed that Julia didn't want to lose touch with him.

'No, I mean to the *trenches*. Back to the fighting, to "finish the job", he says.'

'Oh, I see,' Rose quickly took her hand and squeezed it. 'Don't fret too soon.

It sounds like he won't be going anywhere for a bit. Anything could happen.'

'Goodness, here you are worried about *my* welfare and I've just given you more terrible news. You must be so disappointed not to *know*—'

'I expected it, really,' Rose stopped her. 'It's nothing we didn't already know.

I suppose I was hoping for some ending, that's all. The rest of the story.'

'I'm sorry it's not a happy ending,' Julia said, dabbing at her eyes with a handkerchief.

'Well, it's not a very nice story, is it?'

***

Another batch of wounded came in as Rose was about to sneak away and grab a sandwich for lunch. It had been a busy morning and she was both desperately tired and starving, but the new arrivals needed immediate attention. Ten soldiers in all had been cut down by one artillery shell landing among them. Two of them wouldn't survive the day. The others' injuries varied. There was one young man whose left leg had been lacerated to mincemeat by the storm of shrapnel.

'You're very pretty, Sister,' he whispered, his face pale from blood loss. 'What's your name?'

'Rose Preston,' she said kindly, checking the tourniquet around his upper thigh. The moment she released it, blood seeped into the filthy bandages. She re-applied it quickly. 'What do they call you?'

'Alistair, Sister Rose.'

'Alistair?' She smiled encouragingly. It looked like he was going to bleed to death the moment they attempted to operate. 'Don't they call you something else? Just about everyone has a nickname here.'

'I won't allow them. My mum would be so upset if they didn't use my proper name. She chose it specially.'

'Good for her.' She went to feel his forehead for signs of fever. He surprised her by gripping her forearm fiercely, his young face screwed into painful defiance.

'I'm a drover, like my dad. I can't ride no horses with only one leg. Don't let them take my leg off, Sister Rose.'

That was exactly what the surgeons would do. Removing the shattered limb and cauterising the stump was the only chance of staunching the blood flow.

'I can't tell the doctors what to do, Alistair. I'm sure they'll know best,' she told him gently and prised his fingers away.

'Without both legs, I don't want to live. I'll be no good to anyone.'

'You shouldn't be worrying about things like that. We need to get you well, first.'

'*Please*!' His anguished cry made people close by twist round to look. It was only another soldier calling for help and they just as quickly turned away again.

Rose felt helpless. He needed to calm down. 'All right, Alistair, I'll do my best. But it's really not up to me.'

He was already nodding gratefully and thanking her weakly as his eyes closed.

Rose had no intention of telling any surgeon how to do his work. Despite herself, she watched the progress of the wounded men being taken one by one into the surgical wards. When two orderlies finally picked up Alistair's stretcher and carried him to the nearest theatre, she told herself that the matter had been taken out of her hands. Then minutes later she followed them and stood inside the door, scanning the half-dozen tables for him.

The surgeons were renowned for amputating hands, feet and even entire legs and arms with the smallest excuse. It was quicker than trying to repair damaged limbs and gave them time to save more lives. But Rose was appalled when she recognised one of the surgeons on duty examining Alistair. He was a man faster than most to pick up one of the ugly saws and start cutting. A blade was handy, lying across the boy's chest as they waited for the chloroform to take hold. She hurried over.

'Doctor Hornsby, may I ask how will you be treating this man?'

Hornsby wasn't old. Rumours said that his medical career had been in disarray through incompetence and that the war had come along just in time to save him. He frowned at Rose over his mask.

'Hello, Rose. I'm sorry, how can I help you?'

'Will you be amputating this man's leg, sir?'

Hornsby glanced down at Alistair. 'I don't see that I have much choice. Most likely.'

Neither the tourniquet nor the bandages had been removed. 'You haven't examined him yet.'

'The amount of damage is quite obvious, as is the loss of blood. The dressings are barely holding the leg together. Is he a friend of yours?' Hornsby's annoyance was growing and others in the tent were starting to take notice.

'He told me he's a drover. He won't be able to ride with only one leg. He asked that we don't amputate it.' Voices inside her head warned her that she was doing a silly thing. She had no right to ask these questions.

'We're trying to save his life, Sister Preston. If that costs him his leg, so be it.'

She tried desperately to think of a way she could stop him. She knew that Hornsby would probably cut the leg off anyway, and now she was afraid that she might have goaded him into it. His pride was suddenly at stake. Everyone in the theatre was listening.

'He wasn't raving, Doctor. He *specifically* asked me to ensure that we didn't remove his leg, sir. He was lucid and completely aware of what he was saying. Couldn't you first try and cauterise the severed arteries without removing anything?'

'And we'll simply have to bring him back tomorrow or the next day to remove a dead limb, young lady. Dead from a lack of blood.'

'Given a choice, he would beg you to try, sir. I'm sure of it.'

'For God's sake, he's just a boy and in no condition to make such decisions.' Hornsby was snapping now. 'You're not much older, as a matter of fact. How dare you tell me how to perform a procedure. I'll be reporting this to Matron Lambert the first opportunity I have. My patience is wearing thin, Sister.'

Mark Cohen suddenly appeared at Hornsby's side, careful not to catch Rose's eye as he asked cordially, 'Is everything all right, George?'

'No, it's *not*, Captain Cohen. Sister Preston is interfering in the manner in which I intend treating this man's wounds. Her behaviour is absolutely unacceptable.'

Rose said quickly, 'Captain Cohen, this man pleaded with me not to allow his leg to be amputated. Without any disrespect, I'm trying to impress on Doctor Hornsby how adamant the soldier was.'

Mark looked at her steadily. 'What if it will save his life?'

'He's already critically ill. If he wakes to discover that he has lost a leg, I doubt he will have the willpower to recover anyway.'

'This is ridiculous. How can you know that?' Hornsby was red-faced and glaring.

'In all fairness, I've been doing this considerably longer than you, Doctor. I would hope that you'd respect my experience.'

'I *beg* your pardon?'

Still calm, Mark interrupted again. 'George, I came over to ask you about a tricky problem I have with some shell fragments near a kidney. You're good at that sort of thing. Why don't we change places? I'll deal with this fellow and get Miss Preston out of your hair. You'd be doing me a favour, actually.'

Everybody knew what was happening. Hornsby would be justified in dismissing Rose's plea if the casualty numbers were mounting up outside. But that wasn't the case and he was possibly guilty of not trying the riskier operation. His incompetence was being exposed.

Mark was giving him a face-saving alternative.

'You're more than welcome to her,' Hornsby said, just as the silence between the two men was becoming awkward. 'You'll be well advised to take the leg off, Captain Cohen. Believe me. Anything else will be a waste of time.' As he walked stiffly away towards Mark's patient, Hornsby added over his shoulder, 'And I'll be having that chat with Matron Lambert, Sister Preston.'

Rose didn't answer. She was watching Mark for signs that he was angry too.

He stayed professional and cool. 'All right,' he said. 'Let's take a look at him. Remove the dressings please, Rose. But not the tourniquet.'

After an hour, Mark had successfully stemmed the bleeding and patched together a lot of the torn flesh and muscle, although it was unlikely that the limb would ever function very well.

'The most he can hope for is a deadweight that will balance him on a horse,' he told Rose wearily. It had been difficult surgery. 'Sometimes a useless limb is more a hindrance than a help. I hope to God you're right. It's what he wanted, yes?'

Rose was light-headed. She had been hungry and exhausted coming into the theatre, and the hour of intensive work hadn't made her feel any better.

'Yes, it is. I believe if he came to and found we'd taken the leg, he would die of a broken heart.'

He gave her an odd look. 'Hardly an accepted medical condition, but one I can relate to,' he said. 'You'll need to watch him closely. He's lost too much blood and he's very weak. Not to mention the possibility of infection and shock. Hornsby will be taking a keen interest in his progress, no doubt. So don't give him any further cause to complain. I have to share a mess tent with him, remember.' He stopped and stared at her. 'Are you all right? You look like you need some fresh air.'

'I'm not the best.' She leaned on the table. The walls were beginning to spin.

'Here, let me help you.'

He guided her outside and found an upturned crate for her to sit on. She nodded her thanks. 'I'm all right now.'

'Perhaps, but I can't stay. I'll have to find someone else to look after you,' he said, moving away. Rose put her head in her hands and waited. The dizzy spell was slowly passing. After a few minutes she sensed somebody standing in front of her and she looked up to see Matron Lambert staring back at her.

'I'll get you a cup of tea, Rose,' she said, not too unkindly. 'And I don't need to tell you who I've just had biting my head off.'

***

The next day Alistair was still alive, but his condition was hardly better and Rose was alarmed to feel some warmth in his flesh, a sign of infection.

'Damn,' she muttered, looking round for some help, then changing her mind. There was little anyone could do except wait and see if the boy had the strength to fight back. She thought about finding Mark and stopped herself. There was nothing he could do either.

An ambulance could have taken the boy away to the rear and a hospital in London. Then the problem would go away for her too. But he couldn't risk the journey yet. Bounced around in the back of a truck, strapped down and cramped with five other sick and dying men, it could be all too traumatic.

Rose asked herself whether she was doing the right thing. *Should she have interfered in the first place?*

***

'Hello, Sister Rose,' Alistair whispered, when she checked on him again at midday. 'I see I got everything still there. I can't feel nothing though.'

'Nothing at all?' She felt his forehead and it was hot.

'Well, just this big lump I can't shift. Like my leg's made of wood.'

'Don't worry. It's too early to tell how much good the doctor did. It could take weeks. I'll be back in a minute.'

She returned with a thermometer and took his temperature. It was over 100.

'You need to rest,' she told him with a forced smile. 'Sleep as much as you can.'

'There's nothing else to do, and it's nice and quiet here.' His voice drifted away. She marvelled that he considered the constant banging of the artillery guns as quiet. What had it been like in the front line?

This time she did search out Mark and found him smoking beside a horse-drawn ambulance. He was patting each horse in turn.

'How's your patient?' he asked, reading her mind as she walked up.

'He has a fever and it's getting worse.'

'Infection,' he nodded, looking grim. 'It will have nothing to do with keeping the leg. You know how it works. It probably would have been in his system well before he even got here.'

Several of the artillery guns fired closely together, a deafening ripple of explosions and she had to wait a moment.

'Still, I can't help feeling responsible,' she said.

'Looks to me like you're feeling *too* responsible. Are you still sleeping all right? If you don't mind me saying, you could do with a good rest yourself.'

She gave him a wan smile. 'Lately, those guns have been firing all night.'

'A few drams of whisky usually helps.' When she didn't seem to find this amusing he said, 'I'll check on your boy later this afternoon and let you know.'

Alistair had lost consciousness by the evening, his fever soaring to 103. Rose sat beside his stretcher, and using an oil lamp for light, constantly wiped down his face and chest with a damp cloth. The sour heat came off him like a dull fire. At least he didn't thrash as some fevered men did. He lay like a corpse and she was able to raise his head and force water down his throat.

Julia found her late in the night. The other wounded men were all asleep and she tried to make her whispering sound stern.

'My God, Rose. You must come and rest yourself.'

Rose was adamant. 'I'm trying to keep his temperature down. His fever is still rising.'

'Just like every other wounded man here. These summer nights don't help.'

She couldn't bring herself to be too angry. 'Look, have you eaten?'

Rose had to think about it. 'I forgot.'

'Then go and grab something while I look after him for a while. Have a break and find a cup of tea too.'

Rose nodded weakly. 'All right. I won't be long. I'll bring back a full lamp and some fresh water.'

Outside, the cooler air hit her like a slap in the face and made her dizzy for a moment. Sudden hunger pains gnawed at her stomach, churning like nausea, and she craved the taste of a sweetened tea. Making her way quickly through the darkness, she found the mess tent and an on-duty cook who cheerfully made her a beef sandwich and a huge mugful. The beef was tough as leather and heavily salted, the bread stale. It all sat in her gut in a solid lump that stopped the pangs. A few minutes more in the fresh air while she drank the tea let her blink away the gritty tiredness in her eyes, and she put on a brave face when she returned to Julia.

'I didn't know how much I needed that. Is he all right?' she said.

'The same as when you left. He is a very sick boy. You shouldn't get your hopes up too high.'

'I just want to make sure he's all right to travel. Then he'll have a much better chance in London.' She busied herself lighting the second lamp.

Julia was tempted to point out that Alistair would be lucky to leave the tent alive. She let it go, sighed and gave Rose a hug as they exchanged places beside the stretcher. Rose sat down wearily, wet the rag in a bucket of water and wiped Alistair's forehead.

'Don't be too late, Rose. Please, or you'll be a wreck tomorrow otherwise.'

'No, I shan't.'

With a final, disapproving noise Julia left.

Without her company, Rose twice discovered herself swaying on the small stool, the tent lurching around her. No matter how hard she kept active with her hands, washing down Alistair and feeling his forehead with her palm, she needed sleep and her consciousness kept trying to slip away.

***

Rose woke up with a start, guilty and at a loss to know how long she'd slept collapsed forward onto Alistair's stomach. It was a wonder she hadn't fallen sideways off the stool. The lamp still burned and outside the guns continued to pound at the enemy. They often fired all night and it could be any time. Jerking upright, with blurred, stinging eyes she peered at the watch she kept pinned to her blouse. It was five in the morning.

'I didn't mean to scare you, Rose.' It was Matron Lambert. 'I was hoping to wake you gently.'

Rose twisted round, feeling her back muscles spasm in protest. Matron stood in the aisle between the stretchers. She looked tired, but this was the beginning of her workday. She had risen early, as always, before anyone else.

'I've–I've been trying to keep his temperature down,' Rose explained with a croak. Remembering, she turned back to feel

Alistair's forehead once more, but her hand stopped, quivering above a pale, still face.

Matron said softly, 'He's dead, Rose. I'll take care of him now. You go to your tent and rest. I don't want to see you out of your bed until tomorrow morning, do you understand?' Rose didn't reply or even move, her hand still reaching for Alistair. And then matron asked carefully, 'Rose? Did you hear me? I want you to get some sleep.'

Inside Rose's head was a roaring sound. A numbing, dull noise that shut everything else out and kept her sight focused on Alistair's closed, dead eyes. The only thing she knew was the sickening certainty that she had let him die.

Someone took her by the arm and lifted her upright, the stool toppling over beneath her legs. She was guided from the tent into the black, pre-dawn night. The helping hands kept a firm grip until the image of Alistair's face was replaced by Julia's, her expression sleepy and deeply worried.

Amiens

'There's no point in being angry about it,' Mark told Rose. 'It's not like I've done anything dishonest. In fact, we have the full blessing of Matron Lambert. I'm merely chaperoning you to safe accommodation in the city, as she asked me to. Afterwards, I'll go my own way. You can even find your own ride back.'

'Exactly. I'm not completely helpless,' she said through her teeth. A rut in the road suddenly threw her towards him, but she managed to avoid the contact.

'I think Matron just wanted to ensure you *went*,' he said patiently, not for the first time. 'You need rest and a few decent meals.'

They were squeezed into the front seat of a lorry bouncing along the road towards Amiens. Rose sat in the middle, with Mark beside the open window so that his cigarette wouldn't annoy her. The driver, an artillery sergeant, seemed undecided whether he was pleased or uncomfortable with her sitting so close to him. For the first few miles, he'd apologised every time the jolting had pitched them together. Finally, Rose said politely that it wasn't necessary. Which was more civil than the way she was treating Mark.

Matron Lambert had confronted her with the ultimatum that she take three days of the leave entitled her, or face an official suspension if necessary. Whatever it took to make Rose rest. And she was ordered to leave the Casualty Clearing Station, to get away from the front line, the wounded soldiers and incessant pounding of the artillery guns in the field behind.

Matron told her firmly, ‘I spoke to Doctor Cohen. I know you are close friends, and he has kindly promised to escort you to Amiens on my behalf. He’s going there himself.’

Rose was too stunned to protest. It occurred to her to explain that it was Mark who had tried engineering her transfer from Lemnos to Cairo, and that with this order Matron was delivering the helpless lamb straight into the wolf’s arms. But she kept quiet. That incident now felt like a hundred years ago and Mark had since redeemed himself many times over.

Still, she couldn’t let the arrangement go unchallenged completely.

‘I’m sorry, Matron. It hardly seems proper to organise such a thing without asking me first. I might be in the middle of a disagreement with Doctor Cohen.’

‘You’re not,’ the matron replied with a dry, knowing look. ‘And the good doctor is well aware of the consequences of abusing my trust in him, believe me. I want you to take this leave, Rose. Do you understand? Relax and try to forget this place for a few days, at least. As your commanding officer, *that* is proper for me to arrange. Your three days begin tomorrow morning. Today you can supervise the ambulance loads. And you will stay well away from the operating theatres.'

She didn't have to add, "And Doctor Hornsby" who, no doubt, had heard the news of Alistair's death and was waiting for an opportunity to make his opinions known.

Mark had sought Rose out that evening and announced that he'd arranged the transport. He didn't even hint at any smugness about the agreement, or his deal with the matron, although Rose watched him closely and had some sharp words ready. Denied the chance to say anything, she contented herself this morning with a disapproving silence, which he kept trying to break.

He rolled his eyes. 'You should *try* and enjoy yourself.'

She shot back, 'I can hardly do that on my own, can I? I was planning to do this trip with some of the other girls. By myself, I might as well have pitched a tent in the next paddock, or taken a room in the village. I'll only be needing a bed to get some decent sleep, after all.'

'Well, perhaps we could have dinner just *one* night?'

She gave him such a glare that he snorted in mock alarm and deliberately faced out the window.

The driver had done the trip many times before and steered a route away from the bustle of military traffic close to the front. It didn't take long and Rose was astonished at how unaffected the rest of France looked just ten miles from the trenches. It didn't seem possible.

When he stopped to let them stretch their legs, she stood in the middle of the empty road and listened to the near-silence of the countryside.

'It's incredible, isn't it?' she asked Mark, who brightened at the prospect of real conversation. 'You could almost believe the war wasn't happening.'

'Nobody really knows what we're dealing with.' He nodded at a young boy herding some goats along a track. 'Only the soldiers who have been there. Even we don't have a clear idea what happens in those trenches, and we hear the stories and see the results more than most.'

'Would you go and look for yourself?' Rose stared at him coolly. 'You could, you know. You're a man and an army officer. Nobody would stop you walking into the front lines to see. Tell them it's research. You're investigating the causes of so many wounds—'

'Yes, I get the idea,' he said hastily. 'And perhaps I will. Why does the notion appeal so much to you? Would it make me as good as your Jonathon?'

She went pale. 'I beg your pardon?'

'I'm sorry,' he said quickly, holding up a hand. 'That was uncalled-for.'

She looked down at her shoe scuffing the soil. 'No, you're right. It isn't what I meant, either. Who on earth would want to visit the front lines if they didn't have to? I'm not very good at saying the right things, at the moment.'

The sergeant had taken his rightful place, as an enlisted man, on the opposite side of the road, though he watched them carefully through a veil of cigarette smoke. Mark knew he would probably call for them to move on soon, so he hurried his next words.

'Rose, I just want you to find some peace, as much as Julia or Matron Lambert want you to. Everyone is worried about you because you're working so hard. You might start by not assuming that everything I say has an ulterior motive. We could go for out dinner and it would be just that, for God's sake.

Keeping each other good company, that's all.'

'Yes, all right. Perhaps we can,' she said. But she still wasn't comfortable.

It was the sergeant who recommended a hotel. One slightly more expensive than others, he said, which guaranteed it usually had some spare rooms. He was right, and Rose was glad of the better facilities. This was her first chance to live in some sort of luxury since leaving home.

The room was small with a single bed and a carved, wooden table beside it. A narrow window looked out on a busy, sunlit street dotted with the khaki of uniforms everywhere. Again, it was hard to believe the front line was only fifteen miles to the north.

Mark had carried up her small suitcase and was waiting at the door. 'Is everything all right?'

'Fine.' She turned from the view. 'Where will you be staying?'

'After seeing this, I might as well ask if they have another room. You don't mind, do you?'

'Of course not.' She doubted that he had planned to do any differently.

'Will you have some lunch?'

'I've already asked for a sandwich to be sent up. I'll have a nap afterwards, I think.'

'Oh.' This obviously affected his next question. 'Well, I'll probably take a walk around the streets. See what's on offer nearby.'

'It's your leave, Mark. It has nothing to do with me. You can do what you want.'

'No, I know.' He paused in thought, and decided to take the risk. 'What about that dinner together? Will you join me for that?'

'I don't want to think about anything just yet. I need to rest. I'll leave you a note at reception.'

'All right.' He nodded uncertainly. 'I suppose I'll send a message up if they don't have a room for me.'

'I'm sure they will. Goodbye, and thank you for the escort.'

He wasn't sure whether she was mocking him and said carefully, 'It's my pleasure.'

Then he left, closing the door gently behind him.

Rose stood still, staring at the timber panelling of the door, and felt the emotions crowding in on her. More than anything, it was strange to have nothing to do.

Then she let the truth out of her heart.

This trip to Amiens was the sort of thing she'd expected to do with Jonathon. Somehow, when they both had leave. Admitting it to herself brought tears to her eyes.

She wiped them away immediately. Jonathon would be disappointed in her, wasting this opportunity with more grief. What would he do, if the situation were reversed?

Perhaps he'd have shed a tear too.

There was the question of what to do with herself over the next three days. She didn't really want to lock herself up in the room and just sleep. That had been said just to discourage Mark—and he was another problem. What should she do? Have dinner with him?

She figured that the plan she'd made up on the spur of the moment was best. Have some lunch, then catch up with a little sleep. Later, she could decide what to do next.

***

She felt almost unfaithful as she penned a note that afternoon to Mark, asking him to pick her up for dinner at seven o'clock. She thought she could get it over and done with now, rather than tease the promise out until the last evening. If it turned out unpleasant or uncomfortable, so be it. They would have a few days to forget it, before returning to duty.

She took the note down to reception herself, dreading that she might bump into him on the way and have to accept his invitation personally, although she couldn't explain why that might upset her. There was also a small chance that he wouldn't get the note in time. She doubted it. He would be checking regularly, or probably had an arrangement with the staff to let him know the moment any message arrived.

He knocked promptly at her door as a town clock somewhere in the street struck seven.

'I'm glad you accepted,' he said, as she opened the door. He was still in the same uniform, pressed and cleaned a little. She had an unexpected vision of him waiting impatiently, dressed only in his underwear, in the back room of some laundry. It made her smile.

'And you're in a better mood,' he added.

'Something like that.' She quickly stopped smiling. 'Where are we going?'

'I found a place not far, and it's a nice evening for a stroll. You can hardly even hear the guns.' He meant this as a joke, but she pulled a face.

They went downstairs and out into the street. If it hadn't been for the French being spoken everywhere and the foreign signs, it could almost have been London. The city was filled with men and women determined to enjoy themselves while they could.

Over the meal, they chatted about the Casualty Clearing Station and the staff there. Hospital gossip was safe, common ground.

Then Mark said, 'God, it's so different from Lemnos. I can't imagine being back there now.'

Rose kept her tone level. 'Tell me, what did you really hope to do, arranging that transfer for us both to Cairo?'

He wasn't as concerned as she'd expected. 'I don't know,' he said easily. 'I was confused—like we all were—and you seemed so young. How old are you now?'

'Twenty-two,' she said, forgetting that Matron Lambert had falsified her enlistment papers. She went on quickly. 'Does it make much difference?'

'Oh, you're a veteran now,' he waved a hand, dismissing it all. Rose suddenly wondered how much he had drunk, and she realised he'd avoided answering her question about the transfer. He added, 'You're one of the best. I wouldn't let you go anywhere.'

'And you? How old are you now?'

'I've got ten years on you. I'm nearly an old man.'

'Nonsense. There are men older than you in the trenches. Jonathon wrote to me about a man called Paul Strand who—' She stopped. 'Well, anyway...'

'Yes,' Mark said with a sudden, forced easiness, swirling his wine glass. 'I suppose we'll all have stories that'll be told for the rest of our lives. I *am* sorry about Jonathon. I've told you that.'

'It's the risk we decided to take.' She looked at him steadily. 'It happens every day, right?'

He gave her a sad smile. 'For God's sake, that doesn't make it any easier to manage. Rose, who do you think you're kidding?'

'No one. I'm not trying to kid anyone.'

'Don't get upset. You should know you have friends who care about you more than you'd like to admit.'

She took a deep breath, then stole another moment to calm herself by sipping on her wine. 'I'm sorry. You're right. It's just that it seems such selfish thinking, feeling sorry for yourself when much worse things are happening to others all the time. Like to wives, and sisters and mothers. Lovers hardly count.'

'Do you ever feel lonely?'

This caught her unaware, then she surprised herself more by nodding and saying quietly. 'Yes, I do. After allowing myself to feel so close to a man, to have that stolen away hurts and makes me feel very alone. None of my friends, like Julia, can fill that space in my heart.'

The mood between them had turned sombre. Mark reached across the table and pressed her hand. 'Steady on. We're supposed to be enjoying ourselves, remember?

Rose shook her head and tried a brief laugh. 'Yes, I'm sorry.'

'Matron Lambert will be rather annoyed.'

'Goodness, don't tell her.' Rose lifted her glass and gestured for him to refill it. 'Maybe this will help.'

'That's very unladylike,' he said. 'Don't blame me for your headache in the morning.'

'We should be glad to *see* every morning we're still alive. I decided that before, in London. Let's never waste a single day.'

Memories made her nearly choke on her words, but she got through them.

When they left the restaurant, it was fully dark and Rose discovered that her footing wasn't quite what it should be. She couldn't help leaning on Mark for support.

'Oh dear, indeed,' he said, stumbling a little himself. 'Perhaps that second bottle of wine wasn't such a good idea.'

'I haven't had a drink since we left London and I'm not used to it. It's gone straight to my head.'

'Perhaps we should keep walking a bit. The fresh air should help.'

'You're the doctor,' she said. 'You should know.'

They took a long roundabout route back to their hotel. Neither of them spoke much, strolling easily and still arm-in-arm, content to be entertained by the nightlife swirling around them. Sometimes Rose saw their reflection in a window and the guilt would twist her stomach. It was supposed to be Jonathon by her side, not Mark Cohen.

But there was nothing wrong with relaxing and enjoying a friend's company either. Even if he *was* an attractive and likeable man.

It was difficult to know where the best argument came from, the pain inside her heart, or the wine in her head. Whatever, Rose knew she had worked hard and deserved some time away from the horrors of her job. No one could argue with that.

'Here we are. Do you feel any better?'

She snapped out of her thoughts when she saw the hotel entrance in front of them.

'To be honest, I'm not looking forward to the stairs.'

'We'll tackle them together.'

After getting their room keys from reception, they headed for the upper floors. The narrow, spiralling stairway had them pressed close against each other. A part of Rose wanted to discourage the contact—the guilty part of her. Another treacherous side took pleasure in the feeling of Mark's body touching hers. She wondered where his room was and suddenly panicked that he might be expecting to share hers, before realising he was only being a gentleman and escorting her all the way to her door.

That was all, and she'd nearly said something silly. She wished that her mind wasn't so clouded.

'Can we talk for a while? I'm not sleepy,' he asked, standing outside her room.

'Talk? What about?'

'Just *talk*, Rose. Have a chat.'

'Oh, I see...' She glanced around, looking for anyone else in the passageway.

'Well, as long as no one sees you coming in—or leaving, for that matter.'

'It wouldn't be proper for a young lady, would it?'

'Don't mock me, Doctor Cohen, or you'll be sent packing straight away.'

'Hurry up, then. Before someone comes.'

The keyhole evaded her attempts to unlock the door for a few moments, then she quickly pushed through with Mark close behind. With a theatrical finger to his lips, he hastily shut the door.

'Don't be an idiot,' she said.

'We can never be too careful.'

'My thoughts exactly. Perhaps you shouldn't be in here at all.'

'Can I sit on the bed?'

There wasn't a chair. 'I suppose you'll have to.'

Mark sat at the end closest to the window, leaned over to open the sash wide, and lit a cigarette. Too late, he asked, 'Oh, you don't mind, do you?'

Perching at the opposite end, Rose said, 'Not with the window open, I suppose. Now, what do you want to talk about?'

He laughed. 'Anything, or everything. Nothing in particular.'

'Well, you'll have to think of something quickly, because I can feel my eyes wanting to close already.'

'Right then.' He frowned. 'What about the stock market?'

'No, I don't care for it. My father might be interested though.'

'Your father, then. What does he do? And your mother?'

With a sigh, she explained first that her mother was dead. Then she told him about her father's business, which according to his letters was considerably more successful since she'd left Australia. He listened carefully and asked questions as if he really wanted to know the answers, which she doubted. When she'd finished, he launched into a description of his own past and his family history. It took some time and he wandered off into stories he, at least, found relevant. Rose was soon fighting a yawn and tried to hide it.

'I've overstayed my welcome,' he said, looking serious. 'I'll leave and let you go to bed.'

He stood up and Rose realised that he needed to squeeze past her to reach the door. The moment was filled with expectation and Mark took advantage of it, taking her hand in both of his as he sidled past. He stood, staring down at her anxiously.

'There's been something I've been meaning to ask all evening. I can't deny that. You've probably guessed.'

She had been too tired to guess any such thing, but she pretended otherwise. 'Are you sure you want to ask now? You might not like the answer.' She tried to return his gaze, the wine and tiredness pricking her eyes.

'Well, I suppose I've started now...' He smiled, then turned grim. He spoke slowly. 'Rose, I want to know... is it too soon?'

He didn't need to explain further. Her weariness vanished as she understood exactly what he was asking. Still, she paused before replying and that caused her a pang of concern. There shouldn't have been any hesitation, or even the slightest moment when he could believe she was encouraging him.

'Yes, it's too soon, Mark. Far too soon.'

'Damn it. That means I've spoiled things.'

'No, not at all. I'm flattered that you're asking.'

'Honestly? We're still friends?'

'Of course. Don't worry.'

'Then will you join me for lunch tomorrow?'

She felt trapped and wondered if this wasn't the result he had been aiming for all along. It would be churlish to refuse him after insisting she wasn't offended by his advances. At the same time, turning him down now could set the right tone for their friendship properly, and for good.

If that's what she wanted.

'If you like. Just lunch, though.'

'What else?' he said, relieved. She didn't have an answer.

He let himself out the door without another word.

Rose undressed, turned out the light and climbed between the sheets. She wanted to enjoy sleeping in clean linen again. It wouldn't be long before it was back to her stretcher bed with only blankets and the tent's canvas walls flapping around her. A good night's sleep wasn't something to squander.

Her head was filled with clamouring words and questions. No one except Julia knew of the ring on its chain round her neck. The other nurses believed Jonathon had been a very close friend. *Perhaps* a sweetheart, but not her fiancé, engaged to be married. All the same, would they disapprove of her beginning a relationship with somebody new? She discovered the question was unexpectedly important to her.

Balancing these arguments were her own notions of living life to the fullest, while they could. The war could kill them all within a week. She whispered at the dark ceiling, 'Why did you have to die? I don't know what to do.'

***

Rose and Mark met for lunch the next day, then walked in bright sunshine through a nearby park. They chatted about nothing special and didn't mention the previous night's awkwardness.

Then Mark said, 'I have to meet with an old friend for dinner this evening. You're quite welcome to join us, but I'll admit you might find it all a bit dreary. We'll be swapping tales of past acquaintances. Medical school and all that.'

At first, she wondered whether he was lying. A concoction to avoid another proper invitation that she might refuse.

She shook her head. 'After last night's wine, I'll be having an early night. Last chance of some real sleep, remember? We're due back the morning after next and I want to travel back tomorrow afternoon. I made some enquiries today. Some ammunition trucks are heading our way, it seems.'

He raised his eyebrows. 'A bit dangerous. Could I cadge a lift too?'

'I don't see why not.'

'Well...' He looked around, dragging out the moment. 'I suppose we could do the same tomorrow. Have lunch and leave for camp straight afterwards?'

'All right,' she smiled. 'One last decent meal before it's back to bully beef.'

She didn't see him again until a planned rendezvous, arranged by written messages, in the hotel reception the following midday. Their last lunch went smoothly, again without any awkward talk about his feelings for her. She was half-expecting another apology. To his credit, he seemed to have accepted the *status quo* and didn't want to upset her by saying any more.

They had to sit around a depot near the railway yards for three hours, waiting for the munitions convoy to move off. The soldiers cheerfully shared tea and biscuits with their passengers as they passed the time. Mark whispered to Rose that he doubted the men would be so charitable if he were alone and without a pretty nurse to escort.

'You're an officer. The *real* enemy,' she reminded him. 'You shouldn't be mixing with them at all.'

The trip back was uneventful, although the air became cold after sunset and uncomfortable because of it. By the time they reached the camp, all Rose wanted was to bury herself under her blankets for warmth and sleep, if the artillery guns would only let her. They now sounded shatteringly loud, the muzzle flashes blinding in the dark. Mark gave her a quick hug and hurried away, leaving her at the truck.

Back in their tent at last, Julia wasn't about to let her friend go to sleep without telling her the full story first. Rose obliged wearily, not wanting to hurt her feelings, although it was a struggle.

'And what about Doctor Cohen?' Julia asked, after waiting for her to get around to the subject the whole time.

'What about him?'

'Did he behave himself?'

'He was the perfect gentleman, as you'd expect.'

'No, that's *not* what I'd expect,' Julia said. 'Are you sure?'

'You'd be the first person I'd tell. You know that.' Rose crawled under the blankets and rolled over, turning her back to Julia. 'Goodnight. I'm absolutely bushed.'

She could feel Julia's eyes on her and smiled, waiting for one last question about Mark. Her friend grumbled something good-natured and left her alone.

Autumn and Winter 1916

The war went on with its remorseless cost in casualties. The Allies continued to attack in the Somme Valley right through until November of 1916, the leaders determined to make their efforts worthwhile at any price. For Rose and her companions in the Casualty Clearing Stations it meant a never-ending stream of wounded and dying men. Days, weeks and months flew by almost unnoticed. The issue of who was winning the war didn't mean much either, as long as the Germans didn't suddenly appear on the camp perimeter. The daily existence of working just behind the front line was more than enough to occupy their minds totally.

As it had done at Lemnos, sheer necessity forced changes for the better. More staff and bigger tents helped, and in some cases the CCS would commandeer an entire farm and use the buildings as a hospital. Rose's hospital did this. They found a large property with a barn and plenty of stables that they turned into makeshift wards. They brought in electric generators and provided power for the important areas. Some stations even boasted X-ray machines. The personnel took regular leave and some, like Julia, hoarded their days to make a trip to London possible. She was seeing a lot of Robert, who was recovering more slowly than expected but getting better all the same. Rose was less inclined to go anywhere and often spent her leave days somewhere quiet and near the station. Julia shamelessly "borrowed" leave days from her with a promise to return the favour, but Rose never asked.

Rose also passed a lot of time with Mark, who accompanied her patiently for walks through the countryside. Sometimes they rode horses. Many officers in the front line had animals kept in the villages and were glad to have the horses ridden in their absence. Rose's friendship with Mark was close and she was comfortable with it, except in the frequent moments she sensed that he was waiting for something more. There was no real intimacy, although they often held hands and sat touching, if they shared a blanket on some outing. Some of these occasions gave Rose a disturbing, surreal feeling that always developed into guilt. Lazing on a blanket in the sunshine with a frugal picnic—it never felt right. There were always the guns, and sometimes the singing of a column of men marching towards the trenches. Once they saw two aircraft dogfighting in the sky above and she recalled that Jonathon's brother, Joseph, was doing the same over the deserts in Egypt. Watching the tumbling aircraft against a backdrop of clouds, she wondered idly whether she should write to Joseph, even though they'd never met.

The idea didn't make much sense. Jonathon had been dead over five months now and she should have written much sooner, if at all. She had little idea how to address a letter to him properly anyway. And what could she say? It might only open old wounds for both of them.

'I wonder why they bother?' Mark broke into her thoughts.

'Who?'

'Those pilots up there. What does it matter if one man manages to kill another way up in the sky, when hundreds are slaughtered within minutes by a single machine gun on the ground?'

'Why do they bother with any of it? And wouldn't it be better if the entire war *was* determined by two men in aeroplanes, instead of millions on the ground?' she said.

'Like gentlemen duelling with musket pistols at ten paces?'

'Something like that.'

'You're an incurable romantic.'

She jabbed him in the ribs. That was the last thing she considered herself.

The planes seemed to move with a painful slowness at odds with the snarling engines that dragged them through the air. The stuttering of the machine guns sounded clearly.

They were surprised when the contest suddenly ended. Rose wasn't sure that she'd wanted to witness either shot down, but the German pilot must have decided he was too far from home and abruptly banked away, diving towards the east. The British plane didn't bother pursuing.

'Did they wave to each other?' Mark asked incredulously. 'Did I see them wave goodbye?'

'Surely not,' she laughed, but thought she'd seen it as well. She was simply glad the fight had finished without bloodshed.

'They did. I'm *sure* they did. This war gets crazier every day,' he muttered and shook his head.

***

A week later, there was an unpleasant reminder that winter was returning. It was October and the Allied offensive had finally stopped in favour of consolidating positions for the change of season. Just in time, because a cold front with heavy rain and early snows swept across northern France and brought the war to its customary halt in the clinging mud. At the Casualty Clearing Station everyone began to prepare for working in wet conditions. The horrors of the previous winter had been forgotten until now. A few days of torrential rain soon reminded them all.

They were followed by weak sunshine slanting down between the clouds. It was, someone said, springtime's last effort. The melting snow chilled everything.

Mark appeared in front of Rose's tent.

'You're off duty, aren't you?' he called through the open flap. She came out.

'Sort of,' she answered carefully.

'There's a cavalry chap who's offered me two beautiful horses if we want to ride this morning. They really are magnificent beasts. Can you come?'

'I don't know.'

'What do you mean?'

'Julia's due back from London any minute, but she's not here. If she doesn't turn up soon, I'll have to cover for her.'

'That's a bit selfish of her, don't you think? If you ask me, she's been traipsing off to London far too often.'

'I'm worried about *her*, not concerned about any roster or missing a damned horse ride.'

'Of course, of course,' he said quickly. 'I'm sure she's fine. When will you know?'

'There's three-quarters of an hour before she's supposed to begin. Matron Lambert will be keeping a sharp eye out too.'

He looked disappointed. 'I'll wait for an hour, all right? If I don't see you, I'll assume you're doing her shift.'

'It's going to rain again anyway,' she called as he turned away.

'Nonsense, the sun's shining. Besides, these animals would be worth riding in a snowstorm.' After a dozen steps he stopped and spun around. 'Then again, I don't know if it's a good idea. They're very spirited horses and you might not—'

'Don't bother teasing me.' She cut him off. 'I'm just as good a rider as you. I'll be there if I can.'

'I hope you can make it.' He smiled and winked, walking away again.

Julia arrived breathless about ten minutes later. She was a mess, covered in dirt. The last three miles had been a ride in an open horse-drawn carriage and the mud thrown up by the animal's hooves appeared to seek her out.

'Where on earth have you been?' Rose said, tersely.

Julia bustled around the tent, hurrying to get changed. 'The rain has ruined everything. A French regiment clogged the entire road—God, those poor souls were dead on their feet. I thought my trip was well planned, but it all went wrong. I'm lucky to get here on the right day.'

'I'll get some water and a cloth. Your face is filthy.'

By the time Rose returned, Julia had put on different clothes. She stood meekly as Rose wiped the mud from her cheeks. Something made her eyes shine.

'Rose, guess what we did?'

'We? Who's we?'

'Robert and I.'

Rose stood back and stared at her, stunned. 'I hope you were careful.'

'No, not *that*,' Julia lowered her voice to whisper. 'Well, not at first... I mean, we got married.'

'You did *what*?'

'We got an army pastor to marry us. Right there in the hospital.'

'Are you mad? You'll be told to resign and be sent home instantly. Unless that's what you want,' she added hastily.

'Not if no one knows. Robert doesn't mind. We *so* wanted to do it, Rose. He loves me, and I love him. Please say you're happy for me.'

Rose couldn't do anything but sit back, her breath taken away by the news. 'My God, I can't believe it.' She realised Julia was waiting and she gave her a big hug. 'I'm sure you'll be very happy. And I'm happy *for* you, too. Perhaps the war will end soon and you can be together properly.' She meant it, although everyone knew the war would never be over during a winter.

'If he doesn't fight again, there's a good chance,' Julia said, her voice muffled against Rose's shoulder.

'Then let's hope. Are you all right? Mark's asked me to go for a ride, and it's maybe the last chance we'll get with this kind of weather.'

'Of course. I told you I'd be back. I'm too excited to want any sleep. Go and enjoy yourself, while you can.'

Rose quickly got a coat more suitable for riding outdoors. She was already wearing her boots and heaviest skirt. Like everyone, she wore the same clothes for everything, and almost every day. This was no place for an extensive wardrobe.

After asking around the officers' mess and getting directions, she found Mark on the edge of camp where a dozen horses were tethered under a tree. The animals were remarkably calm with the artillery pounding out shells nearby. One of the horses was saddled. The gear for another was slung across a branch. Mark waved when he saw her coming.

'Glad you could make it.'

'I knew Julia wouldn't let us down,' she said pointedly.

'So, what was her excuse?'

'The French jamming up the roads with troop movements. Along with the rain.'

'What else? Anyway, wait a minute while I put your stuff on this young lady,' he patted the horse beside his. 'Then we'll be off.'

'Are you sure the rain's going to hold off?'

'We might get a shower,' he said. 'It would have been all right, if you hadn't waited for Julia. Besides, we can always find shelter somewhere.'

She let the comment about Julia go. The news about her friend getting married made his remarks sound so petty.

He helped her into the saddle, then swung onto his own horse. Rose's mount moved skittishly under her and she quietened it by leaning forward and rubbing its neck, whispering kindly into its ear.

'You should be firm,' Mark said.

'I'll do it my way, thank you.'

'As you always do.' He arched an eyebrow. She ignored him.

They set off across the field at an easy canter. The long grass and drifts of remaining snow could hide deep wheel ruts from the guns and old shell craters, so it wasn't wise to ride too fast. Rose let Mark lead the way, since he seemed to have a plan.

For half an hour, they rode without trying to talk and just enjoyed the freedom of escaping from the hospital. He was taking them across open pastures again, winding a way though gates and gaps in the hedges, and she didn't question where they were going. It was nice not having to think or worry about anything.

As they crested a long ridge, they couldn't ignore a squall in the west visibly advancing towards them. A curtain of grey rain swept across the ground beneath.

'Oh dear,' Mark said, standing in the stirrups to look around. 'We're going to take a beating if we don't find some cover. Let's make a run for that farmhouse. It's got a decent barn, see?'

They didn't quite beat the rain, suffering the first patter of large drops as they wheeled the horses to a halt in front of the stone barn. By the time they'd dismounted, opened a door and led their animals inside, a sheet of hail was hammering the yard outside. The barn was empty except for some scattered chickens, roosting and puffed up against the damp.

Rose looked through the downpour at the farmhouse about 200 yards away. 'How are we going to introduce ourselves?' she called above the noise of the storm. 'We'll get drenched on the way.'

'No need,' he said, tethering the horses to a rail. 'If anyone saw us and they're worried, they'll come. It's pretty obvious what we're doing. Hey, look what I've got.' He pulled a bottle of wine and two tin mugs from his saddlebag.

'Always prepared, I see.'

'Always. Come on, let's have a roll in the hay.'

'Very funny.'

But they did, going to lie on a large pile of hay in one corner. Before he sat down next to her, Mark took some feed over to the horses. Then dropping down at her side, he carefully balanced the tin mugs between his legs, opened the wine, and poured drinks for both of them. Rose had already collapsed backwards and closed her eyes. She hadn't realised just how cold it had been riding and now the hay offered a warm, soft embrace.

'Here,' he said, touching her lips with the mug.

She took the cup and sipped, trying not to raise her head. The wine was nice, but she didn't want to make the effort of sitting up to drink it. She murmured,

'Do you think the storm will pass?'

'Not for a while.'

'We can't ride back in the dark. You won't know the way.'

'Don't worry. Let's just see what happens.'

They chatted softly about what it would be like, living here in France without the war. Just a small farm with a few animals and perhaps a field of vegetables to sell at a market. Rose finished the wine quickly because it was impossible to put the mug down without spilling it. Mark refilled it at once, despite her protests.

'Let me rest,' she told him, smiling and drinking again before holding the mug at arm's length away from him. 'No more for me. You can be on guard duty, like a good captain in the army.' She deliberately fell back into the hay again and shut her eyes, feigning instant sleep. She expected him to complain. He stayed quiet, and she heard the clink of the bottle against his tin cup. It wasn't long before the dark shapes behind her eyelids began shift and swirl as she started to doze.

Then as a complete, pleasant blackness filled her mind, somebody's lips closed over hers.

Being so close to sleep, she didn't react instantly—or over-react. She understood what was happening, of course. He was kissing her. It was presumptuous, but then again, lying with him like this in the hay was hardly keeping her distance or discouraging him. What should she do?

Heartened that she didn't object so far, Mark was touching her face as he continued to kiss her. Now his mouth moved more urgently against hers. For a little time she returned his passion with the smallest effort, not staying still and cold, yet keeping short of enthusiastic. She kept trying to decide what she wanted and needed to figure it out soon, because his hands had already slid down to the buttons on the front of her dress.

It was exciting to feel his fingers open the lapels and slide in. His touch on her bare flesh was chilled. It also brought shivers of anticipation. Dangerously, she began to consider just enjoying herself. Nothing to do with his ambitions or emotions—

or her own deeper feelings, for that matter. Perhaps there might be a total escape in making love naked in the straw with the rain pouring outside. A complete removal from the world and its war. The men did it all the time. It was even encouraged. Why couldn't a woman do the same?

He murmured softly, 'What's this? A magic charm to keep away amorous doctors?'

She opened her eyes to look down at herself. The top of her camisole was exposed, the material dull from constant use and washing, and the flesh of her chest and breasts looked an unhealthy white. His hand was resting just above her cleavage, the thin chain entwined through his fingers. Jonathon's ring dangled against his palm.

Abruptly she tried to sit up and push him away. At first her hands sank into the hay, then she finally struggled upright. She saw on his face annoyance and disappointment. If he hadn't spoken, breaking the moment, who knew what might have happened?

'It's my mother's ring,' she lied instinctively. She'd hurt his feelings enough without mentioning Jonathon's name. 'God, I'm sorry. I've suddenly realised I don't want to do this. Really, I'm so sorry...' She busied herself refastening the buttons of her dress.

'I should have asked before kissing you—' he began.

'No, it's not your fault. I can't blame you for trying.' She bit her lip and went still. 'I'm not stupid, Mark. I know you've been very patient with me, but I need more time.'

'More time?' He sighed and stared out the door for a moment. 'How much? I can't go on like this forever. I'm very fond of you, Rose. However, you're starting to wear me down.'

She flinched at the term because it seemed to have nothing to do with affections or friendship. He didn't notice. She said quietly, 'It's nearly the New Year. Will you wait until then? It's less than a few months. It could be a new start for me if I make up my mind to put the past behind me. Anything could happen. Perhaps the end of the war too.'

'All right, let's see what the New Year brings us.' She could see he was giving in easily because he was exasperated and couldn't be bothered making an effort to be understanding. That disturbed her further, and again she wasn't sure who to blame, or whether he had a right to lose his patience.

A voice called carefully in French. A man in dripping oilskins and a wide-brimmed hat stood inside the door. Some of the chickens rushed over to him.

'Oh no,' Mark said dryly. 'You'd better help me. I haven't had much luck learning French either.'

The farmer was friendly. With a broken mixture of both languages and some signs, he invited them back to the house for soup and bread. The rain had eased enough to make the journey across the yard possible and the food was excellent, eaten in a kitchen that was nearly hot from the burning stove. Rose could happily have stayed the night except for the awkwardness it would cause.

At the last minute, having given the rain every opportunity to ease off, she mounted her horse, and waving to the farmer, followed Mark out of the yard. The ride back was cold and wet, and not helped by his stiff shoulders in front of her. At least the journey was quicker than the way there, which made her wonder briefly whether he had deliberately led her to the farm and its hay pile, then circled the place until the weather forced them into shelter.

That seemed too devious and she told herself she was tired, upset and reading too much into things.

Back at the camp, as they tethered the horses under the now dripping trees, Rose didn't know what she wanted to say, though she felt it should be something serious.

Mark said, 'Don't hang about here. Go and get warm and dry. I'll see you later.'

'All right. Try and get out of the weather as soon as you can too.'

Suddenly she couldn't cope with any of it and hurried off towards her tent. As she walked, she thought she could feel his eyes on her. She didn't pause to look back.

***

All the next week, Mark was reserved with her, and she sensed that he was purposely punishing her, teaching her a lesson rather than being genuinely upset. He began to smile eventually and one afternoon they shared a cup of tea in her tent. As at Amiens, neither mentioned what had happened between them, and that was becoming the story of their relationship.

After that, whenever Mark and Rose did meet he was brightly cheerful and concerned about her welfare, always offering to help, but that was all. The timing wasn't right for much else, she guessed.

He seemed satisfied to count down the weeks until 1917, which made her feel like a promised bride in an arranged marriage. She, in turn, couldn't shake a feeling of dread as the days rushed by.

She *liked* him a lot, that was certain. Which meant she could probably love him eventually. He was generous, warm and she found him funny—and she didn't laugh easily. Also, although it was a little mercenary, she had to admit he had a future beyond the army and a good chance of surviving the war.

***

On Christmas Day, 1916 it snowed, a white Christmas. Any hope of enjoying the festive season was ruined by attacks from both sides. In the first year of the war there had been an unofficial truce with the opposing armies joining each other across no-man's-land to exchange gifts and sing hymns. The following year, 1915, had been similar with no fighting, although the troops stayed in their own trenches.

This Christmas, someone fired a salvo of artillery to spoil the enemy's peace, and it provoked a predictable reaction. Within minutes, the whole Western Front was alive with the busiest day of fighting for weeks.

The Casualty Clearing Station was swamped with wounded, freezing men.

Rose worked all day and into the evening, tending soldiers who didn't need surgery. By nightfall, her arms ached from winding bandages around bloody limbs and supporting the weight of men too weak to help themselves. The stink of antiseptic made her throat raw. Worst of all, it felt like the bones in her feet were grating together.

Just after nine o'clock, Yvonne came in and said gently, 'I just brought your friend Doctor Cohen here. He has a mug of tea outside. I'll finish this fellow. You go out and have a break.'

Rose didn't protest. She turned away from a soldier with a bloodied, broken arm, put on her coat, and went outside into the night. She heard Yvonne cheerfully wishing the wounded man a merry Christmas.

Mark was an odd sight. He stood in the half-light from reflected lamps, which made the falling snow shimmer as it passed. His shoulders and hat were powdered white, and he held two steaming mugs of tea.

'Wouldn't you like to go inside somewhere?' she asked.

'No, I desperately need the fresh air.' He sounded exhausted. 'If I breathe in any more chloroform, you'll be able to operate on me.'

She peered at his reddened eyes. 'You look awful.'

'Have you seen yourself?'

'I'd rather not.'

They sipped their tea comfortably for a minute, then he said, 'I was hoping tonight would be another truce. We could all get together and cook up some sort of Christmas dinner. Some people have got ham and turkeys, you know.'

'The girls were making grand plans a few days ago.' She nodded into her mug.

'I've got a grand plan of my own. Do you want to hear it? I was always going to ask you tonight, only I expected better circumstances.'

She went tense, but it was hidden under the bulky coat. 'You might as well tell me. I don't think things are going to get any better, if this is supposed to be a merry Christmas.'

'All right. Can we go back to Amiens together? Next week, after the New Year? Apart from today, the war's been pretty quiet. We might be able to have seven days leave. Can you imagine a different restaurant every night? Celebrating the start of 1917 in style. We could buy some warmer clothing and new boots...' He faltered, knowing that nothing would disguise what he really wanted from her.

She was actually relieved. For one terrifying moment she thought he was going to ask her to marry him. The idea was ridiculous now, but for an instant it had been real.

'I don't know, Mark. Of course, it sounds lovely,' she added quickly. 'I mean, I'll have to ask Matron Lambert. Please don't make any plans until then.'

'When can you see her?' He sounded glad that she hadn't refused outright, which gave her warning voices inside her head.

'Not until later tomorrow.'

She suddenly wanted an escape and saw Yvonne leading the injured soldier out of the tent and beckoning for the next to be brought forward.

'Mark, I'm sorry. I can't let Yvonne do this for me. She has her own duties. Can we discuss it later?'

He took the empty mug from her. 'We've got a week before anything definite has to be planned. Hell, we can just go if we want. There'll be a hotel somewhere.'

She gave him a small wave and hurried away. Back inside the tent, she intercepted Yvonne helping the next casualty onto a table. It was an Australian major with a filthy bandage around his head. His eyes stared blankly.

'That's fine. Thanks, Yvonne,' Rose said. 'Just what I needed.'

Yvonne gestured that it was nothing and left.

Rose turned to the major. 'Now, what have you done? Let's see, shall we?' She began to unwind the bandage from his head and revealed a bullet crease down his left temple. It was a very lucky injury. If fate had moved him a fraction of an inch, he would have taken the bullet directly in the brain. As it was, he was suffering little more than serious concussion and a nasty gash.

'You're very kind,' he said, dully.

'And you're very fortunate,' she said. 'Goodness, this was close.'

'Was it? The buggers can't ever shoot straight, if you ask me. Oh... and merry Christmas, Sister.'

'Thank you. And the same to you, Major.' She was concentrating on cleaning the blood and grime away from the injury and her eyes stung from the disinfectant.

'What's your name?'

'Rose. Rose Preston. I'm not really a sister. I'm a VAD. You'll have to keep still a moment.'

'Preston?' He frowned and she clicked her tongue because he had moved. 'I knew a Rose Preston once—no, wait a bit. I wrote her a letter, when we were at Anzac. Was that you? I'm Frank Willow. Do you recall anything like that?'

Instantly, Rose had tears pricking her eyes that had nothing to do with the antiseptics in the air. 'Yes, that was me. You got Jonathon White to deliver it. Do you remember him?'

'Private White, of course. A fine fellow. One of my best, though you don't tell 'em that. I wonder how he is?'

After a moment of shock, Rose tried to keep the croak out of her voice. 'I'm sorry, Major. Jonathon was lost at Pozieres. Don't you know? Were you transferred from his company?' She stepped to one side out of his vision so he wouldn't see her tears.

'God, who *wasn't* lost at Pozieres?' He grunted an empty laugh. 'I was wandering around for days trying to find my men—'

'*Please* keep still, Major.'

'Yes, of course. Sorry.' Willow stayed quiet for a minute as she dabbed at the dried blood, then he said casually, 'But he popped up again, didn't he?'

Inside, her heart was breaking all over again. This was the cruellest coincidence. 'Major, for goodness' sake. I'm trying to see what I'm doing and it doesn't help if you keep bobbing your head.'

'Sergeant White,' Willow went on, as if she hadn't snapped at him. 'Didn't they find him?'

'No, Jonathon wasn't just *lost* like you. He was officially posted as Missing, Believed Dead. He is dead, Major Willow.'

'No, Rose,' Willow replied with a childlike patience. 'I remember now. They found him about a month later in one of those hospitals in London. For fellows who have gone a bit silly from all the shelling. A bit of mumbo-jumbo, if you ask me. We should send them straight back into a decent fight, like putting a man back on a horse, when he falls off.' His tone changed. 'Still, I wouldn't have picked White as a man to shirk his duty. Perhaps there's something in it... I'm sorry, have I upset you? I'm not *really* saying he's a coward, you know.'

She stepped back, her face drained of blood, and stared at him until he was uncomfortable.

'Are–are you all right, Rose?'

'What hospital?' she whispered, barely audible above the guns outside.

'I couldn't tell you. One of those places where... Well, no. I wouldn't have a clue. We just got word that he was alive. Paperwork, you know. Damned glad to get it, in this case of course, but—' he stopped, suddenly aware that she was gone.

She ran out into the night without taking her coat. She stumbled from one tent and building to another, tripping on things hidden under the snow, twisting her ankle and cutting her shin badly. She didn't feel it or notice the red trail of blood on the snow behind her. All she cared about was finding Matron Lambert and begging for some leave.

Learmont Hospital

It was nothing like any hospital Rose had seen before. She walked through the tall gates and past a miserable-looking guard in his hut, an elderly man who stopped blowing on his gloved hands for warmth to give her a crooked, sympathetic smile. This was no weather for anyone to be outside. On the winding road across the grounds, Rose kept her footing inside a wheel rut to avoid tramping in thick snow. The dark trees on either side were bent under its weight, and the snow falling was grey because of a factory nearby belching filth into the air.

The building beyond was an imposing Victorian structure that had fallen into disrepair in an era when spending money on such things was the last thought on anyone's mind. Bars had recently been added to the windows with little regard for aesthetics. The place looked more like a prison.

At least it was warm inside, and Rose was glad to hurry through the entrance doors, despite the forbidding appearance. The foyer was wide and high with stairways and passages leading off in all directions, unfurnished except for some metal chairs that she noticed were bolted to the floor. The place echoed. A male orderly had let her in, a man also in his later years who looked ill-suited to his white uniform. Most of the staff here would be people too old for active service in the trenches.

'Who do I see about visiting one of your patients?' she asked. 'Do I need permission? I spoke to a Matron Warnsborough yesterday on the telephone, but if she's busy–'

He replied in a voice ruined by countless cigarettes. 'Then Matron Warnsborough is who you want, Miss. I'll fetch her for you if you'll wait here.' He walked away without waiting for an answer, then paused after a few steps. 'Don't mind any of the patients you might see. If they're out and about, they'll be harmless enough.'

Rose nodded, her worst fears confirmed. This was also an asylum for the mentally ill. It wasn't just for soldiers with the mysterious afflictions brought on by the war.

'Hello. Are you a new nurse here?'

Rose spun round to see a young, well-groomed man in pyjamas and a heavy dressing gown. The slippers on his feet had allowed him to creep up on her. With his hands buried in his pockets, he was hunched over and looking at her with a quizzical, friendly smile.

'No, I've come to visit someone,' she said.

'Will you be staying long?'

'I don't know. It depends on how well my friend is.'

'Oh. I don't suppose you smoke, do you? I haven't had a fag for ages. You know, I'd *kill* for a cigarette.' He blinked rapidly. 'Of course, while I was in the army they were quite keen on that sort of thing. But not here.'

Something in the way he said this chilled her. She guessed it was his attempt at humour and she managed a grin. 'I'm sorry, I don't smoke. I should have thought to bring some for everyone. Very selfish of me, wasn't it?'

'That's a pity.' He nodded absently, taking a hand out of his pocket to rub at his mouth. Rose was shocked to see his hand shake so violently that he had difficulty putting it to his lips. His fingers flapped like a wounded bird in front of his face. He didn't seem to notice, and said again, 'That's a pity.' He moved off with shuffling steps, Rose already forgotten.

'You'll have to forgive Peter,' another voice came from behind her. It was as

if everyone was trying to scare her. Now she was confronted by the matron, a small woman dwarfed by her uniform. Her eyes twinkled with knowledge and confidence. 'He rarely has good manners. You might blame his parents.'

'Not his… condition?'

'I doubt that's an excuse for being rude. You must be Miss Preston?'

'Please, call me Rose. Is it still all right to see Jonathon?' She wondered whether the matron had any idea how much turmoil those words caused her. Her stomach was rolling with fear and anxiety.

'Your timing is perfect. He has been recovering his memory rapidly in the past fortnight, after recognising little more than his own name for so long. It's quite common. We have several men here in various stages of remembering their past. I believe it's his mind slowly healing, like any other part of his body would from a severe wound.'

Rose took a deep breath and dared to ask, 'And was he wounded badly?'

'What if he was?' Matron Warnsborough gave her a searching look. 'What if he is missing his arms or legs, or if he's been disfigured? Will you leave again and never come back? That happens, you know. Too often, and I won't allow you to see him if that's your intention.'

'No, I'm just so very glad he's alive. I thought he was dead.'

She stared at Rose a moment longer. 'He was as good as,' she said, gesturing for Rose to follow her. 'You needn't worry. He didn't suffer a scratch on him. Jonathon was found wandering naked on the battlefield asking for his friend Robert. The soldiers who saved him assumed it was *his* name. Anyway, it was a miracle that he wasn't killed, although you'd know better than me that such miracles occur every day in that terrible place.'

'Yes, that's true,' Rose breathed through her relief. 'Naked? From a near miss?'

Matron Warnsborough explained over her shoulder as Rose trailed her through grim corridors and past closed doors with strange, muffled sounds behind them. 'I'm aware that men are frequently stripped by the blast of a nearby explosion, but Jonathon was unmarked. I suspect he took off his own clothes and his identity tags. That's common too. We have patients here who still, after years of treatment, will rip their clothing off at the first opportunity. I'm sure the famous Mr Freud would have something to say about it. I feel it's simply a nervous disposition that makes the sensation of material against the skin irritating.' She half-turned. 'It's only my opinion, of course. Jonathon, by the way, hasn't had a problem with that since he came here. He's quite fine, now. Initially it made identifying him difficult. In fact, we didn't. He volunteered his first name about a month later and a surname shortly after that. It's been a long and patient journey since then. We eventually wrote to tell his parents the good news. Didn't they contact you?' Suddenly there was a hint of suspicion.

‘I know Jonathon mentioned me in his letters home often, but he would never have bothered with an address or perhaps even my last name. I expect they’ll be quite desperate to find me.’

‘These boys never think to take precautions against the worst happening.’ She said this primly, apparently satisfied that Rose wasn’t some sort of forbidden lover. ‘It was sheer chance that you heard about him? I’d say he’s luckier than most, even now.’

It was a lot for Rose to absorb and she only had this brief walk through the corridors ahead to prepare herself. *What would Jonathon be like? What did "quite fine" mean?* Here was a woman battling the mysteries of the insane almost alone, mostly unappreciated and certainly unknown because it frightened the outside world too much.

Rose was grateful to be led into a pleasant, warm study lined with bookshelves and ornate furniture. One wall had a hearth of glowing coals, a luxury in these times. It was a large room, almost a library, and a direct contrast to the stark surroundings in the rest of the hospital. Then with a stab of anxiety, Rose guessed it was a place specially designed for these sorts of meetings. A comfortable environment to soften the blow of an otherwise disturbing moment.

With another start she realised that someone was sitting in front of the fire. A high-backed seat showed only a mess of fair hair, but she knew instantly it was Jonathon. Matron

Warnsborough was standing back, silently waving for her to go in further alone.

She mouthed, *'Be gentle... and patient.'*

Rose walked over slowly until she was close enough to reach out and touch the chair. The head didn't move and she wondered whether he was asleep. Her voice caught in her throat, then it came out in a broken whisper.

'Jonathon? Are you awake?'

The man in the chair jerked a little, then he turned and lifted himself slightly to look around. Yes, it was Jonathon's face that stared uncomprehending at her, and although she expected it and had steeled herself for this moment, the reality of seeing him alive was almost too much and left her speechless. The muscles in his neck were straining, his posture awkward. She could see by the way he gripped the arms of the chair, trembling with the effort, that he was weak and underweight. She was stunned by his appearance. He looked so old. She quickly dropped to her knees beside the chair and he sank slowly down again, still watching her wide-eyed.

His face betrayed a kaleidoscope of emotions. One expression after another, punctuated by shock, and to her dismay, even dread. He didn't make a sound.

‘Jonathon, it’s Rose.’ She carefully prised his hand off the armrest and put it in hers. It felt cold and dead. ‘Do you remember me?’

There was a long, terrible moment when she feared he wouldn’t reply. She hadn’t admitted to herself until this instant just how scared she was that Jonathon wouldn’t recognise her. She didn’t take her eyes off his, willing him to smile knowingly, or give her just the smallest sign of recollection.

Then she felt his fingers carefully entwine with hers, just as they had every time they’d held hands.

He spoke with a painful dry voice and tears started to slip down his cheeks. ‘Rose, Rose... my God. I–I thought you were just a beautiful dream.’

‘I’m real, Jonathon.’ She put his hand to her face and touched her own tears.

‘I’m not a dream.’

Egypt, 1917

Lieutenant Joseph White let the aeroplane slide to the left in its own time, a drunken lurch caused by the four twenty-pound bombs under its wings. He wanted to see how bad it could get. The BE2c was a stable aircraft. It was nicknamed "Stability Jane" except the bombs were playing havoc with the already fragile aerodynamics and making Joseph work for his pay. Still, he wasn't about to complain. Today was a day he would be bombing the German airfield at Beersheba. Finally, after months of reconnaissance flights taking photographs and tearing off for home afterwards, the squadron was on the attack.

The plane's unexpected shift brought a look of alarm from his observer, Roger Calwell, sitting in the forward cockpit between Joseph and the howling engine in the aircraft's nose. Roger's eyes seemed larger under the goggles. The Lewis gun in front of him swung crazily on its mount and nearly whacked the back of his head. He didn't notice as he twisted round to look at Joseph, who laughed and gave his friend the thumbs-up.

They were flying in company with five other BE2c's and a single Martynside, which wallowed in the air even more alarmingly with a solitary hundred-pound bomb strapped to its underbelly. The sky immediately around them was perfectly clear and deep blue, but anvil-shaped storm clouds were climbing magnificently over the horizon in all directions like monstrous, circling predators.

As always, Joseph felt a sheer delight in flying and found it difficult to keep his mind on the dangers. He was one of the squadron's best pilots and had been given one of only two planes that carried a machine gun. It was his and Roger's responsibility to watch for German aircraft trying to intercept them, since the rest would be defenceless. Being attacked was a slim possibility. Even though the enemy had far superior machines, their pilots seemed loath to pick a fight. On the rare occasions opposing aircraft found themselves in the same sky, the Germans always turned tail and ran, and the underpowered Australian planes had no hope of pursuing.

So an elaborate plan was hatched to destroy the enemy aircraft on the ground. The difficulty lay in reaching the airfield at Beersheba to bomb it, plus the railway yards there and the headquarters of the Turkish army. The squadron had flown two hours to Mustabig, refuelled and rested briefly, then taken off on the final leg. Joseph's backside was numb and his back ached. At least they were flying at an altitude that took the edge off the desert heat below. If it wasn't for the 60mph slipstream tearing at his face, it could have been almost pleasant, although Joseph never thought of himself as uncomfortable in an aircraft. Other men joked that they were piloting a rattling, clamouring box made of canvas and wood, but not him.

Their navigation over the desert needed to be precise. By his reckoning, they were less than ten minutes away from El Arish, another German airfield. Part of the plan was to drop bombs there too if targets presented themselves.

He felt his gut tighten with excitement. This was so different from his time at Gallipoli. Up here, he never felt threatened. No one could touch him while he swooped through the sky. The Turkish soldiers guarding the aerodromes would blaze away with their rifles, but their chances of hitting him were small. Most of the enemy didn't understand that to allow for deflection, they had to aim in front of the speeding planes. Only if the German pilots took off to defend themselves might he be in any danger. Then he would welcome a real dogfight. After nearly a year of training and flying, earning his officer's commission as well as his pilot's wings, he had yet to pit his skills against the enemy.

El Arish appeared to their left, the airstrip given away by the lattice of wheel marks in the sand. Joseph guessed that the collection of dirty, green tents would be the facilities. There was just one biplane was parked beside them.

The Australians circled around, taunting the Germans below and hoping they would take off and start a fight. Tiny figures only clustered around the tents and stared upwards. Some of them held rifles, but no one tried shooting. Finally the squadron leader, Captain Baker, waggled his wings for attention and motioned for a pilot called Derringer to bomb the biplane. The others continued to fly a wide arc around the airfield.

Derringer broke away and sideslipped into a deliberate path directly for the tents. Watching, Joseph could imagine the grim determination on Derringer's face. He wasn't one of their better pilots and would be concentrating furiously. It made sense to send him in here against no opposition where he had only to fly in a straight line without dodging real anti-aircraft fire.

The observers on the ground realised what was happening and scattered. Some sprawled on the ground away from the tents and fired their rifles. Derringer was diving at the parked aircraft. As Joseph's own flying brought him in behind, he could see the tiny alterations, then over-corrections, in Derringer's flight. Unconsciously, Joseph squeezed his hand at the moment he thought Derringer should release his bomb. Nothing happened. Seconds later, a black speck detached from the BE2c and wobbled downwards. Derringer banked hard away to avoid any blast, although he was being overly cautious. His aircraft was too high to be in danger.

The bomb exploded a hundred yards beyond the enemy biplane, not even close enough to cause splinter damage.

Derringer's plane laboured back into the sky and re-joined them. Captain Baker must have made it clear that he was allowed just one attempt. The captain raised his hand in a signal for everyone to follow him, and the squadron turned east again.

In the front cockpit, Roger swung round and gave Joseph an exaggerated shrug. Joseph returned the gesture with a grin to say he wasn't worried. There were bigger and better targets further on. Baker was right not to waste too much time or ammunition on a solitary plane.

The town of Beersheba loomed out of the haze and crept towards them across the desert. It was a patchwork of ancient stone buildings surrounded by the pale tents of the Turkish army. The airfield had its own neat pattern of canvas structures beside a cleared runway with nearly a dozen planes lined up nearby. In the distance, a single railway track spread itself into junctions that led to sheds and a water tower. There were Joseph's targets. Seeing them clearly, he let out a whoop and clapped Roger on the top of his head, startling him.

There was a sharp cracking sound and an innocent-looking puff of black smoke to his left. Several more blossomed in quick succession. The airfield had anti-aircraft guns and they were aiming at the bunched squadron. Baker quickly waved another pre-arranged signal. Expecting it, they all peeled off for their objectives. As Joseph flew towards the railway, he could watch his comrades bomb the airstrip.

The first to try was the Martynside with its single large bomb. Like Derringer, the pilot flew his aircraft in a straight line and ignored the antiaircraft fire, which was erratic now. He went low, ensuring that he would hit the easy target of the runway itself. The bomb dropped and erupted spectacularly in the middle of the cleared strip.

Joseph began to focus on hitting his own marks. Anywhere in the maze of railway junctions would do. If he could damage a shed or a locomotive at the same time, that would be a huge bonus.

An anti-aircraft shell burst close enough to shove the BE2c sideways. Both Joseph and Roger leaned out of their cockpits to check the plane, and there were no holes in the fabric. All the wire struts held too, singing with the slipstream. The two men exchanged sombre thumbs-ups. Sign language was easier amid the noise.

They cruised high over the junction yards first, looking for the best place to bomb. Joseph was disappointed not to see any trains or rolling stock. Plenty of sheds were on offer though. What they held would be pot-luck. Joseph chose one at random, put the nose down and swung the BE2c into an attack line. He considered jinking to either side to throw off the aim of the anti-aircraft guns, but the flowering black explosions weren't even coming close. He would be just as likely to steer directly into a shell by accident. The ground rose quickly to meet them and he saw men scattering in panic, mostly wearing long Arab robes. Roger, ready with the Lewis gun, was wisely holding his fire. Fragile alliances were in place with the Bedouin. He even gave some a reassuring wave as they roared overhead. One tall Arab stopped and shook his fist in return.

Pulling the release lever twice sent the bombs on their right wing tumbling down. Joseph had to compensate for the sudden lack of weight and the drag on that side, letting the plane yaw a little as he climbed. He glanced over his shoulder to see what had happened.

The shed and the adjacent tracks were lifting gracefully upwards in a plume of smoke before tearing apart as they fell again. Jubilant, he slapped Roger on the head twice.

'Bull's eye,' he screamed happily. Roger frowned and rubbed at his stinging scalp.

The world spun crazily as the BE2c stood on a wingtip and came back for a second run. Joseph looked for the next easy target. This one had horses tethered close by, so he swerved left, found a water tower smack in his sights and made a hurried judgment. The tower was a legitimate goal, but if the Australian Light Horse captured the town, the water would be useful.

He pressed the joystick to his left knee and headed for the neat rows of conical tents.

He spaced out his tugging on the release lever, spreading the fall of the bombs across the camp. Roger was firing a long burst with the Lewis gun, swinging the barrel left to right. Tents collapsed and men fell. The bombs exploded and flattened more canvas like bursting balloons. It all happened within seconds, and before Joseph could tell how much damage he had inflicted, they were past and climbing again towards the German airfield to find Captain Baker.

In the minutes it took to fly across the town, Joseph and Roger shook hands wildly and traded fierce grins. All four of their bombs had done good work. Judging by the spirals of smoke stretching high into the sky all over Beersheba, they weren't alone in being successful. Joseph started to count them, thinking each swirling column meant a well-placed bomb.

His attention was wrenched back by Roger firing a short burst. He had only pulled the trigger to get Joseph's notice. Now he was pointing frantically to the south and lower.

Despite the huge crater in their runway, two German Fokkers managed to take off and with their more powerful engines were pursuing the Martynside, which had been circling and observing the efforts of the others. It was older and slower than the BE2c's, but by sheer chance it had the second machine gun to defend itself.

That didn't stop Joseph from banking into a steep course to intercept. It was going to be touch-and-go whether they got there in time to match the odds. He saw Roger fighting to maintain his balance, fumbling with the Lewis gun's ammunition drum to put a full one in place.

The next minute dragged impossibly as the four planes converged. Everything else was forgotten, including the dropping bombs and whirling aircraft of the rest of Joseph's squadron. First to open fire was the Martynside, sending a loop of tracer difficult to see in the bright sunshine. It fell short and wide of the approaching Germans. Even so, they reacted by flipping apart in panic, which gave Joseph time to get within range and Roger a hurried shot at both. He didn't come close, his glowing rounds reaching into empty air first on one side, then in a hasty spray on the other. Joseph caught a glimpse of his mouth working on curses and snarled a few himself. Looking around quickly, he tried to decide which of the separated Germans to chase. Aircraft moving away from each other drew apart fast. Already both Fokkers were tiny against the backdrop of the desert and the distant dark thunderclouds.

With a curse of despair and punching the side of the cockpit with his fist, Joseph saw that it was useless. The enemy were fleeing, probably heading for a support airfield deep behind their lines. He would never catch them.

His first dogfight was over and it had lasted less than ninety seconds.

***

The squadron landed at their home base in the last light of the day. One of the storms was close. Buffeting winds moaned as the planes taxied towards the tents. With these gusts adding to the propeller wash, a blinding cloud of sand and debris swirled around them and the planes had to grope their way through to their parking places. Fitters and mechanics waited anxiously with ropes to tie the aircraft down before the squall hit fully. The air smelled damp with impending rain.

Roger yelled as he pulled off his leather helmet, 'The bastards ran for it before the damned barrel was warm. What's wrong with them? Don't the Germans *want* to win the war?' He had tightly curled brown hair that never looked different. Even now, after wearing the helmet for hours and running his fingers across his sweat-soaked scalp, it stayed the same.

Joseph winced at the sand driving into his face. With his goggles off, he had two large rings around his eyes. 'I expect they don't want to be shot down. It's a long way to the ground.'

'That's the best chance we've had,' Roger growled. 'Opportunities like that only come along once in a blue moon.'

'I'll tell you what. Next time you can fly, and I'll knock the buggers down.'

Roger was a pilot too. Everyone shared the tasks of either flying the aircraft or being the observer. He looked annoyed. 'Are you saying I should have hit them? *You* would have?'

'I've told you how to do it—'

'And I did, damn you. I aimed for where he'd be flying. A deflection shot.'

'But you have to remember *we're* moving too,' Joseph explained patiently. 'It all adds up. Look, come on—let's go and celebrate. I'm sure everyone else will be. The bombing was sensational. Maybe the skipper'll shout the whole squadron drinks.'

Roger grumbled, but followed him to the mess tent.

It turned into a party, since the storm prevented them from doing anything else except staying put and enjoying themselves. The pilots got drunk and sang soldiers' songs loudly because most of the men had come from the army. When they weren't hanging off each other's shoulders, they re-lived the bombing attacks, demonstrating their flying expertise with flattened palms waved through the air while the tent around them groaned and flapped with the storm winds. It began to rain heavily and touching the canvas caused the water to seep through, which became the sort of serious issue that could occupy drunkards as the alcohol took hold. Each crash of thunder and lightning brought a chorus of awe, as if from children at a fireworks show. The men's faces, flushed with whisky and good humour, glowed in the flickering lamplight.

Later, they tired and settled down into less animated conversations. Captain Baker sidled over to Joseph and Roger. He motioned them into a hushed discussion.

Peering through the smoke from his pipe, he asked, 'I don't suppose you fellows would want to swap all this for freezing cold and snow?'

'France, skipper?' Joseph guessed straight away. 'Are you joking? A chance to take on the Huns at home? The squadron would jump at the—'

Baker waved him to be quiet. 'I can't offer it to everyone, that's the problem.

And there's a snag. You might not be so keen, when you hear it.'

'It can't be that bad, surely?'

Baker glanced around to make sure that no one was eavesdropping. 'We're sending three more squadrons out from home, and they're going straight to England for training. The top brass want to salt these new units with experienced flyers from squadrons like ours. So while you might be in England before you know it, it could take six to eight months of bringing the new men up to scratch until you cross the Channel and get into the fighting. God knows, we might smash the Turks here and beat you to it, but I doubt it,' he added.

'What sort of kites will they be flying?' Roger asked suspiciously. It had taken their squadron long enough to get the updated BE2c's.

'DH5s, most likely,' Baker said, knowing that would be an incentive. These were single-seater fighters.

'Sign me up,' Roger said immediately.

Joseph was just as keen, but he didn't want to appear so eager to leave Baker and the others. 'I've got a brother in London,' he said pensively. 'In hospital. It would give me a chance to see him.'

'Is he hurt bad?' Baker said.

Joseph had never explained to anyone the nature of Jonathon's illness. Too many people were sceptical of such things in a time when women in London streets were handing out white feathers to men they perceived as cowards.

Now he could say brightly, 'He's just coming good, apparently. I got a letter from his sweetheart last week. He's already talking of going back to the Front, but it's early days, yet. He might have to transfer to the artillery if the doctors won't give him a clean bill of health.'

'He doesn't want to fly, does he?'

'Well, he's good on a horse... I don't think so. I can't imagine it.' He didn't want his brother flying. This was *his* achievement, his own accomplishment that he didn't want to share.

'So, are you sure you want to go?' Baker raised his eyebrows. 'Things will happen pretty fast once I start the wheels moving.'

'The bloody Germans won't put up a decent fight here, will they?' Joseph looked disgusted. 'If I have to go chasing them in France, I suppose I must.'

'That's the spirit,' Baker shook their hands solemnly in turn. A gleam of jealousy came into his eye. 'With a bit of luck, we might be right on your tail. I hope you're not too sozzled, by the way. You and Derringer are flying tomorrow morning. The Light Horse captured Rafa this evening and then retired about ten miles west afterwards. They want pictures of the village.'

'Oh... all right.' Joseph shot an unsteady look at Roger. Derringer's partner was a man called Haines. 'Nothing that a good cup of tea in the morning won't fix, I suppose,' he said with false cheer.

'That's the spirit. See me in the morning for maps and such, will you? I can't be bothered tonight. Fancy a nightcap? My shout.' Baker suddenly beamed at them.

'Of course, we do,' Roger said quickly before Joseph could refuse. 'Did I mention, sir, that this bastard says I can't shoot? I think I did bloody well today, even though I didn't actually hit anything. It could have been the piloting, of course. Were you watching?' He led Baker to the bar, turning the captain away from Joseph's outraged expression.

***

The next morning, their airfield showed the results of the night's storm. Deep channels had been cut into the ground from water running off the tents. Piles of brush and rubbish had been heaped against the canvas. Everything left outside, especially the planes, suffered a coat of sticking sand. In the early dawn light, the mechanics were complaining about having to clean every piece of equipment they owned. The place was a mess.

So, too, were the four men climbing into their aircraft. Two crew to each BE2c. Roger tumbled headfirst into the front cockpit and stayed like that for a while, his legs dangling over the side. With the sun still only a streak of colour along the horizon, it was comfortably dark below the rim of the nacelle.

Getting gingerly into the pilot's seat, Joseph heard him groan softly.

'What was that?' he asked.

'I said, can you start the engine quietly? I want to sleep for a bit.'

'You didn't want to keep things quiet last night. You sang the same bloody song about six times. It's my turn now,' Joseph said unpleasantly.

'That's not the same thing.' Roger's voice echoed from the cockpit.

'It's worse, what you did. You sing like a camel.'

Roger pondered this for a moment. Then, moaning and puffing, he hauled the rest of his body into the aircraft and peered with half-closed eyes at Derringer's plane parked further down the line. 'He's going to do it,' he announced mournfully.

Derringer's engine sputtered, then roared into life. It seemed to bring the whole desert alive, shattering the morning calm. Roger swore and tightened his helmet straps to pull the ear pads into place.

'Here we go,' Joseph shouted and signalled at the fitter standing in front of their plane to swing the propeller.

With the morning air so calm, it didn't matter which way they took off. Joseph opened the throttle and guided the BE2c in a straight line away from the tents. He could feel the wheels breaking through the thin crust made by the rain. Looking over his shoulder, watching for Derringer behind him, it was odd not to see the usual rooster-tail of dust behind them. The aircraft lifted from the earth and gained height, hastening the dawn with an orange sun appearing to the east. Joseph banked in a gentle circle as he continued to climb, still waiting for Derringer. A dark shape was racing across the pale sand below. Five minutes later, the second aircraft wobbled into position behind Joseph's left wing and they turned towards enemy-held territory.

The town of Rafa had been another desperate victory by the Light Horse, who captured the village to secure water for themselves and their horses. The Australians had enjoyed success driving the Turks back across the desert towards Palestine, but after winning each battle the soldiers bivouacked in the open, away from the local Arab population. The Australian Flying Corps were always called upon to photograph the evidence of the captured town, providing proof of the victory and checking whether the Turks came sneaking back. With their supplies destroyed and having sustained heavy casualties, the enemy usually found it easier to keep retreating.

Joseph had done this several times before and Roger was an accomplished aerial photographer. Right now, he was fiddling with the bulky camera to make sure it was ready. Derringer and

Haines were there as a backup with identical equipment, and a token escort, since they weren't armed.

It was a forty-five-minute flight to the target. Joseph used the time and fresh air blasting in his face to clear away the last of his hangover. Captain Baker's nightcaps had gone on for another hour. So waking up hadn't been easy.

When the two planes arrived over Rafa, the town was still smoking in places. Some of the burning stacks were Turkish stores, to the dismay of a group of Bedouin scavenging among the litter for working rifles and ammunition. The Arabs turned their dark faces up at the circle planes and watched them warily. They didn't try to shoot with their ancient weapons. They were supposed to be on the same side, thanks to Lawrence of Arabia, but at the same time the Arabs were renowned opportunists. Joseph was glad to be safely above them.

Gesturing for Derringer to stay high, he went first for his photographic run. He aimed for lines of trenches hugging the town's perimeter which he thought were satisfyingly empty of defenders until he saw they were filled with dead Turks. He held the BE2c as steady as he could with Roger aiming the lens over the side of the cockpit. When Roger straightened and began changing the film plate, Joseph swung them towards the thickest spire of smoke. This picture was followed by one of broken stone walls, behind which lay more dead. Bedouin moved among these, ransacking the bodies. They ignored the aircraft now as they would circling vultures.

Roger held up a single gloved finger to Joseph. He had one film plate to use. Joseph nodded vigorously and looked around, searching for a suitable subject.

A distant stuttering struck him as a sign that something was going amiss in the engine. He tried to identify it, then the truth came with a startling rush.

It was machine gun fire coming from somewhere in the sky—and that had to be Derringer in trouble.

Joseph stared around desperately and saw three swirling crosses behind, silhouetted high against a thunderstorm on the horizon. Instantly he threw the plane into a steep, climbing turn that brought a cry of alarm from Roger when he nearly dropped the camera. He recovered, stored it safely, and glaring at Joseph, demanded to know what was wrong. Joseph pointed forward urgently. Roger followed his line of sight above the propeller's arc and visibly jumped when he saw the dogfighting aircraft.

It was obvious what had happened and Joseph cursed everyone, including himself, for not having expected it. Each time the Light Horse had captured a village, the Flying Corps sent a reconnaissance flight the next day to take photographs. Finally, the Germans figured on sending some aircraft of their own to wait for them. It was an ambush the Australians had made for themselves.

This morning, their arrogance and contempt for the German Air Force, and their belief that the enemy wasn't interested in fighting looked like costing Derringer and Haines their lives. And Joseph and Roger theirs too, if things got any worse.

The Renault engine laboured to haul the plane upwards. Joseph could only hope Derringer survived until he got there to help. There was a chance things could improve if Derringer saw him and tried escaping by diving in Joseph's direction, but he had other things on his mind. Helpless to do anything except wait for his own struggling aircraft to cover the distance,

Joseph watched as Derringer twisted and rolled in panic, rather than with any evasive skills. Each move saw him lose height, which made Joseph's task of reaching the fight easier except soon Derringer would be trapped against the ground. The Germans, in two-seater Aviatiks with the armed observer in the rear cockpit, were both trying to manoeuvre close enough to get a decent shot, which showed inexperience or too much enthusiasm. Disciplined pilots would have worked together with one herding their prey towards the other. As Joseph willed Derringer to stay alive just a bit longer, he saw the tracer fire from one German go perilously close to his comrade. The second

Aviatik skidded away in alarm. The German's incompetence might just be Derringer's lifeline.

Then Joseph saw the deadly stream of tracer run across the Australian plane, making it stagger in the air before it nosed into a shallow dive.

The loud chatter of Roger opening fire with his Lewis gun dragged his attention away from Derringer's plight. The design of the BE2c with the observer in the front cockpit meant Roger had only a limited field of fire. He couldn't shoot forward through their own propeller. His weapon was a loose mount, not a fixture with the interrupter gearing that allowed other types of aircraft to fire between the blades of the spinning airscrew. Nor could he aim directly behind without the risk of killing his own pilot. It meant that they needed to be so near their target that Joseph could *turn away*, and let Roger shoot sideways.

Their pursuit of Derringer and the German attacking him had presented Roger with the chance of a burst at the other Aviatik, still recovering from dodging his countryman's bullets. It was a long shot, the tracer from the Lewis arcing wide and harmlessly past. At least it had the effect of telling the German that Joseph and Roger had arrived. Not only that, but unlike Derringer, they were armed and looking for a fight.

The Aviatik again corkscrewed violently away, the pilot taking no chances, and kept turning until it steered for the enemy lines.

Deserting his partner, the German ran for home. Joseph saw Roger raise his hands in amazement.

The remaining enemy aircraft was flying a half-hearted chase now, plotting a course that gave him a choice between finishing Derringer off and fleeing for safety too. A final stream of tracer curved out and ran over Derringer's aircraft. It was good shooting and the Germans, apparently satisfied, banked hard away from Joseph's approach and headed for their own lines too.

Joseph yelled a curse of frustration and tried to cut the corner. It brought them within range for a single burst. Roger emptied the entire drum in a hopeful wide spray before the superior Aviatik quickly gained distance. The German observer even offered a farewell wave.

'Cheeky bastard,' Joseph shouted angrily, then nearly choked when he saw

Roger raised a friendly hand in return. 'Don't do that, you stupid sod!'

Roger didn't hear him.

Frustrated, Joseph flipped them onto a course to find the other BE2c.

Derringer had landed beside the trenches they had photographed earlier. The plane had pulled up with no mishap, but Joseph wouldn't risk the same without a close inspection first. He flew down and skimmed the sand, checking that the ground was free of obstacles and hidden ditches that might trip him up. He spotted both the crew walking around their stationary BE2c. It seemed everything was all right, after all. Joseph knew that they had been lucky.

They landed in a swirl of dust and taxied over next to the stricken plane. Derringer and Haines turned their backs to the hail of stinging sand and grit, then Joseph switched off his engine and everyone peered at each other anxiously through the haze. When he took off his helmet, Joseph heard a loud buzzing. It came from an enormous cloud of flies feeding on the corpses in the trenches nearby.

Stiffly, he climbed down and waited for Roger before walking over to the others.

'Are you hurt?' he asked, seeing Derringer so deathly pale and Haines not much better.

'No, we're fine,' Derringer said hoarsely.

'Are you sure? He gave you a good pasting twice. We saw it.'

Derringer looked really ill. He and Haines exchanged an odd, guilty look. 'We went over to the trench for a quick look, that's all. Not knowing what to expect really.' He wiped at his mouth, betraying the fact that he'd been sick. 'It's bloody awful.'

Neither of these men had seen action in the army. They'd transferred and arrived at the airfield after the Anzac evacuation. In the background, Roger wore a mocking expression.

'You'd better get used to it,' Joseph said grimly. 'That's what the damned German was trying to do to *you* before we caught up and spoiled things.'

'Thank God you did,' Derringer nodded.

'No, thank God the Huns ran for it. We were outnumbered and outgunned. How's your crate?'

'It's buggered, Joseph,' Haines said. 'They shot a dozen holes all through the fuel tanks and we're dry. It's bloody lucky the tracers didn't turn us into a flamer. Come and have a look if you like.'

The four of them went over to the damaged plane and examined it, poking their fingers into the bullet holes and kicking sand over the dribble of fuel that had pooled underneath. There was no doubt Derringer and Haines had been lucky to avoid being hurt. The aeroplane couldn't be repaired or flown.

'What are we going to do?' Derringer asked timidly.

Joseph slapped the fuselage. 'We can't guarantee we're still behind our own lines, and the Light Horse might have buggered off in any direction. We'd better burn her, just in case. There's no choice.'

'How will we get back?'

'How do you think? You'll each have to ride on a wing either side. It won't be the first time and bloody uncomfortable—'

'Ah, Joseph,' Haines interrupted, calling from the other side of the plane.

Joseph shouted back, 'What would you rather do? Walk?'

'*Joseph.*'

Haines was worried about something else. Exchanging a look, the other three hurried around the BE2c's motor and ducked under the hot cowling. There they stopped in surprise, confronted by a daunting sight.

Ten yards beyond Haines, a tall Bedouin tribesman stood dressed in full traditional robes. A hood shielded most of his face, but there was no concealing his ugly glare. Haines was right to look terrified. This man was a true warrior, proud and with no fear of these airmen. He held an ancient rifle loosely in one hand. Joseph guessed it could be brought to bear very quickly. And it reminded him that his own revolver was still in the cockpit.

'Christ,' Roger whispered. 'He must have been searching the bodies. Does that mean he's on our side?'

'The Bedouin only have one side, Roger. Their own.'

'So what the hell do we do? Do we just shoot him and run for it?'

'Keep your voice *down*. Shoot him with what?'

'For God's sake, they can't understand English,' Roger said. 'Where's your damned gun?'

Haines hadn't moved a muscle. He called tremulously, 'Do you think I can move over towards you fellows?'

'No, you'd better stay there for a second. We don't want to alarm him.'

Haines groaned but didn't move.

The Arab spoke in a deep voice that made them all jump. In excellent, accented English he said, 'You ask am I on *your* side? Why should I care which army you belong to?' He swept his arm wide. 'You are all squabbling over land that is ours. One of you is as bad as the other.'

It left them speechless. Then Joseph said, 'Actually, we're trying to get rid of the Turks for you.'

The Bedouin snorted, then spat on the ground.

Roger added, with a rush of bravado, 'That's right. You should be bloody grateful.'

The Arab regarded Roger as if he were sizing him up for a meal. 'The Turk is here because *you* are here, so I say it's your fault.' He let that hang threateningly, then gestured at the corpses behind him. 'And they make poor pickings for scavengers like me. Your soldiers are fatter and are better equipped. It's a shame they don't die more often.'

Joseph gave his companions a warning look. 'Why? What do you need?'

A thin smile showed under the hood. The Arab had perfect teeth. 'A good horse?'

'We don't ride horses. We're not cavalry. These are our horses,' Joseph jerked a thumb over his shoulder at the aircraft.

'I am not a fool,' the Arab replied with dry contempt. 'It is a British Experimental Mark 2, and the Germans are shooting them down like flies in France.'

'Oh, well...' Joseph groped for words while Roger simmered with sudden outrage. 'I'm afraid we don't have anything we can give you.' Joseph noticed Haines sidling towards him. 'It's the weight, you see. We can't carry much.' There was a silence while the Arab ran his eye over the aircraft.

'Why should you give me anything? Are you trying to buy my loyalty?' he said slyly.

'No, it's because you're our ally, I suppose. We should be helping each other beat the Germans—and the Turks too.'

'Really? And what do you give your *other* allies to appease them?' The thin smile returned.

Joseph turned to his comrades, looking for suggestions, but he got none. He turned back to the Arab.

'Well, there's horses... and food too. Rifles and ammunition, of course.' He sighed. 'It's not my job to know exactly. I'm sure it's everything you need.'

The Arab fingered the handle of a large dagger tucked into his sash. Its blade was bloody from cutting away the uniforms of dead Turks. His smile turned to a humourless grin.

'You give them Lewis guns, perhaps?'

***

Joseph patiently checked his gauges and prepared to take off.

Roger twisted round and shouted at him over the roar of the engine. 'How are you going to explain losing my bloody Lewis gun? Baker will have our guts. What if he docks our pay?'

Without looking up, Joseph yelled back, 'I'll say we needed to lose some weight. To get these blokes home.'

Roger glanced at Derringer clinging to one wing, then at Haines on the other. Both of them looked frightened half to death.

‘I think he’d rather we brought back the machine gun than these two jokers.’

‘Then go and ask for it back.’

Roger stared glumly after the distant figure of the Arab striding easily towards the village. His robes flowed magnificently as he moved, the Lewis gun slung over his shoulder. The spare ammunition drum he’d tucked under his arm, and he still carried the old rifle.

‘What’d he say his name was?’

‘Prince Amman. He got a rowing blue at Oxford, or so he told me.’ Joseph tapped one of the gauges to make it work.

Roger settled back into his seat. ‘Fat lot of good that’ll do him in the fucking desert, the thieving bastard.’

***

Two days later, following another long night of dedicated drinking in their honour, Joseph and Roger left the airfield. They were bound for Cairo and then Southampton. When they headed off, the temperature was 105 degrees Fahrenheit in the shade. It didn’t help their hangovers.

In France and England, where they would arrive within a fortnight, people were calling that winter the worst in living memory. It hadn’t stopped snowing for three months.

1918

The restaurant was crowded, as always. Despite the rationing of all kinds of food and drink, London's nightlife still thrived on the war. Lately, a fresh wave of men had arrived with plenty of money in their pockets. Robert was observing some of them now from the corner seat of the booth with Julia pressed happily against him.

'They're full of shit, these Yanks,' he muttered. 'They reckon they're going to win the bloody war, but when will they do some fighting?'

Jonathon was scraping at a sauce stain on his lieutenant's uniform. Sometimes he felt acutely conscious of his new status. He thought of himself as a soldier, not an officer. Robert had advanced to sergeant when they allowed him to transfer into the Transport Corps to drive ammunition trucks and ambulances, and kidded him about it mercilessly.

Jonathon gave up scrubbing and said, 'They don't have to. It's enough that the Americans are here. The Kaiser's shitting himself.'

Rose took out her handkerchief, rubbed at the stain for him and Jonathon grinned. 'I'll be happy if the Doughboys do all the fighting from now on,' she said. 'Our men have done enough.'

He shook his head. 'No, they're going to wait until the entire Yank army's here and do it in one push, not before. They're already saying that the American public won't stand defeat the way we've been hammered for years. At the first sign of failure, all the support back home will disappear.' Jonathon raised his hand at a passing waiter and pointed at their empty wine bottle. 'We'll still be doing all the work until the Yanks are good and ready,' he added.

Rose wasn't happy. 'It's only two days before you go back. I've got so used to not worrying about you, and now it starts all over again.'

'It's different this time, though,' he said.

'Too right, it's different,' Robert snorted. 'He's as safe as Lloyd George himself. The bloody artillery just rush all over the place like headless chickens, causing trouble and bringing hell back down on the heads of the poor bastards in the trenches. They don't stick around to cop it themselves.'

Julia didn't see the gleam in his eye. 'Now, don't you two start arguing,' she said.

'Where's your depot again, Robert?' Jonathon asked innocently.

'We store ammo',' Robert told him smugly. 'You're not allowed within cooee of us in case you start any trouble.'

Jonathon could have teased him about his own safe posting to the Transport Corps. But it was still an unkind reminder of the permanent limp Robert bore and his stiffened back, both of which prevented him from being a front-line soldier again.

Julia quickly changed the subject. 'Everyone's saying the Germans are preparing to attack us before the Americans can build up to full strength.'

It had a dampening effect on their mood and she was annoyed at herself.

'It makes sense,' Jonathon said. 'They might come out of it even worse off. It's probably just another silly rumour.'

Rose smiled brightly. 'For God's sake, let's not get all maudlin. Have you heard from Joseph again?'

'Our own family Red Baron? Not since his last letter about finally being posted to France—you've read it.' He explained to Julia, 'Only five victories and he officially becomes an ace. If he's as good a pilot as he was a sniper, it shouldn't take long.'

'Joseph the Assassin, remember?' Robert pulled a face. 'If he gets as many Hun pilots as he did Turks in the...' he changed his mind. It wasn't a good story to tell in front of the girls.

‘It seems a little macabre to keep count, doesn’t it?’ Julia asked.

‘Maybe,’ Jonathon answered first. ‘The newspapers can’t get enough of these flying heroes.’

‘Flying idiots, if you ask me,’ Robert said. ‘It’s a bit hard to get out and walk home if something goes wrong.’

They were interrupted by the arrival of the full bottle of wine. With the place overflowing with American "Doughboy" soldiers waving their money and tipping heavily, service consisted of the bottle being hastily dropped into the centre of the table.

‘I’m surprised he bothered to uncork it,’ Robert muttered as he poured for everyone. ‘Let’s drink a toast to Joseph and his personal flying circus. Good luck to him.’

Rose was lost in a memory of lying in an open field with Mark Cohen, watching the two aircraft dogfight above them, and their conversation about the point of it all. Even now, thoughts of Mark still gave her twinges of guilt, but only about how fate had dealt him a losing hand. In the year since Jonathon had come back into her life with his long road to recovery—during which she’d spent every minute she could helping him—Mark had graciously accepted defeat. Apparently, anyway. They remained close friends and worked well together, but there were still days when Rose suspected that he was still waiting for *his* chance. She couldn’t help believing that he would secretly welcome the news of Jonathon's battalion being finally posted to France. And sometimes Mark made odd comments about joining the fighting himself, as if that might impress her, or as if he had something to prove. She ignored them.

'You'd better say something soon,' Robert broke into her thoughts cheerfully. She saw that he was filling her wine glass slowly and waiting for her to stop him.

'Goodness! Stop,' she smiled, feeling bad about musing over Mark, innocent though it was. That wasn't right, while she was here with Jonathon.

He had his arm round her shoulder, and misunderstanding her quiet reflection, he gave her a squeeze. 'Don't worry about me,' he said softly, so the others didn't hear. 'Robert's right. We'll be staying well out of trouble. You'll be closer to the front lines than me, half the time.'

It was a lie, but she knew what he meant. Jonathon's guns were light artillery, always on the move and behind the network of trenches to allow them fast deployment. They dashed to trouble spots just the same.

They were all staying in the same hotel. As usual, it was more expensive than they would have preferred. The invasion of friendly troops from the huge armies training and resting in England meant cheaper accommodation was impossible to find at short notice. Tonight, no one really minded, since the four of them would be going their separate ways back to France within days. Rose and Julia were due back at the Casualty Clearing Station, still in the same farmhouse after nearly two years, and Robert was going to his base depot a few miles to their north. With all the Australian forces now formed into a single command structure, autonomous from the British Army at last, Jonathon's battalion was going to the same sector of the Western Front.

The couples' parting wasn't going to be as wrenching as it might have been. Meeting each other in France for days off wouldn't be that hard. Robert had managed it once already.

They split up in the hallway upstairs, going to rooms either side.

'About bloody time,' Jonathon said to Rose with a grin, kicking the door closed behind them and sweeping her into his arms. 'What's the point wasting time in some stuffy old restaurant when we can be here together?'

She laughed as he pressed her back against the bed. '*You* ordered the last bottle of wine.'

'Just to get you drunk, in case you were thinking of putting up a fight.' He wrestled her down onto the quilt covers.

They made love passionately, as lovers do when they're aware that their time together is limited. He was strong and kind, fully recovered from his illness and again the man she'd fallen in love with right at the start. Perhaps… there were moments when she looked into his eyes and wondered if the insanity could return.

Would he ever be *exactly* the same person he had been, before he'd lost those months of his life to some dark, unreachable place inside his own head? Did someone who suffered a complete, mental breakdown like that ever heal completely? Sometimes, Rose warned herself that it just wasn't possible. A remnant of the damage done had to be there, and it was wise to be prepared.

That was a risk she was more than happy to take, and in one way she welcomed the slight doubt over Jonathon's wellbeing and mental state. The army shared the view and had refused him a return to the infantry and front line duty. Retraining as an artillery officer had been the best he could do.

***

Four days later, the soft bedding and Rose's warm presence were a distant, difficult memory.

Jonathon stood in a freezing wind, the paddock around him crowded with guns, shouting men and horses stamping through the snow. It had been a long time since everything he said or did was to the deafening tune of the Western Front's heavy artillery hammering like angry gods nearby. Overhead it was threatening rain or more snow, another grim reminder of army life.

Jonathon huddled deeper into his greatcoat and tried to recall why he'd been so enthusiastic to return to all this. For the first time, he was honestly glad he didn't have to stand knee-deep in a stinking trench somewhere.

Watching soldiers march past, he was impressed by their equipment. When he'd arrived in France for the first time back in 1916, fresh from Gallipoli and convinced like everyone else that the Australians would quickly win the war for Britain, their uniforms and gear had still been those of simple soldiers. They had clothing to suit the weather, basic implements for living, and each had a rifle with its ammunition.

Now many men carried Lewis guns over their shoulders, while just about everyone had a brace of grenades and small mortars. Added to the burden were a gas mask, spare ammunition for their weapon, water bottles and a clatter of personal gear for eating and sleeping. Their uniforms were covered in bulging pockets and hanging implements. Jonathon saw that everyone carried his trenching spade and many had been wickedly modified into another killing tool, just as the British sapper Sinclair had shown him so long ago.

Lieutenant Chalmers came up to him and broke his thoughts.

'The boys are raring to go, John,' he said cheerfully. 'Just dying for a chance to shell somebody with sausage on his breath.'

'You should be more careful what you wish for, Geoffrey,' Jonathon replied, unsmiling. Chalmers was in command of a gun section, the same as Jonathon.

Their battery had eighteen pieces in all with junior lieutenants each in charge of six.

'I'd say we've got the bastards on the run already. The Huns are worried. The Hindenburg Line won't save them from the Yanks.' Chalmers gave a satisfied nod. 'I got into this show just in time. It'll all be over soon.'

'What stopped you before?' Jonathon looked at him sideways. Chalmers was the same age and had joined their battalion only recently, and no one knew much about him.

He had the grace to appear guilty. 'I was in charge of a crew of lathe operators in a munitions factory outside Geelong. My father's one of the company partners. He convinced me I was doing better work making shells than shooting them, and I'd always supposed someone had to do it. Place is filled with chattering girls now, of course.'

'Really? Is that what changed your mind?' Jonathon's attention was caught by a motorbike labouring across the field. Their company commander, Captain Faulkner, had broken away from a group of men to wave the courier down.

Chalmers took a moment to reply. He sounded slightly bitter. 'Actually, some bitch started putting a white feather on my desk every morning. I never found out who, although I tried.' He paused. 'Those women can be quite... unpleasant, when they get an idea inside their heads, you know?'

'Yes, some of them. But not all,' Jonathon said tersely to finish the discussion. 'Look out. I think something's happening.'

Now a runner was heading their way, sent by Captain Faulkner. He stumbled in the holes and mounds hidden by the snow and arrived breathlessly in front of Jonathon. Steam clouded around his head as he gasped, 'The captain's compliments, sir. Can you limber up and take your section to these positions?' He handed over a piece of paper. 'Open fire on the target as soon as you can. He said to take a wireless. There's a plane overhead to give you fall-of-shot.'

'Thank you. I'm on the way,' Jonathon snapped.

He snatched the signal and stopped only to wave across the distance at the captain, who was watching. Then he turned to yell orders to his men. As he strode towards his horse, he heard Chalmers call after him.

'Give 'em hell, John, you lucky bugger. Our turn next time.'

Jonathon's gunnery section was still horse-drawn and as their lieutenant he had an animal of his own which he'd named Rosie. Right now, his men were reacting to the urgency of his orders, frantically tightening the last of the harnessing on the horses so they could move off. The six guns would be followed by two carriages of ammunition. Jonathon always kept Rosie saddled with the girth strap loosened until she was needed. He was buckling it when his sergeant, Carlton, hurried over.

'We're heading north, Edgar,' Jonathon told him before he could ask. He showed him the signal which included references to landmarks. 'Sound familiar?'

Carlton read it quickly. 'It's a fair way, past the Casualty Clearing Station in that farmhouse. Beyond that, sir, I don't know for sure. The church spire should be easy to spot.'

'If it's still there.' Jonathon nodded. Map references vanished, blown away by German artillery. He'd purposely put the proximity of Rose's CCS out of his mind. 'Are you ready to move?'

'Ready when you are.'

'Then I'll take the lead.'

With Jonathon riding at a fast canter, the procession of horses, guns and ammunition rushed as best they could along the ruined tracks. The situation might have called for a gallop, but other traffic on the road and the winter conditions made it too dangerous. As it was, his crews clung precariously to the gun carriages and ammunition carts.

Ten minutes later, there were the original farmhouse, barn and buildings of Rose's CCS. They'd all survived despite several brief errant attacks by the German artillery. Clustered closely around were large canvas structures with huge red crosses emblazoned on their roofs. Spread further was a sea of smaller white tents with everything inadvertently half-camouflaged by the snowfall.

Behind the CCS, the heavy battery was letting off regular rounds. Jonathon could tell the emplacement had been there for a while, the one Rose had told him about several times, joking and complaining. Finally witnessing it, he frowned at the logic of placing the guns there in the first place—or at least of keeping them at this stage of the war. If the Germans counter-attacked in force, it would be a prime objective and the CCS would be overrun on the way. The German air force was capable of large bombing raids now too, even if with questionable accuracy. So the Casualty Clearing Station wasn't as safe as it had been in the past.

His horse shied away from a motorbike coming the opposite way and Jonathon couldn't worry about Rose any longer. He had other things on his mind. The CCS slipped from sight as they continued down the road.

Their destination proved to be an open field with an infantry battalion camped miserably at one end. Thin smoke drifted up from fires. The soldiers stopped and watched the battery arrive in a flurry of snow and mud kicked up by the horses. The skyline to the east was a dirty haze with half a dozen observation balloons floating ghostlike above the earth.

With the guns wheeling into a line and being anchored down, other men started passing the ammunition from the carts. Jonathon dismounted and let Rosie roam free while he walked up and down the emplacement encouraging his crews. They would be opening fire within minutes.

He heard an angry voice.

'Hey you! Yes, *you*! Fuck off out of here. My blokes haven't had any decent rest for bloody days.'

A group of soldiers from the infantry camp were advancing towards him with a sergeant in the lead. All of them were clearly angry.

'I've got orders,' Jonathon shouted back. 'There's nothing I can do about it.' He pointed at the trenches. 'Someone's in trouble. They need some artillery support.'

The sergeant snarled, 'You'll bring a hail of the bloody things back down on us, you bastard. What do you think those observation balloons are, fucking pork sausages? They're probably calling in shots on us now. You don't have to start shooting to attract their bloody attention.'

'Then perhaps you should break camp now, while you can?' Jonathon knew it wasn't the right thing to say. He didn't know what else to suggest. He actually sympathised with the sergeant.

'Move now? This is the first chance my men have had in fucking days for some hot grub and to get almost dry.' The sergeant came up to him and the two men stared at each other a long time, while the others looked on.

'Jesus Christ,' the sergeant said. 'They told me you were dead. Then they found you in a madhouse. What the hell are you doing *here*?'

'*You* can ask, Tom?' Jonathon said. 'I never thought you'd get off the hospital ship *alive*. How can you be fit for active bloody duty? You wanted me to leave you for dead, remember? For God's sake, you're at least supposed to be back home safe and sound.'

Sergeant Tom Carter grinned savagely and pumped Jonathon's hand. 'It took a while to convince 'em I was fine. And I've got a hell of a war wound. I can shit sideways.'

'You must be mad.' Jonathon was still amazed.

'No, that's what they told me about *you*.'

'Well, that's a long story–' Jonathon checked to see his gun crews almost ready. 'Shit, Tom. I *have* to do this. You know I do. Every second counts.'

'Damn it.' Carter wiped a hand across his face. 'Maybe if you're quick they'll leave us alone.'

One of his men grunted, 'Fat fucking chance of that, sarge.'

Carter shoved one of them on the shoulder and sent him back towards their camp. 'Come on, you blokes. Let's prepare for the worst. Jonno's right. If it was us out there yelling for artillery support, we wouldn't want him to stop just so we could get some damned sleep.' Over his shoulder he called back to Jonathon, 'Where are you camped? I'll try to find you for a drink.' Then he added, 'Hang on. Am I allowed to fraternise with bloody officers?'

'If it's your shout.' Jonathon told him the battalion's location and waved. Inside, he felt shaken. It might have turned into a nasty scene.

Carlton called from the nearest gun. 'We're ready to go, sir. Robbo's got the spotter plane on the wireless, but it's not good. We can hardly hear him.'

'Then we'd better open fire while we still can.' Jonathon nodded. Carlton pulled the lanyard and his gun crashed backwards with the recoil. The other crews took their cue and began shooting too. All six pieces fired and reloaded as fast they could.

Robertson on the wireless screamed, 'The flyboys reckon up another fifty yards, sir! Then we're on the money.'

Jonathon turned and jogged along by the guns, calling out the correction.

On target, there was nothing else for him to do. He watched the sky anxiously as if he might see incoming rounds, aware that Tom Carter was right and retribution would come soon. He glanced towards Carter's camp. It looked like the men weren't moving. There was still food cooking on the fires and soldiers wouldn't abandon hot food unless they absolutely had to.

Enemy shells finally screeched out of the leaden clouds and landed with a ferocity and accuracy that took Jonathon by surprise. At least ten rounds exploded in a shattering salvo between his guns and Carter's camp. Behind the emplacement their horses bucked in panic.

'Keep firing, keep firing,' Jonathon yelled, already thinking about pulling out. The German shelling was too close for comfort for a first salvo. *Was it luck or skill?* He stared at the nearest balloon, a grey blimp shrouded by wisps of low cloud. The men in that tiny basket didn't have the luxury of looking straight down at their target like the Allies' plane above them could. Did they see how close they came?

Why the hell didn't Joseph and his damned newspaper heroes shoot the bloody things down?

The next salvo erupted in almost the same place except for one round that hit Carter's camp and killed two men. Jonathon saw them thrown high into the air by a shell that hit the ground beside them. The rest of Carter's company had abandoned their equipment and run for a line of trees beyond the road. The pair who died had lingered too long, straggling behind to snatch a last mouthful of food.

Jonathon found Carlton beside him, the sergeant screaming to overcome the noise and his own deafened ears. His face was streaked by gun smoke.

'They're getting bloody close, Jonno. How much longer do we stay?'

'Four more rounds per gun,' Jonathon shouted back, and saw the startled expression on Carlton's face. Four more shots would obviously give the enemy time for the same, and they were already too close. As Carlton turned away Jonathon grabbed his arm.

'No! To hell with it. Let's get out of here. Leave any ammo on the ground. We'll come back and get it later. These bastards are going to bracket us any minute.'

His gun crews didn't need any urging to harness up and run for it. A fresh salvo landed in front of the emplacement and sent a curtain of earth into the air between them and the front line. Jonathon thanked God the Germans were shooting in disciplined volleys with all their guns firing together. The interludes provided a chance to escape.

One gun crew didn't make it. The next rounds came near enough to throw their howitzer onto its side, the wheels and carriage instantly a twisted wreck. Three men lay still beside it while the horses reared crazily in their harnesses, trying to pull the dead weight.

Jonathon rushed forward, pulled a bayonet from his belt and tried to cut the horses loose before they trampled the gunners. Pushed and jostled by the animals, he sawed at the leather and they finally galloped free of the gun, still in harness. Jonathon dropped down at each man bleeding in the snow. They were all dead.

He felt someone tugging at his coat. It was Carlton. 'Come on, Lieutenant,' he pleaded. 'We'll get these blokes later.'

'Go! Run for it, Edgar,' Jonathon gasped, staggering to his feet. Nearby an anxious-looking corporal clung to Rosie's reins. Jonathon hauled himself into the saddle and the corporal sprinted for the trees.

The gunners gathered on the road and reorganised themselves. Jonathon ordered one wagon to stay and collect the dead. The rest began a slow march back towards their main camp. As they passed, he saw soldiers from Carter's company emerging from the trees and he saw Carter himself standing on a knoll and holding his rifle high in a gesture of farewell. Jonathon waved in return, although thick smoke drifting on the wind put a barrier between them, and he couldn't be sure that Carter had seen him.

***

Back at base, Jonathon reported to Captain Faulkner and heard that his bombardment had done its job. They'd destroyed a German mortar unit that had been in the process of wiping out a critical fortification in the front line.

Outside the captain's tent, Jonathon saw Chalmers approaching and gave the other lieutenant such a glare he hastily turned and walked away. Jonathon wasn't interested in telling him some gallant story of their success. He had other things to think about.

Ten fierce minutes of battle had left him exhausted and numb. Worse than he'd felt after eight months on Gallipoli. Was it because he wasn't used to it? Were the pressures of command greater than he'd realised? He was worried that he wasn't as mentally fit as he'd believed.

At the same time, he resolved not to be too harsh on himself. Every man in this war needed to remember exactly what he was doing—the horror of it. Perhaps he should be glad that it affected him so? It might actually make him a better officer.

Suddenly he wanted to ask Rose. She would tell him honestly. And in this insane world of total warfare she was only a twenty-minute ride away. How strange was that? With Captain Faulkner's permission, he would try to visit her that evening.

He headed back to the captain's tent, suspecting that he'd just invented an excuse to visit his sweetheart, and Faulkner would let him, he knew.

Rank, as they said, apparently did have its privileges.

A Knight of the Sky

A line of men was advancing slowly across the field, their heads bent to the task of flattening the ground in front of them with shovels. Occasionally someone stooped to pull a large stone out and hurl it aside. They had started early in the morning. Now, close to midday, the line had barely got halfway along the makeshift airstrip.

Watching from where he leaned on the wing of his plane, Joseph was exasperated.

'Never thought I'd miss Egypt,' he said, patting his pockets for a smoke. 'At least there we just took off and landed wherever we wanted. None of this rubbish.'

'Or those bloody guns firing all day and night,' Roger agreed morosely beside him. 'Christ, imagine being in the trenches. Putting up with that racket the whole time.'

'It's a bit more intense than Big Bertha spoiling a swim in the ocean.' Sudden memories made Joseph's expression whimsical.

Their squadron's new airfield was seven miles behind the front lines, well within hearing range of the guns. The base was a converted horse stud with plenty of barns, stables and extensive living quarters for the farm workers, none of whom were left. The war had taken them all. There were no horses either, although the stud's owners still lived frugally in the main house and had so far ignored the swarm of noisy aircraft that descended upon them. The squadron's officers invaded the living quarters and adjacent kitchen with its long dining table. The enlisted men made themselves comfortable in the stables, which suited them, being close to the barns where they could work on the aircraft under cover if necessary. Altogether, a fine arrangement and for Joseph and Roger much better than the sand-blown tents outside Cairo. If only they had a flat landing strip.

All they needed was a chance to fly and start doing their job. The squadron commander, Major Judith, had picked the most suitable paddock and ordered the enlisted ranks to find a shovel each (of which there was no shortage in an old horse stud), form a line and begin flattening every tussock, filling each hole, and removing any rocks.

Roger asked, for what seemed the tenth time, 'Do you still reckon we'll get up today?'

Joseph nodded at the line. 'Look, they're stopping for bloody dinner now.'

'Bloody hell, they only had morning tea five minutes ago.'

'You shouldn't be so keen to get yourself shot at.'

'I just want to have a look, that's all. The famous Western Front at last. The war'll be over before we get there.'

'We could take a walk and see it for real,' Joseph said innocently. 'You know, I think maybe we *should* take a tour of the trenches. It'd let us know what it's really all about.'

'Pig's arse,' Roger spluttered around lungs full of cigarette smoke. He coughed painfully, tears in his eyes, and needed a minute for the spasm to go away. 'Are you mad? I only want to see it from a grandstand view, safe in the cockpit of my kite, thank you very much.'

Joseph nodded wisely. 'Thought as much.'

The squadron's "kites" were SE5a's, single-seat biplane fighters regarded by many as the best the Allies had and much better than the DH5s the pilots trained in over England. They were easy to fly, fast and stable. They carried two machine guns, one mounted on the engine cowling and firing forward through the propeller and the second a fixed Lewis gun attached to the upper wing, also shooting forward. Several German aircraft could match them, but they certainly weren't inferior. For the Australian pilots, it was a dream come true. The men couldn't wait to take them into battle.

'Come on, we might as well eat too,' Joseph said, pushing himself away from the wing. 'The strip won't be finished for ages.'

'I'm too nervous to eat. I'll chuck the whole bloody lot up again.'

'Have a few tots of rum first. That'll settle your guts down.'

Roger brightened. 'There's a thought. Might warm me up too. Tell me, what do the Germans want France for anyway? The weather's bloody awful.'

***

Major Judith, affectionately called "Judy" by those he allowed, ordered the first patrol at 1600 that afternoon. Given that it was late January, the day was short and the four aircraft he sent would only have an hour in the air because they needed to land before dark. The mission was a token gesture, a thin excuse to get some of his men familiar with the territory, since they were so keen to go. Otherwise, he could have waited for the next day and flown the full squadron.

As he'd hinted he would all day, Judith sent Joseph, Roger and two less experienced flyers called Dunlop and Parker. Everyone had been training together for months, but neither Parker nor Dunlop had ever flown in action.

'Stay close to these blokes,' Judith told them sternly, poking a thumb at Joseph and Roger standing nearby. 'They know bugger all, but at least they've been shot at and should have the sense to run if things go wrong. And by the way,' he turned around to the others, cutting off their grins. 'Just have a *look* and come back.

There's no need to take on any bloody flying circus on our first day.'

'Back in time for tea, sir,' Roger saluted needlessly.

'You'd better be.'

Despite the enlisted men's day-long efforts, the airstrip gave them a bumpy ride. Especially at the end, where the men had grown tired and keen to finish thc work. The aircraft left in pairs, one close behind the other, and the first thing Joseph did was lead them in three full circuits of the airfield. He wanted to learn the landmarks and make sure he could find home again, even in the gloom of evening. Then he waved an arm and set off towards the north-east, climbing slowly and feeling the chill slipstream turn colder as they gained height. Before him, the sky was clear beneath 10,000 feet. Above this were enormous cumulus clouds like huge dumplings, drifting slowly and casting sharply defined shadows onto the earth below, their crowns orange with the late sun.

They'd heard and read about the Western Front for years. For soldiers, this was the real fight, the place where the war would be won and lost.

Joseph was still unprepared for the incredible landscape that rolled underneath his wings. It took his breath away and he swore softly, over and over again.

The green countryside was split as far as he could see, east to west, by a wide strip of twinkling, moving mud, the trenches jagged lines winding through it with thousands of men in them. The ground seemed to boil like a thick stew. Glittering sparks were rounds igniting on impact and streams of tracer flickered across the dark ground.

He couldn't even begin to imagine what it was like down there. Somewhere his brother Jonathon was a part of it, although he wouldn't actually be in the trenches. His battery was made up of light calibre guns, the unit dashing like cavalry from one trouble spot to the next.

A black cloud appeared with a vicious crack to the right. A sound like pebbles thrown on a tin roof came from his fuselage. Then further explosions, dozens of them around the four aircraft in quick succession. It was German anti-aircraft fire and the first shot had been uncomfortably close. Joseph took the flight in a wide s-shaped turn to throw off the gunners' aim. The shells kept coming, nothing too near. The men had been warned that it was a fact of life over the front, not something that might be avoided or predicted as in Egypt. As long as they flew close to the main trenches, somebody would try to shoot them down. Even their own troops sometimes, and especially the French, who were so sick of being bombed and shelled that they shot at anything in the sky just in case.

Joseph deliberately steered along the front, inviting the anti-aircraft guns to have a go so he might get used to it. It was rare that any aircraft were seriously damaged. Not unless they flew low, straight and so slow that even the worst gunner could score a hit. The hail of shells always greeted them. It even helped the pilots during their patrols. A cloud of friendly anti-aircraft fire could be seen from a distance a lot more easily than the enemy aircraft the ground crews were shooting at.

A flash of colour, a glimpse of red moving through a shaft of late afternoon sunshine, made him suddenly tense. He used his peripheral vision and saw three tiny aeroplanes flying above the Allied reserve trenches, so close to the ground that the British anti-aircraft weren't firing. The redness gave the lead aircraft away as an enemy. Only the Germans painted their planes in individual vivid patterns.

He banked to intercept and took the others with him.

Major Judith had ordered them not to get into any fighting. Joseph figured this was different. The enemy were blatantly over the Allied trenches, possibly engaged in artillery spotting or reconnaissance photographs. He couldn't ignore it.

Keeping high, drawing rapidly closer, Joseph recognised the red aircraft as a two-seater Rumpler, definitely the sort of plane to be doing something unwelcome as far as the British troops on the ground were concerned. The other two enemy aircraft were

Albatross DIIIs, fighters providing an escort. With the Rumpler at a real disadvantage to the Australian SE5a's, the Germans were outnumbered, although the Albatrosses weren't to be treated lightly. Joseph and his flight would drive them away and if they scored a victory or two, it would a fine feather in their cap to take back from their first patrol.

It was almost too good to be true. The German flight still hadn't seen them and were flying closer than the Rumpler to the Australians who were about to pounce from above. Joseph held off diving into an attack until the last possible moment to get the maximum surprise and the easiest kills.

He spat out a curse as the Rumpler suddenly flicked into a roll and headed for their own lines, the Albatrosses immediately following. The pale face of one of the pilots looked over his shoulder in panic. A few seconds more and Joseph would have been attacking. Now he had to chase them. With his superior height it wouldn't take long and he would be quickly on their tails, but it wasn't the same. He swung onto a course after them.

As his flight roared down and drew level with the trenches, Joseph was shocked to have white bursts of friendly anti-aircraft fire erupting around him. Already angry at missing his best chance at the Germans, he yelled over the side of his cockpit. 'We're on *your* side, you bloody fools! Are you blind?'

Weaving violently, partly to throw their aim and to show off the roundels on the fuselage too—as if the ones under the wings weren't enough—he glanced round to see if Roger and the others were doing the same. Being shot down by their own troops would be disastrous.

What he saw behind him turned his stomach cold with fear. Beyond the careening SE5a's were six—no, eight, aircraft falling out of the sky towards them. Colours glittering in the sunshine said that these were Germans too. More Albatrosses and gaining fast. The anti-aircraft shells hadn't been shooting at them after all.

'Christ, look out! It's a fucking *trap,*' Joseph snarled, aloud.

He hauled on the control stick, pulling his plane into a tight turn that made the wings shudder. Out of the corner of his eye he watched Roger try to follow. He could already taste his first victory, but had the discipline to stick to his flight leader whatever happened.

Parker and Dunlop didn't react as fast. They kept flying straight after the Rumpler. Dunlop managed a waving puzzled gesture at Joseph, who frantically pointed back towards their own territory. It was unlikely Dunlop saw the urgency. The planes were separating fast. Dunlop was also doing the right thing by staying with his wingman, Parker, who should have instantly followed Joseph, his flight leader. His first kill was the only thing on his mind. As the two SE5a's shrank into the distance, the Rumpler and its escort still escaping in front of them, Joseph could see the indecision in Parker as his head turned constantly towards him, trying to understand why Joseph and Roger had abandoned the chase. It was inevitable that the diving Germans closing their trap would also come into Parker's field of vision.

Too late, the silhouette of Parker's plane flattened and his wings caught the lowering sun in the west as he mimicked Joseph's manoeuvre to turn inside the diving Albatrosses. Dunlop did the same.

The German pilots were surprised by Joseph's sudden breaking away. Only two of them managed to change course quickly enough to fire at him and Roger, sending tracer bullets past both the Australian's tail-planes. The other Albatrosses wavered, then plunged on towards the easier prey, Parker and Dunlop. It was a real "flying circus", the Albatrosses painted in a variety of bright colours and designs. It spoke of arrogance and confidence, the pilots shunning the conservative camouflage the SE5a's wore. The German on Joseph's tail was enthusiastic and no novice, judging by the closeness of the tracers now crackling past either side of his plane as Joseph zigzagged desperately. With each turn he craned to look. He was beginning to outrun the Albatross now that it had lost the extra speed from its dive.

All Joseph had to do was survive his opponent's marksmanship a little longer and he could pull clear. His aircraft was faster. He saw an aircraft far behind turn into a ball of flame and curve gracefully downwards. He was sure it was an SE5a but didn't know which one. Roger was to his left, doing exactly the same thing, using his plane's superior engine power in a flat-out race to escape his pursuer. The problem was that both Australians had to weave and twist to present a difficult target, while the Germans had the luxury of flying straight and level.

Within a minute, Joseph was skimming just above the ground across no-man's-land. He had to pull up to avoid a muddy crest covered with barbed wire. His plane trembled as bullets chewed at his wingtip and he banked hard right yet again. In front of him, he could see the Allied front trenches filled with waving men, encouraging him on. Machine guns opened up and their tracers gave him a nasty fright as they passed beneath him, aimed for the Albatross. He jinked to the left now before straightening and roaring across the trenches as if it was a finishing line. Faint cheering came from below. At least if the Albatross shot him down now without killing him, he would land in friendly territory.

It occurred to him to try fighting back instead, now that the advantage was on his side. With an angry oath, he sent the SE5a into another tight turn, meaning to complete it and confront the Albatross head-on, if he could.

But the German had vanished.

Taken utterly by surprise, Joseph stared around until he spotted the plane leisurely climbing over no-man's-land, heading for the enemy lines. Fierce anti-aircraft and machine gun fire chased it, but the pilot flew straight. Another aircraft was trying to join it, and being lower it got most of the attention from the troops on the ground.

Joseph's opponent apparently turned for home the moment they'd crossed into Allied airspace. It was good disciplined flying and gave Joseph the bitter thought that it was a lot more than he'd done. With a guilty start, he searched around for Roger. He saw a faint biplane silhouetted against the setting sun on a course for their airfield. Now he took a last long look towards the east. A few of the early brighter stars showed low on the darkening horizon under the cloud base. There was no sign of the Albatross flight.

Two curved plumes of smoke, one more ragged than the other, ran across the sky all the way to the ground.

Joseph landed in the last twilight of the day and taxied his plane to a position beside Roger's. His friend was there, leaning against the fuselage and smoking, while he chatted with Major Judith. The other pilots were milling about at a discreet distance. It seemed the bad news was already known. The way Roger put the cigarette to his lips in sharp, jerky movements belied his casual stance. In the gloom, his face was white as he watched Joseph's aircraft approach and shudder to a halt.

A mechanical fitter climbed onto the wing to help Joseph out.

'Are you all right, sir?'

'I'm finc,' Joscph told him wearily, tearing his helmet and goggles off. Every muscle in his body ached, but he wouldn't say that. He needed a moment just sitting in the cockpit to summon the strength to get out.

'Are you sure, sir?' The fitter checked up and down the length of the plane.

'Yes, I'm just... I'm just getting my breath back.'

When he clambered down, cursing his weak knees, he understood why the fitter had asked him twice. The SE5a was riddled with bullet holes from behind the cockpit to the tail. The damaged wingtip was a splintered mess.

Several other hits showed over both wings.

'My God,' he said. 'How the hell did he miss me?'

'I didn't fare much better,' Roger said shakily. 'I didn't think I was going to get away from the bastard.'

'More to the point,' Judith asked with clipped, nervous words. 'Did Parker and Dunlop get away?'

Safely on the ground, the enormity of what had happened began to sink in. Joseph shook his head, feeling numb with the tragedy. 'I saw two smoke trails. I saw one of them go down in flames, but I wasn't close enough to see who. It doesn't bloody matter, I suppose. They both got shot down. Over German lines too. I doubt we'll be seeing either one again, even if by some miracle they survived.'

'Roger's told me what happened,' Judith began.

'Then he's probably told you the best version he can think of, sir,' Joseph interrupted harshly. 'The truth is, I got sucked into a trap. That Rumpler was doing nothing except waiting for an idiot like me to take the bait and get jumped by the rest of their Jasta overhead.' He gestured angrily at his plane. 'We got surprised when they didn't even have a sun to hide in. We've lost two good men and had the hell shot out of another two machines—and look. I didn't even fire my fucking guns.'

Judith said coolly, 'You disobeyed the orders I gave you. I said not to look for trouble. Instead, you went chasing bloody Germans over their lines. I expect to lose men and aeroplanes. It's part of the game. I *don't* expect to have my pilots do as they bloody well please.'

'I thought they were artillery-spotting,' Joseph said, the excuse sour in his mouth. 'I shouldn't have chased them when they turned tail and ran. I lost my head.'

'So we lost Parker and Dunlop, who also disobeyed my instructions to stick close when they didn't turn to follow the moment you and Calwell broke off the pursuit. Christ, how clear do I have to make it? Was there something you blokes didn't bloody understand?'

'You were clear enough, Major. I just didn't obey.'

He waited stiffly for the real reprimand. A punishment of some kind. What should be done to a flight leader whose foolishness had caused the death of two fellow pilots?

The major turned and walked heavily away. He said over his shoulder, 'Just tell everyone what happened today. Everyone, all right? I want you to *teach them the damned lesson*. Perhaps we should be glad we got to learn it now, at the start.'

'What shall I put in my report, sir?' Joseph called, confused by the sudden let-off. Their intelligence officer, Lieutenant Lockyer, would be waiting in his tent to hear the details for the squadron's record.

'Exactly what bloody happened. You won't be the first pilot who got jumped during a patrol.' The set of his shoulders didn't encourage any more questions.

Roger waited until the major got beyond hearing, then sidled over to Joseph and offered him a smoke.

'Jumped on a patrol, did you hear that? It means he's not telling anyone we fucked up. Just that we got unlucky.'

Joseph took a deep breath. 'I'd say that's to protect the reputations of poor bloody Parker and Dunlop, not us. The damage is done, isn't it? I feel bad enough. He doesn't need to kick my arse anymore. Judy knows we took a hiding today. What's the point in making me feel worse? I couldn't, as a matter of fact.' He lit up with a trembling hand. 'I suppose we'd better get it over with and tell Jim Lockyer the damned details.'

***

Later that evening, as the pilots gathered in the mess drinking toasts to Parker and Dunlop, Joseph and Roger found themselves minor heroes who had escaped the Hun's devious trap. No one blamed Joseph. Mostly, they had to explain over and over again the dogfight itself, even though it amounted to nothing more than the Australians fleeing desperately for home. The other pilots' enthusiasm for the fight couldn't be dampened.

Half-drunk and still angry with himself, Joseph understood what the major meant when he'd insisted he wanted the pilots to learn a lesson from these deaths. If the mood around them was any indication, the men weren't learning a thing. The story was just whetting their appetite for getting into the fight.

***

The next morning, the entire squadron of eleven remaining SE5a's, including Major Judith, flew a patrol up and down the Western Front for an hour, putting up a show of force for the troops below and introducing the rest of the pilots to the battle zone. Joseph was again flight leader of three aircraft, which surprised him until he caught himself nervously scanning the skies with a diligence verging on paranoia. After the tragedy of the day before, he was the best man for the job. Experience counted for everything, even with bad mistakes.

They saw plenty of German aircraft, but not in large numbers and none willing to take on nearly a dozen enemy planes. Major Judith flew a wide zigzag course that brought them regularly over the lines and close to the Germans, on each occasion prompting furious salvoes of anti-aircraft fire that stained the air ominously black around the Australians. No one was damaged. It wasn't long before the novelty wore off for Joseph and was replaced with something that was to become familiar. An exhaustion caused by doing so many things at the same time. Flying a plane in formation needed constant attention. This was secondary to watching for the Germans, especially the preferred attack from above and behind.

It was said that hearing the enemy's guns before you *saw* him was the way you met the pilot who killed you. Joseph's neck ached from looking over each shoulder every few seconds. The controls took their toll too, although in this regard the Australians were luckier than some. The SE5a didn't need a lot of effort to fly straight and level. Other types, like the Sopwith Camel and Nieuport, demanded constant pressure on the controls to stop them wandering or even flicking into a deadly spin.

Joseph was annoyed with Major Judith, who seemed to be taking his responsibilities for this section of the front too literally. He led the squadron into a wheeling turn to retrace their course at precisely the same points of every leg. Four times the formation droned steadily along the trenches, swerving to the east and back again, attracting anti-aircraft fire with a dangerous predictability. Making things worse, the squadron maintained height as well. It could only help the enemy gunners.

The patrol seemed to be serving one small purpose. Three German observation balloons just behind their lines were all hastily winched to the ground as the squadron approached, then relaunched as it moved on.

Their frantic activity made Joseph grim. Right now, the Huns were probably getting heartily sick of hauling the balloons down, only to be ignored.

On the fourth circuit, one of them was dragged just a hundred feet lower, bobbing nervously on its cable and prepared to escape lower. The faces of the observers in their basket were clear as they watched the approaching aircraft. Judith still ignored it and swung the squadron away at exactly the same moment as before.

When they flew the course for the fifth time, the same balloon wasn't lowered at all and Joseph couldn't believe the squadron didn't try to shoot it down. The German ground crews would be surrounded by machine guns and anti-aircraft batteries. Still, the balloons were vulnerable at this height, unless they had fighter protection, which didn't seem to be the case today.

'What the hell are we here for?' he growled, watching the balloon slide past his starboard wingtip unharmed. A sudden shiver from the cold made his teeth chatter and he swore about that too.

At the end of this leg, Judith signalled yet another steep bank into a reverse course, then added an extra wave telling them that it was the last. When the planes reached the opposite waypoint the squadron would set a course for home.

Joseph couldn't really complain. In many ways, the patrol had done its job. The Australians now all had a taste of the Western Front and been subjected to heavy anti-aircraft fire, getting used to it just as the troops below learned to accept artillery bombardments and sweeps of machine gun fire. They had seen German aircraft somewhere in the sky almost the whole time. Judith's lesson for the day was over.

This time, two of the balloons stayed high in the air. Joseph stared, pleading, at Major Judith's SE5a in front, willing his leader to move into an attack. As the last balloon again fell behind and the moment was lost, he punched the cockpit rim and looked over to Roger's plane. His friend wasn't watching.

When Joseph looked back, Judith had flipped over and was heading in a fast, shallow dive back towards the closest balloon, madly waving and telling his pilots to follow him in a line-astern attack.

'You bloody sneaky bastard,' Joseph yelled, exultant. He could imagine that the Germans below had already left their winches and guns, relieved that the squadron had passed once more. Maybe they were even annoyed at having their routine disturbed yet again, dragged away from comfortable bunkers with newspapers and letters from home, and warm coffee with a dash of schnapps. Their minds would be switched off from thoughts of defending the balloon or hauling it desperately to the ground. How long would it take them to realise that the Australians had altered course at the last moment?

Not long. The SE5a's were howling down on full throttle, trying to reach the balloon while it was as high as possible. The sudden change of angle made it hard for Joseph to judge, but he saw that the balloon was sinking towards the earth. The winch crews had returned quickly.

A storm of defensive fire lifted from the trenches around the spot where the cable touched the ground. Too soon, the curling tracers fell uselessly away, but there were many guns firing. Not the anti-aircraft howitzers nearby, for fear of hitting the balloon. This didn't stop the guns directly below the Australians as they crossed the trenches. They added their own deadly black blooms in the air.

Judith kept their interception course high, aiming for the top of the balloon and using its bulk as a shield from the guns underneath. He started to weave when the German machine guns had his range, their tracers drifting past his wings. The other pilots did the same, while Judith was getting the worst of it.

By the time the major started shooting, the rest of the squadron was strung out in a ragged line. They could see his bullets punch into the soft skin of the balloon and vanish without effect. Behind him, a pilot called Metter started hitting the target. Again, the balloon seemed to absorb the attack. It was getting dangerously close to the ground now. Within a minute, the volume of defensive fire the Germans could provide at short range would make it suicidal to continue.

The major's plane zoomed across the top. Pieces of fabric were torn and trailing from his aircraft. Metter was staying close to him. Third in line was Waterhouse, a young pilot who everyone believed had lied about his age when he enlisted, only no one could get a confession out of him. He was small and dwarfed by his plane, but he made up for this with sheer aggression. Pressing his attack all the way and firing both guns, he caused a small tear in the balloon's skin, which spread quickly.

Next was Joseph. His point of aim was the hydrogen spilling out. He ignored the hail of bullets snapping past him, knocking against his plane with innocent tapping sounds. Something clanged dramatically off his engine, but it didn't miss a beat. He centred his sights, reached up and pulled the trigger for his upper Lewis gun. The SE5a shuddered with the firing. His tracers disappeared satisfyingly into the growing black hole in the balloon's surface.

The flames started rapidly and lasted only seconds before the balloon erupted into a spectacular fireball. The heat of the explosion flung Joseph's plane upwards, and tossed like a leaf, he fought for control. The rest of the squadron broke in all directions, the job done. Each SE5a curved away to head back to the Allied lines. Unhindered now by the risk of hitting their own balloon, more German anti-aircraft guns opened up in a fury and chased the Australians home. In scant seconds, the fight was over and everyone was running for safety.

Joseph's own efforts to turn around and get his aircraft flying properly took him further east than the others. At one point he glanced anxiously around to see Roger grimly staying with him for protection. They flew wide over a shattered forest and Joseph had time to look down at the awful destruction of the trees. Something about them, not just their starkly burnt and naked limbs, struck him as strange.

With a shock, he saw that it was the ground around them. The place was teeming with troops. Thousands of reinforcements in a thick grey mass, their helmets and polished rifles glinting dully in the sunshine.

'Bloody hell,' he breathed, trying to guess how many were there. It was impossible. Rumours warned about a big German offensive coming before the Americans got seriously into the war. And about a million enemy soldiers being released from the fighting in Russia. It looked like they were true.

He put the nose of his SE5a directly for home and left the throttle fully open, diving for his own lines. Roger was only too happy to follow.

The two were the last to land, taxiing into the line of SE5a's surrounded by their pilots. With no one hurt, the atmosphere was triumphant and the men were comparing damage to their planes as if each bullet hole and fabric tear was a trophy to be bettered. Only Major Judith was missing. He had gone straight to his office to call through a preliminary battle report. The pilots had cheered as he passed, agreeing that his aircraft won the prize when it came to battle scars. A bullet had even gone through his dashboard and shattered half his instruments.

A pilot called Fletcher ran up to Joseph's plane as he climbed stiffly out of the cockpit.

'How'd you go?' he said. 'Did the bloody Huns take a decent pot-shot at you too? You delivered the killing blow, you know. That sausage went up like all hell let loose!'

'I suppose so,' Joseph smiled, not wanting to spoil Fletcher's enthusiasm. 'I took a big whack in the engine. I'd better make sure the grease monkeys take a good look. Where's Judy, do you know?'

Fletcher was poking his finger into a bullet hole in the lower wing. 'He bolted for his office as soon as he landed. Probably wanted to tell the top brass the good news.'

'Thanks.'

With a wave to Roger, who was sitting in his plane, Joseph hurried towards the buildings. He found the major in the tiny office that was a converted pantry, shouting into a telephone. Judith held up a hand to stop him as he came close.

'Yes! Yes, it was us. We bagged a balloon. The last in a line of three—couldn't miss it.' Then he listened a moment. 'I don't care what the fucking British army is saying. How can they mistake us for a bunch of Camels, for God's sake? It was our sausage and don't let anyone else claim it, understand?'

Joseph interrupted, 'This is important, sir. You'll need to tell them.'

The major frowned at him and barked into the phone, 'Hang on a second, will you? What is it, White? Is somebody hurt?'

'When I was recovering from the balloon going up, I flew over that burned-out forest just to the south. It was full of troops, sir. Thousands of the bastards.'

Judith absorbed this, tapping his finger against the receiver. 'All right,' he said, then returned to the conversation on the phone. 'Listen, I've just been told something else. Are you listening? Can you hear me properly on this bloody thing?'

Joseph turned and walked out. The major's shouting followed him into the yard. He went back to the planes and Roger met him halfway.

'Did you see all those buggers hiding in the trees?' Roger asked immediately. His face, streaked with oil and smoke apart from the white circles of his eyes, looked like a clown's. 'Half the German army was there, I reckon.'

'I just told Judy. He's calling it through.'

'Those stories about a big push must be right. I hope they attack somewhere else, the bastards. We only just got here.'

Giving him a quizzical look, Joseph said, 'They've got to break through the front lines first, remember?'

'Hell, that shouldn't be hard,' Roger said. 'We'll run out of bullets before we can shoot that many. The rest'll just keep coming.'

***

That was the only patrol for the day, even though it finished well before lunch. Major Judith wanted a complete check-up of all the aircraft before they flew again. It was about getting the ground crews used to war on the Western Front too. They would be fixing damaged planes daily, sometimes more than once.

The pilots hung around the airfield, their adrenalin still high as they swapped stories or annoyed the fitters trying to repair the aircraft. The day was heading for another celebration once the sun had set, this time of their first squadron kill, the observation balloon.

The evening began as the one before had with the pilots heartily toasting themselves and their success. Not just the shooting down of the balloon, but surviving the first patrol over the enemy lines. It wasn't long before somebody offered a salute to Dunlop and Parker as well, which was greeted by a cheer of grim satisfaction. Revenge had been dealt out, especially since nobody recalled the balloon's observers jumping to safety in time.

Joseph's heart wasn't in it as much as he'd expected, although this was the sort of stuff all the men had wanted since joining the flying corps. The camaraderie of the mess and enjoying victories over the Huns—reliving the dogfights. He had a feeling that their jubilance was premature. This had been a lucky initiation into flying over the Western Front that could have ended up a lot worse. The anti-aircraft fire had been fierce and the fact that nobody got hurt was freakish. The lack of any German escort was amazing. And everyone was forgetting the agonising deaths of Parker and Dunlop, offering solemn toasts to the dead as if they'd lost an honourable game, rather than died screaming.

He soon begged off from staying in the noisy mess, saying he was tired from having flown the extra patrol. A weak excuse, but he didn't care. Roger was loudest in protesting because he had done the same, while Joseph used the uproar to duck out the doorway and wave goodnight.

Instead of going to bed, he decided to ride a bicycle into the nearby village and find a quieter drink on his own. He knew that his fitter, Corporal Finlayson, had brought a bike and he went to the stables to ask if he might borrow it. After disturbing the mechanics, who were playing a hushed game of two-up, and ignoring a litter of empty wine bottles, he found Finlayson working on his own aircraft, huddled under a tarpaulin with an oil lamp and tinkering with the engine.

Joseph called out as he approached, so he didn't startle him. 'You're not a gambling man, Corporal?'

Finlayson pulled his head out from under the tarpaulin and squinted at him.

'Lieutenant White?'

'I've come to ask if I can borrow your bicycle.'

Finlayson didn't answer. He nodded at the engine. 'You were bloody lucky today. Look at this.'

Joseph crowded under the canvas with him. The cramped space smelled of heat from the lamp, motor oil and Finlayson's own sour odour. The corporal ran his finger along a bright silver groove on the exhaust, the scoring from a bullet. That must have been the loud clang that Joseph had heard during the attack on the balloon.

'It couldn't have hit in a better place,' Finlayson said with a grunt of relief. 'These engines are easy targets. Plenty of places a single round will stop the damned lot and bring you down.'

'I think I heard it hit.' Joseph fingered the mark.

'You were lucky,' Finlayson repeated.

'We all were. To come back in one piece, I mean.'

The story of the brief battle over the balloon would have been circulating among the mechanics. That every aircraft suffered at least some minor damage told a tale of its own.

Finlayson nodded slowly. 'The lads are running a sweep about who'll be the first not to come back—after Mr Dunlop and Mr Parker, of course,' he added.

Joseph was shocked. 'That's a bit rough, isn't it?'

'You know these blokes. They'll bet on anything. There's no real harm in it.'

'And what are the damned odds on me?' Joseph asked, before he could stop himself.

'Very long, sir,' Finlayson said, so dryly that Joseph couldn't tell whether he was sincere. 'Don't you worry.'

'I reckon you should keep the whole bloody thing quiet, if you can't stop it. Some of the pilots could take it the wrong way.' He calmed down and matched Finlayson's tone. 'Especially if they're favourite to win.'

'It'll be over by the end of the week,' Finlayson said simply. 'Someone will collect.'

'You're too damned cheerful for me.' Joseph backed out from the tarpaulin. 'So, can I borrow your bike?'

'Be my guest, sir. It's behind those drums.' Finlayson fumbled in his pocket and produced a key. 'You'll be needing this.'

Joseph discovered a thick chain and padlock threaded through the spokes. He unlocked it and draped the links awkwardly over the handlebars. They threatened to slither off straightaway. Joseph thought about leaving the chain behind, but Finlayson would probably be annoyed if he found it.

It was a long time since he'd ridden a bicycle and the rutted farmyard ground didn't help. He wobbled alarmingly off into the dark, down the track to the village. The bike didn't have a lamp, and only a half-moon provided enough light to let him stay on the road and give the distant village a jagged, dim silhouette about three miles away. Behind him, the Western Front flickered and thumped intermittently. It was a quiet night, in the way these things were measured, and he thought uneasily of the thousands of German troops waiting in that forest. Silent, a dark and patient horde ready to crash like an ocean wave on the Allied lines. He shivered and pedalled harder, the effort making him sweat under his heavy clothes. With the Americans now in France, it seemed like the whole world was lined up against the Kaiser's troops, but the Germans still refused to go away. Worse, it seemed they were even more determined to win the war. Such single-mindedness in an entire army was frightening.

By the time he reached the outskirts of the village, he was too exhausted to worry about much more than pedalling and getting somewhere. Then he struck the main street, which was cobbled and rattled his teeth. It made a racket as the bike bounced around crazily. There were plenty of people to notice his comical progress, and no one seemed to care. The village had a large square with an impressive fountain in its centre, a flying angel with wings spread, poised over a circular pond. Joseph could see everything, thanks to plenty of light washing out from cafes, bars and restaurants around the square, each of them doing a poor job of maintaining a blackout to guard against enemy bombers. Perhaps the Germans knew that the village had no military value apart from providing recreation for the hundreds of soldiers, mostly Australian, who milled drunkenly around the streets. Bringing the lock and chain for Finlayson's bicycle was suddenly a good idea. Joseph doubted it would last a minute unattended if it wasn't secured.

His notion of finding a quiet drink was looking foolish, and he was annoyed at himself for not having given it more thought. Every bar was crammed with soldiers on leave, downing the local red wine fiercely as if it were their last chance. And for many, it might have been.

Disappointed, Joseph decided it was silly to come all this way with such an effort and not have a drink somewhere. He wondered if he could quickly gulp down just enough alcohol to dull the ride home without getting so drunk that he didn't finish the journey. He chose the nearest tavern and locked the bicycle against a tumbling wrought iron fence. Some passing soldiers jeered at him good-naturedly.

The tavern was a converted house with almost everything except the walls removed to allow maximum space to squeeze in drinking soldiers. The air was thick with cigarette smoke and the smell of soiled and damp woollen uniforms. Chatter and laughter competed loudly. Self-conscious that he was on his own, Joseph pushed his way through the crowd to find out how he was supposed to buy a drink. He was already regretting having picked this particular bar but guessed that the others would all be the same. Finally he got to a rickety trestle table staffed by two young French girls. They watched the customers with a practised caution and expressions of weariness beyond their age. No doubt, wine wouldn't be the only thing the girls were asked to sell, and with monotonous regularity.

He held up a single finger and waited to see the result. A bottle of wine, uncorked, was dumped on the table in front of him.

'What, the whole bottle?' he yelled against the noise, although he knew the answer. 'Don't you have something smaller, like a glass?'

He was given a Gallic shrug by one girl and blank stares by both. He handed over what he thought was enough money, kept his hand held out for change, and was amused rather than outraged by how little he got.

There were no empty glasses or mugs. Most of the soldiers were using their own tin cups or just drinking straight from the bottles as they roared conversations at each other, so he took a sip and immediately gasped and swore at the sharp taste. It was going to be hard work finishing the whole bottle.

He looked around. Four years of war had changed the eager and innocent adventurers of Gallipoli into wiser, resigned soldiers who were doing a difficult job. Sprinkled among them were the newer recruits. Their uniforms weren't so untidy or frayed. The leather strapping was in shape, not stretched and twisted. They looked both keen and frightened about the things everyone was discussing. The near-miss that killed someone else. A savage hand-to-hand fight someone survived. Brutal subjects that these men chatted about as if it were just a game of football.

He felt strangely excluded. It wasn't just being alone tonight. Most of the worst fighting in France by the diggers had happened while he was flying above the Egyptian desert. He played a small game, studying some of the faces closely and trying to judge just what each man had been through.

It was then he realised that he knew one of the nearest soldiers, so he went over and tugged at the man's sleeve.

'Aren't you Craig Heath?' he asked with a smile, in case he was wrong. 'We were in the same section at Anzac. I'm Joseph White.'

Heath broke off his conversation with three mates and gave him a cautious look. After a moment his expression turned into a relaxed grin. 'Shit, of course I remember you. The Assassin himself!'

They shook hands awkwardly, swapping bottles and cigarettes. Heath introduced him to his companions.

'So what mob are you with now?' Joseph asked.

'The same. Your old section.' Heath offered a salute with his bottle, the gesture betraying the fact that he was drunk.

'Really? That's a bit of luck, bumping into you. Where are the others? Hell, I haven't seen Dexter since we split up after Gallipoli, the little bastard.' He looked hopefully around the room.

'Dexter? From Anzac?' Heath was puzzled. 'You've got to be joking. I'd have to be the only one left out of those blokes, I suppose.' He frowned at his friends for help. 'Since Pozieres, I guess? Late in '16?'

'At least.' One of them nodded, uncaring.

Joseph felt himself go cold. 'So what happened to Dexter, do you know? He was a good mate.' He hoped the answer was a wounding. Something that took Dexter safely home.

'Dexter Bell?' Heath was thoughtful. 'The skinny little bloke, right?'

'That's him.'

'Yeah, he got machine-gunned, if I remember right. A lot of blokes got killed that day.' He scratched his head with the top of his wine bottle.

Joseph's straight face hid his distress. 'He's dead, then? For sure?'

'Now that I think of it, yeah. I know they brought him back, cause some funny bastard said he only needed half a hole to bury him in, the bugger was so small.' Heath let out a bark of laughter that the other three joined without noticing that Joseph stayed quiet.

'So, where are you?' Heath asked. 'Artillery or something? I can't pick the threads you're wearing—shit! You're an officer.' He finally saw the lieutenant's tabs.

'Only because I'm a pilot.' Joseph tried to dismiss it. A part of him wondered if he should have come into this tavern at all. Perhaps it was unofficially reserved for enlisted men. 'In the flying corps,' he added.

‘A flyer,’ Heath said blandly. ‘In one of them planes.’

‘That’s right.’

Abruptly, a feeling that nothing really mattered swept over Joseph. Hearing of Dexter’s death affected him too much and the rest was trivial. Besides, Heath and the others were never going to be comfortable with an officer suddenly among them, regardless of the past. It was pointless for him to try. ‘Right, then,’ Heath said. ‘It’s all right for some. So, you’re out of the trenches?’

‘Looks that way.’ A gulf between them was widening and Joseph didn’t feel like bridging it. ‘Look, I need some fresh air. I’ll catch up with you blokes later, right?’

‘For sure.’ Heath raised his bottle again.

They were both empty promises, a means of going their separate ways without the embarrassment of admitting it.

Nursing his wine, Joseph headed for the first door he could see. It went out to the rear of the house. Outside, the grass and brick wall stank of urine. Hundreds of soldiers relieved themselves here every night. A few were here now, their backs to him as they pissed on anything suitable, mainly a broken, wooden fence around the garden. He needed to get away from the stench and stepped through a gap in the palings, only half caring that it probably took him into private property.

It didn't help. Other men before him had obviously had the same idea and the ground here also reeked of vomit, tobacco and urine. He pushed on, scrambling over a stone wall this time, and left behind the noise of the bar. Now he was in darkness behind another house. It appeared to be a private dwelling, or at least a business that didn't operate in the evenings. A single lamp burned inside, showing though a tiny window.

He wanted the comparative quiet and anonymous shadows. As his eyes adjusted, he spotted a chopping block with an axe buried in it. He wrenched out the blade, sat down wearily and pulled his cigarettes from a top pocket.

He felt guilty about Dexter's death, as if he'd abandoned his friend to die when he'd transferred to the flying corps. He remembered asking Dexter to come with him. He should have insisted or tried harder.

With the rasping of his match to light the cigarette, someone spoke softly from the gloom.

'Please, if you are very drunk, you must move on. Or I will have to call the gendarme.'

'Bloody hell.' He let the smoke drop unlit from his lips. It was a woman's voice with a strong, French accent. A slight tremor betrayed her nervousness.

Scrabbling at the ground between his feet for the lost cigarette, he mumbled an apology and added, 'I'm not drunk. Not yet, anyway. Who are you?'

'Who are *you*? You are in *my* garden, monsieur.'

'If this is your yard, why are you standing outside in the cold?' He found his smoke, smoothed it out with his fingers and put it back in his mouth.

She answered as he lit up. 'My daughter is sleeping inside. She's afraid the soldiers from the *estaminet* will come here with all their noise and drunken behaviour. So I promise to keep watch out here in case someone like yourself appears.'

Now he could see a slim figure, a black shape against the greater darkness of the house behind her. She had taken care not to be given away by the lamp in the window. Unexpectedly, it made him think of his brother Jonathon, who would have seen her straightaway with his keen night-sight.

'If she's sleeping,' he asked, 'how does she know you're still out here in the dark? Why don't you go back inside?'

'Michele can awaken during her first few hours in bed.' Joseph could tell she was reluctant to be lured into a conversation. 'It's a matter of faith with children.'

'Have you explained that we're here to help?' He wanted to see this woman, to know what she looked like. She sounded young and somehow gentle. 'I'm Australian. I've come a long way to fight the Germans for you.'

'She is only four years old, monsieur. One soldier is just like another, and she only knows that the army took her father away.'

'Where is he now? Posted somewhere nearby?'

She took a moment to reply. 'Dead. At Verdun. Who *wasn't* killed at the fortress? Michele doesn't know. The future is too uncertain with the enemy so near. For now, I let her keep the dream that her father will return.'

Joseph stayed quiet, filling the moment with a swig of his wine. He was surprised to find how much he needed to tip the bottle. Without realising it, he had drunk a lot. 'I was only looking for somewhere quiet. I didn't mean to scare anyone—and I didn't think the village would be the way it is, crowded and loud. Stupid of me, really,' he sighed.

'You wanted peace and quiet, monsieur? It's become a rare thing.' A trace of sympathy came into her voice. 'What is your name?'

'Joseph.'

'Have you come out of the front line, Joseph?'

'No, I'm a pilot. With the flying corps. We just arrived the other day.' A spinning sensation warned him that the wine was getting well inside his head.

'Ahh... a flyer?' She said this with a breath. Her soft exclamation struck him as such a *French* sound. 'Michele has seen you overhead. She loves the aeroplanes.'

'Then perhaps she won't be afraid of me? If she knows I'm not a soldier?'

He was surprised to hear a short, quiet laugh that was somehow edged with sadness. 'Do you have wings sprouting from your back, Joseph? Like the angel in the fountain?'

'No, I'm afraid not. You could tell her I take them off when I'm on the ground.'

There was another silence. He wondered whether she had taken offence at his sudden familiarity and was trying to find the courage to again tell him to leave. Before she could speak, he took a risk.

'Look, have you got something I could buy to eat, mademoiselle? To be honest, I *have* drunk too much of this bloody horrible wine. Something else in my stomach would be a help.'

'*Bloody horrible*,' she mimicked him. 'Australians all talk the same. You say all the same words.'

'Well, just the bad ones.'

She hesitated so long he thought she would say no. 'I have some bread and eggs. I'll make you an omelette and toast, but you must pay for the eggs. Otherwise I won't be able to replace them tomorrow. It's bad enough the armies take everything unless we're quick.'

He was surprised, especially after he'd owned up to being a bit drunk. 'Are you sure?' he asked, worried that she might have felt forced into it. Perhaps she believed he wouldn't take no for an answer. 'I don't want to be any trouble.'

'I think you sound nice,' she said matter-of-factly. 'So it would be rude of me to refuse. If Michele wakes and takes fright, please leave at once.'

'Of course.' He stood and brushed splinters of wood from the seat of his trousers.

As the woman moved towards the lit window, he saw her in some faint light for the first time. The profile of her face was sharp with fine-boned features. She was small, almost petite.

He couldn't help expecting something to be wrong. She would be disfigured, or crippled. It just seemed so unlikely that a young woman, even a recent widow, would be alone in a place like this. A village filled with soldiers of all kinds, desperate for company. He knew that even a woman determined to keep her good reputation was almost expected to entertain officers. It was the way of things in their strange war-torn world.

But there was nothing. She was older than he'd guessed—thirty, perhaps, and as he suspected from her silhouette, a very pretty woman. A thick pile of black hair was pinned up and forced under a loose cap. Strands escaped untidily over her cheeks. He couldn't believe his luck, then quickly told himself that that sort of thinking was exactly what would get him thrown back out again.

He stepped inside what had to be the village bakery. Large benches white with flour were against the walls. The centre of the room was dominated by a huge oven. He could feel the heat from a steel chimney that disappeared into the roof.

'You work for the town baker?' he asked, staring around.

'I *am* the baker,' she said. 'Now my husband is gone. It was his business.'

'I'm sorry. I might have guessed that for myself and avoided any offence.'

She gave him a steady, measuring look. 'My name is Katherine,' she said finally, the last syllable drawn out.

'Katherine,' Joseph repeated slowly. 'I'll bet your daughter is as pretty as that angel in the fountain.'

Katherine twisted her lips. 'Don't begin by being too clever, Joseph. You'll spoil things.'

'I had to say something,' he apologised. 'I can't understand why half the Australian army isn't knocking on your door. Most of those blokes won't have a lot of respect for you being a widow, when you're as lovely... I mean, well, not these days, anyway,' he ended awkwardly.

'My father is the village gendarme and takes guarding his daughter and granddaughter very seriously. I told you I could call him. He's standing outside the *front* door.'

'Oh?' He quickly lost his bravado. 'What would he do if he found me here?'

She turned away, taking a pan down from a hook and putting it on top of the stove. Next, she took a loaf of bread from a cupboard. As she worked, she said, 'That depends on whether he's remembered to load his pistol. He's old, and might have forgotten again. That's why he hasn't been taken away by the army.'

Joseph winced as she clattered the pan around, lifting a metal ring to check the fire beneath before letting it clang back into place. 'Is he deaf, as well?' he asked hopefully.

'A good gendarme is always deaf and blind to some things.' She put an apron on and he resisted an urge to help tie it.

What she made wasn't just an omelette. She put in onion and herbs as well. The smells that filled the bakery were delightful. When she put a plate in front of him, apologising that she had no butter for the toast, he couldn't wait to taste it. A second later, he was nodding gratefully with his mouth full. Then he noticed she wasn't eating with him.

'You're not having any?' He panicked that he'd eaten her last eggs.

She shook her head. 'I pick at the loaves and cakes all night as I bake. It's more than enough.'

'When do you start work?'

'Soon, or nothing will be ready for the morning.'

'You'll work all night?'

'No, sometimes I bake late, or I start very early in the morning. Tonight, with all the noise and soldiers around, I won't sleep. I might as well begin.'

'Can I help you?'

She took it as an offer that he felt obliged to make. 'No, I'm happy to work on my own. Besides, your friends will be wondering where you are.'

'I told you, I didn't come with any friends. I'm in the village alone.'

'Then shouldn't you return to your *esquadrille*?'

Joseph shrugged. 'Sometime. It would be nice not to be surrounded by soldiers for a while, and do something different. Really, I'd like to help you. And I'll still pay for the eggs,' he added, in case she thought he had no money and was trying to pay with work.

'Have you ever made bread?'

'I've helped my mother.'

He was obviously young. She faltered, and he sensed it. He said quickly, 'Come on. Just for an hour or so. Don't forget, I might not be around tomorrow...'

This was the sort of glib thing the pilots said to each other. A crude joke they enjoyed when they borrowed money from one another or begged a cigarette. He instantly regretted having said it. It had been from habit, but Katherine wasn't to know that. Her face fell and she stood still, staring at him.

'I'm sorry. I didn't mean that,' he said, holding up a hand to placate her. 'It's just something we say as a joke.'

'That would be funny in Australia? That you might be dead this time tomorrow?'

'No, but it's funny for *us*. For the soldiers in the trenches too—it's hard to explain,' he floundered, annoyed that he had ruined the mood.

She turned away again, took a kettle from the stove and poured water into the frying pan to clean it. He watched her stiff back and waited for her to tell him to leave. In the silence, he felt in his pockets for money and put a handful of francs quietly on the table.

She said carefully, without looking at him, 'You can help me mix the cakes. We'll make one especially for you to eat tomorrow evening. As an incentive to keep yourself alive. We must try and send you back to your mother in good health, so you can show her how to bake like the French do.'

He made some comical attempt to help her around the bakery. She seemed to enjoy his foolishness and often scolded him for trying to make her laugh, which she rarely did, saying it might wake Michele. He made a mess and probably cost her much in precious rationed supplies, but she didn't complain. After an hour, everything had been placed in the oven. Katherine stepped back and looked at him. His uniform was dusted in flour and there were white streaks on his face.

'Now you must leave,' she said calmly. 'I'm going to bed, and so should you, no doubt.' She glanced towards the front of the bakery. 'By the back door. I'm not ashamed, it's simply too late to explain things to old gendarmes, that's all.'

Joseph slapped at his clothing, raising small clouds of flour. 'Can I really come back tomorrow night? To eat my cake?'

They had made one in the rough cross-shape of a biplane. Too much like a crucifix for Joseph's liking, although he didn't say so. She was going to ice it with roundels for Michele.

She inclined her head. 'Can you bring something from an aeroplane for Michele? Anything will do. A piece of wood or a scrap of leather. She's only a small child.'

'I'll find something,' he promised. 'And if I get the chance tomorrow, I'll fly low over the village and wave.'

'We'll listen for you, and try to run outside in time.'

There was an awkward moment, too brief to be sure what caused it. Then the front door began to rattle ominously.

'Quick,' she hissed. 'My father will either shoot you, or keep you here all night listening to his stories.'

He was tempted to linger. She gave him a shove towards the back door and he had no choice, snatching his coat and cap as he passed them. She even closed the door in his face as he turned to say goodnight and found himself abruptly outside and in the dark. It was bitterly cold after the warmth of the bakery.

He shrugged into his extra clothing gratefully.

Wanting to avoid the *estaminet* and its raucous crowd, he climbed fences and worked his way through several other gardens until he reached a street. From there, he made his way back to the bicycle and happily wobbled off towards the airfield, oblivious of the jarring cobblestones and chilling breeze.

For the moment, he had forgotten all about Dexter Bell being killed.

First Kill

'So, come on. Where the hell did you get to last night?' Roger asked him as they walked towards their planes. It was a fine morning. Cold, but clear. All the pilots had risen early in anticipation of flying a patrol, which Major Judith had promised them the night before despite the fickle February weather in the last days of winter never guaranteeing anything. Today, they were in luck.

Roger had been looking at him strangely all morning, over breakfast and when they lingered outside the mess waiting for a decision from Judith.

Someone else had always been with them, so he hadn't been able to ask anything indiscreet. Finally, he had his chance in the minutes while they manned the aircraft.

'What are you talking about?' Joseph asked innocently.

'We all decided last night that you were a bit of a party pooper and I was dispatched to bring you back to the mess. For a proper drink to celebrate bagging the Hun sausage. Of course, you weren't in your bed, were you?'

'Ah, I see.' Joseph could imagine the sort of drunken debate among the pilots that determined he should be forcibly returned to join the fun.

'What sort of an answer is that?'

'Sorry, actually I went into the village for a quiet drink.'

'You what?'

Roger stopped in mid-stride, staring at him.

Joseph said, 'It's nothing to start a fuss over. I simply wanted somewhere peaceful for a while.'

'Peaceful? In the village? It's full of stinking trench rats trying to swindle you out of your money.' Roger had had an unhappy experience playing cards against some soldiers in a London pub, and held a long grudge.

Joseph started walking again. 'Steady on. I was one of those trench rats, remember? And so was my brother. So were *you*.' He recalled what he'd found out about Dexter Bell. A surge of guilt caused his step to waver for an instant.

Roger didn't answer straight away. Like Joseph, he'd joined the army before transferring to the flying corps, enlisting in time to see just a week of action before the Gallipoli evacuation. Hardly enough to call himself a veteran, though it wasn't something he liked to admit.

They were about to split for their own aircraft and he said triumphantly, 'I've got it. Some of the lads have told me there are a few tasteful girls in the village. Quite inexpensive, they say. Is that where you went, you old rogue?'

Joseph couldn't be outraged. Roger had accompanied him on several visits to whorehouses in Cairo.

'No, I ran into some blokes from my old section at Anzac. Time got away from me, that's all.' He clicked his fingers. 'That reminds me. I owe one of them five bob and I promised I'd get it back to him tonight.'

'In the village? I might come with you for a look.'

'There's no need,' Joseph shouted as they moved farther apart. 'We'll probably be celebrating in the mess again tonight. I'm only going to borrow Finlayson's bicycle and dash in, give him the money, and come back. I'll be faster on my own, on the bike. Back before you know it.'

One of the SE5a's started up with a coughing roar and stopped any chance Roger had to argue.

It was another patrol with the full squadron. This time, Judith separated them into four flights of three each, then sent half the pilots into a high position at the limit of their aircraft's performance. It was similar to the trap Joseph had fallen into on his first day, with the other half of the squadron dawdling over the front lines slowly to allow the SE5a's in the thinner air above to keep pace. Judith hoped to lure a stronger force of Germans into an attack. As one of the better pilots, Joseph was flying in the lower group. They would have to survive the initial assault by the enemy, probably in much greater numbers.

There was no chance to over-fly Katherine's village as they took off, although Joseph led his flight of Roger and a man named Leaver in long, lazy circles around the airfield, giving the upper flights time to gain altitude. It was ten minutes before he judged that the specks high above were moving towards the Front and he set a similar course. The other three SE5a's of their flights, led by Metter, fell in behind.

The Western Front was sharp in detail this morning. The festoons of barbed wire in front of the forward positions resembled a fine black spider's web strung between twigs. In the still early air, Joseph could even see countless cooking fires sending up thin columns of blue smoke. He tried to imagine the miserable soldiers huddled around the flames, seeking out the heat and waiting for a hot tea, perhaps their only warm meal for the day. He'd had a bacon sandwich for breakfast, the night before he'd enjoyed Katherine's omelette and toast, and tonight he expected cake and fresh bread. It hardly seemed fair.

He shook his head and turned his attention to the sky around them. He was certain they'd find trouble today. They were asking for it, and he had to be ready.

He was a bit worried about Leaver, one of the pilots who didn't get to shoot at the balloon because he was near the end of the line-astern attack. Leaver had made a lot of noise in the mess about making up for that. He yearned to be a part of the next celebrations with good reason. He simply wanted to shoot down a German as soon as he could. It was a dangerous enthusiasm and he'd been warned about doing anything foolish in pursuit of a victory. Joseph had seen a veiled deceit in his nodding agreement.

Despite his sense of foreboding that there would be a fight, the sky remained empty. Nothing like the day before, when aircraft were in sight everywhere.

He checked Roger, flying just behind his right wingtip, gazing down at the trenches below, perhaps thinking again that he lacked something because he hadn't spent enough time as a foot soldier. Leaver was staring at his instruments as if something was wrong. Joseph watched him for a while, looking for a sign. Leaver finally scanned the sky unaware that he was being watched.

The chattering of a machine gun from behind made Joseph jerk violently in his seat. A second later, it was more than one gun. Four or five were hammering somewhere. Tracers were glittering past Metter's flight and the three aircraft scattered apart. A dozen brightly coloured aircraft appeared, plunging down behind both formations and instantly pulling into a climb to zoom beneath Joseph's plane. He didn't wait for anybody to start shooting at him, breaking desperately to the right, praying that Roger would do the same or they might collide. If Leaver knew what he was doing, he would follow.

The attackers were German Pfalz DIIIs, and they had come from the best angle of all. Above and behind, where even the most experienced pilot looked the least because of the tiring effort of turning in his seat. Still, in his frantic manoeuvring to get away from this dangerous initial strike, Joseph found breath to curse the fact that no one saw them coming. Everybody had assumed that everyone else was taking care of it. Judith and the rest of the squadron had let them get jumped too. Surely the major had seen the Germans and tried to follow them down?

That was the last chance he had for idle thinking. Two Pfalz's were on his tail and taking turns to fire, sending tracers streaming around Joseph to vanish in a gentle curve in front. Some passed between his wings as he rolled, then rolled again.

Gritting his teeth at the risk, he hauled his aircraft into a tight turn and hoped the Germans weren't good at deflection shooting. He felt bullets ripping through his fuselage and holes magically appeared in the upper wing letting daylight through. The Pfalz's went skidding past on a wider bank, unable to keep with him. He snapped his plane over into an opposite turn and suddenly had a choice of targets. Both Germans were trying to recover. One had begun to climb and was stalling, almost stationary in the air. Joseph could see into the cockpit with the pilot pushing and pulling at everything in sight, but with no airspeed his aircraft wallowed like a sinking ship.

It couldn't have been a simpler shot. The Pfalz was close and hardly moving, hanging motionless in the moments before dropping into a controlled spin downwards. Joseph opened fire and let out a yell of triumph as he watched his tracers spray all over the German. Nothing smoked or caught fire, but as he flashed past in pursuit of the other Pfalz, he knew that the first pilot was dead or mortally wounded. He had shot too many men as a sniper, given only a fraction of a second to see the result, to be mistaken.

Lifeless arms hung from the cockpit as the Pfalz slowly turned onto its back and fell.

His next quarry knew he had made a mistake letting Joseph out-manoeuvre him in a turn. This time it was pure instinctive skill. A natural hunter's ability that always brought rabbits home for his mother to cook. The same expertise that had let him kill over 200 Turks on Gallipoli, many of them unaware that they were about to die.

The German in the second Pfalz must have believed he would escape. Both aircraft were moving fast and at different altitudes—a difficult shot for any pilot. Normally, an impossible one for a pilot in his first real dogfight. Yet, Joseph's tracers smashed into the Pfalz's petrol tanks and the aircraft erupted in a ball of flame. It happened in an instant, and like the Turkish soldiers, the German didn't even have time to realise that he was about to die.

Joseph felt a moment of searing heat from the exploding Pfalz as he passed. He was pulling into a climb to gain back precious altitude, a golden rule he didn't forget even through his intense exhilaration at scoring two victories. Given a moment to claw back some height, he took it, and looked round to see what was going on around him.

Judith and the others had joined the fight, which was scattered far and wide.

As always, it was only a matter of a few minutes before any dogfight was spread out all over the sky. It was vital that a pilot didn't find himself lured well beyond the enemy lines.

He spotted a lone Pfalz low against the ground, struggling to get back home. It flew slowly with a stream of oil or smoke coming from its engine. He was tempted, only it would take him too far into German territory and low, so he wouldn't be able to dive for home afterwards.

Then he saw an SE5a doing exactly what he'd decided himself was too dangerous. It wasn't much higher than the German and was going to take an age to overtake it. Worse, the Australian pilot was either ignoring or hadn't seen two Pfalz's sweeping in from the east to protect their comrade. Joseph only saw them when the SE5a caught his eye.

'You bloody idiot,' he yelled over the cockpit rim. 'Give it up!'

The other SE5a bore on, seemingly oblivious of the danger.

'You useless bastard.' Joseph threw his aircraft into a dive to join the chase. Instead of aiming for the stricken Pfalz, he went for the SE5a. If he could put a burst in front of its nose, the pilot might look round and see the other Germans.

Seconds dragged by into a minute. Joseph swore loudly when he saw that he wasn't going to get there in time. Feeling almost sick with the frustration, he watched the intercepting Pfalz's open fire on the SE5a, which lurched like a startled horse and banked away, pieces flying off in its wake. He read the identification marks. It was Leaver. He should have guessed.

Leaver was trying to complete his turn and head back towards friendly territory. This gave the Germans plenty of opportunity for deflection shots at his exposed wings. Their tracers hosed around Leaver's plane with plenty of rounds passing through the fabric, sending more shreds behind him as if it was shedding its skin. The SE5a dropped alarmingly, putting Joseph's heart in his mouth as he watched, then it staggered a few crucial feet upwards again.

He had an instant to see Leaver in his cockpit as he rushed past to meet the Germans head-on. Leaver looked all right, but didn't acknowledge his passing. Now Joseph had to see what the Pfalz's would do with him on the scene. If the Germans were confident, one could keep him occupied while his companion finished off Leaver. Otherwise, they'd fight each Australian in turn as a pair.

Opening fire at long range, Joseph wanted to split the Germans. It worked, even though his bullets didn't come close, and he followed the Pfalz banking left and moving closest to Leaver. He needed to do something fast because chasing one German left him open to the other. Joseph had a chance for another burst, and the enemy took the safer option and twisted away. It gave Leaver some breathing space. Joseph stared around, trying to locate the second Pfalz. It was probably on his tail and about to kill him.

He let out a hoot of triumph and relief, seeing the other German fly low and to the east, heading for home. The first enemy didn't try to come back for more either, keeping his own turn away from Joseph until he was headed in the same direction as his comrade. Apparently, they'd had enough. Perhaps they were low on ammunition.

The danger wasn't over. All the way, Leaver flew home with the same fierce concentration he'd used to attack the Pfalz. He didn't waver from a straight line and didn't even look at Joseph, who stayed above and behind him. Leaver's plane was badly damaged. He could see that even from a distance. The fabric was holed and torn everywhere. As they crossed the last of the trenches a thin line of blue smoke blossomed from the motor. Without flames, it didn't look too serious at this stage. Leaver could make it home even if he glided the last mile on a seized motor.

Joseph started to think something was seriously wrong when Leaver approached the landing strip in the same dogged manner. He made no attempt to slow down and aimed for the ground as if he wanted to strafe it, not land. Joseph watched with growing horror as Leaver dropped lower, flying much too fast.

The SE5a slammed into the ground at the perfect place for a landing on the strip, except nothing else was right. The undercarriage collapsed instantly, the propeller shattered, and the plane skidded crazily over the grass and left dark furrows in its path. Bits of the aircraft ripped off and spun dramatically to either side. Joseph could even hear the motor, unburdened from the airscrew, screaming at high power before it stopped abruptly. At the end of a long sliding path, the SE5a came to an almost gentle halt just off the landing strip. Leaver stayed slumped in the cockpit.

Joseph landed quickly and taxied towards the wreck. He could see plenty of other aircraft parked at the stalls, so he must have been among the last to return. Men were running hard across the field towards Leaver.

Half a dozen people reached the wreckage at the same time he did and crowded around him, eagerly grasping at the pilot's straps and clothing.

Urgent questions about Leaver's wellbeing caught in Joseph's throat as he saw that the man was dead.

He'd been shot several times through the chest. The lambs wool lining of his jacket had soaked up the blood and hung heavily, bright red, from his shoulders. Leaver's face was splattered with droplets that had been thrown up by the slipstream. All around him the cockpit was a bloodied mess of splintered wood and broken instruments.

'How the hell did he fly home?' someone asked quietly, as everyone went silent.

'He might have been dead before he landed,' a corporal rigger suggested. 'The poor bastard. What do you think, sir?'

Joseph came out of a daze to find that he was filled with a sudden unexpected anger. He said sharply, 'The fucking idiot got himself killed, and nearly got me shot down with him, that's all I know. Don't just stand there, you blokes. This thing could still catch fire.'

That whipped them into action. Someone produced a knife and cut through Leaver's safety strap. Joseph reached down beside his leg for the revolver and Very Light pistol. As his fingers searched for the guns, he noticed the aircraft's compass was dangling from the ruined timber of the dashboard. The instrument itself was undamaged, though spotted with blood. He wrenched the compass away from the wood easily and put it inside his jacket. Then he found the two weapons and the spare flares, and handed them to Finlayson, who'd appeared at his side.

***

'It's called a compass,' he told the wide-eyed little girl sitting in front of him. Michele didn't understand any English. He explained anyway, 'See? The needle always points to the oven where your mother is working, so you know where to find her.' It was true. The compass was far more attracted to the massive iron in Katherine's stove than magnetic north beyond the bakery walls.

From where she worked at a bench, Katherine turned and said something in rapid-fire French to her daughter. Then she asked, 'Where did you get it, Joseph? Did you steal it?'

'It's a spare. We have plenty, and this one doesn't work accurately anymore.'

'Are you sure Michele can have it? It's far more than I expected.'

'Really, it's worthless to the bloke who gave it to me. He won't want it back.'

Michele was cradling the compass in her tiny hands. She turned it backwards and forwards and smiled, seeing the needle point faithfully towards her mother, who had moved next to the oven.

'Have you eaten?' Katherine asked.

'Yes, thank you.' It was a lie. He didn't want to impose again on her meagre rations. He was plotting to bring her some supplies from the airfield, if he could manage it. 'I've just come to taste my cake and meet Michele. I'd better not stay long.'

'Oh? One night's work as a baker's assistant was enough?'

'I'd rather be here, but tonight the squadron commander wants to present me with something.' He said this happily to Michele, who giggled at his enthusiasm, even though she didn't understand him.

'What have you done, Joseph?'

He put his hands gently over Michele's ears and she squirmed at his touch.

'You can guess.'

'A successful day?' Katherine looked sombre.

'Twice. I got lucky.'

'And two Boche were unlucky?'

'I suppose so.'

She busied herself making a pancake for Michele. She rattled and scraped at the pan for a minute, then said, 'I should be glad. I hate the Germans and what they've done to our lives, our country. This whole war is their fault. But I cannot hate the two men you fought today. They were probably just like you. Young and adventurous. Except today you won, and they lost. Isn't that right?'

'That's the way it is. It might be the other way round tomorrow.'

'Exactly.'

Joseph realised it was the wrong thing to say. 'It won't be. You'll be glad to know I'm the first to turn tail and run for my life. I'm a coward, really.'

She took the pancake from her pan, put it on a plate and dropped it in front of Michele. The little girl grabbed a spoon and started cutting. Katherine leaned over her shoulder and helped her, saying to Joseph, 'Which is why your commander wants to pin a medal on you this evening. Is there such a thing as a coward's decoration? Are you sure you won't eat something? I have plenty.'

'Will you sit with me and eat, too, or fuss around the oven all the time?'

'No, I'll sit with you.'

'Good.' He was pleased.

'My father always sits at the head of the table. Don't let him find you in his chair.'

'Oh.'

'I'll call him in and you can meet. Mind, he speaks very little English.'

His name was Henri and he frowned at Joseph when Katherine led him inside from the front door. His gendarme uniform was frayed and ill-fitting, but he wore it with pride. Joseph suspected he'd been brought out of retirement to resume his policeman's duties because there weren't enough younger men, and the uniform was tailored to fit a more youthful Henri, or perhaps it belonged to someone else altogether. They shook hands warily and Henri poured him a glass of red wine without asking whether he wanted it. He seemed uncomfortable. It might have been the language barrier. More likely, it was finding a strange man inside his daughter's home.

Then the old man's face lit up in a wide smile after Katherine explained something to him. He grabbed Joseph's hand again and shook it vigorously this time. At Joseph's puzzled smile he portrayed with his flattened palm an aircraft falling to crash onto the table. He made a loud, explosive noise, spraying red wine. It startled Michele, who looked up from her plate in fright. Katherine hurried over to comfort her.

'She's terrified of the big guns,' she told Joseph. 'She thinks Father is talking of a bombardment. The bombs have come close to the village in the past.' She said some soothing things to Michele, then quietly scolded Henri, who threw his hands helplessly into the air, the gesture of all grandfathers wrongly accused of upsetting their grandchildren.

The meal was pancakes with the smallest smear of honey, fresh bread without butter again and some of the cake, which tasted of cinnamon. The icing was very thin, due to the shortage of sugar, but Katherine had managed to create two red, white and blue roundels on the "wings". It all combined to make Joseph thirsty and he gladly accepted a second glass of wine. He tried to drink it at a civil rate and would have liked to stay, especially if Henri was going somewhere. That didn't look likely.

'I'd better go and get my medal,' he said, standing up and apologising to the old man with a gesture.

Katherine gave him a knowing look, after a glance at her father. 'Of course.

Or they'll come looking for you.'

'Can I come and see you again?'

She shrugged demurely. 'If you like.'

'Tomorrow night?'

She hesitated. Three visits could be the start of something more than a casual acquaintance.

She shrugged again. 'All right. But later, like last night.' Her eyes went to Michele. 'Come in the back way again.'

Joseph had the sense to exchange a formal handshake with Henri, who looked pleased with the respect shown. Then he took Katherine's hand. Her fingers were warm and dry from the flour, and he held them a fraction longer than he needed to. He did the same with Michele, who accepted it solemnly, her whole arm moving up and down with his hand.

Out of the corner of his eye, Joseph saw the hint of a smile on Katherine's face.

***

'Where the hell have you been?' Roger asked from the shadows outside the officers' mess. 'Bloody Judy's been itching to make you a hero and you've been missing for hours. I told him you wouldn't be long.'

'I got side-tracked.' Joseph stopped beside him and took a deep breath, preparing himself for the chaotic celebration inside.

Roger looked at him suspiciously. 'It is a girl, isn't it? You may have been paying off your debts to some pongo soldier, but I smell a woman involved, too.'

Joseph saw no sense in denying it any longer. 'I have met someone, yes,' he said.

'You bastard. You don't waste any time. We haven't been here longer than a bloody weekend. Has she got a sister?'

'She's got a *daughter*, Roger. It's not what you think.'

Roger thought it was funny. 'Oh dear. And where's the hubby? Off fighting the Hun?'

Joseph said calmly, 'Killed at Verdun, like the rest of the French army.'

'A widow? Even better, they say a pot that's been cooked in always adds more taste to the—'

'I told you, it's not like that,' he cut in irritably.

Roger was surprised. 'All right, steady on. I'm just having a bit of fun.'

'Sorry, she's not some whore that anyone can pay for. I don't want you to get the wrong idea. And don't blab about her to everyone else either, understand? Or, by God, I'll shoot you down myself.'

'Ah, that's right. Our own Red Baron,' Roger gave him a sweeping bow and gestured at the doorway. 'Well, Your Grace, the rest of your servants await you to help celebrate your magnificence.'

'I can hear it,' Joseph muttered. As he reached for the handle, he suddenly feinted a jab at Roger's midriff, then changed and knocked his friend's cap flying. As Roger swore and scrambled after it in the darkness, Joseph said, 'You're my wingman, remember? It's your job to make sure I don't buy any drinks tonight.'

'Don't worry.' Roger slapped the dirt from his hat. 'Our fledgling ace will be treated like royalty by everyone.'

The mess was crowded with all the Australian pilots and some from a British reconnaissance squadron based nearby. Several army officers had been invited along for the party. News of a novice flyer who'd shot down two Germans within days of first arriving had travelled fast. The noise in the room doubled as Joseph entered. Hands reached out from everywhere to slap his back. Drunken faces confronted him, loudly demanding to know where he'd been. He was given two drinks with instructions to catch up.

Another pilot apart from Leaver was missing, a man called Soames. He was last seen on fire and crash-landing into no-man's-land just short of the Allied trenches, so his fate wasn't entirely beyond hope. No one talked about him, or Leaver. This was a party to enjoy Joseph's victories and no one was interested in acknowledging the fact that the scores had probably been evened by the enemy. Besides, Major Judith was claiming a kill too. Without smoke or wreckage and with his victim vanishing somewhere behind the German lines, getting it officially confirmed was unlikely. That didn't stop the pilots from declaring it definite, of course.

Joseph let himself roll with the flow and relaxed, drank too much and got rowdy himself. He had, after all, achieved something significant, worth celebrating. Most rookie pilots took weeks to even get a shot in at an enemy—if they survived that long. Shooting down two Germans in one patrol was the stuff of legend, like the Englishman McCudden, or Albert Ball.

And he had met a lovely woman called Katherine, who cooked him pancakes and baked him a cake, and didn't mind him visiting on any night.

For Joseph, things were looking good.

***

Over the following week, he flew every day, but didn't get a chance to improve his score. The Germans were reluctant to venture into Allied territory, while they protected their own in force. Large Jastas of enemy aircraft lurked just behind their lines, chasing away any attempts at reconnaissance and discouraging patrols by any Allied squadrons with the sheer weight of numbers. As a result, the opposing air forces teased each other across the expanse of the Western Front below, like neighbours arguing over a fence but never crossing it. Brief and almost accidental skirmishes occurred and planes were shot down, their tall spires of smoke seen for miles. Joseph's squadron didn't get into any fighting. They always arrived too late, or left before anything happened.

At night, he went to bed early after only a few drinks in the mess, a ritual event that most of the other pilots indulged in until late. Their lives were one long adventure to be celebrated each evening. Joseph had no problem with that, however he suffered in the mornings from too much of the local red wine. There was always whisky which cost twice as much.

On three occasions he quietly pedalled away to Katherine's and helped her bake the next day's bread. He timed it so that Michele was in bed and Henri had taken up his post outside the front door. He had established a small barter system with Katherine, exchanging fresh bread and sometimes cake to take back to the squadron for sugar, butter and other things the army supplied that were strictly rationed to the locals. With this occurring, even Major Judith tactfully ignored the solitary figure riding off into the darkness so often. All the major cared about was a timely return so he was prepared for flying in the morning.

Joseph and Katherine shared the tasks of the bakery with an intimacy enforced by the small space around the oven. They chatted about anything and everything. Katherine told him about her husband and how they had been almost destined for marriage from an early age, living and growing up in the same village. She spoke with only a trace of melancholy. Even with that sadness, Joseph loved to hear the melody as she spoke, no matter what she was saying. He asked her to teach him some French and she smiled in her soft way at his tortured attempts to emulate her. He saw that he could often make her smile, but it was rare that she laughed with any real joy. It was like a rule she wasn't prepared to break.

In turn, he described his home and the farm, and it didn't seem so different from the land they were in now. He knew only a little about other parts of Australia, places that she might find interesting. Then he discovered she was instantly fascinated with his stories about Egypt and its ancient landmarks. She asked him repeatedly about the size of the pyramids and the shape of the stones. Anything to do with the desert, its other strange and glorious monoliths, and the Arabs themselves all made her eyes shine with excitement.

One night as they talked and he was trying again to make her laugh with a lurid explanation of a camel's stench, a rattling noise interrupted him.

'What the hell's that?' he asked, and went to the tiny window in the back door and peered out. In the dim light reflecting outside, water cascaded off the edge of the roof. 'My God, it's pouring down. Where did this come from?' Faintly, he heard men shouting in alarm. The soldiers in the streets were scattering for shelter.

'The north,' she said easily. She came close behind him to look too, her breath warm on his neck. 'The bad storms always come from the north. They can last for days.'

'Damn it, I'm going to drown on the way back to the airfield.'

The front door burst open and Henri shuffled in, brushed water from his uniform, and nodded him a greeting. Without a word, he turned out a lamp and sat down in a chair near the window. He was in deep gloom and able to observe the outside world unseen. This was his foul weather station. He was still on guard—more so, with the yelling soldiers running for any open door to get out of the rain.

Joseph whispered, 'He *knew* I was here? He didn't look surprised.'

Katherine was puzzled. 'Yes. What did you expect?'

'Each night I've come?'

'Of course.'

He sighed at her.

'Back to work,' she said. 'We've nearly finished.'

He always delayed the final job of the night so that he could stay longer. When they were done, the two of them always drank a glass of red wine together at the table, and he drew this out to its last possible minute as well. Tonight he did as usual, also in the hope that the rain might ease before he began the trip back. There didn't seem to be much chance of that. It continued to hiss loudly on the slate roof and the garden at the back was flooded.

Finishing the last drop of his wine and running out of reasons to linger more, he grimaced at the ceiling. 'I'm not looking forward to this.'

Across the table, she spoke softly over the rim of her glass. 'If you stay the night, can you return to your *esquadrille* in the morning in time? Will you get into trouble?'

His nerves jumped. *Where did she expect him to sleep? On the floor beside the warm oven, or in her bed?* 'I'm sure Major Judith would understand,' he said with a calmness he didn't feel. 'As long as I'm back in time, yes.'

'Will you fly at dawn?'

'Not in this weather. I suppose it might clear as quickly as it came.'

'It might,' she nodded, easily. 'I always wake early enough to send you on your way, if it does.'

'All right, then. Where... ah, where could I sleep?'

She smiled without answering and stood up, walked quietly over to her father and whispered something to him. Henri was startled out of a doze and grunted back sleepily. She quietened him with a kiss on his forehead and returned to Joseph, turning off one light and picking up the remaining lamp as she came.

'This way,' she said, climbing a narrow staircase and stopping after a few steps to make sure he was following.

With his heart pounding, he went after her, trying not to let his boots clomp on the wooden stairs. He found himself in a single room that was the entire upper floor of the bakery. The steel flue of the oven in the centre provided warmth. Everywhere were the personal touches of a home. Pictures, hanging drapes and ornaments on the furniture. A dressing table with a decorated mirror was obviously Katherine's own place. In one corner was a narrow bunk. A mound under the blankets had to be Michele. She didn't stir.

Katherine stood at the other end of the room beside a double bed covered with an impossibly thick bedspread. She had turned the lamp low to make herself just a dim figure in the gloom. Joseph knew she was watching him intently, waiting to see his reaction.

'Shall I—' he began in a hushed voice.

‘Shhh.’ She put a finger to her lips, then crooked it at him. ‘Come over here.’

With an exaggerated tiptoe so as not to disturb Michele, he went to her. He cursed his heavy boots. When he was close, Katherine reached out and began undoing the buttons on his shirt.

‘Don’t ask me anything,’ she whispered. ‘I don’t know the answers.’

She undressed him completely, even stooping to untie his shoelaces while he stood self-conscious in front of her. Completely naked and acutely aware that she was still fully clothed—and that Michele might wake at any moment and see him—he grasped for her blouse at the first chance. She stopped him by pushing his hand away gently and staring into his eyes for understanding. Then she slowly disrobed, revealing a beauty that took his breath away. She even smiled gratefully at the look of awe on his face. Last, she unpinned her black hair and let it tumble down almost to the small of her back.

Finally, she pressed herself gently to him. The top of her head came under his chin. He could feel her warm lips against his chest and panicked in case she felt him trembling.

‘We mustn’t make any noise,’ she said.

‘In case we wake Michele,’ he nodded, his voice quivering treacherously.

'No, so my father doesn't know where you are when he comes looking to shoot you.'

'What?'

He felt her shaking, and after a moment of alarm, realised that she was laughing softly.

***

Afterwards, they lay in each other's arms, comfortable with their silence, and stared up at the exposed beams of the roof. The rain still hammered down. Joseph wondered whether Katherine would send him away when it stopped. He would refuse, he decided. It was the most comfortable bed he'd ever been in, quite aside from having this beautiful woman in it. If this was love—and he suspected it might be—he would never leave unless he absolutely had to. He wanted to know how she felt, but he was afraid to ask. Everything felt perfect and he didn't want to spoil it.

She asked him in a whisper, her mouth against his shoulder, 'Joseph, would you take me to see Egypt?'

'Just you?' he said.

'And Michele, of course.' She sounded almost annoyed that it needed saying.

'Of course,' he said hastily. 'Sorry, I was confused.'

She bit him and said, 'Well, would you?'

Under the covers he ran his fingertips down her back and made her shiver.

'I'd take you to see the whole world. Honestly.'

'Would we see the pyramids?'

'We could climb them. Together.'

'And the Sphinx?'

'You can let Michele pull its tail.'

She laughed again. 'What about the whores in the bazaars? Will we see them?'

He frowned in the dark. 'Did I tell you about them? I don't remember.'

She snuggled into him. 'You make love like a man who has known only whores. Quickly, to make room for the next customer. And without any... expertise.'

With his ego and feeling of goodwill crumbling fast, he said, 'Well, I'll admit I haven't had much practice at this sort of thing. It's all right for you to say. You've been married.' It came out before he could stop it, and he wished he could take it back.

She didn't sound offended. 'I *am* married, remember,' she said.

'That's what I meant.' He was floundering and hated himself for it. 'I mean, you've got an unfair advantage.'

She pulled herself closer and kissed him on the cheek. ‘Perhaps I can teach you,’ she said with a smile. ‘I hope you can learn this better than your terrible attempts at speaking French.’

‘Practice makes perfect, you know,’ he grumbled. It didn’t feel like he’d had the last word.

The Approaching Storm

Over the next three weeks, Joseph shot down four more enemy aircraft. All of them were two-seaters and relatively easy, but nobody cared about that. The Germans seemed intent on gathering information with reconnaissance flights and often a single plane was caught trying to snatch some photographs. After the first three of these, he officially became an ace with five victories. The squadron celebrated wildly that night. The rest of the pilots combined had only four kills to their credit.

He joined in the partying as always, but as often as he could during the evenings he sneaked away to visit Katherine. They did the baking every night and chatted long afterwards. She didn't invite to him into her bed as much as he would have liked and he soon learned not to ask to sleep with her—that was a sure way of being told no. He almost always returned to the squadron. Winter was fading fast and it was rare that the weather promised a poor morning and prevented him from flying.

One night, they lay together in her bed after making love and he again felt everything was perfect. Even better, he was amazed by how peaceful it was outside. Someone in High Command was taking the threat of a German offensive seriously and the number of drunken soldiers in the streets was greatly reduced, the men being kept in the front lines. At the other end of the room, Michele slept undisturbed. Katherine seemed subdued, although she often became quiet at this time. Joseph amused himself by curling a strand of her hair around his finger and tugging gently, keeping her awake.

She asked him in a hushed voice, 'What will happen with us, Joseph?'

'I told you, we're going to see the world. Egypt, anyway.'

'No, seriously.'

'I am being serious.'

She said, 'But we cannot win.'

'Bullshit. The Huns are on the ropes and soon the Yanks will put a huge army in the field—'

'No, I meant us. We cannot win.'

Joseph thought about this for a moment, then gave up. 'What do you mean?'

'If we lose the war, you'll be dead. The army that fails doesn't survive the battle. You'll be killed or taken prisoner.'

'You're bloody cheerful tonight,' he said. 'What if we win?'

'Exactly. You'll go home to your Australia. I'll be left behind.'

'No, you can come with me,' he said.

'Oh? Have you asked me whether I want to leave my village? My father?'

He suddenly felt he was on dangerous ground and said carefully, 'You haven't said anything about this before. I haven't had time to give it any thought. What do you want me to say?' When she didn't answer he said, 'What if the Germans got just this far and we had to pull back? What would *you* do? Follow our squadron to wherever we went?'

'I would go to Paris.' She was firm, ignoring the idea of going after him. 'I couldn't stay here under the enemy.'

'You have friends in Paris?'

'I've never been there, but I could find work. There is always a need for a good baker.'

'You've obviously got it all figured out,' he said. 'It sounds like you'd be leaving *me* behind.'

'You would be retreating with the rest of the army. I'd be forgotten.'

'Don't say things like that,' He was almost angry. 'I wouldn't forget you.' Again she didn't reply and he couldn't understand her mood.

'Look, there's a Casualty Clearing Station on a farm outside Pozieres. It's only a few miles away. My brother's sweetheart is stationed there. Her name is Rose Preston and I'd want you to go there, instead. I'm sure she'd look after you until I caught up.'

Since he had never actually met Rose, it was a rash thing to promise. But from the letters he'd received from Jonathon and his mother, she sounded like someone who was sure to help.

Katherine explained patiently, with the authority of someone who had endured the entire war within a few miles of the Western Front, 'Poor Joseph, you don't know what it is like to lose. Perhaps it's good for France with your soldiers so ignorant. I can tell you there is no room for civilians when the battles are going bad. Even a nurse is in the army too and must obey her officers.' She gave a tiny shake of her head. 'No, it would be best if Michele and I fled to Paris.'

'You're a stubborn ass.' He pulled her hair harder. She let out a small yelp and poked him hard in the ribs. It relieved some of the tension. The conversation had become too serious about things they didn't really want to think about. But the glum mood wouldn't go away completely.

She asked, 'So, what *will* you do after the war? Back home?'

'The farm, of course...' His words trailed off as a thought struck him. As young boys, both he and Jonathon took it for granted they would live their entire lives on the farm, sharing the burden and the profits. Now, the war brought them maturity and he understood that things wouldn't be so simple. His brother, as the eldest, probably had first claim to the property and even the closest ties between them wouldn't prevent a clash of interests eventually. There wouldn't ever be room for two wives or separate families. Someone, most likely he, would have to find a life for himself—or perhaps Jonathon would leave, if he chose. Nothing was certain anymore.

Katherine sensed his confusion. 'Is there anything else you'd like to do?'

'Keep flying,' he said, and frowned. 'I can't imagine any reason for aircraft, if there's no fighting.'

'You could stay here and become a French baker.'

'I suppose I could...'

'But you won't.'

'All right, hang on a second,' he said, exasperated. 'I need time to think about this. You've been mulling it over for a while, I can tell. It's not fair.'

'Then don't think for too long,' she said quietly. 'Tell me, before the Americans come, or the Germans.'

It was his turn not to answer. Who knew for sure when either occasion might be? A few minutes later, he reluctantly rolled out of the bed. 'I have to go back. Judy's a bit touchy at the moment. All sorts of rumours about a Hun offensive are scaring everyone.'

'Be careful,' she said. There wasn't much warmth in her words and she'd turned her back.

Unseen under the covers she put a hand to her belly. She had missed her periodic flow, though she was normally predictable. She believed that he was too young to face such news calmly, and she wanted him to think about their future without the added pressure of knowing that she might be pregnant. There were days, with the war all around them, when everything looked so bleak and impossible. A new child could only make things worse.

'I'll come and see you tomorrow and we'll talk,' he was saying as he dressed. He hated the way she was shrinking away from him, and he didn't know what to do.

As he rode back to the squadron in the dark, he was amazed at how quiet the war was tonight with just an occasional flare arcing across the horizon.

Without warning, he began calling himself all kinds of fool. She was the most wonderful woman he'd met and he'd pay any price to keep her. Jonathon was welcome to the farm, all of it. Nothing was more important than being with Katherine.

He was tempted to turn around and pedal back. He wanted to tell her right there and then that he loved her—really, not just in the pillow-talk of lovers. He was certain these were the things she wanted to hear, and the reason she was acting strangely. He *was* prepared to do anything to stay by her side. Could they get married? Was he allowed to live in France after the war?

He kept the bicycle rattling on to the squadron. Major Judith was sympathetic towards his ace pilot and his frequent disappearances, but tonight it would be best not to test his good humour. He would tell Katherine tomorrow of his heart-felt decision, and together they could decide what was best for both of them.

***

Joseph was woken by a shattering, indescribable noise. It was so loud and he jerked awake so violently that he fell from his bunk and hit his head on the floor. He raised himself painfully, uttering curses that couldn't be heard above the racket. He sensed the door opening and saw Roger's white face. His friend was opening and closing his mouth, but nothing made sense.

'What the hell is happening?' Joseph yelled, pulling himself up and close.

The floor was trembling under his bare feet.

'A bombardment,' Roger screamed back. 'It's fucking incredible.'

'The Yanks mean business,' Joseph managed a rueful grin. 'Christ, they must have every gun in France firing.'

'It's not ours. That's bloody *theirs*. Those shells are landing on our lines.'

'Oh no, not *now*,' Joseph said.

They both went out and stood in the yard, staring to the north-east. Around them, almost every man in the squadron, pilots and ground crew alike, was doing the same. They could actually see each other in the light of the distant artillery barrage.

'What time is it?' Joseph asked.

'Three... in the morning,' Roger added unnecessarily. 'What are they doing, do you reckon?'

Joseph felt his stomach churning. 'Blowing us to bits,' he said, quietly. 'Like they never have before.'

Major Judith appeared and pushed his way through. He shouted urgently, 'Fuel up the damned planes. Every one of them. Then load all the stores into the trucks and be ready to run like hell towards Amiens. The squadron will take off in the first available light, provide ground support for the army, then refuel and re-arm as you can. Don't bet on that being here! Have a good look, before you land.'

Joseph grabbed him as he passed. 'It's only the guns, Judy. Surely they haven't broken through already? Maybe our lines will hold?'

'Not a chance, Joseph,' Judith said grimly. 'They're pulling back now, what's left of them. This has become a disaster in the first five bloody minutes. No one expected anything this big. You'd better pray we get in the air before the German army arrives.'

Judith hurried off. Despite his orders the men stayed still, watching the bombardment with its fiery, leaping glow. Already their hearing was dulled by the constant roar.

Only Joseph looked elsewhere. His eyes were turned helplessly in the direction of the village.

And in the Morning

More violently than his brother, Jonathon was hurled from his bed by the first German shells landing. The barrage was aimed at him, or his battalion at least. No doubt they'd been targeted by one of the many balloons or reconnaissance planes that had flown nearby over the past week.

The monstrous explosions made the ground shift under him as he staggered to his feet. The sudden transition to this shattering, terrifying chaos left him numb and unable to think clearly. Then, as he desperately pulled on his boots and extra clothing in the dark, a hot blast slapped his tent flat and smothered him. He swore over and over, tearing at the canvas to try and find a way out, too panicked to reach for the knife on his belt. All he could see were flashes through the material and he felt oddly more exposed, trapped in the fallen tent, than he would have out in the open. Darker shapes seemed to be at the edge of his mind too. Shadows he hadn't seen since his days in the hospital. The suffocating embrace of the canvas brought back memories of being buried alive in the mud at Pozieres.

That frightened him more than anything—the thought of slipping back into that madness.

Suddenly the tent opening collapsed around him and he was standing in the clear, the canvas gathered around his feet. His relief was immense as he took a huge breath, but the sense of wellbeing was short-lived. The scene in front of him was out of a nightmare.

The bombardment was erupting everywhere. The stunning blast of the shells came so frequently that the landscape was lit with a surreal flickering light.

'Save the horses,' Jonathon shouted. 'Men! Save the damned horses! Get them out of here.' His feet caught in the canvas as he stepped forward and angrily kicked himself clear. Then he grabbed the arm of the next man stumbling past. It was a corporal, someone he didn't recognise. He shouted into the man's blank, shocked face, 'Tell everyone to take the horses back. It's too late to limber up the guns. We'll never save them. But we'll need the horses later.'

The corporal nodded frantically and ran away, echoing his orders in a high wavering voice that hardly cut through the roar of the explosions.

Most of the animals were corralled under trees in a corner of the field. Jonathon went that way, trying to run, but he kept tripping over things strewn across the ground. Once he went sprawling straight into a new shell crater. The hot soil stuck to his face and he could smell the cordite. As he got back on his feet, a near miss detonated a few yards away and sent him reeling again. He kept going, instinctively bent over to protect himself and zigzagging from each new explosion, which was pointless, he knew. There was no telling where the next shell might land. It was a matter of sheer luck who would be killed and who lived. The deafening reports made him cry out or swear each time the invisible waves punched at his body.

Luckily for the horses, the German shelling in their sector was accurate, aimed at the men and guns in the centre of the field. The corral had so far been spared. Still, the horses were rearing among themselves in terror and tugging wildly at their tethers. Men dodged between them, slashing at the ropes to lead bunches of three and four animals away at a run.

Now he remembered his own knife. He pulled it out as he ran among the horses. Hooves flailed everywhere. One caught him a painful blow on his thigh, then he was jostled sideways and almost fell, which could have been fatal. Grabbing a handful of tethers he sawed at the leather until they parted, then dragged them backwards and found himself coming clear with four animals. He led them towards the road, beyond the verge of the shelling where the others had gone. It looked to be safe—for now.

The horses calmed as they left the field and the explosions behind. Jonathon kept going and reached a group of a dozen more being held by dazed, shocked soldiers. No one was speaking. The noise was still too great. He handed over his animals to a man standing alone, then he set off to climb a crest behind the road. It was hard in the dark. The slope was covered in loose rocks that kept breaking away under his boots. He didn't need to get too high before everything was revealed to him.

The sight stunned him. The bombardment wasn't a solitary attack on their position alone. The entire Western Front was lit up by a massive barrage as far as he could see in both directions. The constant roar of guns made the air shiver. Even though he'd been lucky to live through the last few minutes, he could feel sorry for the soldiers in the front lines. They were getting a shelling of unbelievable ferocity.

Shaken and weak-kneed, he made his way back down the crest to the waiting soldiers. Their group had grown much larger and other officers were there trying to re-establish order. He started looking for his own men. A few minutes later, he felt guilty about his joy in finding that Rosie was one of the unharmed horses. Guilty, because some of his men had been killed and that didn't disturb him as much as Rosie's death would have.

The bombardment in their sector stopped, the German guns changing target, and for the next two hours Jonathon and his men searched in darkness among the wreckage and bodies in the field, looking for wounded and equipment that might be salvaged. Some soldiers had torches, but not a single lamp was found in working condition. Much of the hunting was done by hand. Men prodded blindly at the corpses of their friends, looking for signs of life and finding only their awful wounds. The officers examined the guns as a priority. Nobody was under any illusion that their part in some battle was already over. It had only just started. The Germans would be attacking with infantry soon and the Allies would need every gun and shell to stop them.

The barrage had done its job well. Not a single artillery piece was usable and the men required to crew them hadn't fared much better. A third of their number had been killed or wounded.

Captain Faulkner was alive. Jonathon heard him calling out his name as he gathered together an undamaged saddle and strappings from an untidy pile of salvaged gear.

'Lieutenant White? Where are you? Has anyone seen Jonathon White?' Faulkner's voice was almost lost.

'Over here, sir.'

Faulkner loomed out of the darkness. He looked pale and defeated.

'Glad to see you're all right, Jon.'

'One of the lucky ones, sir.'

'Yes, I suppose so.' Faulkner looked around at the dim shapes moving through the field with all its debris. He said bitterly, 'Christ, we've been wiped out before we even got started.'

'They'll put us back together, sir.'

'No doubt, if we survive the main attack. It must be coming. You saved the horses?'

'Most of them. I wasn't the only one who had the idea.'

'Well, someone else wants them now, and they're no good to us. We traced the telephone lines back to an undamaged section and got through to headquarters. Absolute bloody madhouse there, of course. They want us to take our animals to the heavy field gun unit near Pozieres. They've been in place for God knows how long and don't have any means of pulling back, if need be. They've given us the job of standing by, just in case. It'd take tractors normally, and they're sending horses anyway. Who am I to argue?'

Jonathon's gut tightened. That was the heavy battery behind Rose's Casualty Clearing Station. Was she in danger? Were they getting shelled too?

'I'll take them, sir,' he said instantly.

'That's what I want. I need to stay here until daylight and see what's left of our inventory. You'll have to go south first. They say the road's impassable on the direct route.'

‘I’ll try anyway.’

‘No, do as I say, damn you.’ Faulkner’s flare of temper was uncharacteristic. It made Jonathon take notice. ‘There’s no sense in losing you and bloody everyone else through stupidity. Take a detour south beyond the shelling. You’ll still get there by dawn. Take as many men as you need and all the harnessing you can carry. They’ve probably got nothing to limber up the horses with. In fact, I’ll wager it’s all going to be a waste of time. Those guns aren’t going anywhere.’

‘I’ll get Sergeant Carlton to round up whoever he wants. We’ll leave as soon as we can.’

‘We’ll be falling back,’ Faulkner said gruffly, hating the taste of retreat the words brought him. ‘I’ll try to let you know where we go.’

It took them an hour to assemble a functional ammunition wagon from the wreckage of everything in the field. Labouring in the night, it was difficult to achieve. When the cart was finished, they piled it high with harnesses, yokes, tools and anything they might need, and with thirty horses in tow Jonathon took a dozen mounted soldiers with him on their rescue mission.

Silently, he agreed with Faulkner that it was all most likely a waste of time. He had seen those guns and knew they were well entrenched, and had been for years. Generally they used tractors or a team of eight horses, properly limbered, to move the guns over good ground for a parade. To shift them quickly under duress, since the whole point was to help them fall back only if the Germans broke through, was asking too much. But to mention any of this risked Faulkner rethinking the order and changing his mind.

Jonathon wanted to go. In his heart, he was more concerned with rescuing Rose from the hospital nearby. He was afraid she was in serious danger.

***

The timing of the German barrage meant everyone was caught in their beds, Rose included, still sleeping in the tent that she shared with Julia. After they'd been so close to the front lines for nearly two years, the sudden bombardment didn't cause that much alarm. Nevertheless the two women exchanged a worried look across the tent.

'My God,' Rose said, calling out to be heard, though Julia was just a few feet away. 'That's awfully heavy.'

'Those are shells landing on our lines,' Julia said, in a small voice. 'I can tell. Besides, those guns behind us aren't firing. If it was our bombardment, wouldn't they be a part of it?'

'You're right,' Rose nodded grimly, swinging her feet to the floor. 'We're going to have some work to do very soon.' She paused to peer at her watch. 'What an unearthly time to start a battle. It's only three o'clock, for goodness' sake.'

Julia stopped as she was about to rise too. She looked worried. 'Do you really think it's the start of a big battle? The German attack that everyone's been talking about?'

'Don't panic. That's not supposed to happen here, even if it is. This'll be just a diversion away from the real attack. They all do it.' Rose offered a smile and a light-heartedness she didn't really feel. 'I don't know why they bother trying to trick each other anymore.'

'That sounds like a lot of guns just to fool us,' Julia said, unconvinced.

'I'm right. You'll see.'

They went outside to find many of the CCS staff gathered in the open and staring north at the kaleidoscope of colour, the flashing from thousands of explosions. Occasionally a curling tongue of flame would lash across the sky. There was plenty of ammunition to set off, and fuel for the flame-throwers. It appeared the Germans were scoring direct hits on supply bunkers. With the volume of fire they were laying onto the forward trenches, they could hardly miss.

Someone shouted that the large urn had boiled and there was a rush to make mugs of tea. This brought the doctors and nurses together in the converted barn which had become an open area for triage and emergency treatment. For a change, the unreliable electricity supply was running. The extra naked bulbs hanging down from wooden beams made a harsh yellow light. Everyone stood around and chatted noisily to be heard above the gunfire. It was an incongruous scene. In their uniforms and white coats they were calm and relaxed, as if they were waiting for an ordinary meeting of some kind. Really, they were preparing to do the most gruesome and disturbing work.

Mark Cohen was there. He still spent time with Rose, and he confided in her when the need arose and they were good friends, though there were barriers between them. Right now, he looked agitated. He came over to stand with Rose and Julia, who were clasping their mugs two-handed, and he gave them both a tight smile.

'Perhaps this is it?' he said.

'An attack?' Julia asked instantly. 'Do you think so?'

'I don't think there'll be an attack around here,' Rose said quickly, and shot a warning glance at him.

'No, probably not,' he agreed absently.

'Really, you two treat me like a child sometimes,' Julia snapped. 'And I let you. Neither of you knows where or when the damned Germans will advance, so don't pretend that you do.'

Rose apologised. 'I'm sorry, Julia. It's just that I don't like you worrying so much. The Front is over 120 miles long, after all. The chances of them attacking right here are quite small, when you think of that.'

'Except they're dropping thousands of artillery shells on this part of the line,' Julia reminded her.

'Well, yes, that's true.' Rose thought it best to change the subject. 'Those poor men in the front lines. God, what must it be like to be bombarded so? I feel terrible saying this, but I'm glad Jonathon and Robert aren't out there anymore.' She avoided looking at Mark.

'It still makes me feel like a bloody sham in this uniform,' he admitted quietly.

'Don't be silly,' she said. 'You're a doctor doing a very good job.'

'But I'm not a soldier, am I? Even though they've made me an officer in their damned army.' He spoke sharply. 'You know, Rose, you asked me once if I'd ever go to the front lines to have a look. To see what it's really like—'

'I didn't say that exactly.'

He cut her off with a wave. 'Whatever you said, it doesn't matter. Sometimes I *do* feel like I should spend some time there. Do my bit of the fighting too.'

'That doesn't make sense,' she told him firmly. 'Your work is here, as a doctor.'

'You don't understand, being a woman. It's all about... about bravery. And cowardice, I suppose. About knowing you've done your share of the hard stuff. Hardly anyone in this war is a professional soldier. Everyone's got a real job at home, just as I'm a doctor. They're not excused their time in the front line, are they? Why should I be any different? God, *you* talk about feeling terrible. Some days I can't even look at myself in the mirror.'

'Rose is right. You mustn't think like that,' Julia said. 'The lives you save here are far more important than going out and shooting Germans in the trenches.'

'See? You don't understand either. It's got nothing to do with—'

He was interrupted by a commotion at the door. A stretcher-bearer appeared with his burden.

'Got nine wounded coming in,' he shouted.

The medical staff hurried into action, their conversations and half-finished cups of tea forgotten.

The casualties arrived fast. All of them were shrapnel and blast wounds, unspeakable injuries much harder to deal with than the more precise bullet holes or bayonet stabs. Concussion from the explosions didn't help, sometimes making the men delirious.

Some soldiers were covered in the gore of friends who had taken the brunt of a bursting shell beside them.

With such a flood of injured, the Casualty Clearing Station began to lose its normal rhythm. The nurses found themselves rushing to help wherever they could. Matron Lambert tried her best, but the demands were so great that she couldn't avoid constantly changing the girls' duties. Which was how Rose found herself unexpectedly assisting Mark in one of the operating theatres. As she quickly tied on a mask and approached the table, she heard him talk soothingly to his patient. He was waiting for a male nurse, a corporal, to prepare his anaesthetics.

'We haven't got a hope, sir,' the soldier was whispering. 'There's millions of the bastards. We could see 'em under the flares, all waiting for the barrage to end. It's the fucking Russians' fault. If they hadn't caved in when they did, giving the Kaiser all these extra troops...'

It was a soldier's simple understanding of the revolution in Russia, both wildly mistaken and completely accurate.

'Calm down, please,' Mark said firmly. 'You're not helping yourself fretting like this. We don't need the Russians. Your mates back in the line will stop them. We always do.'

'There's no one bloody *left*, mate,' The soldier half-laughed and tried to lift himself, but failed. He had a gaping stomach wound and the morphine gave him false strength. 'If they're not here wounded, the buggers are dead and buried by the shelling. I'm telling you, there's hardly anyone left to put up a fight.'

'It always looks worse than it is,' Mark said with a trace of desperation.

'Come the sunrise,' the soldier said. 'The bloody Germans are going to swarm out of their trenches like fucking rats, you'll see. There's no one to stop them. They'll be here for breakfast and kill me in my bed...' His last words were lost.

The corporal was ready, quickly slipping a mask over his face. He nodded at Mark.

'All right,' Mark said to Rose. 'Cut the rest of his clothing away. I'm just going to sew him up as quickly as I can and hope someone gets a chance to do more further down the track. We haven't got the time here for—'

'Oh, fuck it,' the corporal interrupted him suddenly. 'I think he'd dead. He's stopped breathing, hasn't he?'

'Watch your language,' Mark snapped as he felt for a pulse, then he tore the mask off to check for breathing. 'Christ, you're right,' he snarled. 'He's gone.'

Mark turned away and strode out of the tent without a word, leaving the other two staring after him in surprise.

'Come on, 'Rose said, after a moment. 'Let's clear him out.'

They removed the dead soldier and cleaned the operating table. After that, Rose had to linger, making excuses for not bringing in the next casualty and hoping Mark would return in time. Eventually she ran out of options and had to go looking for another doctor to take his place. Reluctantly, she found Colonel Asquith, the hospital's commander. Asquith wasn't medically trained, and he was trying to help out in the barn.

'Colonel, I think Captain Cohen's been taken ill,' Rose told him calmly. 'He left Theatre Two and hasn't come back. It's been vacant for some time.'

'Ill? What do you mean?' Asquith was stooping beside a patient. The colonel was in his sixties and he got to his feet painfully.

'I'm not sure, sir. It came on very quickly, and I was busy...'

'All right, thank you, Rose,' Asquith was already searching about, looking for a surgeon to take Mark's place. He saw someone nearby and went over to speak to him. Rose used the moment to slip away.

Over the next half-hour, as she went about her work, Rose could see the undercurrent of something else happening apart from the drama of the incoming wounded. People were sharing guarded comments as they passed each other, or whispered over the injured soldiers they tended. A rumour was moving fast among the staff, she could tell, and it wasn't hard to guess what it would be about. Colonel Asquith was questioning everyone he came across and Rose did a deft job of evading him. Finally he cornered her as she was washing her hands in a stone tub. The lukewarm water was tinged with pink. It was never replaced often enough.

'There you are, Rose,' he said. 'You'd better tell me again about Captain Cohen. He was ill, you said?'

'I think so, Colonel. He walked out of the theatre as if he was going to be sick.'

'Are you sure? No one can find him anywhere. I've wasted precious men and time looking.'

'As I said, he went very quickly.'

Asquith gave her a long look. She avoided his eyes by pulling a towel from where it hung and drying her hands fastidiously. Then she met the colonel's questioning stare.

'Where do you think he's gone, Rose?' he asked quietly.

She took a deep breath, thought for one last moment about staying silent, then let it out in a resigned sigh. 'I think he's gone forward into the trenches, sir. To help with the fighting.' Saying it aloud took away her own final doubts.

Asquith's eyebrows shot up. 'Are you serious?'

'Very, sir. Mark—Doctor Cohen—was talking about it just before the wounded started arriving. He was feeling helpless and wanted to do his bit. So he's not deserting, if that's what everyone thinks.'

'It's desertion, no matter which *way* he goes,' Asquith exploded. 'The bloody fool. He hasn't been trained for that sort of thing at all. He doesn't know one end of a rifle from the other. What in God's name does he think he can do?'

Realising that Asquith was probably right, Rose felt dreadful. The army could be so stupid about these things. Mark might well be charged with desertion, an extremely serious crime, despite the fact that he'd gone forward to fight. The British army summarily executed their deserters and were pressuring the Australian commanders to do the same.

'It's because he was feeling a–a coward that he's gone, Colonel.' The word stuck in her throat. 'He wants to get into the fighting and stop the Germans advancing at daybreak.'

'It will take more than a damned-fool doctor to do that,' Asquith barked, but not at Rose. He knew it wasn't her fault. 'Still, perhaps the first Hun mortar to land near him will change his mind and bring him running back. It had better. He's a surgeon, for God's sake. We need him here.'

'I know, Colonel. I wish I could do more.'

Asquith went to walk away, then he paused and gave her a grateful look. 'I'm glad you told me, Rose. We were all starting to assume much worse.'

'I'm not *certain*, Colonel. He could be anywhere.'

'Yes, but it makes perfect sense why we can't find him.'

The casualties continued to pour in. The medical staff had dealt with worse, especially during the massive Allied offensives of the previous year when thousands of men had been killed every day, but those frantic times had been during daylight hours. There had been lulls in the night that had allowed them to take stock. These wounded were coming in fast and at a time when things should have been quiet. If the Germans launched an attack at dawn, the hospitals would become hopelessly overloaded.

The gossip about Mark Cohen's whereabouts was soon replaced by a new rumour. One that Matron Lambert soon confirmed.

'We have to start preparing for a sudden withdrawal,' she told Rose.

They were standing outside one of the theatre tents where Rose had just finished assisting another doctor. She blinked in surprise and felt the gritty tiredness in her eyelids. 'Do they really think the Germans will break through?'

'Asquith has been told on the quiet that our front line is a shambles. The shelling has completely wiped away our defences. Officially, of course, the men have been told to stand firm at all costs. In reality, there are very few soldiers left to man forward trenches that have all but vanished.'

'So we're going to retreat?' As the truth sank in, Rose felt appalled.

'We need to be ready at a moment's notice. The wounded are being sent straight on further to the rear. We'll deal only with those already here and try to clear the tables.'

'I can't believe this. We're supposed to be on the brink of winning. The Americans are here.'

'Not soon enough, it seems. If the order is made, be ready, Rose. I don't want any of our girls being taken prisoner.'

That thought put a shiver down Rose's spine. She suddenly remembered a long-ago conversation, when she had had afternoon tea with Emily Strathbury and the others. Someone had mentioned with almost perverse delight the stories of German soldiers raping nuns in Belgium. Too late, they had upset Tiffany Schultz, who had German ancestors. At the time it had been shocking, but too distant and impossible. Now, maybe one day Emily would tell a story of Rose's capture with such wicked relish.

She nodded. 'We'll be ready at the drop of a hat.'

'Good.'

Matron Lambert left and Rose could see the fatigue in her walk. The war had aged her fast and she often limped after a few hours' duty because of a bad knee.

'Rose? Is that you?'

She turned gladly at the familiar man's voice. It would have been better if it had been Jonathon. Rose was still delighted to see Robert hurrying towards her.

'Robert? What are you doing here?'

'I'm a bloody ambulance driver, aren't I? What do you think I'm doing?'

He gave her a hug that lifted her feet off the ground, and she kissed him on the cheek.

'Hurry up,' he said. 'I've been looking everywhere for ten minutes and there's going to be hell to pay. Where's my wife?'

'Shh!' Rose jammed a finger against his lips. 'No one's allowed to know, remember? Do you want to get us all discharged?'

'Right now, I wouldn't mind,' he said, wearily. He glanced at his watch. 'Damn it, I haven't got more than another minute. This isn't fair. Do you know where she is?'

'Julia could be anywhere. Will you be coming back?'

'Yes, the round trip takes about an hour.' He fidgeted, worried that he would get into trouble.

'Then go, and I'll make sure she's here in an hour's time.'

Robert was both relieved and unhappy about leaving without seeing Julia at all. He could see the sense in Rose's plan. 'All right,' he said. 'Don't let me down, will you?'

'Promise. It'll be daylight by then. We'll be able to find each other much more easily.'

He waved and trotted away. She could see by the way he moved that his back was hurting him.

The tension in the hospital grew palpably over the next hour. Dawn was breaking, washing out the flickering gunfire. Oddly, now the German bombardment was a welcome sound. As long as the shells continued to fall so heavily, the enemy hadn't left their own trenches to attack.

Although no official order had been called, Rose suspected the hospital was going to be abandoned anyway. It was just a matter of time to see if they could clear out the wounded first. No more casualties were being brought in and a steady stream of ambulances were emptying the wards and removing the lines of lesser casualties laying on the ground. After hearing that Robert had visited, Julia was excited about snatching a few minutes with him and the two of them watched the clock keenly. Right on the hour, waiting until the last moment to minimise the time they might be seen lingering for no apparent good reason, Rose led her to the exact spot where she'd met him.

He wasn't there.

'Oh damn,' Julia looked around anxiously. 'Do you think he's been and gone?'

'No, we said an hour. He's running late, that's all. It must be difficult to be punctual in all this.' She made it sound casual.

It was broad daylight by now. To the north and towards the Front, an amazing pall of smoke and dust smothered the trenches on top of a drifting mist. Beyond it, German observation balloons hovered. Tiny black shapes, aircraft too far away to identify, slid through the sky.

As Rose and Julia waited, other staff from the hospital passed by. Everyone looked haggard with exhaustion and frayed nerves. Some of them were derigging equipment to load into the ambulances with the last of the wounded.

Matron Lambert caught them.

'Is something wrong here? Have you both got nothing better to do?' She had come from the other side of the tent and surprised them.

'We're meeting someone, Matron,' Julia said meekly.

Rose wasn't so daunted. She explained easily, 'We won't be more than a few minutes.'

'I can imagine who it's going to be, Julia,' Matron said. 'You don't need a wedding ring. It's been written all over your face for a long time.'

'Oh dear,' Julia was stricken and for once, Rose didn't know what to say.

'As you can see, we are definitely leaving here,' Matron said dryly, changing the subject for them. 'At least in an orderly fashion, not as we feared. When you've finished your *brief* liaison, come and see me in the barn. There's a lot of work to be done within a short space of time.' She didn't wait for an answer, turning quickly away so she wouldn't witness any meeting between Julia and her forbidden husband.

'Yes, Matron,' Rose managed to call after her.

Julia turned to her with wide eyes, her hand over her mouth. 'Oh God, she *knows*. How long do you think she's—'

There was an odd noise like large hail striking a tin roof. Rose could hear it rapping on the canvas of the tent beside them. Holes magically appeared in the white cloth and a red flower blossomed over Julia's breast. She stopped talking and wore a surprised, breathless expression. Her legs folded and she collapsed to the ground almost gracefully.

The roar of the Fokker's engine and its chattering machine guns swamped everything as it swooped over the Casualty Clearing Station. Soldiers and staff scattered in panic, and for some it was too late. Five people lay where they'd been cut down by the Germans' strafing.

'Julia,' Rose was paralysed by the sight of her friend, fallen and bloodied at her feet. Then she fell to her knees and examined her desperately for signs of life.

Julia's eyes were open, fluttering with shock, and her face was deathly pale. A single bullet had hit her high in the chest and exited lower down her back. Rose's first fear was that it had pierced the top of her lung. She watched Julia's lips for the frightening, tell-tale sign of frothing blood. So far, there was none.

'Oh my, what have I done?' Julia whispered painfully, her sight glazing.

'You haven't done anything. Keep still and be quiet,' Rose told her softly. 'You've been shot, but it's not too bad.' She tried to smile encouragement, tears filling her eyes. She wiped them away angrily and tried a laugh. 'God, it's not *pretty*, Julia. You should know. But it's *not* bad, I promise you. You just have to be calm.'

'It hurts quite a lot,' Julia said with a disturbing calm.

'Well, now you know.'

Rose cried out for a stretcher and two soldiers were already running towards her with one. Before they arrived, someone else dropped down heavily next to her.

It was Robert.

'Christ, what happened?' he said, fumbling for Julia's hand. He was trembling and going into a form of shock himself. 'Is she going to be all right?'

Julia's eyes focused on him, and she said in a childish voice, 'Hello. You're late.'

'Keep her quiet,' Rose told him firmly, her self-control coming back. 'It's not too serious, trust me. We need to keep calm so she does too.'

'Jesus, this is my fault for being late. For telling her to meet me here.'

'Don't be bloody stupid,' Rose snapped, forcing him to listen. 'If you were here a minute ago, you might *both* have been killed.'

For that matter, it made her think of the minor miracle that she herself had escaped unharmed.

'All right... all right,' Robert choked back his shock. 'What the hell do we do?'

'Get out of the damned way.'

She supervised the men lifting Julia onto the stretcher. The pool of blood that had come from her exit wound was worrying.

'Let's take her to the Dressing Station,' she told them. Including Robert, she added, 'We need to stop the bleeding, then get her out of here to another hospital. This place is getting too dangerous. Can you take her?'

He looked puzzled until he understood that she was asking whether he had room in his ambulance. 'I'll make sure there's a place left,' he said, and ran away through the tents.

She wasn't going to bother with the other casualties at all. With the hospital emptying of wounded, there was more than enough medical staff to deal with them. As Julia's stretcher passed a group of people huddled around a fallen figure, Rose saw among them the sprawled shoes and stockings of another nurse. With her heart pounding, she left Julia for a moment and quickly pushed through to see who it was.

It was Matron Lambert. Three bullets had hit her across the back. She was alive, although in a serious condition. Two doctors were debating loudly what to do as she was being put gently onto a stretcher. As terrible as Rose felt, she had to tear herself away again. Matron Lambert was in good hands and Julia needed her help. She hurried on.

Ten minutes later, the situation had calmed and Julia's chances of surviving looked good. Rose stopped all the bleeding, dressed the wounds thickly to counter the jolting of the ambulance, and Robert had secured her a place in his own vehicle. Grace was allowed to ride with Julia since many of the staff, the women nurses especially, were being evacuated at every opportunity. It could have been Rose, except she felt compelled to stay and try to make sure Matron Lambert was all right. It was silly, she knew. There were plenty of others to do it. A loyalty born from years of working with the matron made her wait behind.

Then she learned that the news was much worse.

Colonel Asquith explained to her, 'Matron's wounds are too bad. I'm told she won't survive the journey in an ambulance unless we operate and try to repair some of the damage first.'

'Can we still do that?' Rose asked, looking around. The hospital was being dismantled as they watched.

'Theatre One is being left untouched. They'll operate there.'

'Who's going to do it?' She wished that Mark was still with them.

'Hornsby has volunteered to stay and do it.'

Hornsby. It couldn't have been anyone worse. 'I'll stay back and help too,' she said.

'Gwen Hampshire is the senior nurse now and she'll be deciding—'

'Has anyone else volunteered?'

'No, because there's no need. Everyone is obviously willing to—'

'Then let's say I *asked* first.'

Asquith looked at her helplessly and started to argue.

Beyond the hospital, the German guns all fell silent within the space of a few seconds. An order that had obviously been pre-arranged. The sudden silence, after so much of the mind-numbing roar, was disturbing and unreal. Everyone in the hospital stopped what they were doing and stared around, wondering.

'Now they'll be advancing,' Asquith said quietly. 'If they break through quickly, you could get caught in the middle of the operation and you'll be taken prisoner.'

'I'm more skilled and faster than any of the male nurses,' Rose said stubbornly. 'There's a much better chance of getting the matron's surgery completed if one of the girls does it. It might as well be me.' Unseen, Hornsby walked up behind Asquith.

'She's right, Colonel,' he said flatly. 'Rose is very good, one of the best. We'll have better odds in our favour if she helps me.'

Asquith knew that the decision had been made for him and that nothing could change Rose's mind. 'All right,' he said heavily. 'It took four weeks in 1917 to advance 250 bloody yards. The German have to capture a mile-and-a-half to get here today. That should be enough time. As soon as the soldiers tell you to leave, put the matron on the ambulance and go, even if it kills her. I'll be commanding a platoon of cooks and cleaners, for God's sake, in a trench line just beyond the fences. The enemy will have to get past us first, if they come this far.' He paused, then sighed. 'All in all, it's not as risky as it seems if you run at the first sign of trouble. Isobelle Lambert deserves the best chance we can give her.'

It was the only time Rose had ever heard her first name and she smiled. 'Thank you, Colonel.'

They began operating with a full medical team, which was rare. As the surgery progressed and some people finished their work, Hornsby sent them away. They could see outside the tent the grounds filling with front line soldiers. Muddy and exhausted men with blank expressions from the hours of constant shelling. They were trickling backwards in a retreat faster than Colonel Asquith had imagined. Sounds of fighting came slowly closer. Machine guns hammered, and the cracking of grenades got louder.

Hornsby kept working at a deliberate pace, his hands steady as he tried to suture the awful wounds Matron suffered. At times, Rose wanted to snap at him to hurry, and she could see similar thoughts in the faces of the others. The conditions outside were making everyone very nervous. Each time he said, 'Thank you, you should leave now,' the ones left behind watched with undisguised envy as that person rushed away.

Five members of staff still remained, including two stretcher-bearers, when Hornsby started closing the wounds. He had removed two of the three bullets. The third would have to stay until the matron was strong enough to endure more surgery.

'Just another ten minutes or so,' Hornsby told them, with a nod at the man doing the anaesthetic. His name was Brown, an older nurse, who had also been a picture of calm.

'Rose, your work has been excellent, as always,' Hornsby said. 'I'm glad you stayed.'

'It was the least I could do,' she said, surprised by his praise. They hadn't exchanged anything other than professional comments the whole time. Hornsby hadn't spoken to her kindly since their disagreement over the young soldier's leg.

A rattle of small-arms fire quite nearby made them all jump. Somewhere men started yelling and rifles fired raggedly. The stretcher-bearers both stared anxiously at the tent flap.

'*One* of you check that the ambulance is still there,' Hornsby said coolly. The inference was clear. He was hoping one man wouldn't panic and run without his friend.

The stretcher-bearer looked worried as he came back from the entrance. 'It's still there,' he said. 'They've got the engine running and the doors open. I reckon they're keen to get moving.'

'Aren't we all?' Hornsby said. 'Just a few minutes more.'

Someone rushed into the tent and startled them again. It was a soldier, difficult to recognise with the sun behind him. Rose knew his voice immediately.

It was Jonathon, and he said without greeting or apology, 'For Christ's sake, the Germans are only 200 yards away. You'll have to leave *now*.'

Hornsby managed to look outraged above his mask. 'Who the hell are you?'

Before Jonathon could answer there came the unmistakable sound of the ambulance's motor revving and the doors slamming. With a crunch of gears it left, the motor fading into the distance. Then came a splintering crash and the truck's engine died abruptly.

'Oh *shit*,' the stretcher-bearer groaned and ran past Jonathon out of the tent. His partner followed. Moments later they could hear a howl of curses.

Jonathon came close and grabbed Rose by the arm. 'We have to run. You've waited too long.'

She stared desperately at the matron lying in front of them. 'Can we move her?'

Hornsby told them calmly, 'There's no point without an ambulance to carry her. You people go. I'll make sure they treat her properly.'

There was an awful silence as they understood what he meant. He was willing to be captured, and he didn't let them think about it.

'Go, for Christ's sake,' he yelled, suddenly hoarse with fear. 'Before they get here.'

With a brief nod of acknowledgement of Hornsby's courage, Jonathon pulled Rose towards the tent entrance. He sensed Brown close behind. Outside, the rifle fire was becoming furious.

'Listen to me, both of you,' Jonathon said. 'We're going to run for the fence line and that trench beside it. From there we can reach the woods and work our way roughly north-west, all right?'

'Are you mad?' Brown hissed. 'We have to go at least south towards our rear.'

'Right now, the Germans are heading for our heavy artillery behind the hospital. There're still a dozen guns left. We don't want to get mixed up in *that* fight, believe me.' He was gripping Rose's arm as if she might agree with Brown and leave him. 'Besides, this is a break-through, and a bloody big one at that. They're already past us in some places. It might be quicker to travel sideways across their advance and sneak through their flanks, than try running in front of them all day.'

'I'll do whatever you think,' Rose said. She was so frightened her words shook, and she could hardly get them out.

Behind them Hornsby shouted, ‘Get moving, damn you.’

‘Run,’ Jonathon told her. ‘I’ll be right behind you.’

Rose literally picked up her skirts and dashed out of the tent. In the open air, she felt terribly exposed and expected to feel a bullet slam into her. The sounds all around were of shouting men and cracking rifles. After a few yards, she dared to look round as she ran, earning a rebuke from Jonathon.

‘Forget about everything else,’ He was running at her heels. ‘Just get to the fence.’

She had seen enough anyway. She’d imagined the farm would be overrun with German soldiers, but it appeared Colonel Asquith and his men, and others retreating would hold them off for the moment. As she reached the fence, she baulked, uncertain whether to climb it or squeeze through the railings. She decided to go over the top, then felt herself lifted and almost thrown over.

‘In the trench,’ Jonathon told her, dragging her with him as they rolled over the parapet. They landed awkwardly at the bottom, and it knocked the breath out of her.

They used precious seconds to recover.

‘Are you all right?’ he asked, panting.

‘Yes, I think so...’ No one else was there. She had lost her veil and her hair had tumbled down around her shoulders. She had been growing it again since coming to France. Mud clung to it in lumps. 'How did you know where to find me?' she asked, raking at her hair with her fingers.

'I didn't,' Jonathon said absently. He was peeking over the edge. 'I had to ask every bloody stretcher-bearer between here and Paris before someone knew what you were doing and where. I could have *throttled* you. Where's that other bloke? Didn't he follow us?'

'Brown,' Rose said, raising herself to look too. 'He didn't like your idea of going this way.'

'The bloody idiot. Where did he go?'

'Jonathon, look!'

Soldiers dressed in the grey of the German army were appearing between the remaining tents and buildings of the hospital. They moved warily, their weapons held ready. In the background, Colonel Asquith was still fighting at their trench, but these Germans must have been confident that battle was over. They ignored it. Three men paused at the entrance to Theatre One, then went rapidly inside.

Rose closed her eyes and prayed.

Two distinct rifle shots rang out.

'The bastards,' Jonathon said bitterly. 'The murdering *bastards*.'

Rose felt stinging tears come and she couldn't breathe. His arm wrapped around her shoulder and crushed her to him.

'Hang on, Rose. You've got to hang on, do you understand?'

'Are they coming this way?'

'I'm afraid so. Damn it, they're supposed to go for the fucking *guns*. That would give us a chance.' Jonathon sounded beaten, and that scared her all the more.

He was angry at himself. It was only a matter of ten yards from the trench before some outbuildings and the remaining mist would obscure their run to the woods. It might as well have been a hundred with the Germans taking their time like this. Somebody would see them for certain. They shouldn't have rested in the trench for a moment. Getting their breath back was going to cost them their lives.

He saw a flurry of action near the crashed ambulance. It was Brown, making a run for it from the wreckage. By now, a dozen Germans were milling in the open space of the farmyard and they all reacted to the running Brown. A chorus of shouts ordered him to stop at the same time as they raised their rifles, and a flurry of shots brought him down with his arms windmilling crazily. Some of the soldiers trotted over to check that he was dead. The rest began to spread out, searching the rest of the property—the last thing Jonathon expected them to do.

A new sound jerked his head up. An aeroplane roared into sight from behind the woods and banked sharply, flying directly over the top of Jonathon and Rose. It was an Allied single-seater, that's all he knew, but it gave him hope. It seemed like the scout was going to strafe the Germans in the yard. There was even a moment when he believed he was staring right into the eyes of the pilot as the man's pale face looked down at them trapped in the trench. He didn't dare wave in case the German soldiers saw his hand.

'Jesus, did he see us?' Jonathon half-prayed. 'Just give them one spray, my friend. Just one. Keep them busy for ten seconds. For Rose's sake, not for me.'

His prayer was answered. The plane sideslipped and dived towards the farmyard. The Germans had been undecided and many still stood in the open. Perhaps they didn't realise it was an SE5a, and not one of their own. In this unfamiliar war of advancing beyond the trenches, nothing was certain.

Both machine guns opened fire and sent the enemy soldiers fleeing in all directions. The pilot must have had Jonathon and Rose in mind because he veered slightly to kill three Germans sprinting for the fence line and their trench. As the plane raced overhead, two bombs detached and landed in the centre of the farm. Everyone flattened themselves as the explosions erupted.

Except Jonathon.

'*Go, go*! *Run for your life*!' he yelled, boosting Rose out of the trench and sending her running for the woods. He followed, catching her by the arm to make sure she didn't slow down.

It only needed seconds before they were hidden from any soldiers around the buildings. After that, it was a desperate race across the paddock to the trees. Behind them, the Germans still sheltered from the strafing aircraft. It was already turning steeply and coming back for another run.

The Germans weren't going to be caught twice and a storm of rifle fire tracked the SE5a as it powered over their heads. Still, it gave Jonathon and Rose enough time to escape. In the end, the enemy never knew how close they'd come to discovering them.

The SE5a wasn't so lucky. As it climbed away from the farm a streamer of smoke began pouring from the motor. It seemed to hop in the air, flying an odd dipping course to the north and towards the old front line. Then it nose-dived for the ground

Jonathon turned at the last second, as they reached the safety of the trees, to see the SE5a disappear behind a distant rise. He felt sick. It had probably crashed close to the forward trenches, or what was left of them. Right now, that was well inside enemy-held territory.

'Good luck,' he muttered. 'I hope to God someone saves you now.'

Rose was sitting with her back against a tree. She was trying hard not to cry, and he put his hands under her arms and picked her up. 'We haven't got time to stay here. With the Huns dallying around the farm, we've still got a chance to stay ahead of them if we hurry.'

She screwed her face up hard, reining in her fear, and said, 'So Brown should have stayed with us. He'll get himself killed because he didn't trust you.'

He realised that she hadn't seen Brown gunned down. 'Well, I'm glad he didn't,' he said. 'We can do better without him.'

'That's a terrible thing to say. He was a good man for staying with us.'

'No, it's not.' He kissed her hard on the forehead and startled her out of her misery. She was amazed to see him grin and wink.

'Because only two people at the most can ride a horse,' he said. 'And if

Brown was here, I might have to leave you behind to walk home on your own.'

She stared at him. 'A *horse*?'

He jerked his thumb in the direction of the woods. 'Come and meet your namesake.'

***

During the hours of darkness after the bombardment started, Joseph could only wait. He desperately wanted to go and see Katherine. She wasn't so far away. But the risk was too great. If the Germans broke through or sent over night bombers, and the squadron was sent into the air minus a member and betraying Joseph's absence, there would be hell to pay. He might be charged with desertion.

One thought helped to keep him at the airfield. He was of more use to her if he was in the cockpit of his SE5a trying to stop the Germans advancing.

Taking off at night wasn't such a problem, however there was almost nothing the pilots could achieve once they were up there. Chances were good that they'd collide with a zeppelin creeping through the sky, rather than shoot it down. And landing in the dark was a real skill. The night bombers used flare paths and specially trained flyers.

The pilots had to content themselves with annoying their fitters and rechecking the aircraft. Twenty-pound Coopers bombs were loaded, four to each plane. These were for small ground targets like machine gun nests and bunkers, but the extra drag on the plane was a disadvantage during a dogfight and the whole squadron would be looking for quick targets to lose the bombs early. If the pilots weren't staring moodily towards the north and the fantastic glow of the barrage, they watched the east instead, looking for the faintest sign of dawn. The moment it came, they would fly.

Half an hour before the first rays of sunshine were expected, Judith called them all together in the mess. He handed out large tots of rum—mugs of tea at this time would only fill bladders and do nothing to keep out the cold.

'We're still panicking,' he announced, his face serious so that no one would laugh. 'This bombardment has caught our army with its pants down, make no mistake about it. The front lines are gone. Luckily the Germans don't know that yet. When the shelling stops, the Huns are going to stroll over no-man's-land like a walk in the park. The official orders say to hold the forward trenches at all costs. Reality is, it can't happen. Of course, we're expected to do our damnedest to try.'

Someone asked nervously, 'How far are we going to pull back?'

'God knows,' Judith said. 'Ask me something I can answer.'

'Is somebody going to provide cover overhead?'

'*Everyone* is doing ground support,' Judith fixed them all with a stare. 'Anything that can fly is being mounted with a gun with orders to kill soldiers on the ground.'

That kept them silent. Ground support was dangerous enough. Normally the anti-aircraft fire was inaccurate at higher altitudes. Close to the ground even the most inept German private could put a bullet into a passing plane. Add to this the German air force trapping them against the earth, and surviving the day looked unlikely.

'Any more rum left, Judy?' somebody asked, raising a laugh.

'Help yourselves, we take off in twenty minutes.' He waved at the wooden cask on the table. 'We'll fly formation to the Front and see what's happening. At my signal we'll go down and you select your own targets. Stick with your wingmen as long as you can. God help you, after that.'

The minute there was sufficient light from the growing dawn to see each other in the air, Judith ordered a squadron take-off. A mist made things difficult, and it was heavier to the north, but it didn't prevent them from getting off the ground. Normally they would circle the airstrip and climb until everyone was airborne. Joseph made sure he was one of the first to go and he took the chance to swing wide and low over the village. What he saw alarmed him.

In the dim pre-dawn light, a procession of civilians was streaming down the road towards the south. They pushed carts piled high with belongings and were bent over with loads on their backs. He flew over them and saw a mass of frightened, upturned faces. Nobody waved. They reminded him of rats leaving a sinking ship. In desperation, he tried to fly straight over Katherine's bakery to see if he might glimpse the glow of her oven from the chimney, a thin hope. The village was a black silhouette against the unlit streets with no windows shining anywhere. The place was almost deserted.

He couldn't linger, and feeling wretched with worry for her, he flew back to join the squadron.

They flew in full formation for three-quarters of an hour, cruising up and down the forward trenches. Below them the ground on the Allied side of no-man's-land boiled under a mist as if it were some enormous hot spring. On the German side a token artillery response was pitiful by comparison.

Enemy aircraft were plentiful, flying in large groups. They were disciplined and didn't try to attack the Australians. Joseph guessed they were waiting for a pre-arranged time to strike simultaneously. It would be one huge, orchestrated attack.

The bombardment ceased so quickly and with such precision, it caused an awesome moment of its own. The mass of explosions stopped abruptly, and the millions of tons of soil churned into the air for so long fell back for the final time. Suddenly, everything below was still.

Until seconds later, under the mist, tens of thousands of men in grey uniforms spilled from cracks in the earth and moved forward towards the shattered Allied lines.

It was happening on such a broad front that Judith simply dropped towards the trenches. Anywhere would do. The pilots had a better chance of attacking the German soldiers than their own army, since looking from above they only had to see through a single layer of fog. The shifting mass of men was impossible to miss. Any troops still facing them weren't so fortunate.

A Jasta of German Fokkers lurking nearby reacted instantly to the diving SE5a's and came plunging down on their backs. Joseph watched them coming, and despite the strict orders to concentrate on troop support, couldn't bring himself to let the Fokkers have an easy shot. He waved at Roger before pulling up and around to meet the Jasta head-on. Two other SE5a's did the same. The rest of the squadron flew resolutely on.

There was an instant of snarling engines and colourful aircraft flashing past, machine guns firing. Joseph fired both his guns hopefully at spinning propellers that appeared and vanished in front of him. Nothing was hit that he could see. Then he was through the enemy into clear air, banking hard to come onto the Fokkers' tails instead. The question was, would some of the Germans come back and try to fight him, or would they continue to chase the more vulnerable SE5a's now strafing the soldiers?

The answer was no surprise. None of the Fokkers bothered to slow and climb again towards the more aggressive Australians. They continued on, running down the other SE5a's like hounds trying to reach a fox before it went to ground. Joseph pursued them.

It turned into a dogfight with the opponents frighteningly low, so there was no margin for error. The SE5a's skimmed the fog, churning the white mist with their slipstreams as they dipped and swooped to fire into the advancing troops. Small hills, ruins and festoons of barbed wire all threatened to trip up the planes' undercarriages. Repeatedly the pilots climbed sharply to avoid obstacles and weaved to throw off pursuing enemy aircraft. The Fokkers had the luxury of staying higher and firing down at the Australians, although their own bullets also continued on and into their own countrymen below.

Joseph picked a German with a bright green fuselage and yellow tail. The Fokker was close behind an SE5a that he couldn't recognise. He arrived too late. A stream of bullets from the Fokker touched the SE5a and it changed instantly from a flying aeroplane into a wreckage cartwheeling across the earth, smashing into running soldiers as it went. It was impossible to tell whether the pilot had been hit or struck the ground in his efforts to escape. The German flyer triumphantly watched the crash over his shoulder as he flew past, and this gave him a second to see Joseph threatening behind before he was killed by Joseph's tracers shredding his cockpit. The Fokker nosed straight into a shell crater to stop dead.

Scared he might share the same fate, Joseph looked behind and saw his tail was clear. In that moment, a clutch of broken trees on top of a ridge materialised out of the fog. Crying out with the shock of it, he hauled on the joystick and narrowly missed the stripped limbs reaching for his wheels. It reminded him that the aircraft was too sluggish for this sort of flying and he quickly toggled the bomb-release twice, not caring whether any deserving target was below. He heard a tapping noise, the sounds of bullets from the infantry below hitting his plane, and he climbed higher.

He roared past a wooden bridge across a small stream and Joseph recognised he was close to a farm and the Casualty Clearing Station where Rose Preston nursed. He doubted the medical staff was still there. Surely they would have been evacuated at the first signs of trouble? He also remembered telling Katherine to head that way if she was running from the Germans.

It was a crazy, remote possibility that he might spot her, and it still might be worthwhile helping keep back the enemy in that part of the line in case she was among the refugees in the area.

As he stayed low and set a course, he was shocked to see Germans crossing the open green paddocks. Watching *any* soldiers fighting over clear ground without trenches was so strange. The fact that they were the enemy and Allied troops were retreating fast in front of them was even harder to accept.

The farm appeared in the distance, half-shrouded by the lifting mist. He recalled with a guilty start that a heavy artillery battery was emplaced behind the hospital, so the Germans no doubt would be keen to capture that and the Casualty Clearing Station by default. He raged at himself a moment. Telling Katherine to come here had been a stupid mistake. What was he thinking?

Flying low across the farmyard and the white tents emblazoned with the red cross, he could see enemy troops creeping between the buildings already. The farm was about to fall into German hands.

Perhaps it was lingering thoughts of Katherine escaping uselessly here, or concern for his brother's fiancée whom he'd never met, that made Joseph's eye catch the distinctly female-dressed figure with long, dark hair crouched in a trench on the farm's boundary. A khaki-clad soldier was with her, probably Australian in this part of Front. It looked like their freedom wasn't going to last. German soldiers were spreading out and couldn't miss them much longer. Unless he gave them something else to worry about.

He sideslipped and aimed directly for the middle of the farm. He had to assume that everyone had run. Only Germans were among the tents and sheds now.

He opened fire, sent the soldiers scampering for cover and left many sprawled on the dirt. Then he swore as some of the Germans ran for the very trench he was trying to protect. Touching his rudder, he swung the SE5a's nose slightly and cut them down. Then, as he swooped upwards again, the two remaining bombs fell perfectly onto the chaos below.

'Run like hell,' he shouted savagely, seeing the nurse and her companion sprint for the trees nearby. None of the Germans seemed to notice and he wanted to keep it that way. He banked around for another run. Part of him suffered a momentary pang of disappointment. The woman was obviously in a nurse's uniform, so it couldn't be Katherine. Then again, he should be grateful that Katherine wasn't in such danger.

On this run he could only strafe the area. It would distract the soldiers a minute longer. He tore across the farm and watched his bullets smash into the tents and wooden walls, hoping enemy troops sheltered behind them and were hurt. The volume of rifle fire that snapped at his plane alarmed him. He wouldn't do this again.

The instant he made that decision the aircraft kicked sideways and his engine lost its smooth bellow. Smoke poured past his cockpit. Hot oil splattered at his face.

'Oh shit... shit!' He wrenched at the controls, and his heart sank as they felt all wrong. He tried to climb and the plane obliged, but his rudder pedals offered no resistance. They lay flat and broken on the cockpit floor.

It was cruel damage and he didn't know whether to laugh or cry. His SE5a was flying steadily back towards the front lines, now in German hands, and without rudder controls he had no way of turning around. He could try and bank into a turn, but there was no guarantee the aircraft would straighten again. Quite simply, the longer it took him to dive and crash into the ground, the deeper into enemy territory he would fly. He couldn't rush into a crashlanding either. The odds of surviving depended on how slowly and gently he hit.

He started a series of swooping manoeuvres, experimenting, which only confirmed his suspicions as to how much control he had. His best chance at coming out of this alive, aside from possibly being shot by any Germans after he landed, was by continuing to swallow-dive until his final plunge flattened him to the earth.

And the sooner the better.

'No time like the present,' he muttered through his teeth.

As he got closer to the bombardment zone, he hastily hauled back on the stick and shut down the labouring engine. The aircraft seemed to hang in the air for a second, then it crashed down with a bone-jarring impact that threw him against his lap belt. His arms, crossed over his face in the last instant smacked into the dashboard so painfully that his hands went numb. He had the presence of mind to worry that his wrists had been broken. Around him the aircraft cracked and splintered like a falling tree. It stayed upright and stopped nose-down in a shell crater.

It took him a while to realise that the crash was over. It had only taken a heartbeat to happen. He'd expected some long, drawn-out disaster.

He allowed himself a second to marvel that he'd survived, then told himself to listen to his surroundings carefully as he flexed each muscle and limb in turn, searching for injuries. He ached all over, but nothing felt serious apart from his hands which were beginning to tingle. It seemed strangely silent after the constant roaring of the engine, then reality cut through. Machine guns and small arms fire came from everywhere. A few ticking noises told him stray rounds were striking the SE5a in places. He wasn't so safe after all. Isolated pockets of resistance, he guessed. British or Australian soldiers who didn't know just how far the Germans had advanced beyond them.

Stinging needles of pain came back into his hands now and he fumbled with the strap. He almost laughed—a little madly he expected—finding he could stand in the cockpit and simply step out onto the ground. Without the undercarriage and being half-buried in the crater, it was that close. His good humour vanished as the last of the mist suddenly dissipated before his eyes and he was exposed to the world.

Old habits from Gallipoli came back as he dived away from the wreckage into another shell hole. Several bullets zipped past him and this time he figured they were aimed at him. Perhaps the previous shots had been blindly directed into the mist, the shooters knowing the stricken plane was in there somewhere.

The shock of his abruptly altered circumstances began to wear off and he took stock of his surroundings. He was in a large crater, the soil loose and smelling of explosives and the overall frightful stench of the Western Front.

Then someone called out in a voice that sent him cold with fear. It was in English, heavily accented by German.

'*Flyer*! Show yourself and come out. The war is over.'

He made a quick judgment. *Show yourself and come out*. The enemy didn't know where he was, and he sounded quite far away. That probably meant the wreckage of the SE5a had hidden his movement. If he went the same way, he could stay out of sight for a distance, and the further he got away from the aircraft, the better his chances of escaping.

He didn't give himself time to think about it. He crawled over the lip of the crater to roll into another only three feet away. He almost shouted in fright, seeing it was occupied. It was only the body of a British corporal. The man was missing half his head. No further calling out or shooting came from the Germans. Again they hadn't spotted him.

The glimpse of his surroundings as he crossed the gap was shocking. The world was an endless plain of shell craters, the churned earth littered with debris, broken equipment and hundreds of mutilated bodies from both armies. A cheerful sun, the beginning of a beautiful spring day, showed everything too clearly.

He slid over to the corpse and prised a rifle from the man's death grip. It was undamaged and loaded with five cartridges. There was no extra ammunition. The man had been on his last clip when he was killed. The water bottle had two tepid mouthfuls, which Joseph greedily swallowed. It gave him heart. After a deep breath to steady his nerves, he pulled himself up to the edge of the crater and looked out carefully.

The forlorn remains of the aircraft now served to block the view that he needed most. The Germans calling him to surrender were most likely on the opposite side of the plane. How many, he couldn't begin to guess, or why they weren't advancing with the others.

Then he saw a helmeted head poke cautiously above the earth about a hundred yards away. It was just visible beyond the SE5a's tail-plane. This told him the Germans were being extra careful, apparently not revealing themselves even when they'd called for him to come out. Otherwise, they would have seen him move. Perhaps they weren't even sure he'd survived the crash.

The enemy soldier lifted himself higher. One hand showed itself for an instant. He was hefting a grenade nervously. It was too far to throw and reach the plane, and he was considering a dash across to somewhere closer. His thin face turned and he spoke to someone invisible. Something about the soldier convinced Joseph he was very young. Perhaps that was why they lagged behind the main assault. These were young conscripts, inexperienced and terrified, despite the offensive going so well.

Still, they outnumbered him and had hand-bombs. When their courage grew, he was in trouble.

'Let's give you a little surprise,' he said aloud, cocking the rifle.

For him, it was an easy kill. He shot the German in the face as the youth took another wary look around.

The cries of dismay coming across the battlefield were at once satisfying and worrying. There were too many different voices for Joseph's liking. More than he had rounds left in the rifle, at least.

One of the Germans was louder. Harsher, and more demanding. Plainly, he was in charge and now exhorting his comrades with vengeful outrage to hunt down the pilot. Joseph sighted his rifle on the same place and waited for another shot. He'd started something he had to try and finish now—and his chances seemed less. He was facing more of the enemy than he'd gambled on.

The top of a helmet became just visible above the soil. It was stationary. Either the wearer didn't know he'd exposed himself, or it was a trick. He thought about this hard. The slightest miss and the bullet would glance away and be a waste. Only a direct hit would punch through the steel, assuming that a man was in fact wearing it.

He pulled the trigger and heard the clang of the bullet striking. Someone screeched horribly. The helmet had vanished.

'Three left,' he told the rifle, patting it. 'But damn it, how many Huns?'

A minute later a grenade came spinning out of the Germans' trench. He grinned, seeing it was going to fall well short. They were panicked or trying to force him into a silly move. His smile snapped off when he saw that it was a smoke bomb. A white haze billowed out, mocking the mist that had recently evaporated.

Dimly beyond it, too obscured for a reliable shot, he saw four figures scamper out of the ground and spread out, heading his way.

'Oh, aren't you just so fucking clever, Joseph?' he told himself angrily. Things had suddenly got much worse. He couldn't keep looking in four directions at once without revealing himself. The closer the Germans came, the more widespread the angles he had to watch.

'One at a time, one at a time…' he reminded himself tightly. With only three rounds, it didn't offer a means of killing the last German. The best he could hope for was to shoot their leader among the three. The survivor might be too discouraged to keep coming. After all, they didn't know he was running out of ammunition.

Christ, he thought desperately. *Where's the rest of the war*? *Can't someone else join in*? *Where the hell is everybody*?

Really, he didn't want that. Chances were too good that *someone else* would be German as well. Right now, he was in a vacuum, the war having moved on at a pace no one understood after years of stalemated trench warfare. This was a small, private battle surrounded by the greatest military offensive ever known.

The smoke grenade ran its course and the view cleared too slowly, and he had little idea where to watch. At least two of them would use the aircraft for cover as long as they could. That left two of the enemy to his right only risking themselves above ground as they traversed between the countless shell craters.

There came a noise of disturbed metal—a kicked food can or discarded helmet. Joseph snapped the rifle to his shoulder. A grey shape rolled across the ground briefly, the blob of a face looking his way.

Again, it was the fleeting rabbit behind his parents' house. The hint of a Turkish turban between sandbags. He fired and the soldier's controlled rolling turned into flailing arms as he toppled into the next crater.

With a grim satisfaction that ignored his near-empty rifle, he said, 'Now, where's your friend?'

His next opportunity came from where he least expected it. The other side, where the soldiers had the crashed SE5a for concealment. A shadow of movement behind the aircraft wreckage betrayed one of the Germans using it for cover. The soldier seemed ignorant that apart from the motor, the SE5a was just flimsy wood and treated fabric. Joseph couldn't believe his luck as glimpses of a helmet, then a rifle barrel, shifted along the crumpled fuselage. He guessed the soldier was going to peek inside the cockpit. The youth wouldn't be able to resist it.

There was a flash of wild eyes below the brim of the helmet, scanning the inside of the plane before the German dropped down again. He had shown enough to tell Joseph that he was squatting out of sight. Aiming calmly, Joseph put a bullet just underneath the rim of his cockpit. He even felt guilty doing it, shooting at his own plane.

Another scream marked his success.

Rather than feel exultant, he felt a wave of defeat, resigned that he'd done all he could, but it was over. He wouldn't come out of this alive. With an ounce more luck he'd kill one more of the Germans. When he'd done that, the remaining soldier would never let him surrender once it became obvious that he was helpless.

He waited, aware that he had an enemy closing in on either side and wondering whether they guessed that it was a life-or-death lottery which one showed himself first and took this last bullet.

An animal yell of madness came from somewhere and a young soldier burst out of a shell crater and came running straight at Joseph, his rifle with a bayonet extended in front at full stretch. The German's face was contorted with fear and intense anxiety. Instantly a second man jumped up from another hole and rushed forward too. His bayonet wasn't fixed, and he ran awkwardly with the rifle at his shoulder, aimed right at Joseph.

Joseph used his last shot to kill the man who was ready to shoot him. The soldier was thrown backwards when the bullet hit him square in the heart.

The remaining German stumbled with the shock of seeing his comrade fall. Impossibly, his feet tangled, he went flying and landed so heavily that the breath was driven from his lungs. There was a moment when he couldn't move, couldn't roll safely into any of the shell craters, and he watched Joseph with utter dread, knowing this pilot was a man too skilled with his rifle to let the opportunity pass by.

That was when a thread of understanding passed between them. Joseph's own look of calm acceptance betrayed the fact that he was out of ammunition. He hadn't even shifted the rifle. He was at the German's mercy.

Sobbing with relief and an almost childish rage, the soldier climbed unsteadily to his feet and slowly walked closer, his finger tightening on the trigger. He shouted a string of angry words, with tears in his eyes, that Joseph didn't understand. He could only stare at the muzzle of the rifle pointed straight at him. A distant part of his mind prayed that the German would shoot, not bayonet him.

Less than ten yards away the soldier stopped, shouldered his Mauser and screamed an incoherent demand again. Joseph didn't move. He was sure that the youth would pull the trigger.

The next shot to ring out came from somewhere else, behind Joseph. The German's throat opened into an ugly red wound and he fell backwards with a gargling noise. He writhed in agony on his back, blood pumping out between his fingers clasped at his neck.

Stunned, Joseph turned around slowly to see who had fired the shot. All he could see was a dirty face and a hand gesturing feebly above a crater. He scrambled from his own hole, his instincts reminding him to stay low. There were still a million more Germans hoping to kill him.

It was an army officer, a captain, and he greeted Joseph with a grateful smile. Joseph felt instantly angry that the captain hadn't come to his aid sooner.

'Where the fuck did you come from?' he said ungraciously.

'I–I've been here all the time. I didn't know what to do.' The captain sounded so exhausted it took the edge off Joseph's anger.

'Are you hurt? Wounded?'

'No, no–I don't think so.'

Joseph looked at him suspiciously. 'What are you?' He looked at the unfamiliar shoulder tabs. 'Medical corps?'

'Yes, I'm a doctor, a surgeon. Captain Mark Cohen.'

'A surgeon?' He couldn't believe it. The captain obviously wasn't a field officer. Very few medical teams worked under fire. 'What the hell are you doing here?'

Mark tried to grin, but it appeared ghastly. 'I wanted to do my bit to fight off the Germans. Come out and give my opposite numbers a little work to do for a change, understand? Impress the nurses, perhaps,' he added this blithely, like a bad joke. 'Things didn't go as planned.' He gestured at the soldier still thrashing weakly as he died from the throat wound. 'That's the only one I've managed to shoot. All night, I've been pretending to be dead while thousands walked past, and that's the only one I've killed.' His attempt to be casual wasn't working. Shock glittered in his eyes.

'Lucky for me,' Joseph said, watching him carefully.

'It seems so.' Mark said. 'I don't suppose you have any idea what to do next?

I'm actually lost.'

'That's easy. We walk home, if the Germans will let us.'

***

Mark told his story breathlessly as Joseph led him in a direct, dangerous route to the south. Often, they had to dive for cover as groups of German infantry came too close. Mostly no one took any notice of them. The enemy was in too much of a hurry to catch up with the victorious troops at the front. Stories of captured hordes of food and wine for the taking had everyone rushing forward. Mark and Joseph were just another two filthy, exhausted men, almost unrecognisable, who were making their way in the same direction as the triumphant advance. Their audacity at walking upright among the enemy fooled everyone. However, Joseph knew it wouldn't be so easy when they go closer to the fighting.

Doctor Cohen explained that he had left his hospital in the hope of erasing a festering deep guilt. To take risks with his life, like everyone else, and yes, to prove himself in some people's eyes. The best way to do that, he figured, was journey up the stream of wounded soldiers coming into the Casualty Clearing Station until he found the source of their pain. He hadn't bargained for the sheer terror that came with walking into the bombardment. When the shelling shifted and began falling all around him, pounding at his body and with his hearing instantly gone, he became disoriented and so frightened that he'd crawled into a trench and stayed there, curled into a pathetic ball in the mud. He didn't mind admitting that. He had no idea where he was, how close to the front lines he'd come, or even how to get out again. All the other soldiers appeared to have disappeared into the night when the savage barrage had come down on them.

He'd lost all sense of time. He remembered a moment of absolute horror as the trench gave in to the heaving earth and the walls fell inwards to bury him. He had dug his way out and crawled into a crater. He had prayed that someone would find him, take him out of this hell, but nobody came. When gas shells started falling he'd remembered an old tale, ripped part of his shirt free and urinated on it, pressing the stinking cloth to his nose and mouth. It worked, apparently. He was still alive.

He woke to the morning sun with no idea whether he'd been sleeping or knocked unconscious by a near miss, or even a taint of the gas. The bombardment was over, then his joy at surviving was shattered as he saw thousands of enemy soldiers walking out of the mist towards him. He'd grabbed a discarded rifle nearby, then immediately changed his mind. Instead of shooting his enemies, as he'd been so passionate to do, he'd lain pretending death for hours, his face pressed into the soil to prevent anyone seeing him breathe or his eyes fluttering.

Joseph's crash-landing and the shoot-out with the German soldiers had been the first time he'd dared to look beyond the shell crater again.

'I'd say you're a very lucky fellow,' Joseph told him dryly, his tone suggesting what he really thought. It was an account of stupidity and selfishness. Good men might have been killed trying to save this captain from himself. Mark having inadvertently rescued Joseph himself hardly excused anything.

Mark finished the last of his story as Joseph dropped behind a low stone wall on top of a hill. On the other side of the wall was a road cutting, dissecting the hill neatly in two. Awful sounds came up to them from the road itself. Joseph risked a look and pulled hastily back.

'It's full of wounded,' he said. 'Theirs, mostly. They're using the cutting for protection from any shelling we send over.' He closed his eyes and scratched at his face wearily. 'Worse than that, the field beyond them is absolutely full of fucking Germans. Thousands of the bastards. We're going to lose this war if we don't stop them soon.' He put his back against the wall and tried to figure out what to do next.

'I've been such a fool. Perhaps, if I help them, they'll treat us well. I can tell them I'm a surgeon.' Mark said in a defeated voice.

'What?'

'The Germans wounded down there. Maybe I should go and help them. It could save our lives.'

'For God's sake, you came out here to kill them, remember? Didn't you just walk out of your hospital?' He was getting sick of Mark's self-pity. Perhaps he was shell-shocked. Despite this, Joseph wasn't interested in trying to treat him gently. Right now, their problems were simple and there was a straightforward answer. They needed to avoid capture and get back to their own side. 'I don't know about you, but I'm not interested in being a bloody prisoner-of-war.'

'I didn't know what I was doing, when I left.' Mark yawned and pressed at his ears which had started to ache. And his head pounded.

Joseph had a thought. 'Were you at the Casualty Clearing Station near

Pozieres?'

'Yes, that's right. Have you been there?'

'I was bombing the bloody thing when they shot me down.'

Mark looked appalled. 'My God, had everyone gone? Were the nurses evacuated, do you think?'

'It looked like it.' He didn't mention the couple he'd seen barely escaping. 'By the way, did you know a girl called Rose Preston? A nurse?'

The question had the opposite effect. Rather than calm Mark further with chatter, he went pale. 'Rose? Of course, I did. She's a VAD.'

'Well, whatever she is—really? What's she like?' He was suddenly only half-listening. His instincts were prickling.

'She's a lovely girl. Absolutely beautiful.'

If Joseph had been paying attention, he might have heard something more. ‘Good. I haven’t met her. She’s my brother’s fiancée, or so he tells me.’

‘Are you serious? Your brother’s Jonathon White? And he’s engaged to Rose?’

‘You know Jonathon?’ Something was odd. Joseph would have sniffed the air like a dog if it could have told him what was happening.

‘I met him while he was wounded on Lemnos. Rose and he are *engaged*, you say?’

‘Didn’t you know?’

‘Nurses aren’t allowed to be married or even engaged.’

‘Shit, then don’t tell anyone.’ Joseph shifted so he could see some of the road. He still couldn’t understand his sudden sense of unease. ‘Bloody hell, it’s a small world, isn’t it?’ He looked up at the sky.

A tremendous salvo of artillery ripped down to explode among the troops in the field. It felt like the whole world was lifted and shaken. Bedlam broke out everywhere. Joseph’s whoop of joy was drowned out.

He yelled savagely at Mark, ‘*I knew it*. It’s about bloody time we sent something back. I hope the lads give them a fucking pasting. Maybe Jonathon's shooting some of those shells—hey! Where the hell are you going?'

Mark had stood up quickly and climbed over the wall. As he was about to slide down the cutting face to the road he called back, 'Now there's going to be more wounded. I'm a doctor, for God's sake, not a soldier. I should be down there helping. We won't make it back through the lines anyway. Are you coming?' His calm acceptance was strange.

'Are you mad? Not *now*.'

'All right. Tell Rose I was every bit as good as your brother, won't you?'

That took Joseph by complete surprise. 'What? What is that supposed to mean?'

Mark he was gone. With his next step he lost his footing and slithered uncontrollably down the steep face until he fell to the road. Landing among men who were expecting a barrage of shells to explode wasn't helpful. From where they lay on blankets and stretchers, they stared at him in bewilderment. He calmly picked himself up, rubbed at a sore knee, and faced a German sergeant who came running, goose-stepping almost comically over all the prone bodies.

'It's all right,' he shouted to be heard above the shelling and spread his arms in a gesture of welcome. 'I'm a surgeon. I want to help the wounded.'

The sergeant stopped, staring at him with an odd expression. His attention was taken momentarily by small rocks, dislodged by the shelling, that began trickling down the cutting face to fall among the injured soldiers. Some of the men called out in fear, imagining the entire cutting collapsing to bury them.

'Really, I can help,' Mark insisted. 'Do you understand English?'

With a disgusted snort, the sergeant pulled a revolver from his holster and shot him twice in the chest.

Watching from above, Joseph's reaction wasn't much different from the German sergeant's.

'You bloody idiot, Cohen,' he said. 'The last thing they want to see, when we're dropping shells on their bloody heads, is somebody looking for a safe bed in prison camp. What a fool. Thank Christ, you never had to fix *me* up.'

He pulled back and took a breath. He was willing to admit that he felt more than a bit relieved. His chances of sneaking back through the lines were infinitely better without the shell-shocked Captain Cohen tagging along. The man had been a nervous wreck and obviously couldn't be relied upon.

'I must ask Rose what she thought of *him*,' he said, curious.

Seven Days Later

'Look what the cat's dragged in,' Roger announced morosely to no one. He was the only one in the officers' mess. A thick bandage was wrapped around his head. He looked pale and tired. A large glass of whisky was in one hand.

'Don't be so glad to see me,' Joseph croaked. He closed the door and collapsed into another chair.

'I can't be. You're dead. Well, missing and presumed so. Are you? Dead, I mean?'

'Not quite.'

'Then you'd better fish that letter I wrote to your parents out of the pile on the sideboard.' He pointed unsteadily. 'Very complimentary it is, too. Lucky for you I couldn't be bothered posting it.'

Wearily, Joseph hauled himself back to his feet and went over. He sorted through a sheaf of envelopes and notes, looking for his parents' name. Instead, first he found Jonathon's name on a piece of paper. 'What's this?' he held it up.

Roger squinted at it. 'Your brother's contact information, in case we heard anything about you. Bloody miracle he found *us* to ask. No one else has, like the damned mailman or the fucking paymaster. I'm absolutely broke, skint. So are you, probably.'

'Is he all right?'

'Disgustingly cheerful, seeing we were still losing the entire war when he dropped by. Had a stunningly pretty nurse with him, the bastard. Upset about you, of course, when I told him,' he added with a shrug. 'Then again, he wasn't so keen to write you off just yet. You'd better call him, if the bloody French telephones are working. Where have you been, by the way?'

Joseph had found the whisky bottle and a glass, and he poured himself a generous measure. The neck rattled against the rim and he made a conscious effort to stop it. Roger held his glass out for a refill. Somewhere nearby an aircraft roared into life and made the walls shiver. It also half-smothered the noise of artillery firing from a field beside the airstrip.

'I've been visiting the Germans,' Joseph said.

'We figured as much,' he nodded wisely. 'Either that, or you were seeing my

Aunt Mabel. She's been dead since 1910, by the way.'

'Who else is gone?'

'Judith went the same day as you, and there's no doubt he didn't walk away. I saw it myself.' He pulled a serious face at last. 'And a few others. Have a look at that blackboard and see who's missing. There's a few names you won't know, of course. Replacements already.'

'What about your head?' Joseph sat down again.

'It only hurts when I wear a hat.'

'Fair enough. Nothing serious, then.'

'No, nothing to worry about.'

There was a silence between them, then Roger sighed.

'All right, I *am* glad to see you back. I was beginning to think I'd be left alone with no friends for the rest of the war.'

'No chance of that,' Joseph sipped his whisky. 'I've got to go and see Paris.'

'Really? Isn't that where the Germans are going?'

'Not if I can help it.'

'Ah...' He considered this. 'Paris, then. Any particular reason?'

'I've got to find somebody. You wouldn't know how many bakers are in

Paris, off-hand?'

'Wouldn't have a bloody clue. Is it important?'

'Very.'

'Then Paris it is, when we get a spot of leave. I can help you look.'

'I'd appreciate that.'

Roger suddenly gave him a solemn look, then raised his drink. 'Seeing that you're now *not* among them, here's to the blokes that won't be going home. There's been a few lately.'

Joseph met his friend's eyes. The bellowing aircraft outside abruptly switched off. The artillery was between salvoes. For a moment, there was a peaceful quiet.

'All right, then,' Joseph nodded, lifting his glass. 'To the blokes who won't be going home. God bless every bloody one of them.'

Epilogue: 11th November 1918

Joseph eased back on the throttle and let the engine cackle. The SE5a's nose lowered, as he wanted it to, and beyond the spinning arc of the propeller he saw the empty trenches and the litter of abandoned positions. The battles moved on now more quickly than military intelligence could tell the Flying Corps. The Germans were running as fast as they could, with the Allies in hot pursuit, and there was not much digging in.

Although, today of all days was a time to stay low and alive, not to be running out in the open. It would be ironic to die in the last twenty-four hours of the war.

Fifty miles behind him, the wasteland of the Western Front was being picked over by Graves Commission troops, salvage teams, and even tourists. Joseph had heard that French civilians were venturing into the horrific mess to see what all the fuss had been about. And scavenging, of course, for souvenirs and anything else of value.

Like many men who'd fought for so long, he had mixed emotions about the armistice that would be in place only minutes away now, at eleven o'clock. With the Allies decisively winning and putting the Germans to flight, their long-held dream of entering Berlin triumphant seemed the only fitting way to end the war. Instead, the enemy had sued for peace even before one Allied soldier had set foot in Germany. It felt unfair, as if the hated Hun had cheated them yet again in the last hours. No wonder artillery battalions to the north-east were still pounding enemy positions and intended to keep firing until the very last second. Frustration and spite were pulling the guns' lanyards and loading the shells, more than any real strategic need.

Joseph was flying for a similar reason. He'd wanted to be in the air during the last moments. Roger would have come with him, if his engine had not failed utterly on the runway and left him stranded. The mechanics, already drunk and celebrating, didn't give a damn and Joseph had continued on, laughing as he saw Roger slap the side of his cockpit like an enraged child.

Not that Joseph wanted to kill anyone. He wasn't hoping to shoot one last victim out of the sky this morning. Common sense warned him to stay well clear. He had good reasons to survive this war. In his top pocket, close to his heart, was a tattered letter from Katherine. She was in Paris, working in a tiny bakery near Notre Dame. It told nothing of her terrifying escape from the advancing Germans in March, or how she was coping with her new life away from the village. It only asked that he come to see her whenever he could—and added with simple understatement that she was pregnant.

The news stunned him, and then made him glad in an almost selfish way. He figured that she would have to marry him now for the sake of the baby, and that was all he wanted. They might even live in France, if it suited her. He'd written back every week since then, never knowing whether his letters would get through, wanting to reassure her that he was still alive.

During the past months there had been no way he could get enough leave from the squadron to travel to Paris. The German offensive had been relentless throughout 1918, on several occasions almost winning the war. Katherine's replies had become less regular and he was certain that some of her letters had been lost. Now, though, he believed that she was still in Paris and waiting for him. Her last note only a few weeks earlier had said so.

It was her first letter, the one that had eased his anxious, breaking heart, that he always kept with him.

Thinking of it, he smiled. Of all the bizarre and unimagined things this war brought him, now he was in a race to see whether the fighting would end in time for him to find her and see his first child born. He would never have dreamt such a thing, four years back, when he'd headed off for the great adventure of Gallipoli.

He suddenly brought his mind back to the job. Daydreaming would have killed him a month ago. It could still get him shot down today before he knew it. The Germans weren't going to be good losers.

'One last look,' he told himself, powering the engine again and turning north. Distant flashing turned out to be a line of light-calibre howitzers behind a hedge. They were blazing away at a forest. Nothing he could see among the erupting shells suggested that there were Germans hiding among the trees, but the artillery barrage was fierce as the gunners exhausted themselves trying to send as many rounds as they could in these final minutes. The unit's horses were grazing contentedly, unlimbered, only fifty yards away. Clearly, the battalion wouldn't be moving again.

Joseph glanced at his watch and was shocked. Only five minutes of the war remained.

He flew low over the gunners and waved to them. The crews didn't stop, however several officers threw cheerful salutes back up at him. He strained to see whether any of them was Jonathon, who he guessed would be doing something similar right now, firing his last shells while he could for his men's spirits, if for no other reason. None of the men below looked familiar. His brother would survive the war, without doubt. He was too careful an officer to take risks with his men at this late stage, and besides the artillery were struggling to keep touch with the fast-moving front lines.

'Lucky sod,' he grumbled, as he did almost every time he thought about Jonathon. Because it made him think of Rose, who he thought of as achingly beautiful and sweet. It was fortunate that he had thoughts of Katherine to temper his jealousy. Rose was safe at Cambrai in a makeshift hospital. Like the artillery battalions, the Casualty Clearing Stations had almost given up staying in contact with the fighting. By the time they set up equipment, the lines were far to the north again. The medical corps were concentrating instead on transporting the wounded to established hospitals. Men like Robert were exhausted from driving hundreds of miles every day over ruined roads and through endless convoys of soldiers, many of them prisoners of war going south.

Joseph flicked the SE5a into a bank and came back for another pass. He figured there was nothing else to do but encourage the gunners labouring below. As he flew past the second time, however, rocking his wings and holding his gloved hand high in salute, the howitzers fell silent.

Just like that, with no fanfare.

The war had ended.

His slipstream chased away the cordite smoke of their last shots. Looking over his shoulder and wondering whether it was the true reason the guns had stopped firing, he saw the men embracing and shaking hands.

A range of emotions hit him. It *was* over. The war had been won and the victory was theirs, not the Germans'—a frightening possibility that had been too real for comfort most of the year.

And he was alive. There had been many times *that* might have ended differently too. It made him shiver to think how close death had been. He felt a mixture of euphoria and a flat emptiness that came from not knowing exactly what he should be feeling at all. It was a strange and unexpected reaction. As if he was missing something.

Suddenly, he was in the wrong place. He had wanted to be flying, fighting to the last. Now, being airborne was robbing him of the wild celebrations below. He wanted to be sharing this moment with his friends, or anyone, since going back to the airfield would take too long. He needed to be a part of the victory sooner. He decided to touch down near the horses and join the gunners, at least for a few minutes.

They greeted his arrival with a fresh enthusiasm, running and gathering around the aircraft as if he'd landed at a country fair. They waved bottles of wine and scotch, and he felt obliged to have a drink as he sat in the cockpit, spilling it on himself as soldiers climbing on the wings shook the plane. Then they helped him out and onto the ground.

'Well done, my good chap,' a captain yelled at him as he pushed through the men. 'Well *done.*' It was as if he had won the war single-handed.

'The same to you, sir,' Joseph shook his hand among a dozen others thrust at him.

They shared more alcohol from bottles passing around in all directions, and the captain offered him a cigarette. In that exhilarating moment, Joseph swapped stories with him—about when he'd enlisted, and how many wounds they'd each suffered. They spoke in a rush, excited and filled with adrenalin.

The other men moved away, whooping and hollering thanks to God, fate and anything else that occurred to them. Watching as he listened to the captain, Joseph felt briefly annoyed about that. These gunners hadn't really been under any threat for some months. It wasn't as if they'd been likely to suffer a sniper's bullet between the eyes in the last seconds of the war. Not like the men still pushing the Germans back at the front lines until the very end. Then, angry with himself, he thrust the unkind thought away.

'I'd better get going,' he broke into the captain's story. 'It wouldn't do to get pissed and prang my last landing. Can someone swing the propeller for me?'

'Of course, of course.' The captain had a habit of repeating everything, and he had a nervous tic below one eye. He ordered a sergeant to stand by and helped Joseph into the cockpit.

'Good luck,' Joseph called as he tightened his straps. He felt now that it had hardly been worth getting out, his stay had been so short.

The captain jumped down off the wing and turned round. 'Yes, and the same to you. Never again, eh? Never again.'

'I bloody hope not,' Joseph laughed.

The captain beamed up at him. 'The war to end all wars, that's what they called it. Must never happen again, after all this.'

'Well, not while we're around, you'd think.' Joseph wanted to get going back to the squadron and find Roger. He flipped a salute at the captain as he called for the sergeant to swing the propeller. The roar of the engine prevented any more conversation. The captain stepped back and lost his cap in the wash, then scrambled after it.

Joseph took off and zoomed over the artillerymen one more time, waving out one side before he set his course for the airfield.

Today would be one, long celebration. Tomorrow was for Paris and

Katherine. It was the first time in years that he had dared to think of the future beyond the next morning.

> In a world at peace.

End

Please see the Historical Notes that follow.

Historical Note

And in the Morning is a novel based on true accounts of the First World War, coming mainly from books specialising in reproducing personal diaries, letters and the memories of people who took part in the conflict. I have tried to keep as faithful to history as I can with almost entirely fictional characters. It's said, "Never let the truth get in the way of a good story", but I found many of the anecdotes and stories uncovered during my research were so amazing that it's worth confirming here some events that actually happened, or pointing out that something very similar took place. At the same time, I'd like to acknowledge the few occasions I've strayed from the truth too.

The battle scenes and subsequent truce described where the Turks lost 10,000 men overnight did happen. The casualty figures are correct, although it's hard to find out how many were actually killed—about half, it seems. Also true is the story of Australian soldiers fighting among themselves, or haggling with money, over the best places from which to shoot. A similar circumstance, where the defending soldiers sat with impunity above the trenches to fire, is shown in Peter Weir's film *Gallipoli*, except in that attack it was the Anzacs on the losing side. However, in that action the Australians lost fewer than 400 men, compared to the Turkish losses earlier. And remarkably, the scene where the Turkish soldier risks crossing no-man's-land to apologise for shooting the truce flag is factual.

A kind of folklore has grown up around the idea that the Anzacs and Turks admired and even liked one another. It was this truce for burying the huge number of Turkish dead that started the comradeship. Until then, the Australian hatred of the Turks had been based on images of their brutality in propaganda. The truce began a period when troops in the opposing trenches would exchange gifts and murderous fire on the same day.

There were many girls like Rose Preston, volunteering to nurse the wounded and risking their own lives in Casualty Clearing Stations not far behind the main lines. But in fact, the Australian government decided not to send any VADs overseas at all, only registered nurses. The solution for many young women, frustrated by this decision, was to travel to Britain and join the VAD system there, or the FANYs (First Aid Nursing Yeomanry) and almost predictably, these girls were eventually seconded back to the Australian Imperial Forces anyway.

As for Rose's youth, an official history offers figures that of 2229 nurses who served during the war (this is a sample, not the accurate figure of how many actually enlisted) seven women were under 21 years old (how they crept into the system is a mystery, considering the 25-year-old minimum age*)*; 1184 were aged between 21 and 30 (most you'd assume were the required 25 or more); and the rest over 31 years old. So girls as young as Rose were undoubtedly out there and serving.

Her posting to Egypt and the hospital ship *Gascon* are events taking from real-life stories of Australian nurses, including the Anzac Day events (Sister Ella Tucker worked for 33 hours out of 36 aboard the *Gascon* during the landings). Only Rose's status as a VAD, rather than a nurse, is dramatic licence on my part.

The animosity between the regular army officers and the nurses was very real, if unexplainable. The complete lack of consideration for the nurses from the men isn't understated here. Conditions for the women were often terrible, mainly because they were ignored. The rift in Cairo between the Commanding Officer and the Principal Matron became a serious scandal. It wasn't until Lieutenant General Fetherston arrived on the scene in October 1915 that things improved—albeit almost too late for nurses working in the Gallipoli campaign. The regulations against married nurses existed.

During the Gallipoli fighting an Australian sniper dubbed "The Assassin" really existed. His name was Trooper Peter Williams and he accounted for over 200 Turks in the manner I've ascribed to Joseph White. Williams became a cult figure among the troops and the diggers eagerly awaited his latest body count. Among the misery and frustration of the failing invasion, he represented a small daily victory. The real Assassin survived the war, although Williams apparently suffered from a gas attack in France and never behaved the same afterwards. He died a pauper's death in 1953, a forgotten hero.

The Western Front and the Australian armed forces' participation in that conflict is a daunting subject for any novelist to cover. I enjoyed the challenge immensely, yet it was often a puzzle to decipher which research was likely to be the most reliable. Millions of men and women were involved in the war over its five years, and the sheer scope of what happened to them means that any well-intentioned attempt to tell their story will provoke contradiction and argument among historians today. My own efforts to make *And in the Morning* as accurate as possible kept encountering information that was at odds with similar histories from alternative sources. Small things that are important to the flow of a book like the weather, the time of day, the location of certain attacks—all these were hard to pinpoint. Mostly, this is because so much of the real history of the time comes from personal diaries and memories. And understandably, some of those recollections vary. The dreadful conditions, the awful and unimaginable situations that soldiers of both sides found themselves enduring, can't be exaggerated. The Western Front was, and still is, the largest man-made structure ever created when you realise it was a line of hand-dug trenches stretching the entire width of France and Belgium, exposed to summer heat and winter snows, and filled with men passionate about killing each other. Anything was possible. Incredible things happened every day and night.

The Australian attack at Fromelles, which failed and resulted in 400 diggers being taken prisoner, did happen. It was a nasty wake-up call for our forces, who had arrived believing that they were going to win the war quickly for King and Country.

Rose's Casualty Clearing Station in France presented interesting problems for me. Mostly, the research showed me nurses and doctors working under primitive conditions because better facilities were constantly ruined by shelling and bombs. Being placed forward of the heavy artillery was common—a result of the ballistic capabilities of the guns, rather than any rash courage from the medical staff. Some parts of the Western Front also enjoyed CCSs with uninterrupted electricity and even X-ray machines, based in converted churches or mansions with comparative comfort. Again, the differing experiences of people depending on where they were stationed provide conflicting stories. I've tried to make Rose's war show aspects of them all. Her working environment seems to have been common, while the better-equipped CCSs seem to have been the exception.

The severe shell-shock and memory loss suffered by Jonathon was, of course, a frequent occurrence. His sudden recovery, prompted by the stimulus of Rose's appearance, is also very likely. Today, we wouldn't question anything like this, but in the 1914-1918 war it was always suspected as a ruse by the patient to avoid further fighting, and a form of cowardice. It's interesting to think that while we do accept that such a mental injury exists, modern medicine will hopefully never have to deal with the effects of such extreme, constant shelling. We'll never really know just how much these men endured and suffered.

In Egypt 1917, it was true the German Air Force was oddly reluctant to attack the British aircraft, even though the Germans were undoubtedly superior in strength and technology. I've been able to find no explanation for it.

The story of Australian troops in France abusing Jonathon's artillery battery came from several accounts of similar events. The infantry hated the mobile guns that arrived at trouble spots, sent off salvoes towards the enemy, then disappeared before any fire was returned. It wasn't unknown for fist fights and all manner of arguments to break out between soldiers and artillerymen in an effort to stop these fast-deployed bombardments.

The enormous German offensive described in the final chapters did take place. It was one of several in March and April of 1918 as the Germans tried to win the war before the Americans became a powerful presence. The initial bombardment that wakens everyone came from 6500 guns, and 4000 mortars, aimed at 70 miles of Allied trenches. That's 150 guns for each mile of front line. When the infantry swept forward, the Germans gained unheard-of territory over the old trench systems, and this was their undoing. Despite all the planning, the hope, and their will to win the war, they coped badly when they actually succeeded.

Supply lines were stretched beyond working. The troops were exhausted and suffered huge casualty figures. Incredibly, a large number succumbed to drunkenness as they found wine and spirits plentiful. Pockets of resistance such as Joseph encountered were common. The novelty of finding themselves fighting over open country, away from the trenches, caused incredible scenes everywhere. One famous counterattack, prompting the letter extract at the beginning of this book, came from a division of Australians who went forward against the advancing Germans without any supporting bombardment of their own, disdaining the inaccuracy and unpredictability of their own gunners. It resulted in the diggers forcing the enemy back beyond the original lines.

Finally, having both Jonathon and Joseph survive the war was a long and soul-searching decision for this writer. Realistic? In fact, yes. Of the 50,000 men who fought at Gallipoli during 1915, approximately 7,000 served for the entire war and lived through the worst of the fighting in France. Sadly, in some ways, that means a lot of the casualties were newcomers who didn't know how to stay alive—but that happens in any war.

Graeme Hague

If you enjoyed this novel, leaving a considered review or rating will help both myself as the author, and other readers looking for guidance as to what to read next. I'll appreciate any feedback, good and bad, and if you'd like to discuss anything in detail, don't hesitate to drop me a line through my website at www.graemehague.com.au

Also, you might like a similar novel I've written called *At the Going Down of the Sun* which depicts the Allied RAF bombing offensive during World War II, and the men and women involved. Yes, it's also a love story. You'll find it on Amazon, also available in Kindle Unlimited, and right at this moment I'm completing an audiobook version for release in the near future.

Printed in Great Britain
by Amazon